The Roya*l*
Se

Andrew Taylor is the _____ er of crime novels, including the ground-_____ _king Ro___ Trilogy, which was adapted into the acclaimed TV drama *Fallen Angel*, and the historical crime novels *The Ashes of London*, *The Fire Court*, *The King's Evil*, *The Last Protector*, *The Silent Boy*, *The Scent of Death* and *The American Boy*, a No.1 *Sunday Times* best-seller and a Richard & Judy Book Club Choice.

He has won many awards, including the CWA John Creasey New Blood Dagger, an Edgar Scroll from the Mystery Writers of America, the HWA Gold Crown, the CWA Ellis Peters Historical Award (the only author to win it three times) and the CWA's prestigious Diamond Dagger, awarded for sustained excellence in crime writing. He also writes for the *Spectator* and *The Times*.

He lives with his wife Caroline in the Forest of Dean.

🐦 @AndrewJRTaylor
www.andrew-taylor.co.uk

By the same author

The Last Protector
The King's Evil
The Fire Court
The Ashes of London
Fireside Gothic
The Silent Boy
The Scent of Death
The Anatomy of Ghosts
Bleeding Heart Square
The American Boy

A Stain on the Silence
The Barred Window
The Raven on the Water
The Second Midnight

THE ROTH TRILOGY: FALLEN ANGEL
The Four Last Things
The Judgement of Strangers
The Office of the Dead

THE LYDMOUTH SERIES

THE BLAINES NOVELS

THE DOUGAL SERIES

The Royal Secret

ANDREW TAYLOR

HarperCollins*Publishers*

HarperCollins*Publishers* Ltd
1 London Bridge Street,
London SE1 9GF

www.harpercollins.co.uk

HarperCollins*Publishers*
1st Floor, Watermarque Building, Ringsend Road
Dublin 4, Ireland

First published by HarperCollins*Publishers* 2021
1

Prelims show a reduced copy of Fisher's Ground Plan of the Royal Palace of
Whitehall, 1680, (1881) © The Print Collector/Alamy Stock Photo

A catalogue record for this book is available from the British Library

ISBN: 978-0-00-832556-5 (HB)
ISBN: 978-0-00-832557-2 (TPB)

Typeset in Fournier MT by Palimpsest Book Production Ltd, Falkirk, Stirlingshire

Printed and bound in the UK by CPI Group (UK) Ltd, Croydon CR0 4YY

MIX
Paper from
responsible sources
FSC™ C007454

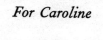

For Caroline

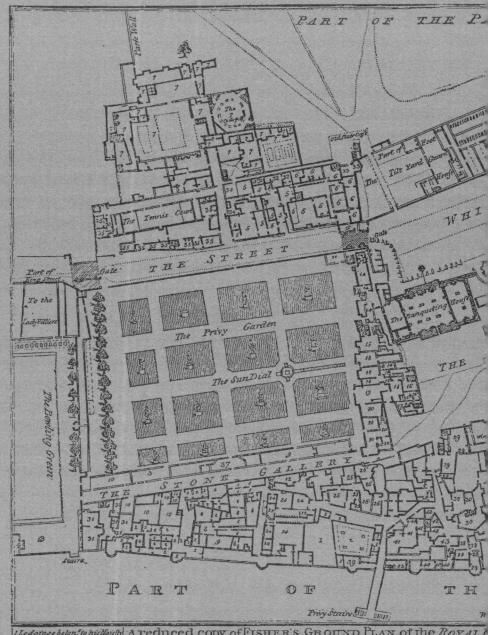

PART OF THE PA

Park Wall

Gilestar Gate

Part of the Tilt Yard

WHI...

THE STREET

Part of King Street

Gate

To the Lady Villiers

The Bowling Green

The Tennis Court

The Privy Garden

The Sun Dial

The Banqueting House

THE

THE STONE GALLERY

Stairs

Privy Stairs

PART   OF   TH

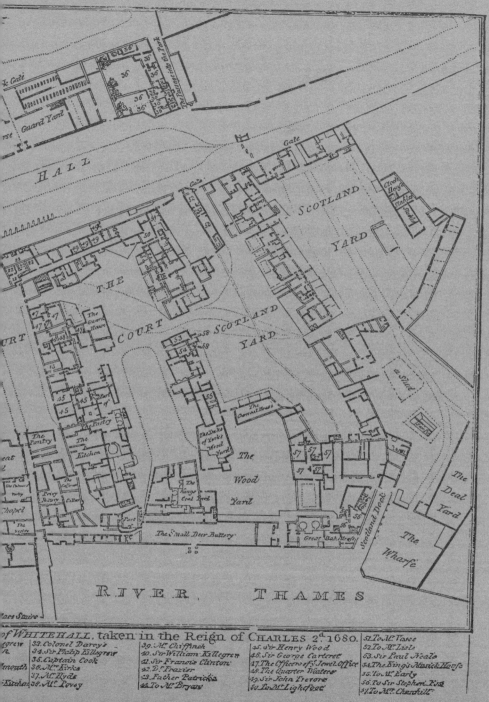

of WHITEHALL, taken in the Reign of CHARLES 2.ᵈ 1680.

RIVER THAMES

NOTE

In 1670, England, Scotland and Ireland still used the Julian calendar, which dated back to the time of Julius Caesar. Since 1582, however, most of Europe had adopted the more accurate Gregorian calendar of Pope Gregory XIII. As a result, the date in Paris was ten days in advance of the date in London. For example, Sunday, 6 March 1670 in England was Sunday, 16 March in France.

During this period, dinner was the main meal. It was usually eaten at midday.

Extracts from letters written by Charles II to his sister, Madame, the Duchess of Orléans (Minette)

Whitehall, 20 January 1669
. . . I send you heere a cypher, which is very easy and secure, the first side is the single cypher, and within such names as I could thinke of necessary to our purpose. I have no more to add, but that I am entierly Yours
C.R.

Whitehall, 25 April 1669
. . . I . . . shall be in the meane time very impacient to heare from you, for I can be at no rest when you are not well, and so my dearest sister have a care for yourselfe as you have any kindnesse for me,
For my Dearest Sister
C.

CHAPTER ONE

TWO GIRLS AT a window, and a rat scratching behind the panelling.

The sky was a cold, hard blue. If you looked carefully, at exactly the right angle between the blackened buildings and snow-patched roofs of the Temple, you could see a section of the river twitching in the distance. The whole scene, including the sky, was blurred and tinged with green, because of the glass.

'I hate this house,' Maria said. 'And I wish he was dead.'

'Master whipped you again last night,' Hannah said. She was two years older than Maria, and much taller, which compensated to some extent for the difference between their stations, at least when they were alone.

'I hate him. I didn't know you could hate someone so much.'

'He don't look well, do he?' Hannah said, as if at random. The maidservant had a freckled face, and her hair looked fair or ginger according to the light. 'Maybe he'll die.'

'Abbott's a devil. He'll live for ever. Just to spite us.'

Maria always called her stepfather Abbott when he wasn't there, as if he were a dog or a servant. Hannah rested the tip of her nose against the glass. The window was rimmed with ice. Her breath condensed on the cold surface. The Temple and the river vanished.

'No one lives for ever.' With her finger she rubbed at a lozenge of glass, making the Temple and the river return. 'What would happen if he did die?'

'My mother and I would go back to Slaughter Street, I suppose. And everything would be right again.'

'And me?'

'You'd come too, of course,' Maria said. 'With me.'

Hannah turned to look at her. 'You swear? Bible oath?'

Maria crossed her fingers behind her back in case the promise later proved inconvenient. 'I swear.'

'Really?'

'On my father's grave.'

Hannah rubbed the glass and watched a crow swooping from the sky. It perched on the wall of the garden. She said, 'There might be a way.'

'How?'

'You can't tell anyone. Ever. And it might not work.'

Maria's eyes widened. 'Have you – have you seen it done?'

'I heard how Ganga did it.'

'Who?'

'Old woman I knew. There was a boy in the village. They said he did things to children and animals . . . he had to be stopped. Ganga knew what to do. The boy swelled up and died.'

'She killed him? Didn't they hang her for it?'

'Why? Didn't touch him. No one touched him, they didn't need to. But Ganga made him die, sure as the sun rises. She said she'd do the same to me if I didn't stop my clacking.'

For a moment neither spoke. The rat stopped scratching, as if he too needed to digest the implications of what Ganga had said.

'I . . . I don't believe you,' Maria said, her voice barely above a whisper.

'I don't care.' Hannah threw her a contemptuous glance. 'I know it works. I know what I saw.' She paused, and a smile spread slowly across her face. 'And I know how it's done. She told me.'

'How?'

'That'd be telling.'

'Could—' Maria took a deep breath. 'Could you do it to someone? If you wanted?'

'People fall ill and die all the time,' Hannah said. 'Young and old, rich and poor. Nothing strange about it. Only natural, ain't it?'

Maria nodded. She could not take her eyes from Hannah's face, from the mouth where these words emerged, one by one, slipping between the smiling lips.

'That's why this is a good way,' Hannah said patiently, as if to a very young child. 'On account of it looks natural.'

'Would you . . .' Maria swallowed, gathering resolution. 'Would you do it for me? Make him go away?'

'Oh no. I couldn't.' The maidservant watched Maria's face for a moment. 'But you could. If you wanted to make things better. It's quite safe. I'd help you. I'd tell you how to do it. If . . .'

'If what?'

'If you make me your maid when we go to Slaughter Street. And look after me. Always.'

'They wouldn't let me have a maid of my own. Not for years.'

'They will if you make them.'

'All right. You can be my maid.'

'For ever and ever. You must swear it. A blood oath.'

Maria nodded.

Hannah drew a small bundle from her pocket, unwrapped it on the table and took out a pin. She lifted Maria's right hand and pushed the point of the pin into the pad of the forefinger. Maria squealed, from disbelief as much as shock. Hannah squeezed the wound until a bead of blood emerged. She repeated the process on herself, drawing blood from her left hand.

'Hold up your finger,' she commanded.

Maria obeyed. Hannah mirrored her movement until the two spots of blood merged into one.

'Say after me,' she said. 'By this blood, and God, and Jesus Christ, and the Devil . . .'

Behind her back, Maria crossed the fingers of her left hand. 'By this blood,' she mumbled, her breath coming shallow and fast, 'and God, and Jesus Christ, and the Devil . . .'

'I swear to make Hannah my maid. I'll treat her as kindly as a sister for the rest of my natural life.'

'I swear to make Hannah my maid . . .' Maria hesitated, aware that this was not in her gift. But the crossed fingers absolved her. The promise meant nothing. 'I'll treat her as kindly as a sister for the rest of my natural life . . .'

4

'Sit down,' Hannah said, her voice unexpectedly gentle. 'You look pale.'

Maria obeyed. She rested her elbows on the table. 'What must I do?'

'First, we need something of his. Best of all, something he gave you.'

'I know.' Maria stood up. 'Wait.'

She went away, into the closet where she slept, and opened the box where she kept her belongings. She rummaged through the contents until she found what she wanted: a piece of coarse linen with something wrapped inside. She returned to Hannah, who was still standing at the window, hugging herself to keep in the warmth.

She glanced at the object that Maria put on the table. 'What is it?'

'A doll. Can't you see? Abbott gave it me.'

Hannah wrinkled her nose. 'I never seen it before.'

'I forgot I had it. He gave it me when he was courting my mother. He must have thought me a little child.'

'Don't look much like a doll,' Hannah said.

Maria laid it on the table. 'It came from him.' She looked up and bit her lower lip. 'That's what counts, isn't it? You said we needed something from him. This must be good because it's meant to be like a person.'

Hannah craned her head over the table. The doll consisted of a cylinder of wood about six inches in length. It had a bobble carved at the top to represent the head. At the other end, the legs were divided in the manner of a clothes peg. There were no arms. An irregular square of linen had been glued to the cylinder to represent its clothes. It had neither hat nor hair. Someone had used the tip of a knife to scratch

5

a mouth on the bobble, and to gouge above it two holes to signify the eyes, one placed higher than the other. The holes had been blackened with soot.

'Didn't cost him above a penny, did it? Ha'penny, maybe, if he haggled.'

Maria shrugged, as if to say, What do you expect? Aloud, she said, 'Now what?'

Hannah poked at the doll with her fingertip, depositing an almost invisible speck of blood on the linen. She squinted at Maria with half-closed eyes. 'You could have me hanged for a witch.'

Maria fought back her panic. She said, as calmly as she could, 'Then they'd hang me too, wouldn't they?' She touched Hannah's arm. 'Tell me what to do. Pray, I beg you.'

Hannah lowered her voice to a whisper. 'Bang a nail into it. No, not a nail – that's too big, might split the wood – we'll use my pin. Then wrap it all up in another bit of cloth. But first we put in something of his.' She sucked in her breath and whispered with sudden urgency. 'I know what will do. Wait.'

She left the room in her turn. Maria waited. Despite the cold, her skin was clammy. She heard a step in the passage, and then Hannah was back.

Her eyes glinted. 'Look.' She held out her clenched hand and unfurled the fingers. Lying on the palm were three nail clippings and half a dozen hairs.

'Are they *his*?' Maria asked, backing away. 'How did you get them?'

'Easy. He wanted his nails trimmed last night. The trimmings were still on the hearth. And I had to cut the hair under his wig the other day . . . still some on the brush I swept up with.'

'What do we do then?'

Hannah took a rag from her pocket. 'You tie up the doll with . . . his *things*. You make a parcel of it. Tie it top and bottom. Like you tie a shroud. Then you put it in the mattress on his side of the bed—'

'Me? Can't you? Wouldn't it be easier?'

'No. I told you, it has to be you. But you must take the thing out once it's done its work, in case they find it and burn you to ashes. And then—'

There were footsteps in the passage. Hannah swept the doll into the pocket of her apron. Maria's mother paused on the threshold. She towered over the two girls and made the room seem smaller than it was. She frowned at Hannah.

'Why haven't you cleared the ashes? You haven't even started the sweeping. And if you don't look sharp, the kitchen fire will go out for want of coal, and then I'll have to beat you again.'

Hannah curtsied and sidled towards the door.

'As for you' – Mistress Abbott rounded on her daughter – 'why haven't you worked at your sampler?'

'I beg pardon, madam, truly I do.' Maria cast down her eyes and curtsied, for an appearance of complete submission was always the safest course with her mother. 'I was . . . thinking about tomorrow.'

'You won't be going anywhere tomorrow if you don't mend your ways. Let alone to Slaughter Street.'

Mistress Abbott left the girls alone. They listened to her footsteps in the passage. The door of the bedchamber opened and closed.

Maria looked at Hannah, who put down the shovel and took the doll from her pocket. Smiling, the maid twisted it in her hands as though she were wringing out a dishcloth. Maria stared at it.

'You'll see,' Hannah whispered. 'In a week or two he'll be dead.'

Later, as Hannah was kneeling before the kitchen fire, she paused for a moment to enjoy the heat. It was very cold in this house as there was so little money to spare. Any brief warmth was to be relished.

Money. She set down the empty shovel on the hearth and felt in her pocket for the rag bundle. Her fingers traced the hard, round outline within. She tugged at the knot that secured the bundle.

It was quite safe. The mistress and Maria were in the parlour at their endless sewing, and she would hear the latch if either of them came out. She unfolded the bundle. Inside was the gold coin. It was foreign, like the gentleman who gave it her, but you could tell it was gold by its weight and the colour. There was a man in armour on one side. He held a sword in one hand and a bunch of arrows in the other.

With a piece like that in her hand, Hannah was probably richer than the mistress. Richer than the master, too, who pissed money away like water. And if all went well, there would be more one day. Thanks to Maria. Thanks to her own cunning.

There was something else in the bundle: a small, neatly folded paper package, tied with string. She touched it gingerly, as if it might be hot.

Hannah hadn't planned the business with the doll. She had

thought it all up on the spur of the moment, though Ganga had been real enough in her way. Ganga had said something else too.

'Mark my words, child. A girl has to look after herself. No one else will.'

CHAPTER TWO

' *SHE WOULD IF She Could*?' Cat said tartly. 'A foolish title for a foolish play.'

Marwood stopped laughing and glanced at her. 'It's diverting enough, isn't it?'

'If that's your humour, I suppose it is.'

'I'm sorry, madam,' he said stiffly, his words almost drowned by the applause and the catcalls rising from the spectators in the pit. 'If you wish, we can leave.'

'No – no.' She waved away the suggestion with her fan. 'Now we've come so far, we may as well see it to the end.'

Cat turned back to the stage below. She knew she was being ungracious. Marwood had paid four shillings apiece for them to sit in a box. But the theatre was uncomfortably hot, with four hundred people jammed together in the confined space. She glanced up at the ceiling, where putti and portly shepherdesses writhed beneath the smoky veil that drifted upwards from the pipes and candles in the pit below.

Most of the audience appeared to be enjoying *She Would if She Could* far more than she was. Her eyes roved among them, finding more entertainment there than in the play. Gentlemen and their parasites thronged the pit – the whores and the card sharpers, the pimps and the pickpockets, those who lived by their wits and by the gullibility of others.

In a reversal of the usual order of things, servants and their like packed the upper gallery, throwing down catcalls and orange peel on their betters. The middle gallery was quieter; respectable clerks sat there, together with citizens and a sprinkling of women of the middling class with their maids. Among them she noticed one of her clients, Mr Fanshawe, who was in company with a young gentleman she did not know.

Meanwhile, on the cramped stage, the figures of Mr Betterton and Mr Harris strutted and gesticulated like puppets at Bartholomew Fair.

'Madam! Pray – the honour of a word?'

The voice cut through the hubbub. Cat was sitting at the left end of the row of chairs in the box. She turned her head. In the neighbouring box, only a few feet away from her, a plump, red-faced gentleman was leaning on his elbow and staring at her with bulging eyes. Sweat streamed down his forehead, and he wiped it away with his sleeve.

'I knew it,' he said, beaming. 'A veritable Venus.' He nudged the gentleman on his other side. 'Look, Ned, there's a pretty little rogue next to us.' He blew her a kiss. 'Look at those lovely eyes peeping at us through her vizard.'

'Pricklouse,' she said pleasantly. 'You make any woman that sees you want to spew.' She touched Marwood on the arm. 'Pray change places with me.'

He stood up and moved aside for her. Realizing that she had been pestered, he scowled at the next box. The gentleman, seeing that Cat was not defenceless, had already turned back to the stage and appeared absorbed in the drama unfolding below.

The evening went from bad to worse. It was not entirely the fault of Mr Etherege and his play. In the final act, a pretty orange seller came to their box. Marwood joked with the girl and gave her sixpence over and above the price she asked; she responded pleasantly, as she would to any generous man whose attentions did not altogether repulse her; Cat noticed that the girl allowed her fingers to brush Marwood's hand as she gave him their oranges, and that he smiled, no doubt foolishly flattered, and eyed the curve of her breasts, which were only inches away from his eyes; and Cat felt irritated by the whole episode.

Afterwards, they left the theatre without exchanging a word. The lobby was already dense with people leaving the pit, forcing them to linger on the stairs from the boxes and the galleries. Stephen, Marwood's footboy, was waiting below to light their way, his dark skin gleaming as if varnished in the flickering glow from the candles. As he was approaching them, there was an interruption.

'Mistress Hakesby?'

Cat glanced over her shoulder and saw the tall, stooping figure of Mr Fanshawe behind her. Her mind slipped into another channel. This was business.

She curtsied and he bowed, as well as they could in the confined space.

'And this is Mr Marwood,' she added, as an afterthought. 'Mr Fanshawe.'

'Your servant, sir. And may I present Mr Van Riebeeck?'

The Dutchman bowed in his turn but said nothing. He was

a much younger, fair-complexioned man with a long face and strongly marked features. He towered over almost everyone around them. He glanced at Cat and looked away. That piqued her. She wasn't particularly vain, but she knew that men generally considered her well-favoured.

'And what did you think of the play, madam?' Fanshawe said.

'I didn't care for it,' Cat said. 'I find I have little taste for comedy.'

'I liked it well enough,' Marwood said abruptly, pushing himself into the conversation.

Cat pretended she hadn't heard him. 'Given a choice in the matter, I prefer music. Mr Marwood prefers the theatre. Though whether it is the play he likes or the company he finds here, I cannot quite be sure.'

She knew she was being spiteful. Perhaps Van Riebeeck sensed the awkwardness, for he said something about a song he had recently heard, and she turned with relief towards him while Marwood fell behind. They continued talking as the current of people carried them slowly down the stairs. She began to think better of the Dutchman. He was not a handsome man, but he had considerable presence and he listened with apparent interest to what she said.

'I'm glad to run into you,' Fanshawe interrupted, raising his voice to be heard over the hubbub around them. 'It saves me the trouble of writing. My foreman is uncertain about the doors at the back of the warehouse. And there's some question about their being prone to flooding. Would you be so kind as to inspect the work with me?'

'With pleasure, sir.' Cat made her voice pleasant, though it was always tedious and sometimes expensive when a client raised a difficulty after the work had been done and paid for.

'Excellent. When the weather improves, we shall fix a day.'

Van Riebeeck smiled at Cat. 'Perhaps, sir, you will allow me to accompany you, when you discuss these doors with Mistress Hakesby. I should like to see her . . . work. If I am not otherwise engaged.'

'By all means,' Fanshawe said, glancing at him. 'And indeed, sir, it is in your interest as well as mine that it should be done well.'

'That too, of course.' The Dutchman's eyes strayed to Cat again. 'Though one hardly needs more than one reason.'

She nodded, though the gallantry was unwelcome. She noticed that Marwood was scowling at Van Riebeeck.

'Ah, it's bitter tonight,' exclaimed Mr Fanshawe.

By this time, the press of theatregoers had pushed them across the lobby and into Portugal Street. Torches flaring outside the theatre doors cast a flickering light over a mass of coaches, horses, and sedan chairs, interspersed with the lights carried by link boys. Snow drifted aimlessly down from the darkness above – small, insubstantial flakes that vanished as they reached the ground.

Mr Fanshawe and Mr Van Riebeeck bade them goodnight, and were taken up in a coach. Stephen lit his link from one of the big torches in the brackets outside the theatre.

'Would you care for supper?' Marwood asked.

Cat didn't look at him. 'I think not.'

'The Dutchman seems to like you.'

'Well enough.'

'I thought he had a wolfish air.'

'If he's in business with Mr Fanshawe, I've no reason not to be civil to him.'

'You should have a care with such men.'

'That's my affair, sir,' she said. 'It's growing late, and I must be up early tomorrow. I must pay my Lord Arlington a visit in the morning.'

'Then I should not delay you any longer than necessary,' Marwood said in a colourless voice.

His words felt like an accusation. Cat said sharply, 'It's thanks to you that I have some small acquaintance with my lord.'

In an awkward silence, with Stephen lighting their way, he escorted her back through Covent Garden to the house at the sign of the Rose in Henrietta Street. This was where she worked as well as lived, for she carried on her late husband's business as an architect and surveyor. After a few paces, she took his arm, for the ground was treacherous, though in the event it was he who slipped, and she who prevented him from stumbling into the gutter.

Over the last year or so, Cat and Marwood had fallen into the habit of meeting once or twice a month to listen to music or go to a play or, in finer weather, walk in the Park or go on the river. She found it convenient to have a man's company on these excursions, without having to fend off attempts at lovemaking. Marwood prospered at Whitehall, and during the four years of their acquaintance his manners and his conversation had acquired a polish that they had lacked before. He was well enough looking, too, despite the burns that scarred the left side of his face and neck, and no longer seemed an overgrown boy. His friendship had become agreeable to her, but now his folly threatened to ruin it all.

Cat had long ago settled in her mind that theirs was an alliance of mutual assistance rather than affection. Marwood had saved her from ruin and death in the past, but she had done the same for him: so the account between them was squared. But she didn't like to see him making a fool of himself with little orange girls in the theatre. Or, if all she had heard was true, with women who had the power to make a far bigger fool of him. Marwood grew steadily more prosperous, more secure in the world. It occurred to her that he might already have set up a mistress for his particular use.

At the house, Stephen knocked on the door. They waited for the porter to open it. In the meantime, Marwood turned his head away to avoid looking at her. Usually they would discuss their next excursion at the end of the previous one. This time, however, neither of them mentioned a future meeting.

Cat listened to Pheebs removing the bars and chains with agonizing slowness on the other side of the door. At last it opened. On the doorstep she turned to look back at Marwood. In the dim light from Pheebs's lantern, he looked miserable.

'Thank you, sir,' she said over her shoulder as she passed into the house. 'I won't detain you. I'm sure you are eagerly awaited.'

CHAPTER THREE

'MARWOOD,' RICHARD ABBOTT said, frowning, and added with patent insincerity, 'Your servant, sir. This way if you please. Pray make haste — my lord wants me, and I mustn't keep him waiting.'

I followed him down a long, marble-floored passage lined with mirrors and pier tables. On brackets fixed to the walls on either side stood pale, stern-faced busts of the twelve caesars. Their blank eyes stared down on us.

Despite his desire to hurry, Abbott found time to glance at his passing reflection. He had grown noticeably plumper in the months since his marriage, and I was childishly pleased to note that his gait had acquired a hint of a waddle. I had expected his usual air of condescension — since he had moved to Lord Arlington's office he was rarely without it — but today he had mislaid it. Perhaps something had agitated him.

He paused before a pair of double doors, beside which a footman stood. The servant opened one leaf and Abbott scuttled inside, leaving me to follow.

The room was empty. It was a long, high box that ended

with two windows that looked over a garden with the bare branches of the trees in the Park beyond. A large fire of coal and logs burned brightly in the grate beneath a tall white chimneypiece. There was a large globe in one corner, and the walls were furnished with pictures, bookcases, and a set of hangings showing a deer hunt in a dream landscape populated by figures in flowing clothes. There was also a great desk inlaid with brass, and with many drawers. Marooned in the vast expanse of its top were writing materials and a single sheet of paper.

Abbott stopped abruptly. 'He must be still in conference with Sir Richard Bellings and Sir Thomas Clifford.' He looked back at me, and his eyes were anxious. 'We'll wait for him. He said to attend him here.'

I had the feeling that Abbott's mind was on something quite different. He was standing by the desk in a new suit of clothes and toying with a curl of his freshly combed peruke. For all his new finery, he was still the same Abbott who until eighteen months earlier had worked with me under Mr Williamson in Scotland Yard. He had a round face, doughy skin and protruding, permanently pursed lips that seemed on the verge of kissing the air. He had a good conceit of himself, and usually he was irritatingly cheerful. But not today.

'Are you quite well?' I said.

'Perfectly, thank you,' he snapped.

He had something in his hand, and he was toying with it unconsciously, like a priest with his rosary or a child with a soft blanket. Suddenly it spun away from him – something small and whitish, round like a coin. It fell with a clatter to the floor and rolled in my direction.

Abbott swore. I stooped and picked up the disc. It was made

of bone, and about the same size as a shilling piece. There was a design crudely inked on it. It looked like a tree.

I held it out to Abbott, who almost snatched it from me, scowling as though the episode was my fault. He slipped the disc in his pocket, took up the sheet of paper from the desk and pretended to be absorbed in its contents.

I walked over to the fire and warmed my hands. It was a cold day in February, and old snow still carpeted the Park. I took the memorandum from my pocket and waved it gently to and fro, in case the ink was still a trifle damp. I held the proof to the warmth of the fire. Lord Arlington would not thank me if I made his fingers inky.

'Why has Williamson sent you?' he said suddenly. 'Why not a messenger?'

'It's a digest of the intelligence from Dover. I wrote it, and Williamson told me to wait in case my lord wanted to ask me about it. For some reason it's urgent.'

That was not quite true. In truth I had volunteered to bring the digest myself. But my motive was my own affair.

He grunted. 'I believe I have taken a cold in the head,' he said in a more conciliatory tone. There were spots of colour in his cheeks. 'My wife had to keep to her bed with it last week.'

I moved away from the fire and tossed the conversation back to him out of politeness. 'Is she quite recovered now?'

'Oh yes. Anna's constitution is exceptionally strong. That's what comes of being bred in the Low Countries, I suppose. But I'm not so fortunate.'

Abbott said something more, but I was no longer listening. Something had caught my eye. I had been staring idly past him, through the nearer of the two windows, into the garden beyond, framed like a painting. The grounds of Goring House were extensive and varied. This part was laid out in the Italian style, with paths running between parterres and populated with statues. The snow still lay on the parterres, but the gardeners had cleared it from the walks between exposing the gravel beneath.

A sudden movement had burst into this static world. At first I could not understand what my eyes saw. For an instant it seemed to me that a dark, furry ball was rolling away from the house. It was about two feet in height, and it wobbled violently as it went.

A woman's voice called out, high and alarmed. The ball veered suddenly to its right and collided with one of the low hedges. And then, with miraculous speed, it was no longer a ball. It resolved itself into a very small child wrapped in furs. It was lying on the ground and kicking its legs in the air. It was also wailing, but not, it seemed to me, so much from pain as from anger. Beside it lay a beaver hat and a muff. A woman cried out.

'That wretched girl,' Abbott muttered. 'She escapes her nursemaid a dozen times a day.'

'My lord's daughter?'

'She can do no wrong.'

The portly figure of my lord himself burst into view. He lifted the child and hugged her. Then he fell to kissing the top of her head. Her nurse ran up. She tried ineffectually to brush the dirt from the child's furs. She turned away to pick up the fallen muff. Beyond the child, her nurse and her father, two people were coming down the path, a man and a woman.

'Oh, the devil,' Abbott muttered. 'I had quite forgot the architects were coming.'

But I had not forgotten. With a lurch of recognition, located in an uncomfortable place that lay somewhere between pleasure and apprehension, I took a step back from the window.

There were Mistress Catherine Hakesby and her clerk of the works, the fox-faced Mr Brennan.

CHAPTER FOUR

CAT WAS SURPRISED and not best pleased to see James Marwood. He came out of the house by the side door with one of Lord Arlington's clerks. At least he gave no sign of recognition when they met. The two men bowed, as they would have done to any lady encountered here. She looked coldly at him.

My lord had eyes only for his daughter. 'Poor Tata,' he said in a caressing voice. 'Nasty fall.'

Tata, known formally as the Honourable Isabella Bennet, smiled benevolently at the people around her. She dropped one of her mittens on the ground and toyed with the black plaster across the bridge of her father's nose; he had suffered a wound here during the Civil War, and his critics alleged that he wore the plaster for the sole purpose of reminding the world of his loyalty to the crown.

'Tata want milk?' Lord Arlington enquired, enclosing her chubby fingers in his own. 'A sweetmeat?'

The child ignored him. She was staring over her father's shoulder at Cat with huge, surprised eyes. 'Chick, chick,' she said. She paused and said it again in a more emphatic tone, more a command than an observation. 'Chick, chick. Chick, chick.'

Arlington turned his head and saw Cat, seemingly for the first time. 'Mistress Hakesby. You're before your time.'

Cat curtsied low, bowing her head in a manner that might be taken to indicate both submission and apology. In the distance, across the Park, the clock above the palace guard-house began to toll the hour: eleven o'clock, the precise time that Abbott's letter had given her.

Tata released her father's neck and stretched her arms towards Cat, who fought a powerful desire to retreat.

'Why, my lord,' she said, wishing that her audience did not include Marwood, 'the young lady's understanding is quite extraordinary for one so young. "Chick, chick." She connects me in her mind at once with the poultry house, where the chickens live.'

'Indeed,' Arlington said, his ill-humour vanishing. 'Many excellent judges have remarked upon my daughter's intelligence. The other day, the King himself did me the honour of—'

'Chick, chick,' said Tata, and crowed with laughter.

She pointed across the garden to a line of bushes interspersed with the leafless branches of several apple trees. Behind it were glimpses of a low building faced with stone.

'I believe she wishes to go there with you, Mistress Lovett,' Arlington said with a smile. He chucked his daughter under the chin. 'You naughty little one. Well, let us all go and admire the chick-chicks.' He glanced at the nurse, and his face hardened. 'Put her hat on, you fool, and her muff. She'll catch her death of cold if you're not careful.'

Abbott cleared his throat. He was shivering, and Marwood's

face looked grim and pinched with cold, which made the scarring on his left cheek more noticeable than usual. Neither man was wearing a cloak, and because they were in Lord Arlington's presence they carried their hats in their hands.

'What is it, Abbott?'

'Should we attend you, my lord?'

'You might as well.'

Arlington transferred Tata to her nursemaid and motioned that Cat should walk beside him. The others followed behind, walking in silence apart from Tata, who emitted a steady, chuckling gurgle punctuated with the occasional squeal.

The poultry house was sheltered from the north by the garden wall. The design was austere, but on a classical model. There was a small portico topped by a pediment on which a stone cock crowed silently, night and day. Both the doorway and the windows were on a miniature scale, as befitted the size of the building's patron. Behind it, concealed from the windows of Goring House, was a pen constructed from hurdles, which in better weather served the hens as a run. At present they were undercover, their bright feathers dulled.

The keeper, a small, wizened man with a large nose and no teeth, appeared from his shed and bowed low. No one took any notice of him. Tata pushed open the door and ran inside, where the nesting boxes were. The nursemaid picked up her skirts, wrinkled her nose and followed. She had to bend almost double to pass through the doorway.

'Dr Wren called on me the other day,' Arlington said. 'While he was here, he desired to inspect the poultry house. He told me he considered it in its small way to be something of a triumph, an ingenious and elegant use of the space available for the purpose required.'

Cat curtsied, hoping that her pleasure was not obvious in her face. 'How very obliging of him, my lord.'

'He tells me that your late husband trained you well. And that he has even asked you to work up his designs for the rear facade of the Customs House.' He looked at her. 'It seems that you have achieved a great deal for one so young. And more especially for a member of your sex.'

'I've had the assistance of Mr Brennan, my lord.' She gestured towards the draughtsman. 'My clerk of the works. Dr Wren employed him at Oxford for the Sheldonian before he came to Mr Hakesby's Drawing Office.'

Arlington ignored Brennan. 'I've nearly finished rebuilding my house in Suffolk. Euston Hall.' He spoke as if this followed on naturally from their conversation beforehand, as for him perhaps it did.

Cat hardly missed a beat, for she made it a rule to study her clients: 'It's in the style of a modern French château, I understand, with pavilions at the four corners? Dr Wren described it to me only the other day. A fitting palace for a nobleman: those were his very words.'

'We're still working on the stables.' The flattery had had no effect on Arlington's expression, but his voice became softer, almost confidential. 'I've a design from a man in Newmarket – a capable fellow, by all accounts; the King has used him – but I have my doubts whether his plan is perfectly suited to the house. The parts should always complement and fulfil the whole, as at the Escorial or the newer work at St Germain and Versailles. Would you be kind enough to cast your eye over his plans while you're here? Dr Wren is coming to advise later as well.'

Cat curtsied again, and said that nothing would give her

greater pleasure. She was aware that as an architect she had one advantage that went some small way towards compensating for the drawback of her sex. Like Dr Wren himself, she was gently bred; she had studied the great architects past and present; and clients like Lord Arlington preferred to patronize, in both senses of the word, an architect who appreciated their taste, and one whose manners in company were not disagreeable. Perhaps, Cat sometimes thought, her sex even worked to her advantage: if nothing else, it gave her the desirable virtue of rarity. After all, my lord had the reputation of being a collector, a connoisseur of fine and curious things; a man who prized the uncommon.

He looked over his shoulder and clicked his fingers. 'Abbott – fetch the Euston plans and lay them on the desk.'

The plump clerk bowed and hurried away. Marwood's eyes met hers, and the corners of his mouth twitched with amusement. She wished he had not overheard her flattering Arlington. Such tactics did not come easily to her, but necessity was a hard school.

Arlington laid his beringed fingers on her arm to guide her back to the house. It was a familiar, possessive gesture, something that within limits Cat accepted as an inevitable hazard from a certain sort of client. With her other hand she touched the knife she carried in her pocket and allowed herself to imagine stabbing it in Arlington's arm.

My lord had not given me leave to go. I was forced to await his pleasure along with a dozen others, while he and Cat examined sets of plans and drawings.

Abbott laid them out one by one on the great desk. Arlington, who loomed over Cat like a bear over his victim, stood so close to her that sometimes their arms brushed each other.

The rest of us simply stood there and watched in a respectful silence. What else could we do? This, I thought not for the first time, is an attribute of power: the ability to force others to wait patiently on your convenience.

Arlington and Cat talked of cartouches and columns, of Juan Bautista de Toledo and Andrea Palladio, of the desirability of a *cour d'honneur* and the layout essential for a suite of royal apartments. I heard fragments of Latin, of French and Italian, and I had not the slightest idea what it all meant.

Notwithstanding my lord's rank and Cat's lowly position, there was a strange equality in this conversation. Like a game of tennis, it was enclosed within its own borders, and the players played as equals. I was impressed, despite myself. This was a side of Cat which I had not seen before.

Meanwhile, however, I cultivated my irritation with her like a flower. Why was she being so objectionable to me? Then there was Arlington. Ten to one, I told myself, she would gain nothing of consequence from this discussion. The truth of the matter was this: I hated to stand by and watch a man like my lord pawing at Cat and talking to her as a man talks to an intimate – or even an actress. All he was offering in return was the bare possibility of receiving the occasional crumb from his overladen table. What made it worse – for me, that is – was that I had no right to feel aggrieved on Cat's behalf.

I watched Abbott as he moved to and fro between the chest where the plans were kept and the desk. He was clumsy in his movements. On two occasions he brought out the wrong folder. The second time, Arlington snapped at him. Abbott had the sort of fair complexion that is cruelly revealing: the blood rushed to his cheeks as he apologized, and as he turned away his lips drooped and trembled like a child's. He looked as if he were trying to hold back tears. I smiled ruefully at him as he passed me, a clumsy attempt to show sympathy, but he ignored me and blundered towards the chest.

At this point, the door opened and the footman announced Dr Wren. I had never met him, though I knew him by sight. He was a trim, handsome man with neat, regular features and a well-bred air, like the sort of dogs that noblemen like to have about them. Arlington greeted him with evident pleasure.

'Thank you for joining us, doctor – I would be glad of your opinion. I have taken the opportunity of consulting Mistress Hakesby too. She was here about the poultry house.'

Arlington swept him into the discussion over the Euston Hall stables, and soon the three of them were leaning over the desk and talking with animation, while the rest of us stood by. Wren was a comely man. It seemed to me that his manner towards Cat was remarkably easy and confidential.

A clock chimed, catching Arlington's attention. 'Ah – almost time for dinner. Will you join us, doctor? My wife and I dine at home today.'

Wren declined, claiming another engagement. To my relief, the invitation was not extended to Cat, and the party broke up. Abbott was ordered to put away the plans.

As Cat was making her farewells to Lord Arlington, he raised his hand to stop her. 'There's another project I would like to discuss with you,' he said. 'But it's not convenient now.'

She inclined her head. 'Whenever your lordship wishes.'

He nodded. 'I'll have someone write you a note to fix a time.'

He turned away towards his desk, where the plans were still laid out. This was my chance at last. I moved towards Cat, intending to offer to escort her back to Henrietta Street once I had presented the memorandum to my lord. I hoped I might clear the air between us on the way, and perhaps fix a day for another excursion. But I was too late. Wren cut in front of me. I heard him offering to walk with her through the Park to Whitehall, where they might find her a hackney.

He offered her his arm, and they left the room, Brennan trailing at their heels like a dog. Cat didn't even look at me.

Arlington, who was telling Abbott how he wanted the plans to be stored, was about to leave himself, but I contrived to come between him and the door.

'Marwood,' he said, pausing. 'Why are you here? Remind me.'

'I have a memorandum you requested from Mr Williamson, my lord. About the condition of Dover, and its harbour and the castle. Together with recent shipping reports. I—'

'Dover?' He waved his hand at me. 'That's of no moment. Leave it with Abbott.'

His voice was elaborately casual. But I had the strangest feeling that, somehow, for some inexplicable reason, Lord Arlington wanted me to think that his sudden interest in Dover was of no particular importance.

CHAPTER FIVE

TOWARDS THE END of the afternoon, I was working in Mr Williamson's outer office in Scotland Yard. Williamson was Lord Arlington's Undersecretary of State. He used his Scotland Yard office for the management of the government's newspaper, the *London Gazette*, and for the gathering of intelligence.

The light was already fading from a heavy afternoon sky the colour of ashes. I was reading, and the informant's writing was foully crabbed. My mind wandered back to Cat. I was not in love with her, but I confess that over the years of our acquaintance a sort of bastard affection for her had grown up within me. We had been thrown together in several difficult and dangerous circumstances, and we had come to depend on each other during these crises. I felt a certain responsibility for her well-being, for she was a woman, alone and unprotected in the world. When I saw men like Lord Arlington or even Van Riebeeck with her, I felt a natural, indeed praiseworthy desire to protect her.

I had just reached this reassuring conclusion when the office boy came round with a taper to light the candles. He scuttled away, almost bumping into Mr Williamson himself, who had just come in.

'The lad grows clumsier by the day,' he said. 'Marwood? A word if you please. And bring a candle.'

I followed him into the inner office, closing the door. Williamson gestured for me to set the candle on the desk. The flame swayed in the twilight, deepening the shadows in the corner.

'You were a long time gone this morning.'

'As you desired, sir, I took the Dover memorandum to Goring House. My lord was engaged, and I had to wait.'

Williamson did not have an expressive face but I fancied, even in the poor light, that I saw him compress his lips. He did not take it kindly when time was wasted unnecessarily, either his own or that of his clerks.

'My lord was much engaged in business?'

'Mistress Isabella's poultry house,' I said, seizing on the opportunity to turn the conversation away from me. 'And the stables at Euston Hall.'

'With whom?'

'Mistress Hakesby, mainly.'

'He favours her?'

'He's pleased with her work, sir,' I said primly. 'So is his daughter, which matters to him. Since Mistress Hakesby was there about the poultry house, my lord asked her to look over the plans for the stables. Dr Wren came in while they were discussing them.'

'Ah, this strange humour for building,' Williamson said. 'It's all very well, Marwood, but in the meantime there's real work to be done, and it won't do itself.'

* * *

It was fully dark by the time I left the office. The ground was hard with frost. I set off on foot towards my lodging in the Savoy.

I was approaching the brightly lit New Exchange in the Strand when I saw a familiar figure, the small, stout shape of Richard Abbott, about thirty yards ahead of me. This was not unusual – I saw him by chance at least once a week; his lodgings were in Fleet Street somewhere, so he passed the Strand entrance to the Savoy every time he went to and from Whitehall.

Abbott had a characteristic way of walking – with his nose in the air, straight-backed, and so upright that it sometimes looked as though he were defying nature and leaning backwards. His feet were turned outwards in a manner uncommon among humans, though accounted perfectly natural among ducks.

Beside him strode a much taller man, who was shortening his strides to match Abbott's. They paused by the open flap of a shop. It was an expensive establishment that sold china imported from the East Indies and painted in Holland. They turned their heads to look at the wares on display. I had only a glimpse of Abbott's companion, and the light was poor. I caught a fleeting impression of a long, horselike face with a large nose. There was a sword by his side, and he carried himself like a gentleman. He reminded me of someone, but for the life of me I could not recall whom.

I paused, not wanting to catch them up. A moment later they moved on from the New Exchange. They crossed the Strand and went into Blue Bush Alley off the north side.

The alley led only to the Blue Bush itself. I had been to this tavern with friends soon after I had come to Whitehall, but only once. It was called a tavern because you could eat and drink and make merry with your friends there. But the real purpose of the Blue Bush was the rattle of the dice box, the play of the cards, and the winning and losing of money. On that drunken evening, I had lost more than I could afford and I had sworn never to return. Since then I heard it said that they cogged the dice and marked the cards when the play was high.

Abbott's folly was none of my business, and I walked on. I had almost reached my house when I remembered the bone disc that Abbott had dropped in Lord Arlington's study that morning. The design on it was not a tree, I realized, but a blue bush.

CHAPTER SIX

MR FANSHAWE PROVED as good as his word. In the afternoon of the day following their chance meeting at the Duke's Theatre, Cat received a letter from him proposing the following Wednesday for the inspection of the work on the new warehouse, and naming ten o'clock as the hour. He would be there to watch the unlading of a ship in which he had an interest.

She accepted the invitation, wondering if Mr Van Riebeeck would be there. In the interval between the invitation and Wednesday morning, she found herself thinking of the Dutchman on more than one occasion. Both his conversation and his manners had been agreeable.

The day was dry, and she walked down to Thames Street in company with Brennan.

'I saw Mr Marwood again last night,' Brennan said. His voice was elaborately casual.

'Oh yes.' Cat hoped she sounded equally unconcerned. 'Where?'

'Same place. Corner of Vere Street and Clare Market.'

'Then he must have got soaked if he was out for long. I thought the rain would never stop yesterday. If we go right here, we can cut down St Bennett's Hill.'

They went the rest of the way in silence. Brennan and Marwood didn't dislike each other, not now, but they were still mutually wary. Since the beginning of the year, Brennan lodged in a court off Vere Street. He had mentioned seeing Marwood there more than once in the last few weeks. Cat could guess all too easily why Marwood went there. Vere Street was barely five minutes' walk from the Duke's Theatre on the edge of Lincoln's Inn Fields. It was where many players lodged.

Fanshawe's warehouse was set back on one of the legal quays between London Bridge and the Tower, a few hundred yards east of Billingsgate Dock. The new building stood on the same ground as its predecessor. After the Fire, he could have taken the opportunity to move downstream, beyond the Tower, where land was cheaper and navigation easier, but he had declined.

'We are safer here,' he had told Cat, 'within the walls of the City, and the docks are better regulated. Besides, you know the nature of my business – I have more than enough space for the goods.'

She and Brennan turned down towards the river. To the left was Wren's half-built Custom House, its brick and stone almost garishly bright in the cold, pale sunlight. Fanshawe's warehouse was a far less ambitious affair, a plain, brick-built rectangle whose walls were broken by small barred windows set high above the ground. Even so, its capacity was more than he could use himself, which allowed him to lease out a portion of it.

The tide was high. The ship, a square-rigged two-masted brigantine, was moored alongside the quay. The riverside doors of the warehouse stood open, and piles of boxes, barrels and bales were stacked on the quayside. Teams of dock workers were carrying them into the warehouse, under the watchful eyes of the warehouse keeper. Time was of the essence, because of the tide. Two Customs officials were on hand, with Fanshawe himself talking to them. There was no sign of Van Riebeeck. Cat was part-relieved, part-disappointed.

No one had seen them yet, and Cat and Brennan made a detour into the blind alley that gave access to the doors at the landward side of the warehouse. Sunlight rarely penetrated here at this time of year, and the old cobbles were slimy with damp.

'There's the problem,' Cat said, pointing at the base of the warehouse wall, where water had puddled into a long, irregularly shaped pool. Some of it was seeping under the closed doors of the building.

'A drain's probably backing up somewhere,' Brennan said, scowling at it. 'There's nothing wrong with the footings we put in, or the slope of the ground. We allowed for all that.'

'If it's an old drain, it must run into a culverted stream, mustn't it?' Cat said. 'Not directly down to the river.'

He nodded. 'I wager that's the problem. There must be one running down from Thames Street. Which means it's not our responsibility.'

Brennan and Cat continued down to the quay. A change had taken place. No one was talking now. Sailors lined the side of the ship. The workmen were standing idle. Their eyes were turned towards the ship, as were those of Fanshawe and the Customs officers. A tall man now stood beside Fanshawe. Cat's attention quickened. Van Riebeeck was there after all. He seemed to sense her presence, because he glanced over his shoulder at her. She was struck afresh by his size. He gave no sign of recognition.

Everyone on the quay was watching a large box being winched ashore with the help of a sling made of rope and canvas. The box was about five feet square and constructed of roughly cut planks, set slightly apart from one another. It swayed and turned as it descended slowly to the quayside.

Suddenly, just before it reached the ground, there was a tearing sound as the canvas ripped. The box tilted violently to one side. One corner slid from the sling and hit the stones of the quay with a crack. There was a gasp from the watchers. The impact dislodged one end of a plank. A nearby workman leapt forward and tried to push the plank back into place.

Van Riebeeck shouted something and made to intervene. But he was too late.

There was a blur of movement at the side of the box. The workman screamed. He jumped back so quickly that he missed his footing and sprawled on his back. A puddle of blood spread from him across the grey stones of the quay. For a moment no one paid him any heed. Their eyes were on the box. Something was moving behind the dislodged plank.

A large paw appeared. It clawed the air.

Wednesday was the day for Maria's weekly visit to Slaughter Street. On this occasion, her mother did not tell her to take her sampler with her to show her progress to her grandfather, Mr Fanshawe. This was a relief, because Maria hated her sampler almost as much as she hated Abbott. Her mother, a

37

notable needlewoman, had high standards, and Maria's work this week had fallen even more woefully short of them than usual. But her relief was tempered by the fact that her mother was to accompany her today.

'Your uncle will dine there with us.' Her mother glanced at her and made a moue of distaste. 'Study to look more cheerful when we're there. You're as dreary as a funeral.'

'I didn't know he was in England.'

'There's a great deal you don't know.'

As they left their lodgings at the sign of the Black Boy, Hannah opened the door for them. Maria followed her mother along the passage that led down the side of the house to Fleet Street. At the end, she looked back. Hannah was still there, watching them.

The two girls had not talked again about the doll. But Maria had followed Hannah's instructions to the letter. It had been harder than she had expected to open up the mattress and push the doll inside. Sewing up the hole she had made was even more difficult; the thread was thick, the material heavy and stiff, and the needle far larger than she was accustomed to use. Now there was another worry: that someone might notice that the mattress had been tampered with.

Mother and daughter walked to Slaughter Street to save money. Mistress Abbott had planned their arrival for half an hour before dinner at midday. They had little conversation. When they reached Smithfield, the market was largely over for the day. Men were clearing away the hurdles. A waggon drawn by oxen crawled across the open space, with several men walking beside it.

Her mother gave an exclamation and stopped. She muttered something in Dutch. One of the men turned towards them and waved. Maria recognized the tall figure of her uncle. He broke away and walked rapidly towards them.

'Anna,' he said, as he drew nearer, 'and Maria too. This is well-met. How do you do?'

'Well enough,' her mother said.

He embraced her, and she responded with a warmth she showed no one else. He turned to Maria and gave her a smile and mock bow. 'Your servant, little madam.'

She curtsied and looked at the ground.

'Fanshawe has gone before us to prepare for our reception,' her uncle continued, speaking in Dutch, as her mother had. 'I said I'd walk with the waggon to keep the lion company.'

'A lion?' Her mother frowned at him. 'Henryk, what nonsense is this?'

'No nonsense about it.' He pointed at the waggon, which was still lumbering ahead of them towards Slaughter Street. 'We've been watching them unload the cargo for most of the morning. The bulk of it is stowed in the warehouse, but Fanshawe wanted some pieces of furniture brought up to Smithfield. And also the lion. He's in the box at the back.'

'Is this some freak? This lion is not amusing.'

'No, he isn't amusing, Sister, not for some people. The box broke open on the quay and the damned brute could have escaped. As it was, it almost tore off a man's arm.'

'Then I wish Mr Fanshawe would not take the savage beast into his house.'

He smiled at her. 'He wants to show it to the world. You know what he's like when he has something novel and curious. A child with a new toy.'

Maria watched them while they talked. Their two faces were very alike, especially in profile. Her mother and Henryk had been taken for twins, though in fact he was six years younger than her, and they had been born to different fathers. She treated him sometimes as if he were still the child he had once been. Maria thought it probable that her mother loved Henryk more than anyone else in the world. Possibly he was the only person she loved.

He offered his sister his arm, and the three of them walked after the waggon.

'Where will Mr Fanshawe keep the beast?' Mistress Abbott asked, still speaking in Dutch.

'He has a place made ready in the stable. One of the captains we deal with brought it back from Africa, and I had it shipped over from Amsterdam.'

They passed among the sheep pens. Her mother and uncle were in front, talking to each other, while Maria trailed behind. She tried to hear what they were saying. Her spoken Dutch was adequate but not fluent, because she had spent most of her life in England. But her ear was attuned to it, and she understood the language well enough. Fragments of conversation drifted back to her.

'Have you seen my husband?' her mother said.

'Two nights ago . . .' Henryk said something that Maria couldn't catch. '. . . the Blue Bush.'

Her mother made a harsh, barking sound, the nearest she came to laughter, though there was little amusement in it. Her uncle said something else, but lowered his voice.

The waggon was negotiating the narrow turning into the lane that led to Mr Fanshawe's stables, which lay at the other end of the garden from the house. One of the nearside wheels caught on the raised edge of a large, rectangular stone on the corner of Slaughter Street. The stone had a criss-cross pattern of runnels cut into it. According to Grandfather, in olden times they had killed the beasts there, and their blood had drained down the runnels. That was why it was called Slaughter Street.

The driver whipped the bellowing oxen mercilessly until they gave a great heave that tugged the waggon over the obstacle and brought it down with a jolt and a clatter on the other side. There was a deep-throated roar from the box, creating a sudden, brief silence. Maria cried out before she could stop herself. The men nearby gave a ragged cheer.

'Ah,' Uncle Van Riebeeck said, looking back at Maria and smiling. 'Our lion grows peevish.'

CHAPTER SEVEN

ON 21 FEBRUARY, Cat received a second summons from Lord Arlington, desiring her to call on him. She was at Goring House at the time he fixed, two o'clock in the afternoon, and was left to wait in an anteroom. My lord kept her waiting for nearly an hour. When at last Abbott ushered her into the study, she found his lordship stooping over his desk. He was poring over another set of drawings. He did not look up as she entered.

Abbott left her marooned in the middle of the room and went to sit at a small table in the corner furthest from the fire. Without waiting for an invitation, Cat drew nearer to Arlington's desk. Almost at once, she recognized the drawings as her own work: these were the preliminary plans and elevations she had done nearly two years earlier for Tata's poultry house in the garden. Her spirits sank. Was it possible that some structural flaw had become apparent? In a flash, she imagined that during the last few months the weight of snow on the roof might have put an unexpected stress on the structure, causing the trusses to—

Arlington looked up. 'Mistress Hakesby.' He bowed to her in a cursory manner and waved at the drawings. 'I have been examining these again.'

'Is there something amiss, my lord?'

'No, no. Quite the reverse.' He rubbed the black plaster across his nose, the gesture so automatic that he was unconscious of it. 'I want you to design another poultry house for me. But one that is altogether larger in scale and more magnificent in decoration.'

'For Euston Hall?'

'Oh no.' Arlington smiled and waved his finger at her; for some reason, he was clearly delighted with himself. 'I have quite a different situation in mind for it. This design – and possibly even the cost of the building itself – will be a gift – a token of my most profound respect and admiration.' He paused. His eyes slid away from Cat towards the chimney piece, though she had the sense that he was seeing something else entirely. 'Perhaps we should envisage this as a double poultry house, partly for the symmetry of it, and partly for the separation of various kinds of bird. We might have an archway between the two blocks, leading to a commodious yard where the fowls may run about in safety. And, as I say, the whole to be suitably ornamented.'

Arlington fell silent. He looked up at the ceiling and smiled as if he saw something pleasing there.

'Suitable for what, my lord?' Cat said.

'Not for what, Mistress Hakesby. For whom.' His gaze returned to her. He was no longer smiling. 'Suitable for a princess of the blood.'

* * *

It was almost a fortnight after our last meeting that I saw Abbott again. It was towards three o'clock on Wednesday, 23 February. I was walking from Scotland Yard to my lodgings in the Savoy. The afternoon was damp and foggy. The recent snow had turned to slush. The streets were crowded. Despite the gloom and the muck underfoot, it was faster to walk than to take a coach, even if there had been a hackney available to hire.

I was on the north side of the Strand, waiting in a group of other foot passengers for a gap in the traffic. I heard a sharp intake of breath beside me and turned my head. And there he was.

For an instant Abbott stared blankly at me, as though I were a stranger. We were not twenty yards from the mouth of Blue Bush Alley, and I guessed he had come from there. He had seen me first, I think, and he must have been trying to back away before I saw him.

His blankness of expression gave way to an uncertain smile when he realized that it was too late to retreat. He seized my arm and wished me good afternoon as if we were the best of friends. As he did so, the wine on his breath reached my nostrils.

The traffic parted and the crowd swept into the Strand, bearing the two of us with it like twigs in a current. Abbott staggered against me. He would have fallen if I had not held him up. It was only then that I realized how drunk he was.

On the other side of the road, he propped himself against a wall, breathing hard. He did not release his grip on my arm.

'A good dinner, sir?' I said.

'Dinner? I don't recall.' His voice was louder than usual,

and the consonants less clearly defined. 'But there was wine, Marwood, take my word for it, by God there was wine.' The words tumbled out of him, each bumping into its neighbours. 'And we gave the dice box a devilish good rattling. Dame Fortune was with me at the start, but damn me she's a fickle jade.'

He forced a laugh. His expression changed. He turned his head and vomited copiously down the wall. After a pause he vomited again. 'Oh God,' he mumbled between his retches, 'oh God.'

'And my lord?' I said when the vomiting had stopped. 'Does he expect you back this afternoon?'

Lord Arlington was strict with his inferiors. He worked them hard. Moreover, he had lived for many years in the Spanish court and he placed a high value on dignity, both his own and that of his servants, whom he considered as remote representatives of himself. In a state like this, Abbott would do himself no good and probably much harm if he staggered off to Goring House or Arlington's office in Whitehall.

Abbott wiped his mouth with the hem of his cloak. 'My lord can go to the devil. They can all go to the devil. Especially that damned rogue I played with. Talking of which, shall we take a glass of wine together?'

'I think you should go home.'

He appeared not to have heard me. He blinked, and his face twisted itself into a look of low cunning. 'And what about a game of something while we drink, eh? Not dice – they don't love me today – cards, eh? That's the thing.'

'You've played enough for one day.'

He patted my shoulder and for a moment his usual condescension bobbed to the surface. 'You're a good fellow at heart,

Marwood, I've always said so. But too sober in your ways. That's your drawback. A word to the wise suffices, my friend. I tell you this, gratis: you'll never get anywhere at Whitehall if you don't learn to drink like a gentleman.'

He belched lingeringly and I pulled away from him, fearing he was about to vomit afresh.

Abbott's spirits plummeted again. 'I'm going to the devil,' he confided, seizing my arm and leaning heavily against me. His lips were trembling. 'Marwood, I don't deserve it. On my oath, I don't. I've been so unlucky.' He turned his face towards the sky, or rather towards the overhanging gable above us. 'Oh Lord God! Deliver me from evildoers.'

He crumpled against the wall and began to cry. Several passers-by threw us curious glances. I cursed my ill-fortune. Had I been a moment earlier or a moment later I might have missed Abbott altogether. As it was, I could hardly leave him to the tender mercies of beggars and bullies and thieves. Within a quarter of an hour, someone would have dragged him into an alley and stripped him of everything he had, including his shirt.

'Come,' I said, 'I'll see you to your lodging, and all will seem better anon. Lean on my arm, eh?'

His weeping subsided to a gentle snuffling as we staggered along the Strand. The fight had seeped out of him, leaving behind a wine-sodden wreck; he had hardly more control over his limbs than Arlington's Tata.

'I'm a fool,' he muttered. 'I'm a cursed fool.'

'Very likely,' I said. 'But the sooner you get home, the less of a fool you'll be.'

We blundered on a few more paces, lurching from side to side.

'But you don't understand, Marwood. No one understands.'

I couldn't see his face under his hat, but it sounded as if the tears had returned.

'No one understands me either,' I said. 'We'll go faster if you don't talk. You live by Temple Bar, don't you? Near the Devil?'

'I – I meant no harm, you know.'

'I'm sure you didn't. Everyone takes a little too much wine now and then. Sleep it off, and it will right itself in the morning.'

'Will it?' His grip tightened. 'Will it? I fear this business will never come right.'

I wondered how much he had lost at play today. 'If you stop gambling it might.'

'Not that.'

'Then what?'

He ignored the question. 'It wasn't like this at first, you know.'

'When you first called for wine and the dice box?'

'But I didn't call for them.' Briefly triumphant, he wagged his finger at me. '*He* did.'

By now we were approaching the place where the road narrowed to pass under Temple Bar into the City, and the din of traffic and shouting was louder than ever. The Devil Tavern was here. On the other side of the road was the church St Dunstan-in-the-West, with Clifford's Inn beyond. I had unhappy memories of this neighbourhood and I did not want to linger.

I shouted in Abbott's ear: 'Who did? Who called for the dice box?'

'Ah. Here. The black boy.'

'A black boy?' For an instant I thought he must mean my

47

boy, Stephen, had called for the dice box, which was an absurdity. 'What do you mean? What black boy?'

Abbott stopped abruptly. He flung up his arm so wildly that his hand almost hit me. 'That one. Look.' He burst out laughing and then turned to vomit for a third time.

By then I had seen the sign hanging above the house we were passing. It was a clumsy carving of a blackamoor with a pipe in his mouth. There was a window beside the door, and the candles were already lit in the room beyond. The shop sold tobacco and snuff.

'Oh God,' Abbott said, his melancholy returning. 'Down there. 'Swhere I live.'

There was a covered passage beside the shop. He pulled me into it, his pace increasing like that of a tired horse with its stable in sight. It was my turn to stumble, for the way was dark, unfamiliar and slippery underfoot. We came to a door on the left-hand side. He drummed on it with the heels of both hands. 'Servant's a lazy slut,' he said. 'I've a good mind to throw her out.'

After a while, he grew weary of knocking and leant against the jamb.

'We shall have wine,' he said, his mood swinging back again. As dogs return to their vomit, so drunks return again and again to the subject uppermost in their minds. 'I shall send to the tavern directly. We must have a toast.'

'No more wine,' I said. 'Not today, eh?'

'Marwood. Do you believe in forgiveness?'

'What did you say?'

'If a man's shorry – sorry – for what he's done, truly sorry, should he not be forgiven? He should, shouldn't he? Everyone knows that, eh?'

Bolts rattled on the other side of the door. There was the scrape of a bar withdrawn from its socket.

'Forgive us our trespasses, Marwood, that's what it says in the Prayer Book, as we forgive them that trespass against us.' He pawed at my sleeve. 'I need to talk to you,' he said with sudden urgency. 'I need advice – pray say you'll help me.'

Suddenly the door opened. A servant woman looked out at us. She was strongly built and unusually tall. It was too dim to see her clearly, though something about the shape of her face was familiar, though I had never seen her before. She wore a long, drab apron.

'Pray don't look so stern,' Abbott said, stretching his hand towards her. 'I'll not have it, do you hear? I'll whip you, woman, if you don't mend your surly ways.'

With a sudden jerk, she pulled the door fully open. Abbott fell into the house and sprawled on the floor, with his feet trailing over the threshold.

'Your master has had more wine than he intended,' I said. 'If we each take an arm, we can get him to bed.'

'No,' she said.

Head swaying, Abbott raised himself to his hands and knees of his own accord. The maid took him by the collar of his coat and with a sudden, powerful heave tugged him over the threshold. He turned his head.

'Shorry,' he said. I wasn't sure if he was speaking to me or someone else.

The woman shut the door in my face.

CHAPTER EIGHT

IT TOOK THE three of them – Hannah, Maria and her mother – to move Abbott up the stairs, along the passage to the bedchamber he shared with his wife. On the way, his hat fell off, then his cloak and then his peruke. He tried to vomit at the top of the stairs, but only produced a dry and painful retching.

'He's brought up the worst of it already,' Mistress Abbott said dispassionately. 'God be thanked.'

Once he was face down on the bed, Hannah and Mistress Abbott removed his boots. By unspoken agreement, they did not attempt to undress him further. They left him lying there, snoring and occasionally breaking wind, while the last of the light drained from the sky.

The master of the house slept for nearly five hours. When he woke, he hammered on the floor of the bedroom with the heel of his boot. Mistress Abbott sent Hannah up to him with a candle. The maid found him sitting on the side of the bed.

'My head hurts,' he said, scowling. 'Bring me the pot.' He commanded her to hold it while he pissed into it. Afterwards, he sank back on the bed. 'A jug of small beer. And mix me a posset. I need something to settle my stomach.'

Hannah left her master with the candle and felt her way down the passage into the parlour, where Mistress Abbott and Maria were sewing at the table, each with a candle in front of her. Hannah told them what her master had said.

Mistress Abbott sighed and put down the shirt and her needle. 'Clear the kitchen table and stir up the fire,' she said. 'I'll come and make it in a moment. Take up the beer when you've done the fire.'

'May I come?' Maria said.

'You haven't finished hemming that shift.'

'But you said you'd show me how to make a posset. Then I'll be able to do it if he calls for one and you're not there.'

Mistress Abbott shrugged. 'Put your sewing away. If you leave it out, it will be filthy in five minutes.'

Maria took this for a form of assent. She followed her mother into the kitchen, where Hannah was wiping the table with a dishcloth. Tallow lamps burned on the dresser, filling the air with their stench and providing a flickering murky light. The fireplace was almost as big as the room itself. In the middle of the recess stood an iron fire-basket, in which a few coals gave off a sullen glow in a bed of ash.

Mistress Abbott sat on a stool. 'Set half a pint of milk to warm,' she said to Maria. 'Don't just stand there, Hannah, fetch some milk. Measure out half a pint.'

Hannah handed Maria the iron pan and went into the scullery for the milk, which was kept in a covered pail on the doorstep.

'Hurry up, girl,' Mistress Abbott called.

'Sorry, mistress. I couldn't find the jug. But I have now.'

When the maid returned, she was breathing hard as if she had run a race. 'Sorry,' she said again. 'Sorry.'

Maria poured the contents of the jug into the pan. Hannah was standing so close that Maria felt the maid's warm, rapid breath on her own cheek.

'Don't spill it,' Mistress Abbott said, fumbling at the ring of keys at her waist.

'And stir it well,' said Hannah softly.

'Hang the milk over the fire and unlock the press.' Mistress Abbott gave Maria one of the keys. 'Find half a dozen cloves and put them in the milk: he says they're good for his toothache. And you'll need a bottle of sack and the sugar. Hannah: the eggs and a bowl for them. And then draw some ale.'

Maria fetched the cloves, the wine and the sugar. Afterwards, her mother set her to beating three eggs in the bowl and sent Hannah to make up the parlour fire.

There was a burst of knocking upstairs.

Mistress Abbott sighed. 'See what he wants, will you? I'll watch the milk.'

Maria gave her mother a startled glance. 'Must I?'

'Do as I say, minx,' her mother snapped.

Maria took one of the parlour candles and went slowly upstairs, dragging her feet at every step. She found her step-father lying on his side and snoring. His legs trailed over the side of the bed. She held up the candle and noted dispassionately that he had somehow managed to overturn the pot. He stirred and opened his eyes.

'Oh. You.'

She bobbed a curtsy.

'Where's the posset?'

'Almost done, sir.'

She went back to the kitchen. Hannah had returned.

'He wants his posset,' Maria said. 'And there's piss all over the floor.'

'Hannah, go and mop it up directly,' Mistress Abbott said to the maid. 'Or the chamber will stink like a necessary house all night. Put a dash of vinegar in the water. Maria, keep the milk moving.'

Hannah fetched rags and a bucket from the scullery and went away again. Mistress Abbott brought the china posset bowl from the press. She added the eggs and the wine. Maria stirred vigorously. When Hannah returned, Mistress Abbott told her to put in the sugar. The pieces were in a twist of paper. Hannah turned aside to blow her nose and then dropped three lumps into the bowl. Her eyes met Maria's over the bowl.

'There,' she said. 'That should do.'

'Stir it until the sugar is quite dissolved,' Mistress Abbott said.

Maria took up the spoon and obeyed.

'There,' said her mother after a moment. She gave her daughter one of her rare smiles. 'Take it up to Mr Abbott. Hannah will come with you and make the room smell sweet. Mind you watch him drink it. I don't want it going to waste after all this trouble.'

The two girls left the room, Hannah with the bucket and a candle, Maria with the bowl. Outside the door of the bedchamber, without a word being spoken, they stopped and looked at each other.

'You first,' Hannah whispered, wrinkling her nose. 'You're the *lady*.'

Maria spat into the bowl. She held it out to Hannah, who did likewise. They smiled at each other. Then Hannah raised the latch with her arm and stood aside to allow her young mistress to enter first.

'Your posset, sir,' Maria said, and advanced towards the bed.

CHAPTER NINE

ON SATURDAY MORNING I was at Scotland Yard, standing at my desk. The other clerks were also at work, more or less in silence. It was shortly before the dinner hour. I should have been preparing a summary of recent intelligence relating to French shipbuilding. Instead, I was trying to write a letter. I was now at work on my fourth attempt to dash off a few lines that would strike a suitably casual but not unfriendly note:

Madam
There is a new Italian castrato singing at the King's Playhouse on Monday next, in the evening. Would it please you to hear him? Pray give me a line—

The office door opened, forcing me to break off. Mr Williamson came in. The room fell silent, apart from the scratching of pens. He paused, looking at us all.

'My lord tells me that poor Abbott is dead,' he said. 'God rest his soul.'

As usual Williamson's face gave nothing away. He might have been telling us what the weather was like outside or about a change in the way we were to docket incoming reports before filing them.

Abbott had died the previous afternoon, he went on to say, after a short but violent illness during which he had suffered acute pangs of pain. A physician attended him on the morning of his death, but he could do nothing to relieve Abbott's agonies. He had told Mistress Abbott that her husband had probably expired after a severe bout of flux, perhaps brought on by drinking more wine than he was accustomed to take. Alternatively, he might have eaten food that was bad; such cases were sadly common even in winter. Cholera was also a possible cause. Or he may have suffered from a growth in his belly, a canker whose malignancy had suddenly increased owing to the cold, damp weather.

'A sad business, however he died,' Williamson concluded. 'But of course Abbott's death does not affect the work of this office. Not now.'

He went into his private room and closed the door. The rest of us glanced furtively at each other. Abbott hadn't been much liked when he had worked here and there was a general feeling that he had not deserved his promotion to Lord Arlington's office, and the increase of salary it brought him. No one said anything. But I knew the same thought was in everyone's mind. Now there was a vacancy, my lord might find someone more suitable to fill it. Perhaps someone else from Mr Williamson's office.

In silence, we went back to work. Or, in my case, to the fifth draft of my letter.

* * *

The following Monday, Williamson tapped me on the shoulder.

'You're to wait on Lord Arlington this morning, Marwood. Go to his room in the Privy Gallery.'

I bowed, took my hat and cloak and left. Williamson hadn't said why I was wanted, and his manner hadn't encouraged questions. I kept my thoughts to myself. I had no desire to replace Abbott in my lord's private office, and I hoped that was not the reason for the summons.

I passed under the archway into Whitehall and made my way into the palace. Arlington's office was on the first floor of the Privy Gallery range, and its windows looked over the Privy Garden. In the clerks' room, the first person I saw was Dudley Gorvin. We dined together once a week or so, and sometimes went to the theatre.

'Do you know why my lord sent for me?' I asked.

'Yes. But you won't see him now, he's gone out. He told me to pass on his commands. You've heard about poor Abbott, I suppose?' Gorvin sniffed, and his expression told me his opinion of his late colleague without the need for any words. 'The truth is, my lord only took him on to oblige my lady.'

'Lady Arlington?' I said, surprised. 'I didn't realize she was acquainted with him before.'

'Not with him. With Abbott's wife. Didn't you know? Mistress Abbott's Dutch, though she's lived here for years, and so's my lady of course. I believe there's some connection or other – Mistress Abbott was maid to her, or someone in her family, and my lady has a kindness for her.'

'Ah. That explains it.'

Gorvin darted a glance at me. 'You mean it explains why

57

her husband was favoured?' he said drily. 'Yes. Anyway, Abbott's the reason you're here.'

'How so?'

'He removed a pair of files from the office a day or two before he died. I assume he wanted to work on them at home. We need them back.'

'Why me? Can't you send a boy for them?'

Gorvin gave me one of his sardonic smiles. 'The files are confidential, so it has to be someone trustworthy, not an inky lad who might fall prey to a scurvy French spy.'

'And my lord thought Mr Williamson could better spare one of his clerks than he could?'

'He asked for you by name, Marwood. That's all I know. You must have made an impression on him. For good or ill. Is that possible?'

'I was at Goring House a week or so ago. My lord saw me with Abbott. And I suppose he realizes we knew each other when Abbott worked in our office.'

'There you are.' Gorvin's lips twitched. 'Perhaps he thinks you were friends.'

'I had as little to do with him as I could.'

'But do you know where he lodged?'

'Fleet Street. At the sign of the Black Boy, by Temple Bar.'

'So you were well enough acquainted to know that?'

'Only because I met him by chance in the Strand the other day. He was in his cups and I helped him find his way home.'

'Drunk?' Gorvin's eyebrows shot up. 'That's unlike him. He had other frailties.'

'Aye,' I said.

'If the odds were good enough, he'd have wagered that the sun wouldn't rise tomorrow.'

'I'd better collect those files,' I said, finding Abbott tedious even in death, poor man. 'I assume the widow's still in their lodgings?'

'As far as I know. And wasn't there a child as well?'

'A baby?' I said. 'I'm surprised they had time. They can't have been married more than seven or eight months at the outside. Unless they took a tumble beforehand.'

'The child isn't Abbott's. It's the wife's first husband's.'

'And these files — what are they about?'

'Nothing of importance, but you know what my lord is like.' Gorvin shuffled the papers before him. 'Everything in this office is confidential. Everything's important. Everything must be in its proper place. Stay — here's your warrant.'

I said goodbye and left him to his papers. The day was fine, though bitterly cold. I decided to walk. If I stretched out the commission for long enough, I could dine while I was out, thereby snatching a little pleasure from this joyless errand. I might call in at the Lamb, a shabby tavern in Wych Street, north of the Strand. The place had been a favourite of old Mr Hakesby, Cat's late husband, and I had occasionally dined or supped there with her since his death.

On my way I called at my lodgings in the Savoy to collect a warmer cloak and a leather satchel to hold the files.

My manservant, Sam, let me into the house. He bowed as gracefully as he could, bearing in mind that five years ago a Dutch cannonball had removed his right leg below the knee. 'Letter for you, master,' he said. 'It's in the parlour.' Then he spoiled this fleeting impression of servility by giving me a knowing wink. 'Stephen says it's in Mistress Hakesby's hand.'

That caught my attention, though I hoped the fact did not

seem obvious to Sam. I had dispatched the sixth draft of my letter to Cat on Saturday evening. 'I'm going out soon. Send Stephen here, and tell him he's coming with me.'

I went into the parlour, closing the door in Sam's face. The fire had not been lit, and the room was chilly. I stripped off my gloves. The letter was on the sideboard. I broke the seal and unfolded it.

Henrietta Street, 28 February
Sir, I regret I cannot accompany you this evening. CH

I crumpled the sheet of paper in my hand. Cat rarely wasted words, but she could hardly have expressed herself more curtly. It was clear that she did not want to see me. She had thrown my olive branch back in my face. But what did I care? The world was full of women.

CHAPTER TEN

M Y FOOTBOY, STEPHEN, walked a pace or two behind me along the Strand. He was much changed since
I had first known him more than two years ago, when he had
been small, terrified and afflicted with scrofula. He was now
about twelve years old and almost as tall as me. He was an
African, slim and upright, with fine features and watchful
eyes.

Sometimes, Margaret had told me, Stephen had bad dreams
and woke them with his cries. Margaret was Sam's wife. She
brooded over the boy as she would have done a son.

He rarely said much to me, apart from when I asked him
a question. According to Margaret, he talked more when he
was down in the kitchen with the other servants. During his
years with me, he had learned to read and write. He had
proved such an apt pupil that I had begun to employ him
when I was checking the proofs of the *Gazette*.

Stephen was my slave. By the strict letter of the law, I
owned him, as I owned the coat on my back and the silver-
gilt dish I kept locked in the larger of my two strongboxes.

In the same box I kept the documents that would confirm my ownership of Stephen to any court in the land. The boy was mine, body and soul.

In full daylight, the alley beside the tobacco-seller's was even less inviting than it had been on my last visit. There was no answer when Stephen hammered on Abbott's door. We went into the tobacco-seller's. The shopkeeper said that Mistress Abbott, her daughter and their servant had gone away after the funeral.

I showed him Arlington's warrant. 'Where did they go?'

'A friend's, sir, I believe. I have the address somewhere . . . Mr Abbott was in agony for nigh on two days. He'd been ill before but not like this. Oh, the shrieking, sir – you could hear it under Temple Bar. He lost all control of his bowels, too. And their maid said he vomited black bile for hours on end. You wouldn't have thought a man could have so much inside him. Ah me, life is cruel, sir, is it not?'

I cut him short when he showed signs of philosophizing indefinitely. 'Do you have a key for Mr Abbott's lodging?'

He produced the key from under the counter. Stephen and I returned to the alley and unlocked the door.

The smells hit me at once. Sweet and sour, clinging and cloying; the smells of decay. To the right a passage led to the back of the house. The stairs were in front of us. There was a dead rat on the bottom tread. It lay in a small, stinking puddle with its mouth wide, exposing sharp white teeth. Like Abbott, it had voided its belly and its bowels before it died.

Covering my nose with the hem of my cloak, I blundered to the window that lit the passage. I flung open the lattice and leant on the sill. I breathed in the familiar scents of coal smoke and privies and cooking, seasoned with the salty tang of the river.

I pulled back my head and stood up. I hoped to God there was no infection in the air. Breathing through my mouth, I made a quick survey. The kitchen was at the end of the passage, with a scullery beyond. The two small windows looked onto a cramped, high-walled garden, where a skeletal fruit tree was slowly dying. There was also a windowless closet where someone, probably a servant, had slept on a straw mattress. Another dead rat lay there now.

There were some scraps of food in the press, including the mouldy heel of a loaf, and, in the scullery, an almost empty barrel of beer. There must have been other food and drink in the house, but it seemed that Mistress Abbott had taken it with her.

In the scullery, I lifted the lid of the waste bin. A foul smell rose from it. I poked inside with the handle of a broom. There were ashes, rotting vegetables and eggshells. I poked deeper and turned up a piece of coarse paper, and a short length of string. There was a mark on one corner of the paper: a pestle and mortar, drawn by hand in ink, enclosed in the outline of a wavering semicircle. It was clearly an apothecary's mark, but the paper gave no clue to what it had contained.

Stephen followed me from room to room, first downstairs, then upstairs. At my command, he opened windows and flung back shutters. Cold air flowed through the house, stirring the heavy odours that hung like invisible curtains.

The largest room was furnished as a parlour, with a table covered with a stained and crumpled cloth and a fireplace heaped with cold ashes. Upstairs, one door opened into a

63

bedchamber with a closet beyond, another to a small, square room that contained nothing but an old table and a stool.

The smell was worst of all in the bedchamber, where I assumed that Abbott had died. The bed had been stripped to its mattress. Its frame was bare of curtains. The mat by the bed was wet, as though someone had emptied a pail or two of water over it and not troubled to dry it. There were shards of white and blue china by the night table.

Nothing had been tidied away, nothing cleaned. I took care where I trod, avoiding a pool of vomit, an unemptied pot filled to the brim, and soiled bedclothes and nightshirts. The corpse of a third rat lay half concealed under a torn shift. It was obvious that Mistress Abbott had left in a hurry, taking with her anything of value and leaving the rest. Perhaps her grief had been so great that she could not bear to stay in the house where her husband had died.

The neighbouring closet opened out of the bedroom. There was no door between them, only an old blanket, nailed to the lintel. The closet was larger than the maid's, with a truckle bed stripped to its mattress. A small doll lay face down on the floor. It was a crude, battered object which could never have had any beauty. Stephen picked it up. There were a few strands of hair clinging to the skirt. He brushed them to the floor. He laid the doll on the bed, where the pillow would once have been.

'Why did you do that?' I said.

'In case the child comes back for it, master.'

I felt an unexpected pang of pity at the sight of the doll. Not only for Abbott, but for all of them. Mistress Abbott had buried her second husband, and his salary would have died with him. The girl was probably missing her stepfather and

64

her home as well as her doll. Their future must be bleak and uncertain.

By now the stench had diminished to a bearable level. Or perhaps I had simply grown used to it. With Stephen standing by, his face expressionless, I turned over the Abbotts' remaining possessions with my gloved hands. It surprised me how mean they were. Abbott could not have earned less than £150 a year, quite possibly more, together with his wife's dowry, if there had been one. But the place gave the impression that the family had lived as if they found it hard to make ends meet. There was nothing to please the eye – few books, no pictures, no plate.

Not that this concerned me. All I wanted were Arlington's two files. Each, Gorvin had said, was of the standard pattern commonplace in both my lord's and Mr Williamson's office; such files were used for documents in current use, which were often passed from desk to desk; they consisted of a sturdy sheet of paper, folded once, which enclosed a number of letters or memoranda, the whole secured by a string which passed through each item, with the ends attached to the outer cover.

The trouble was, I couldn't find them. I recruited Stephen to help, and we searched everywhere, upstairs and downstairs, even – using the poker from the fireplace – among the soiled bedclothes and shirts. All we turned up was another dead rat, this one in the cupboard that had served as a larder.

Our lack of success soured my mood still further. On another day I might have been less irritated. But self-pity feeds on itself, and so does irritation, its bastard cousin. I was already angry with Cat for sending me such an unfriendly note after all we had gone through together. Now

I felt a strange, not-quite pleasure in the fact that Providence had sent me another reason to consider myself a child of misfortune.

'We'll try once more,' I said to Stephen. 'Just in case we've overlooked something.'

We went from room to room. It was a forlorn hope. We ended our second search in the chamber upstairs which contained a table and chair and little else. The tabletop was spotted with ink and scored with cuts, as if Abbott had repeatedly sharpened his pen with a penknife there. On the windowsill was the stump of a tallow candle, which showed signs of tiny toothmarks. It looked as if Abbott had used this room as a study. Surely, I thought, it was here, if anywhere, that he would have kept the files.

Stephen was poking the ashes in the fireplace in a desultory fashion. I heard a noise and automatically glanced towards the sound. The boy had stepped back from the hearth. A floorboard had creaked under his foot. He shifted his weight slightly, and the board gave another mournful creak.

I was about to order him to close the window when Stephen crouched down. As I watched, he worked his fingertips into the gap between two floorboards. I joined him by the fireplace. One of the boards had been sawn in two at the end near the side of the hearth. The gap was not obvious, for the boards around the fireplace were thick with dirt, dust and ash.

The shorter piece tilted. Stephen lifted it out. He put his hand into the cavity beneath, in the gap between two joists and above the ceiling of the room below.

He looked at me. 'Nothing.'

I waved him aside and examined the cavity myself. I saw fragments of lime plaster and the side of one of the joists that supported the floor. There were no files. Oddly enough, there were no cobwebs, either. I poked a fingertip into the plaster dust. My eye caught on something red, about the size of a groat. I laid it in the palm of my hand and took it to the window.

It was an irregular fragment of sealing wax with an indentation at one corner. I took out my pocketbook and put the wax in the pocket inside the back cover. It was an unusual shade – closer to purple than red.

It proved that something had been hidden under the floor, a document of some sort. Perhaps Abbott had made the hiding place to protect the family's smaller valuables from the risk of theft or the prying eyes of servants. The widow must have taken away the contents, including those cursed files, when she left the house.

The day was slipping away. The prospect of a leisurely dinner, at the Rose or anywhere else, was receding rapidly. Arlington wouldn't thank me if I came back empty-handed.

I told Stephen to close all the windows. 'We must find Mistress Abbott now.'

'Shall I bring the doll, master?'

'What?' I stared at him. 'Why?'

'For the little girl.'

I thought it a good idea and told him so, though my motives were less charitable than his. There was a surprising vein of sweetness running through the boy, for all the pains he had endured in his short life.

I locked up the lodgings, and we went back to the shop. The tobacco-seller showed me the address that Mistress Abbott had given him. It was written in an elegant, upright hand: *Mr Fanshawe's, in Slaughter Street, Smithfield.*

The name struck a chord in my memory. Could this be the same man I had encountered with Cat during our disastrous visit to the Duke's Theatre? The man with the Dutch friend. The man who was having problems with his warehouse doors.

'Do you know Mr Fanshawe?' I asked.

The shopkeeper shook his head.

'So he never came here as far as you know?'

The shopkeeper took a pinch of snuff and sneezed. There was a brown stain on his upper lip. 'The Abbotts didn't have many visitors, sir. They lived privately, you might say. Maybe they thought themselves too good for other folk.' He wiped his lip with the back of his hand. 'Or maybe they needed all their breath for shouting at each other.'

While we had been searching the Abbotts' lodgings, the sky had clouded over. It was now raining, a chilly, relentless winter downpour. I took a hackney to Smithfield. Stephen sat opposite me. In the gloom of the coach's interior his dark face was almost invisible. Drops of water drummed on the roof, competing with the grinding of wheels.

He stirred on the seat. 'Master?'

I peered at him. 'What?'

'There was another rat in the room with the hole in the floor. It was by the fire irons on the hearth.'

I had been looking for government papers, not dead rats. 'So?'

He leant forward, his elbows on his knees. 'I counted them, sir. Five.'

'Did you happen to notice whether any poison had been laid?'

'No, master.'

Nor had I. Of course the rats might have eaten it. Anyway, what did it matter? Everyone had rats in their house. Everyone tried to get rid of them.

As the coach rumbled and jolted through the streets, I counted the dead in my head. Five rats. One man. And they had all died while emptying their bowels and their bellies.

CHAPTER ELEVEN

T HE SMELL OF blood hung over Smithfield and its neighbourhood, night and day. It was a Monday, which meant that the lowing of cattle and the bleating of sheep filled the great open space at the heart of it. There were far fewer animals than there would be when the warmer weather came and the roads were clearer. Scarcity meant higher prices, but rich men were always willing to pay for their meat.

Slaughter Street lay to the west of the market, at its upper end by the sheep pens. It was a narrow but well-kept thoroughfare lined with substantial houses that were older than the Fire.

I paid off the hackney. A crossing sweeper pointed out Mr Fanshawe's house, which had three tall storeys with ornately carved bressummers on the street frontage. There was no sign of a shop or manufactory attached to it.

A heavily built porter answered my knock. With him was a manservant, who civilly asked my business. He was respectably dressed in black broadcloth. I told him I had come from Lord Arlington and desired to speak to his master. The man bowed, his eyes flicking towards Stephen, and begged me to step inside.

He conducted me through an outer lobby to an old-fashioned hall whose plaster ceiling was blackened with smoke. Stephen followed me in and waited near the door, with his eyes cast down. The servant left us.

I looked about me. There was a gallery at the end opposite the fireplace. The walls were panelled, and the wood had darkened, which made the room seem smaller than it was.

The chamber was older than the century but it was furnished with colourful carpets and fine porcelain, with bright, delicate tapestries and some exceptionally fine and curious pieces of furniture, inlaid with precious metals, rare woods and ivory. The room spoke not only of wealth but of exotic, unusual tastes.

I did not hear a door open or even a footstep. But suddenly there was a third person in the chamber, the stooping gentleman I had met with Cat at the theatre. He wore a long gown, fastened high against the cold, and there was a cap on his head rather than a wig. I guessed that I had disturbed him when he was on the verge of sitting down to dine privately.

'Mr Fanshawe – your servant, sir.'

He inclined his head in a bow. 'Mr Marwood. We have met, have we not?'

'Indeed, sir. At the Duke's Theatre a few weeks ago. I was with Mistress Hakesby. Forgive me for troubling you, but I come on business from my Lord Arlington.'

He showed no sign of surprise. 'You're employed by him? I didn't realize.'

'Yes, sir. In the office of his Undersecretary, Mr Williamson.'

'I know Mr Williamson.'

'I think you will have heard of the death of one of my lord's clerks. Mr Abbott, late of Fleet Street. I've been informed that Mistress Abbott and her daughter are staying with you.'

There was a silence, long enough to be uncomfortable. With an effort, I resisted the temptation to obey the universal urge to fill a silence by blundering into speech. At last he said, 'That's correct. Pray sit down, Mr Marwood.' He wore a set of false teeth, and his words emerged from his mouth with a faint but disconcerting whistle. 'May I offer you a glass of wine, perhaps? A biscuit?'

'Thank you, sir. But no.'

Refusing to be hurried, he waved me to a chair, and took another some distance away. He did not look at Stephen, who was standing against the wall, below the great tapestry.

'And what is this business of my lord's?'

'First of all, to convey his condolences to Mistress Abbott.' There was no harm in saying that, though Arlington would have sent a note to the widow as soon as he heard the news of his clerk's death; he was punctilious about such things. 'Also, his clerk has discovered that Mr Abbott was working on two files at the time of his death. He had removed them to finish his labours at home. I've been sent to retrieve them. Pray allow me to show you my lord's warrant.'

At a signal from me, Stephen came forward and carried the warrant to Mr Fanshawe, who studied it carefully and handed it back to the boy.

'I went to Mr Abbott's lodgings at the sign of the Black Boy,' I said. 'But I couldn't find them. No doubt Mistress Abbott took them with her for safekeeping when she and her daughter removed here. Perhaps I might be permitted to ask her in person.'

He stirred in his chair. 'I regret, sir, that will not be possible. Mistress Abbott is indisposed. Prostrated with grief.'

'Then if I might write a few—'

He held up his hand. 'There's no need to inconvenience yourself, sir. Mistress Abbott has already confided these files to my care. I know she is anxious for them to be returned as soon as possible. I had intended to send them to Lord Arlington. But now you have saved me the trouble.'

He rose to his feet and tugged the bell rope to the right of the fireplace. He had hardly sat down again when the servant entered. His master beckoned him to his side and murmured a few words to him. The man bowed and withdrew.

Mr Fanshawe and I sat in silence, another one. It cannot have been more than a few minutes yet such a silence felt like a foretaste of eternity. It was as if my host had withdrawn into himself, into a private space outside the usual passages of time where intruders were not permitted.

The servant returned with the files. He looked to his master, who waved languidly in my direction. The servant handed them to me with a bow.

Two could play this game of stateliness. I held up the index finger of my right hand. 'Stephen.'

He materialized at my elbow and bowed just as the servant had done. Without a word I gave him the files.

Fanshawe stood up, obliging me to do the same. 'I believe that concludes our business, sir. Pray give my humble compliments to my lord, and to Mr Williamson.'

At my elbow, Stephen cleared his throat. I glanced at him.

73

The files were in the satchel. In the palm of his hand lay the crudely made doll we had brought from the Abbotts' lodgings.

'One more thing, sir,' I said. 'Would you return this to Mistress Abbott's daughter? It was left behind in her closet.'

Fanshawe's face briefly changed. It was as though a mask had been removed, revealing something softer and more expressive underneath. At a nod from me, Stephen handed him the doll with a bow.

'Thank you,' Fanshawe said to me. He glanced down at the doll in his hand and wrinkled his nose. 'Goodbye, sir. Joseph will show you out.'

Outside it was still raining, and the air still smelled of blood. Stephen and I walked down the street.

'Someone was watching us, master,' he said.

'In the hall?' I turned to look at him. 'Who?'

'A girl. She was up in the gallery.'

'You've got your wits about you today.' I smiled at him. 'You're a good lad.'

Maria was almost sure that the black boy had seen her.

She remained in the gallery, crouching out of sight of her grandfather, and waited. The house in Slaughter Street had many nooks and crannies, which made eavesdropping much easier than it had been in the Fleet Street lodging. The more you listened, the more you knew. You could never tell when knowledge might come in useful.

In the distance, she heard the thud as the street door closed and the rattle of its chain. Almost at once, there came the sound of her mother's rapid footsteps in the chamber below.

'Has he gone, sir?'

'Yes. He came for those files. He'd been to your lodgings first. A man named Marwood.' Her grandfather's voice was weary. 'One of Mr Williamson's clerks. I've met him before. I gave him the files, and he went away.'

'Abbott didn't like Marwood,' her mother said. 'He thought Williamson favoured him. And the King, even.'

'It doesn't matter, Anna. The files have been returned, and you can be easy in your mind again.'

'You are too kind, sir.' Her mother's voice was gentle, almost sweet. 'Maria and I are so glad to be here again.'

'Where else should you be, my dear? This is your home. I wish to God you'd never left it.'

A chair creaked. Then footsteps. The clack of the door latch filled the empty air below.

'It's all for the best,' Maria's grandfather said. 'The poor foolish man is dead and buried. And now you and Maria are here again, and everything will be pleasant once more.'

After dinner, Mr Fanshawe called Maria to him in his study. It was a square room at the back of the house, with small paintings on two of the walls. Maria liked the paintings because they showed ordinary things and ordinary people: a windmill turning on a hill, a woman sitting with a bowl on her lap and peeling apples, a cart outside a country inn. They had belonged to her dead father, Mr Fanshawe's only son, who had worked in the Dutch Republic for several years. That was how he had met Maria's mother.

Maria took her sampler with her, in case her grandfather wished to inspect her progress. But when she offered to show it to him, he waved it aside.

'How do you like my Barbary lion?' he asked.

'Very much, sir.' Privately she thought it a foul and dangerous beast.

A smile spread over her grandfather's face. 'I thought you would like it, my dear. Perhaps you have inherited my interest in collecting such things. But we must give him a name, must we not? What do you think of Caliban?'

'Yes, sir,' she said. 'It's . . . it is a very good name.'

'I agree,' he said. 'Then we shall call him Caliban. And now I have something for you. A man brought it this morning. It came from your old house.'

He opened a drawer, took out the doll and held it out to her. Maria had expected this, and she had prepared for it in her mind. But she shuddered involuntarily as she took the doll. Witchcraft was a terrible word, and this hideous doll was the word made real. They hanged witches now, but her grandfather had told her that, in times gone by, they used to burn them at Smithfield. According to Hannah, the executioners would chop up whatever the fire did not consume on the Slaughter Stone at the bottom of the street.

'Thank you, sir.' She dropped a curtsy, because her grandfather was a stickler for such things.

The old man looked narrowly at her. 'You don't care for it?'

'To tell the truth, no, sir.' Suddenly she hit upon the right words: 'Besides, it came from Mr Abbott, and I never liked it. He gave it to me when he was courting my mother. To win my favour.'

'Ah. A bad business.' Her grandfather looked at the doll, which was still in her hand. 'And it's a poor thing, isn't it? Do you want to throw it on the fire and be done with it?'

'With all my heart, sir.'

Maria stepped forward and tossed the doll onto the coal. It lay there a moment, its rag covering stirring in the heat. Then a flame streaked along the edge of the cloth, and soon the doll was naked, reduced to a blackened peg. The fire took hold of the wood, which burned merrily for a few seconds and then died to a glowing ghost of its former self.

Something snapped inside her. She knelt by the hearth, took up the poker and ground down the ghost until it was indistinguishable from the fiery bed on which it lay.

'Good,' said her grandfather. 'That's the end of Mr Abbott. You look pale, my child, despite the fire. Perhaps we should send you down to Swaring in the spring and put colour in your cheeks.'

'Yes, sir.' Swaring was a small estate that Mr Fanshawe owned in Kent. Maria had been there once when she was barely out of leading strings. She remembered the place as cold and muddy outside, and cold and damp within.

'Is that your sampler you have there?' Mr Fanshawe asked. 'Show me.'

Reluctantly, she unrolled the horrid thing and spread it on the table beside him.

He put on his spectacles. 'Very handsome, my dear. Is that a mermaid? And that I dare say is a rabbit. Or is it a squirrel? Or a cat?' He looked at her over his glasses. 'Talking of cats, why don't you add Caliban to your menagerie?' He tapped the sampler with his finger. 'He would lend great distinction to your work.'

'Yes, sir,' Maria said, and cast down her eyes.

'Let's find our cloaks.' The old man's voice quavered with excitement. 'It's time for them to feed the lion, and I know you will enjoy that. If you like, you shall throw him a piece of meat with your own hands and watch him tear it to pieces.'

CHAPTER TWELVE

I DINED LATE at a tavern south of Smithfield and within a stone's throw of the City wall. I sat alone in a booth at the side of the common room, while Stephen had his dinner downstairs with the servants. I told him to leave the satchel in my keeping.

While I was waiting for my pigeon pie to arrive, I took out the two files. They should not have been removed from Whitehall without permission from Gorvin or Lord Arlington. Mr Williamson's office had a similar system. But everyone knew that men occasionally took work home with them – when the office was overwhelmed with business, for example, or when a clerk wished to get ahead of himself before a holiday.

Before his death, Abbott had been writing a docket for each file, a summary of their contents. He had completed one but written only the heading of the other. I had nothing else to do while I waited for my pie, so I leafed through the papers that the files contained. It was boredom that drove me to do it, as much as curiosity. Or, as my late father would have said, it was yet another example of the Devil finding work for idle hands.

As Gorvin had told me, the first file dealt with shipping sighted in the Channel during the past month. This was the file that had not been docketed. There seemed nothing of particular significance in a report about a Dutch Indiaman blown off course by a storm and passing the Isle of Wight; or three French fishing boats that had got into trouble in the same storm. Two of the letters had passed through Mr Williamson's office before they were forwarded to Lord Arlington's, and I was already familiar with their contents.

The docket for the second file had been completed. I removed the papers, one by one. They were letters dated between the end of October and the middle of November. They had passed between Gorvin and Mr Montagu's clerk at our embassy in Paris. According to the docket, they related to matters of trade and to shipbuilding.

Underneath, however, were two other letters. To my surprise, neither was entered on the docket. I turned them over. Both had been double-sealed with dark red wax.

So dark, it was almost purple.

I took out my pocketbook and extracted the fragment I had found under the floorboards of Abbott's lodgings. The wax was precisely the same colour as the seals. It fitted neatly into the side of one of them. I unfolded the letters and glanced at the signatures at the bottom. They were from the ambassador, Mr Montagu, himself.

At Whitehall, taken all in all, ignorance was often safer than knowledge. But curiosity got the better of me. I scanned the contents. In the first, the ambassador wrote to my lord at some length of the war between France and the Dutch

Republic, and its implications for England if the French armies overran the whole of the Spanish Netherlands and threatened the United Provinces themselves. After all, Mr Montagu wrote, the Dutch were our allies and there was much speculation in Paris whether we would send troops to assist them by land against the French.

In the second letter, Mr Montagu recorded a conversation he had had with Madame, the Duchess of Orléans. Madame was the sister of our own King, and the wife of the brother of King Louis. Montagu wanted to reassure Lord Arlington that she was still on exceptionally good terms with the French king, a circumstance which Mr Montagu intended to exploit for certain negotiations he had in mind. However, he wrote, Madame was not in the best of health. Furthermore, there were circumstances relating to Monsieur her husband that rendered Madame particularly unhappy, though the ambassador failed to make these explicit. But he did suggest that Lord Arlington should draw this to the attention of the King as a matter of urgency.

I returned the files to the satchel and sat back, sipping my ale and half-listening to the rumble of conversation on the other side of the curtain that separated my booth from the common table. The two letters were clearly confidential. Abbott shouldn't have read them, let alone taken them home.

At this point, the waiter arrived with my pie. I stabbed the crust with the point of my knife. A spout of steam shot upwards and gravy spurted out. I chewed my first mouthful, crunching the small bones.

The last time I had seen Abbott, when he was clinging to my arm and staggering along Fleet Street less than a week ago, he had been as drunk as a brace of lords, slurring his words into a sort of verbal slush. He had asked me a question.

Do you believe in forgiveness?

In fact, he had asked me two questions. The second one had been.

If a man's sorry — for what he's done, truly sorry, should he not be forgiven?

At the time I had assumed that he was referring to the fact that he was blind drunk and on the way home when he should have been sober and at work in Arlington's office.

But what if these letters were the reason?

After dinner, I parted with Stephen in the Strand and went on to Whitehall. Gorvin was at his desk in Arlington's office. My plan was to give him the files and leave as soon as possible. I wasn't sure what was going on in this business, but I knew that I didn't want to be involved in it.

'You have them?' he asked the moment he saw me.

I nodded. Gorvin was not usually so abrupt.

'What took you so long?'

'Mistress Abbott had removed herself to a friend's house, and she'd taken the files with her.' I unstrapped the satchel and gave him the two folders. 'I must return to Mr Williamson. He's—'

'One moment.' Gorvin slid off his stool. 'Pray wait here while I take these to my lord.'

I watched him thread his way among the other desks, knock on the door of the private room and enter. Gorvin and I were friends, but Whitehall friendships are contingent in their nature, not absolute. A moment later, my lord's door opened again and Gorvin beckoned me. 'Mr Marwood, my lord.'

'I know who he is. Come in and close the door, Marwood.'

Arlington was standing by the window, looking out over the Privy Garden. It was still raining, and the candles had been lit. He turned to face me.

'These files. Gorvin tells me that Mistress Abbott left her lodgings, and she took the files with her. Correct?'

'Yes, my lord. She removed most of her possessions at the same time. She and her daughter have gone to stay with a Mr Fanshawe at a house in Slaughter Street, near Smithfield.'

'Fanshawe, eh?' He paused to consider this, but he did not ask me any questions about the man. 'Continue.'

'Mr Fanshawe said she took the files for safekeeping, and she had asked him to return them to your office.'

'Did you talk to her yourself?'

'No, my lord. I understand that grief has overcome her.'

Arlington sighed heavily. Then he snapped, 'It's now the afternoon. Did you look at their contents on your way back?'

'No, my lord,' I said promptly. 'There was no need for me to do that. All I did was glance at the dockets to make sure they were the ones that were missing.'

'Good.' He stared at me, and I stared back. His expression was not unfriendly. It seemed to me that the atmosphere had grown perceptibly lighter in the room. 'Did anything strike you as in any way curious?'

I did not hesitate. 'No, my lord.'

'Very well. Remember, Marwood, a discreet servant is a good servant, and a good servant will have his reward. The reverse also holds true. Go back to Mr Williamson.'

I bowed once more, picked up my satchel and left him in the fading light. I went back to Gorvin, who was looking more cheerful now I had emerged unscathed from the lion's den.

'All well?' he said. 'Do you want to dine with me on Wednesday? I thought we might go to the Axe.'

'All right,' I said. 'Do you know anything about an old man called Fanshawe? He lives in a big house near Smithfield.'

'Why?'

'He's the friend that Mistress Abbott went to when she left Fleet Street. He gave me the files.'

'He's not just a friend,' Gorvin said. 'He's her father-in-law.'

It took me a moment to work out what this must mean. 'You mean his son was Mistress Abbott's first husband? And the father of the girl? Who is Fanshawe?'

'A merchant. Luxury goods, mainly from the East Indies. Spices, silks, that sort of thing. He buys in bulk from Dutch importers, and then sells the goods here. Half the shopkeepers in the New Exchange get their stock from him. I believe my lord himself has patronized him. And Lord Ashley.'

Lord Ashley was a colleague of Arlington's: he was the Chancellor of the Exchequer and another influential member of the government. If you could raise the capital and knew where to go both to buy and to sell, it must be a good business to be in: few risks and relatively few costs on the one hand, and on the other a swift and profitable return on your money.

'She must have come down in the world when she married Abbott,' I said.

'Love,' Gorvin said, and laughed. 'The tender passion

made a fool of her. I saw her with Abbott once, just before they married. She's no beauty, I can tell you, and she's a good five or ten years older than he was, and six inches taller. But there they were in the Park together, and she looked like a lovesick girl clinging to his arm. They were billing and cooing like a pair of turtle doves. That changed fast enough when they married.' He gave a bark of laughter. 'By all accounts they were more like a pair of fighting cocks.'

CHAPTER THIRTEEN

ON TUESDAY, SIX days after her last meeting with Lord Arlington, Cat took a hackney from Covent Garden to Goring House. The rain had continued unabated since yesterday. She did not want to look like a drowned rat while discussing the accommodation proper to aristocratic fowls.

Lord Arlington did not keep Cat waiting above quarter of an hour. When she was ushered into his study, he was not alone. Lady Arlington was there too. Cat curtsied first to her ladyship, who gave her an amused smile, and then to my lord himself.

'A female!' Lady Arlington said. 'My love, how extraordinary.'

Her husband smiled at her. She was a good-natured woman with an air of breeding. Her father had been a bastard of Prince Maurice of Orange, and her sister was married to the Duke of Ormond's son. It was generally thought that Arlington had done well for himself in marrying a lady who was not only amiable but had such an array of useful connections.

At a nod from my lord, Cat unrolled the plans on the

desk. The Arlingtons studied them, with my lady exclaiming over the sketch of the main facade, with its central archway leading to the courtyard behind the main building.

'It is so graceful. And so modern. Wouldn't something like this work well at Euston? For the stables, I mean?'

'For the entrance?' Arlington nodded ponderously. 'Perhaps. With the measurements increased in proportion.' His forefinger stabbed at the detailing around the archway. 'And with less ornamentation. But that's by the by. What do you think? The question is, will *she* like it?'

'Who? The mother or the daughter?'

'Both.'

'Madame is both a mother and a woman of taste. And her daughter is a little girl. A building like this would delight both of them. For different reasons. Just as our own poultry house pleases Tata and me equally, but not in the same way: I like it because she does, as well as for itself. She likes it for the chickens and because it's hers.'

Arlington turned to Cat. 'Are you much engaged with business at present?'

'No more than usual, my lord,' she lied.

'I would like you to work up a full set of plans for this, with drawings of the facades and a note about the necessary materials and any directions you think useful. Pray be as specific as you can, and write in French, not English. The directions and so on must be sufficiently complete for a good builder to work from.'

Lady Arlington coughed. 'My lord, might it be advisable for Dr Wren to cast his eye over them?'

'I think not. It may divert Madame when she learns that a woman has been the sole author.'

Cat coughed in her turn, her mind running ahead to the fee. 'And with whom should I discuss any – ah – practical matters? Mr Abbott?'

There was a silence. Lady Arlington glanced at her husband, her eyebrows raised.

'No,' he said. 'Mr Gorvin will see to all that. Write to him at my office. Now we must not keep you from your other engagements, Mistress Hakesby. Good day.'

In the afternoon, the rain had stopped at last, and the sky cleared to the south; there was even a fitful gleam of sunshine. Cat was alone in the Drawing Office. Brennan had gone to Fenchurch Street, where they were overseeing the building of three houses of the second rate, according to the specifications now laid down in the City's regulations. It was tedious work, but at least – as Brennan had pointed out more than once – the client, who made a comfortable living by importing Canary wines, was prompt in meeting his payments. How unlike, Brennan implied, their nobler clients, some of whom seemed to think their rank absolved them of any need to pay their bills at all.

His absence left Cat's mind free to wander among the possibilities generated by Arlington's extraordinary scheme for Madame, the Duchess of Orléans. In some ways, this was the part of a project that she liked most: when imagination was unfettered by considerations of cost, congruity and practicality. Nothing need be ruled out.

Standing at her slope by the window, she let her pen take her where it would. The work absorbed her, and the sheets of paper mounted up.

So deep was her concentration that a knock at the door took her by surprise; usually she would have heard the footsteps on the stairs. She opened the door and found the tall figure of Mr Van Riebeeck outside on the landing. He swept off his hat and bowed. Instinctively she took a step backwards and dropped a curtsy.

'Sir,' she said, wishing Brennan were with her, 'I—'

'Madam, forgive the intrusion,' he interrupted. His voice was deep and unusually resonant. 'I found myself in the neighbourhood. Mr Fanshawe told me where to find you.'

As he was speaking, he walked into the middle of the Drawing Office. He stood there, looking about him, making no attempt to hide his curiosity.

'What can I do for you?'

'Admirable!' It was as if he had not heard her. 'So light! So airy!'

He stared at the three tall slopes, the two sets of drawers where they stored the larger plans, and the shelves laden with boxes that lined one wall from floor to ceiling. He tilted his head back to look at the long skylight. The sun chose that moment to come out from behind a cloud.

'How bright it is, madam — even on a winter's day.'

'We do a great deal of close work. We must make the most of what light we have.'

He strolled to the nearest window, which was beside her own slope. 'And a fine view of the rooftops of London.' He turned to look at her again. His face was intent and unsmiling. 'I told you an untruth.'

'How so?' Cat said curtly.

'I did not call altogether on a whim.' His eyes drifted down to the slope beside him. 'But what is this? How intriguing.'

His voice had a curious effect: it set something vibrating within her, as a bell will sometimes summon an answering note from another bell, or plucking an octave on a lute will produce an unearthly sound of the same pitch that seems to float in the air, unattached to the instrument that made it sound. She felt the blood rising to her cheeks.

'A few early sketches, sir, that's all.' She had a sudden desire to impress the Dutchman. 'My Lord Arlington has commissioned us to design another building for him.'

'Another, eh? You have worked for him before, then? No doubt you have many clients at court. Mr Fanshawe was fortunate to secure your services.'

'We take all sorts of commissions,' she said primly. 'All are welcome if they pay for our services.'

'And is this another . . . poultry house, perhaps?'

There was a hint of amusement in his voice. Van Riebeeck must have known all along what she had done for Lord Arlington, she realized, which meant that he had taken the trouble to find out. A poultry house – however grand the building, however exalted the client – did not sound quite as impressive as she would have liked.

Her visitor bent over her sketches. 'Two pediments . . . columns . . . is that a row of statues? An archway . . . why, madam, this is not a house for poultry, it is a veritable palace.'

Against her better judgement, Cat succumbed again to the temptation to impress him. 'That is as it should be. My lord intends it for a lady of royal blood.'

'Ah.' He raised his head and smiled. For a moment he stood quite still and said nothing at all. Then he changed the subject, as abruptly and disconcertingly as before. 'I realize you scarcely know me, but pray let me put a proposition before you. I recall that at the theatre the other evening, you said something about preferring music to a play.'

'Yes, sir,' Cat said. 'I like music.'

He studied her as closely as he had studied her drawings. 'I've a proposal for you, madam. Forgive me – I know our acquaintance is short, but then so are our lives, so we should not waste them. It would give me so much pleasure, and do me so much honour, if you permitted me to escort you to Austin Friars tomorrow night. A friend of mine promises us an evening of music. You are aware of Monsieur Grabu?'

'Of course. The Master of the King's Music.'

'He is promised to us,' Van Riebeeck said. 'It's unusual for him to play in such an intimate setting – as perhaps you know. And he rarely has leisure from his royal duties to play privately. But my friend was able to oblige him recently in some business matter he needed to transact, and this recital is by way of showing his gratitude.' The Dutchman gave her another of those dangerous smiles. 'Would such a diversion be to your taste? Will you come with me?'

CHAPTER FOURTEEN

THE HOUSE IN Slaughter Street had a long narrow garden. At the far end there were stables, a sty for the pig, and a run for the chickens. Caliban the lion now lived in the stables, which had been partitioned to provide him with accommodation, making an enclosure, a make-shift cage. The partition had been fitted with a door of two layers. First there was a solid outer leaf of wood. When this stood open, it revealed an inner door made of iron bars for the benefit of those who wanted to view the animal. There was also a small hatch at eye level in the partition.

The lion was an elderly animal that whimpered in its sleep. It had been brought from Africa in the hold of a Dutch East Indiaman. By the time it arrived in England, there were a number of sores on its skin, which wept continually and caused it considerable irritation.

Mr Fanshawe had hired a keeper, a broad-shouldered, thick-lipped man who was accustomed to manage bulls at

Smithfield. Maria had heard him explaining his job to Mr Fanshawe's manservant.

'They're all the same, master, these brutes,' said the keeper, whose name was Brockmore. He spoke in a hoarse whisper that was meant to be inaudible to Maria. 'You can do anything you want with them if you understand them aright. They're scared of fire and sharp points. They eat, they shit, they sleep. They fuck if you give them a chance. That's all there is to them. They ain't like us.'

Brockmore was assisted by his son, who was built on the same design as himself but on a smaller scale. Every day, father and son brought a barrowload of cheap meat from the slaughterhouses of Smithfield and fed Caliban. After eating, the lion was generally sleepy, which allowed the Brockmores to remove some of the excrement, while taking suitable precautions in case the animal grew dangerous. They cleaned out the enclosure only once or twice a week.

At first, Mr Fanshawe visited Caliban two or three times a day. Sometimes he took Maria with him. Though she pretended to be awed and fascinated by the spectacle, she privately thought that the beast was not only disgusting but a disappointment. It stank. It had lost some of its teeth. Its mane was tangled. It spent most of its life sleeping. When awake, it paced listlessly up and down its cage, swaying from side to side as if unsteady from drinking too much ale. It also scratched itself, sometimes drawing blood.

Once a day, before and during its dinner, the lion became lively. It wasn't pleasant to watch the beast eat, but it was undoubtedly impressive. In the first few weeks of its stay, it attracted a stream of visitors to Slaughter Street.

'Caliban is a wonderful specimen of the Barbary lion,' Mr Fanshawe would tell them, rubbing his hands with pride. 'I doubt there's another to match it in England. It puts the King's beasts in the Tower quite in the shade.'

The story of the lion's arrival in London had grown in the telling, and its attack on the unfortunate docker had given it an undeserved reputation for ruthless cunning and bloodthirsty aggression. This added considerably to its attraction for Mr Fanshawe and the visitors he brought to inspect his new acquisition.

Maria's dislike of the lion had increased now that her grandfather had desired her to add him – or at least something faintly resembling him – to her sampler. Mistress Abbott embraced the idea with enthusiasm, and not just because it was politic to keep Mr Fanshawe in a good temper.

'You are so fortunate to have so very interesting an animal,' she said. 'You should put him near the top. Make him larger than the unicorn. I should have loved such a challenge when I was your age. And you have the advantage of a real lion as your model.'

In Maria's opinion, the only thing that the lion did well was roar. Sometimes you could hear Caliban not only in the house but in the street beyond. He made a deep, inexorable sound that was both terrifying and pleasurable. Maria wondered why the lion bothered. Perhaps, she thought, he was hoping that he might find a friend in this benighted place.

When the rain stopped on Tuesday afternoon, Maria went outside. She was not permitted to go abroad in the City alone, so she took the air in the garden, keeping well away from the stable where Caliban lay in his usual post-prandial stupor.

That was when she encountered Hannah. Except at prayers, when the whole household gathered in the hall, Maria had not seen her since they had come back to live at Slaughter Street. They met by chance halfway down the garden, near the summerhouse where gentlemen would drink wine and play music or games on fine evenings.

'There you are,' Hannah said in her hard, toneless voice. 'I wondered if I'd ever see you again.'

Maria smiled weakly. 'How do you do in the kitchen?'

The maid was wearing the stained clothes she had worn at their old house. Tendrils of hair had escaped from her cap. There was a smear of what looked like dirty grease on her forehead. She was carrying a wooden bucket in each hand, scraps for the pig.

'What does it look like?'

In Fleet Street, at the sign of the Black Boy, she and Maria had been allies, united against the world, and in particular against Mr and Mistress Abbott. Towards the end, in the last hectic months before Abbott's death when there had been no money for Maria to have new clothes, they had even been taken for sisters when they were out on an errand. Now all was changed. Mr Fanshawe had seen to that. Maria was conscious of her own carefully dressed hair, the cockled grain of her new camlet cloak, and even the clean skin of her face.

She took a step towards this strange new Hannah, then stopped. 'What do they make you do?'

'Anything that no one else likes. Scrubbing greasy pans in the scullery. Taking the swill to the pig and cleaning out the henhouse. That's when I'm not trying to keep the men from putting their stinking hands up my skirts. Even the kitchen boy tries his luck.'

95

'But at least you're here. My mother could have turned you out after Abbott died.'

Hannah craned her head towards Maria. 'We made a bargain, you and me. You'd take me as your maid, and in return, I'd—'

'I tried. I truly did. I asked my mother if I could have you as my maid.'

('Hannah?' her mother had said. 'Have you run stark mad? Hannah's no more fitted to be a lady's maid than your grandfather's pig.')

'What did she say?' Hannah demanded. 'Tell me.'

('She should count her blessings, that wretched girl. She's got food in her belly and a roof over her head. More than she deserves. Besides, you're far too young to have a maid of your own. You'll wait until you've found a husband to pay for one.')

'She said . . . that I wasn't old enough for my own maid. I'm sorry.'

Hannah came closer, and Maria fought the urge to retreat. Hannah said, 'I kept my side of the bargain. You should keep yours.'

'But I tried, I—'

'I could go to a justice, you know.' Hannah smiled without kindness, showing the gap where two of her teeth had been knocked out by a boy who had tried to steal her basket in Fleet Street. 'Make a – what is it? – an affidavit saying what you did. How you killed him.'

'But I didn't!' Maria wailed.

'Didn't you? Whose doll was it? You got his hair and his nail clippings, didn't you?'

'I didn't! You did.'

96

'That's not what I'll say when I'm under oath. It was you put that thing in his mattress. You sewed it up in there. You wanted him dead.' Hannah paused, contemplating the effect of her words. 'The justice will send someone to arrest you. And he'll charge you with causing death by witchcraft. You know what that means.' Hannah lowered her voice. 'They'll hang you and let the crows pick your body apart.'

CHAPTER FIFTEEN

ON WEDNESDAY THERE was a savage wind from the east that chafed the skin. Shortly before midday, I collected Gorvin from Arlington's office. We hurried down King Street, holding our hats to our heads to stop them flying away. The Axe lay in an alley west of the street. We found places at one end of the ordinary table. A serving man swooped down on us, and we ordered our dinner.

'I told my lord we were engaged,' Gorvin said quietly.

I felt a stirring of alarm. I knew Gorvin well enough to distinguish idle conversation from a remark made with an ulterior motive. 'And?'

'He said so much the better. He bade me show you this.'

Gorvin felt in his pocket and took out a letter, which he passed to me. It was addressed to him at Lord Arlington's office in Whitehall, in a handwriting that brimmed with twirls and flourishes. I unfolded it.

The First Day of March, 1670

Honoured Sir

I have in my possession a Schedule of Debts owed to me by Mr Richard Abbott of your Office, which is countersigned by you, your signature being duly witnessed, together with a note that you promise to stand surety for the full amount on his Behalf. This Debt having fallen due on the first day of this Month instant, I accordingly write to request Payment. Interest at ten per centum per Month is charged daily, so Promptness is advised. The sum total of these Debts is four hundred and twenty-three pounds, eight shillings and nine pence. I am usually to be found at the address below after three in the afternoon, where the Schedule with your signature will be returned to you on payment in full.

I am, Sir, your Obedient Servant,

Jeremiah Johnson, A.M.

At the Blue Bush, off the Strand

I read the letter twice. I looked across the table at Gorvin and raised my eyebrows.

He smiled sweetly. 'Pompous devil, ain't he?'

'Did you sign this schedule?'

'Of course not. Abbott must have forged my signature. The damned scoundrel.'

I did not like the way this conversation was tending. 'It's odd, I grant you. But nothing to do with me.' I left a pause but he said nothing. 'Are you sure that the letter is the first you've heard of this?'

'Yes. Faith, sir, what do you take me for?' Gorvin sounded outraged, which meant nothing; he could play a part as well as any man. 'I wouldn't have lent Abbott a farthing. Let alone stand surety for a debt of four hundred pounds.'

'Could Johnson have forged the whole thing – including your signature?' I answered my own question. 'No. He wouldn't be such a fool. But do you think he knows Abbott's dead yet?'

'I hadn't thought of that. Perhaps not.' Gorvin glanced at me, assessing my reaction. 'All I can tell you is that this letter arrived this morning. I showed it to my lord and he said I should send you to Johnson.'

'For God's sake.' I glared at him. But I had expected something like this, and my anger was partly a matter of form. 'Why me?'

'Because he's convinced that you and Abbott were intimate friends.'

'Then he's been most grievously misinformed.' I wondered if it was Gorvin who had done the misinforming.

'Marwood, you know what my lord's like when he gets a notion in his head. No one can disabuse him of it. And indeed, you were acquainted with Abbott as well as anyone was. It shouldn't cause you much trouble. All you need do is tell Johnson that the signature is forged, and that in any case Abbott's dead, and he can whistle for his money. If the man continues to pester us, we'll find something to charge him with. But, between ourselves, my lord would rather not do that, for the sake of Abbott's widow. Or rather for the sake of Lady Arlington, who's tender-hearted where the unfortunate lady is concerned, for the sake of past friendship.'

We leant apart as the pot-boy came between us to set down our ale. I didn't want to waste my time in going to the Blue Bush and having an unpleasant interview with a rogue who lived by his wits. It was nothing to me how Abbott had ruined himself. Nor did I care for Arlington using me as his errand boy, but there was nothing I could do to alter his mind. Mr Williamson wouldn't like it, but he would not go against his own master.

'Who is this man Johnson?'

'I've never heard of him.' Gorvin sounded cheerful; it was the voice of a man who has shuffled off an unpleasant duty onto someone else. 'A Master of Arts, if you can believe it.'

'In all events, he's a gamester who plays high.'

'Which is an advantage, Marwood. Think about it. If Johnson lives by his wits, he'll know the folly of offending someone like my lord. And the rest of the rogues at the Blue Bush won't thank him for attracting our attention.'

Our dinner arrived. The ground beef was too heavily salted, for my taste, and the beans were hard and gritty. After a few mouthfuls, I pushed my plate aside.

Gorvin sighed. 'Lord, Marwood. You're making a mighty fuss about such a little thing.'

I stared at him until he dropped his eyes. I was almost certain that he wasn't concealing anything, though I couldn't be sure. That was always the trouble with Whitehall. It was one thing to like a man, but quite another to trust him.

From the outside, there was nothing remarkable about the Blue Bush. The alley that led to the tavern door had been swept and cleared of rubbish, and the building itself seemed in good repair. There were respectable-looking shops on the ground floor. On my previous visit, I had gone with a party of clerks, all of us half-drunk, to lose our money in the name of pleasure.

I went inside. Directly ahead at the end of the passage was a big common room. Early though it was, the candles were lit, and a great fire burned in the hearth.

I hesitated in the doorway. A tall, large-bellied man in an apron approached and asked me my pleasure. Noticing my scarred cheek, he tilted his head to see it better.

'I'm here to see Mr Johnson,' I said.

He narrowed his eyes and studied me from head to foot, as a man looks at a horse to assess its value. 'Is that so, your honour?' There was a hint of a brogue in his voice. 'And would that be for business or pleasure?'

'Business. His business.'

'And your name, sir?'

'He won't know my name. But the business concerns Mr Abbott.'

There was a pause. He had one of those smooth, even-featured faces that give a misleading impression of good humour. 'Ah. Is that so?'

The news of Abbott's death might not have reached the Blue Bush. 'You know the gentleman, perhaps?'

His head moved ambiguously. It was neither a nod nor a shake but something between. He beckoned the boy and bent to whisper in his ear. The lad hared up the stairs.

'You can sit down if you care to rest your legs,' he said, waving towards a settle against the wall. 'Or not. Just as you please, sir.'

He withdrew a few paces – enough to discourage conversation, but near enough to let me know that he was keeping an eye on me. He propped himself against the panelling and picked at his teeth with a fingernail.

The common room was low-ceilinged. The air was thick

with smoke from the fire and men's pipes. The customers sat in twos and threes at a long table. All of them were drinking. A few were reading newspapers or talking, but most were playing at dice or cards. In the main, the money on the table was small stuff – heaps of silver and copper and, here and there, the yellow wink of a gold piece. I guessed that the real business of the establishment took place on the floor above.

The boy clattered downstairs, and went over to the man in the apron. I feigned indifference while they talked. At the end of it, the porter or whatever he called himself came over to me and said that the boy would take me up to Mr Johnson.

'You should come here for yourself, your honour,' the porter went on, growing suddenly amiable and gesturing towards the men hunched over their cards and dice. 'For pleasure, that is. Everything's fair and above board in this house, I'll take my oath on it. I've seen some of our gentlemen grow rich overnight.'

I didn't reply. The boy led me upstairs to a gloomy landing with many closed doors. He knocked on one of them, and a voice called for us to enter.

I found myself in a narrow, ill-lit chamber with a single window at the far end. A man rose from his chair and bowed. He was small, made smaller by the fact of his being hunched over as if he carried an invisible load on his shoulders that forced his head forward and down. He wore a suit of dark purple cloth, stained here and there with spatters of wax.

'Your servant, sir,' he said in a light, high-pitched voice. 'My name is Johnson. And whom have I the pleasure of addressing?'

'James Marwood,' I said. 'I come from Lord Arlington's office.'

'Excellent. And how does my lord do?'

'I've no idea. I'm here about the affairs of Mr Abbott.'

'Come, sir, let us be seated. A glass of wine?'

I declined the wine. We sat at a table that was close to the fireplace. There were four chairs around it. Johnson pushed aside a dice box and two packs of cards.

'Mr Gorvin showed me the letter you sent him,' I said quietly. 'Concerning Mr Abbott's affairs.'

'Yes, indeed.' He kept his voice as low as mine. 'A matter of a debt for which Mr Gorvin stands surety. And no doubt he has sent you here to discharge it on his behalf.'

Johnson shifted in his chair, and his eyes flickered. He was trying to assess if I had brought the money with me. Four hundred pounds is a substantial sum to carry about. Gold weighs a man down.

The change in his position threw the light from the candle onto his face. For the first time I saw him clearly. His sparse grey hair straggled down to his collar. His cheeks were networked with veins and blotchy with reddish-purple patches which almost matched his coat. He needed a shave. His eyes were large, shiny and moist, like something half-alive and twitching in the bottom of a rockpool.

'You said in your letter that Mr Abbott owes you money—'

'Indeed he does, sir, as God's my witness, four hundred and t—'

'And that the debt was due to be paid by the end of last month—'

'By midnight on Monday, to be precise, sir.'

'And that Mr Gorvin guaranteed the debt, and signed a schedule to that effect.'

Johnson took a paper from his pocket and smoothed it out

on the table between us. He kept his hand resting on part of it, but I could read the writing, including the addendum at the bottom signed with the name of Dudley Gorvin, together with the signatures of two witnesses, one of whom was called Thomas Connolly.

'As you see, sir, duly signed and witnessed. Thomas was one of the witnesses – you met him downstairs, I think, he keeps the door – and the other is a gentleman who often comes to shake the bones with us.'

'But this is not Mr Gorvin's signature,' I said. 'And this addendum is not in his hand. I am familiar with his hand-writing, you see – I work with him.' I showed Johnson a paper that Gorvin had given me. 'That is a true specimen of his signature.'

'But the signature on the addendum is very like, sir, you must agree.' Johnson leant towards me and took me confidentially by the sleeve. 'There are many reasons for any small differences in the writing that you may fancy you distinguish. Perhaps Mr Gorvin signed by candlelight, and it was a cold night, and perhaps his hand trembled somewhat, or the pen was in want of trimming, so it is hardly surprising—'

'Mr Abbott is dead,' I said, more loudly than before.

He stared at me. I would have taken my oath that the news had come as a shock to him.

'Had you not heard? He died last week, and he's left nothing behind him but debts. You cannot press a corpse for payment, so let that be an end to it.'

'Faith, you're lying,' Johnson said weakly, and his fingers relaxed their grip on my arm. 'Or – forgive me, sir, I did not mean to impugn your honour – I am sure it is merely that you've been misinformed. When I last saw him, he—'

'Ask at his lodging if you don't believe me. At the sign of the Black Boy by Temple Bar. Or ask at Whitehall, if you prefer. It was a sudden seizure. It carried him off in a day or two.'

'Dear God,' Johnson said, surprised into momentary piety. 'We never know when the Angel of Death will tap us on the shoulder.'

He was sweating heavily now. He took a handkerchief from his pocket. It was purple to match his clothes, edged with surprisingly delicate lace, but soiled and frayed. He mopped his face with it, crumpled it into a ball and squeezed it so hard that his knuckles whitened. He sat back and took a deep breath. His former manner dropped over him like a familiar cloak.

'But even if this is the case, sir,' he said, 'I may well have a claim on the estate. There must be something left. Perhaps we can come to an understanding. Consider, sir, what may happen if we do not: I'm a poor man, but if necessary I shall go to law. I cannot take my oath that there will not be a degree of scandal attached to the affair, when I explain poor Mr Abbott's weaknesses to a judge. It will not reflect well on my lord. He will—'

'You've a claim on nothing,' I cut in. 'If you know what's good for you, sir, you'll put that faked schedule on the fire. The signature can be proved to be false. In which case you will be open to a charge of forgery. Mr Gorvin will go to a justice and lay information against you. My Lord Arlington will encourage him to issue a warrant and have you placed under arrest. And you know where all this will end? The hangman's noose.'

At this, the words came tumbling out of Johnson's mouth:

he was trying to excuse himself, to throw the blame on Abbott, on Gorvin, on anyone but himself, to claim that the schedule had been sent to Gorvin by mistake. The irony was that I suspected that Johnson was innocent of wrongdoing, in this matter at least. He would not have known what Gorvin's handwriting looked like – probably had never heard of the man. The forgery had almost certainly been Abbott's doing.

'And so, sir,' I said, interrupting Johnson and rising from my chair, 'there's nothing more to say. I see no reason why we should meet again.'

For form's sake he tried to argue but soon gave it up. He opened the door and preceded me onto the landing. As we were crossing the passage to the head of the stairs, another door opened.

'Have you heard the news about poor Abbott, Mr Wulf?' Johnson's voice was high and unsteady, and the words spilled out as if he had little control over them. 'He's dead. A sudden seizure, this gentleman tells me.'

'Oh. Indeed? God rest his soul.' The newcomer's voice was deep. To my ears, it had a hard, atonal quality, like a hammer striking a stone.

I was descending the stairs, but I glanced over my shoulder. Wulf was already turning away. In the moment before Johnson's body came between us, I glimpsed his profile. I recognized the long-faced man whom I had met with Fanshawe at the Duke's Theatre. At the same time, my mind dredged up another memory: the tall gentleman I had seen with Abbott outside the New Exchange. They were one and the same. The Dutchman. Van Riebeeck. Then why was he calling himself Wulf?

I clattered down the stairs, with Johnson just behind me.

I couldn't be sure, but I didn't think that Van Riebeeck had seen my face. The Irishman was standing below, watching us.

'Pray tell Mr Gorvin it was a foolish mistake,' Johnson said at the foot of the stairs. 'He must not concern himself any further in the matter. This is all down to Abbott's folly.' He took a sudden breath. 'Poor fellow. Still, *de mortuis nil nisi bonum*. We are all of us sinners, sir.'

I came to a quick decision. I caught him by the sleeve and hissed in his ear: 'Meet me tomorrow at midday by Temple Bar. Be discreet.'

Johnson looked like a startled rabbit. Fortunately he kept his mouth shut.

'Dine with me. I'll make it worth your while.'

I turned away. The doorkeeper had come forward and was now much closer to us than before.

'Leaving us already, your honour?' the Irishman said, staring ostentatiously at me, memorizing every crack and contour of my face. 'Shame, sir. But you'll know where to come the next time you've a fancy to roll the bones. You'll always find a welcome here.'

CHAPTER SIXTEEN

I T WAS GENERALLY assumed, at least by men, that a widow was in need of a husband. This was particularly true if the widow was not ill-favoured and enjoyed a financial competence in her own right. Only a husband could provide her with the blessings of his authority and protection, as ordained by God, as well as direct her affairs for her and provide her with those private comforts under the covers which only a man is equipped to give.

In the two years since Mr Hakesby's death, Cat had grown used to fending off the unwanted attentions of men. In the first few months, Brennan had clearly nourished ill-advised hopes of succeeding his former master. She had taught him the error of his ways, and they now worked together for the most part in harmony; meanwhile he found an outlet for his soft and tender passions in the plump arms and saucer-like eyes of a pastry-cook's daughter in St Martin's Lane.

The only man in whose company she felt at ease was James Marwood, with whom she had survived so much and quarrelled so often that she took him for granted, as she might have done a brother, had God seen fit to provide her with one. Marwood irritated her frequently, but at least he had never tried to make love to her or tell her how to run her own affairs.

Now, however, he was in danger of becoming insupportable. She could forgive his unfortunate liking for low comedy, but not the way he had ogled the orange girl in front of her very eyes. It was all of a piece. During the play, he had stared fixedly at the stage, where that shameless little punk Meg Daunt was playing the part of Ariana and making eyes at the gentlemen. Meg Daunt lodged in Vere Street, where she received callers, all men. Including Marwood.

Like all his sex, Cat decided, Marwood was enslaved by the unruly tube of flesh that dangled between his legs. His boorish behaviour towards Mr Fanshawe and his guest had been almost equally bad. Did he not realize that Fanshawe was a client, and that it was necessary for her to be agreeable to clients if she was to make a living?

When Van Riebeeck had called on her at the Drawing Office yesterday, it had taken her by surprise. She knew little about him, apart from the fact that he was an intimate friend of Mr Fanshawe's and clearly a man of some distinction. She had last seen him a fortnight ago, when they dined together at Slaughter Street on the day of the lion's arrival, and he had set himself to be particularly attentive to her.

There was no reason not to trust him – quite the reverse – and it would be foolish to reject the chance of attending a private recital by Monsieur Grabu. Besides, it was pleasant to know that if she needed a man to escort her, she was not dependent on the services of James Marwood.

* * *

Van Riebeeck collected her in a hackney on Wednesday evening. He handed her into the coach with as much ceremony as if she had been Madame herself, not a tradesman's widow who struggled to make ends meet.

'I believe our friend Mr Fanshawe will be there,' he said to her, raising his voice to be heard over the noise of the traffic. 'You will be glad to see him, no doubt.'

After that he relapsed into silence. Neither of them spoke for the rest of the way. Their journey took them east to Ludgate Hill and then around the City wall. Austin Friars lay beyond Moorfields, hard by Broad Street in a part of the City that had escaped the attentions of the Fire. The old church of the monastery had been granted to the Dutch citizens resident in London more than a century earlier, and many of them lived nearby.

The coach dropped them to the south of the church, outside a lighted gateway with a large oriel window projecting above it. The night was cloudy, and it was difficult to make out even the outlines of the building beyond, but it appeared to be a house of some size. A handful of link boys clustered in the street, and their flaring torches dazzled Cat's eyes.

Van Riebeeck took her arm and led her through the gateway towards a door at the side of the house. This stood open, and the soft light of candles spilled down the steps in front of it. The porter bowed low and greeted Van Riebeeck by name. A footman removed their outer clothing. Van Riebeeck repossessed himself of her arm and they climbed a broad flight of shallow stairs.

The sound of voices grew steadily louder. There were discordant squeals as someone adjusted the tuning of a violin.

At the head of the stairs, the manservant opened a door. He did not announce them but stood aside and bowed.

The chamber beyond was large enough not to seem over-crowded with twenty or thirty people. The musicians were at the far end, which was more brightly lit than the rest. Van Riebeeck guided Cat to their host, a middle-aged merchant named Alink, whose English was as fluent as if it had been his mother tongue.

'I grew up in London, madam,' he explained. 'My father's business was here, and so is mine.'

He led her to his wife, a sturdy woman whose eyes were almost submerged in rolls of fat. When she smiled, she revealed a set of teeth so regular and perfectly spaced that they were probably made of ivory.

'You are most welcome here. Come, Mistress Hakesby, you must sit by me.' Her English was almost as fluent as her husband's but more heavily accented. She introduced Cat to a number of the women, who were sitting apart from the men, and nearer to the fire. 'This lady is the guest of Van Riebeeck,' she told them, speaking in English from politeness to her visitor, 'and a great lover of music.'

The news caused a flutter of whispers and twitching skirts. Several of the women glanced over their shoulders at the gentleman himself, who was now standing among grave-faced, soberly dressed men and talking in a low voice to their host. He was younger and taller than most of the others but they treated him with obvious signs of respect.

'Have you known Mr Van Riebeeck for long?' Mistress Alink asked.

'No,' Cat said. 'And you?'

'Oh yes.' Mistress Alink's eyes were still on Van Riebeeck.

'His family is well known in Amsterdam. They are connected to the Grand Pensionary himself.'

'Indeed, madam. I did not know.'

The information explained the respect that the older men were showing to Van Riebeeck. The Grand Pensionary, Johannes de Witt, was the dominant political figure in the Dutch Republic.

Monsieur Grabu signified that he was ready to begin the recital. As the audience was settling, there was a stir at the door, and a latecomer joined the party. It was Mr Fanshawe. He bowed unsteadily to Mistress Alink.

'Forgive me, madam, I am unconscionably late.' He was out of breath from the stairs, and his voice wavered. 'My Lord Ashley kept me. And here is Mistress Hakesby!' He stooped over her hand. 'An unexpected pleasure.'

'Mr Van Riebeeck was kind enough to bring me, sir.'

'Indeed. You and I last met on the day my lion arrived.'

'Is he quite settled now?'

'Oh yes, though not as healthy as I would like. I keep him in my stable and visit him every day. I have named him Caliban, as he is wild, and a monster, and must learn to obey.'

The recital surpassed Cat's hopes. Monsieur Grabu was never still. He was a wiry, sallow-skinned man with very long thumbs that curved backwards. He not only directed the music but took the part of principal violin. There were four singers – two women, together with a tenor and a bass. Grabu played several compositions of his own, adapting his style easily to the more restricted setting of this relatively modest house and the size of the audience.

When the music was over, the party trooped into another room, where supper had been laid out. Cat sat by

Van Riebeeck, and Fanshawe took the chair on her other side.

'Well,' Fanshawe said. 'That was quite ravishing. Don't you agree? Monsieur Grabu's fingering is beyond compare.'

'For myself,' Van Riebeeck said, 'I sometimes grow weary of French music.'

'But – but Monsieur Grabu is a Catalan.'

'Indeed, sir. But the fellow trained in France, and your king favours the French in all matters. I would hear more Italian or even German music.'

Fanshawe cleared his throat and his fingers plucked at a roll beside his plate, reducing it to crumbs. 'Ah yes,' he said after a pause, turning to Cat, 'on the subject of work, madam, Van Riebeeck tells me you are working for a most illustrious client at present.'

She smiled at him. 'We value all our clients alike. But we are particularly attached to those who pay our bills.'

Fanshawe laughed nervously.

'A poultry house,' Van Riebeeck murmured in her other ear. She felt his breath on her skin. 'Pah.'

Still probing, Fanshawe said, 'Another commission from my Lord Arlington. Most impressive. And I understand this one is intended for a lady of royal blood?'

'Doubly royal,' whispered Van Riebeeck.

'And Van Riebeeck has had the good fortune to see something of your plans. He says it's a most magnificent building, fit for a queen.'

Another insinuating whisper. 'Or a princess. Or rather for her hens.'

He was mocking her, and Cat found that she enjoyed it. 'Mr Van Riebeeck is too kind,' she said. 'Of course, much will depend on what my lord wishes.'

Fanshawe smiled. 'Of course. In the meantime, you must permit me to show you my lion now he is settled. He is held securely, and it is quite safe. Would you care to dine with me on Sunday? My daughter-in-law would be charmed to meet you again, and perhaps Van Riebeeck could join us if he is not engaged elsewhere.'

Cat accepted, though there was an air of contrivance about the invitation, and she wondered if Van Riebeeck had suggested it to Fanshawe beforehand. That could be construed as a compliment.

By this time, the evening was coming to an end, and guests were trickling away.

'Are you quite finished, madam?' Van Riebeeck demanded, rising to his feet. 'Shall we make our farewells?'

The Alinks fussed over them as they were leaving, escorting them downstairs to the door, sending one servant out for a hackney and another to fetch their cloaks.

The interior of a coach forces intimacy on a couple whether they wish it or not. They sat opposite each other, Cat with her knees angled away from Van Riebeeck's, as the hackney jolted slowly over the cobbles and the endless rain drummed on the roof and dripped down the leather curtains that covered the sides of the coach. Neither of them spoke. Cat was aware that he had taken a good deal of wine during and after supper.

Her senses seemed heightened by the enclosed darkness. His smell was a blend of wine and sweat and a strangely feral odour that put her in mind of Caliban the lion. She was, she told herself, greatly relieved not to feel a hand fumbling at her skirts or heavy breathing in her ear. But what would happen when they reached Henrietta Street? Would he expect to come in with her?

The coach rumbled through Covent Garden, where the air was raucous with the cries of stallholders, the shrieks of women and the hoarse laughter of men going about their pleasures. Henrietta Street was quieter. The hackney slowed to a halt outside the sign of the Rose. Cat's hands, invisible on her lap, balled together into fists.

Van Riebeeck climbed out and held out his arm to help her down. Her fingers tightened on his sleeve, and she felt the unyielding muscle and bone beneath. It wouldn't hurt to invite him for a glass of wine.

Then, abruptly, the situation changed. Before they had had time to knock, the house door opened. The porter, Pheebs, appeared in the doorway, his head turned towards someone behind him in the hall. He stood back to allow a visitor to leave. Standing in the doorway was the familiar figure of James Marwood.

They saw each other at the same moment. So did Van Riebeeck.

'Madam.' Marwood came down the steps and bowed to her. 'Your servant.'

She curtsied in return.

Van Riebeeck stared. 'Mr Marwood. We met at the theatre. You were with this lady.' His voice made the words sound like accusations.

Marwood looked at him. Cat looked from one to the other. There was enough light to see their faces. Marwood was frowning, and his mouth was slightly open as if something had surprised him. Perched above them on his seat, the coachman said something about his fare, but no one paid him any attention.

'What are you doing here?' Van Riebeeck said, and his tone was a provocation in itself.

Marwood ignored him. 'I called to enquire if you were within. I trust you are well?'

'Perfectly, thank you,' she said. 'But it's late for you to call. Was there a particular reason?'

'Nothing of any moment.'

'How are you acquainted with Mistress Hakesby?' Van Riebeeck demanded.

'The late Mr Hakesby and I were once engaged in some business together.' Marwood's voice was colourless. 'Though why that should be any concern of yours, I cannot begin to imagine.'

'That's for the lady to decide, sir, not you.'

'Nor you, either.'

Cat was suddenly angry. The two men were facing each other like a pair of fighting birds in a cockpit, hooded and spurred, hungry for each other's blood. The rain dripped from the brims of their hats. They seemed to have forgotten her existence. They seemed to have forgotten it was raining as well.

'Well, sir,' she said to Van Riebeeck, 'thank you for an agreeable evening.'

'More than agreeable, madam,' he said, sketching a hasty bow. 'For me at least. Too agreeable to end yet—'

Cat interrupted: 'But it is growing late and I must bid you both goodnight.'

Without a second glance at either of them, she went into the house. Pheebs closed the door with a satisfying bang, shutting out the squabbling men, the grumbling coachman, the rain, the wind and the night.

CHAPTER SEVENTEEN

ON THURSDAY, I loitered by Temple Bar for nearly twenty minutes. By a quarter-past twelve, it was clear that Johnson wasn't coming. The odds had never been in my favour – he had no reason to trust me after I had wrecked his attempt to make Gorvin pay Abbott's gambling debts. Perhaps he hadn't even heard my whispered words as I was leaving the Blue Bush, or perhaps he was too afraid of Van Riebeeck and Connolly to run the risk of meeting me.

It was doubly irritating. When my Lord Arlington had set in motion my investigation of the circumstances surrounding Abbott's death, I had had no choice but to obey his commands. But meeting the Dutchman with Cat yesterday evening had given me another reason to talk to Johnson. I had already known that Van Riebeeck was an habitué of the Blue Bush, which meant he was a gambler who mixed with low company. He went under the name of Wulf there, which was not the mark of an honest man. I also knew he was a friend and associate of Fanshawe, the former father-in-law of Abbott's wife and the grandfather of her child. I had seen him with Abbott.

But now I had discovered that Van Riebeeck was on sufficiently intimate terms with Cat to spend an evening with her.
Worse still, he clearly desired to see more of her. I would
give a great deal to be able to warn her against him. But to
do that effectively, I needed more information.

I cut my losses and walked down the Strand to the Fountain.
I found a place at the common table. I had hardly squeezed
on to the bench when I felt a tap on my shoulder. It was
Johnson, shiny-faced and panting as though he had been
hurrying, and open-mouthed like a gargoyle. He was wearing
the purple suit he had worn yesterday, which looked even
shabbier in full daylight.

'Good afternoon to you,' I said. 'I had quite given you up.'

'Forgive me, sir.' His large eyes were glassy with moisture,
giving the impression that he was about to burst into tears.
'I thought it best to be cautious . . . to make sure you were
alone. I wondered if perhaps . . .'

'I wished you harm? Why should I do that?'

'I'm sure I don't know, sir,' he said, his high-pitched voice
suddenly prim. 'It's not for me to say. But in my profession
I have learned that a man can't be too careful.'

'But you'll dine with me now you're here?'

'Thank you.'

'Then I'll find a booth or a private room.' I disentangled
my legs from the bench and beckoned a waiter.

'And I think you said that – ah – you would make it worth
my while? May I ask how?'

'I desire certain intelligence,' I said. 'And I will pay for it.
The amount I pay will depend on its quality.'

The waiter found us a booth. We ordered our dinner. There
was a window to the left of me, which threw a strong light

on the scars on the side of my face and neck. I noticed Johnson staring at them.

'If you crane your head a trifle,' I said coldly, 'you will have a better view.'

He coloured and started back. 'Forgive me, sir. I did not mean – I did not, on my honour, to——'

'Hold your clack.' I paused, for I had learned in these last few years that there were more ways than one to put a man at a disadvantage; even my burns had their uses. I watched the fear spreading over Johnson's face. There were grey hairs among the black stubble on his cheek. 'Deal with me fairly, and we shall not quarrel. But if you hold back information, or try to cheat me in any way, by God you will suffer the full rigour of the law. A charge of forgery, remember.'

'But . . . but that was all Abbott's doing.'

'A judge won't agree. Besides, Abbott's dead and you're alive. You were trying to profit by the forgery. That means the gallows. Do you understand me?'

He nodded violently.

'Have a care,' I said, leaning back against the wall. 'If you go on like that, your head will fly off your shoulders.'

At this opportune moment, the waiter appeared with a jug of ale. At a nod from me, he poured for both of us. Johnson seized his mug and drank deeply.

'Tell me,' I went on, 'is this how you earn your keep at the Blue Bush? They give you a pigeon to pluck, and you pluck it, and then you share the proceeds?'

He coloured again. 'If a man likes to play, I can't stop him. And he will play with someone, so why not me?'

'The Blue Bush is a species of engine which exists to part

a man from his money. And you are a moving part within it. Correct?'

'There is no law against it, sir. It's like any other profession.'

'It pays well?'

'My income varies. One must be philosophical. Sometimes fortune frowns. Sometimes she smiles.' Johnson extended his left arm and looked coyly at me. 'As you see.'

'See what?' I said.

He stroked his sleeve. 'This suit of broadcloth cost me well-nigh twenty pounds. The mulberry colour is quite unique and it was very expensive.' He smiled proudly at me and fluttered his handkerchief to emphasize the point. There was something childlike about his vanity that was almost disarming. 'Not that I mean to be boastful, sir. I merely show you evidence that Dame Fortune often smiles on me.'

I had had enough of philosophy for the time being. 'You play with marked cards, I imagine, and load the dice. That's perfectly clear, but it's not my business at present and we shall not discuss it.'

Johnson's head snapped up. He glared at me. 'You wrong me, sir. I have a God-given talent for games of chance. It's true that the play at the Blue Bush favours the house, not the customer, and that not every game is as above board as mine. But I have no need to cheat.'

'How so?'

'Have you heard of Monsieur de Fermat and Monsieur Pascal?' His tone had become condescending.

I shook my head.

'They were French mathematicians. They discovered how to calculate which way the dice are likely to fall or the cards to appear. In a word, what is *probable*. I follow their system.' Johnson cleared his throat and smiled, as a man does when he is pleased with himself. 'Most gamblers, on the other hand, are swayed by a foolish superstition or a childish whim. The more they lose, the wilder their actions become. Often they take too much wine as they play, which makes it worse. But I, sir, I am different.' He tapped a forefinger against his forehead. 'I calculate. With every throw of the dice or turn of the cards, I work out which outcome is more *probable* than the others.' He shrugged his thin shoulders. 'Sometimes I lose, sometimes I win. But in the course of an evening's play, I win far more times than they do. That's why I have no need to cheat.'

It was in its way an impressive performance. It is always revealing when you stumble on what a man cherishes about his own attainments. Even the public hangman, I imagine, takes a professional pride in the performance of his art.

'In the end, the result is the same,' I said. 'You fleece your opponents.'

The fire had gone out of him. He said wearily, 'Sir, believe me, they fleece themselves.'

'Was that true of Abbott?'

'He had the fever.' Johnson paused, watching me refill his mug. 'Some men do. Once they start to gamble, they cannot stop. You could say with justice that I made it easy for him to ruin himself. But if it hadn't been me, it would have been someone else.'

We drank in silence. I broke off a fragment of roll and dipped it in my ale. Johnson's eyes flicked to and fro, constantly opening and closing as if they were itching. His body twitched on the bench. He held his mug with both hands. His fingernails were black and in need of trimming. Strange, I thought, that a man with such a talent for winning money should be so pitiable in other respects.

There was a stir of movement behind us. Johnson looked suddenly alarmed. I glanced over my shoulder. Stephen was standing there. He bobbed his head and held out a letter to me.

'Messenger said it was urgent, master,' he murmured.

I broke the seal and unfolded the letter. It was a curt note from Mr Williamson, who desired me to inform him when I would do him the honour of returning to my labours in his office. I could almost hear his hard voice enunciating the words carefully and tipping each one with sarcasm. I stuffed the letter in my pocket and dismissed Stephen.

'Who was that?' Johnson said. 'I thought you said you'd be discreet.'

'That was my footboy, not the town crier. I left word with my people that I would dine here in case there was a message for me.' I watched him drink, and made my voice gentle. 'When I left you yesterday, a man came onto the landing. You told him Abbott was dead.'

Johnson nodded absently. 'Mr Wulf. Herr Wulf, I should say. He is sometimes at the Blue Bush – he keeps a room there, and I believe he owns a share in the business, though he does not care to involve himself in the day-to-day running of it.'

'Herr Wulf? Is he German?'

'Indeed, sir. From the Palatinate, like our own Prince Rupert. But he speaks English well, almost like one of ourselves.'

'I believe he was acquainted with Abbott.'

'Oh yes. He sponsored him.'

I raised my eyebrows. 'Sponsor? As a godparent sponsors a child when he's baptized?'

'In a manner of speaking. At the Blue Bush, anyone may play in the common room downstairs. But if you wish to play for higher stakes, or in private, then you must be invited into one of our rooms upstairs. For that you need a sponsor. Someone well known to the house who will vouch for you.' Johnson looked directly at me, and again I sensed a hint of pride. 'The Blue Bush is a very select establishment.'

'Where does this man Wulf live? What does he do?'

'I've no idea. Sometimes one does not see him for months at a time.'

'But he's a gambler?'

'Yes. Usually with someone he brings to the house. He's cautious, though. He often played with Mr Abbott. In fact, he was there the last time I saw the poor man. Abbott had scraped together a few pounds and was desperate to mend his fortunes. But alas, the dice were against him yet again. It's barely a week ago, but it seems an age.'

'It was Wednesday, the twenty-third of February,' I said, for the date had been lodged in my memory. 'As well as gambling, Abbott dined at the Blue Bush, or rather drank there. He left at about three o'clock in the afternoon.'

Johnson frowned. 'I see that . . . you have made quite a study of his movements.'

'So there were three of you that day – Wulf, Abbott and you? You were in the room where I met you yesterday?'

'Yes.'

'Describe Abbott to me.'

'What?'

'What was he wearing?'

'But if you met him yourself, you must—'

'Answer me!'

He cowered away from the simulated anger in my voice. 'A dark cloak . . . the suit he wore at Whitehall . . . a dark-blue colour, I think. A broad-brimmed hat. That's all.'

'Was he wearing a sword? Carrying anything?'

'No sword. Not even a stick – I remarked on that. Nor even a book for Mr Wulf this time.' Johnson saw the question in my face and anticipated it. 'Mr Abbott sometimes brought a book for him.' He sketched its shape with his long, mobile fingers. 'Wrapped in a parcel, from a bookbinder by Westminster Hall. It saved Mr Wulf a journey. He either left it at the Blue Bush for collection or gave it to him directly.'

'How very obliging,' I said. 'Tell me, on that last day, how did Abbott seem when he left?'

Johnson shrugged. 'I don't know. Mr Wulf lent him a little money. After we'd played a while, I left them alone together. Abbott was in his cups by then, and he asked me to send up another bottle. But he was already in low spirits. Wulf was saying he shouldn't take his losses to heart, and the night was always darkest before dawn, and he would come round soon enough. I knew that was impossible.'

'How so?'

'Faith, sir, in my profession I see it often when a man is reduced to playing with borrowed money. It's something about his face, about the way he shakes the dice box – I cannot quite put my finger on it. But I know that when his spirits sink beneath a certain point, they will not rise again, and nor will his fortunes.' Johnson paused and looked directly at me. His face was as calm as a judge's. 'I know then he is ruined. Beyond all redemption.'

The waiter and his boy brought the trays with our dinner, the dishes steaming under their covers. I called for another jug of ale to wash it down. I ate little, but I watched Johnson. He hacked at his chop with his knife and stuffed the pieces into his mouth. Gravy trickled unheeded down his chin.

I waited until he had almost cleared his platter. 'Could you examine Wulf's chamber at the Blue Bush, if you had a mind to?'

'What?'

'You heard me.'

He sat back, knife in hand, and stared at me. 'Perhaps.' His voice was wary. 'I know where the keys are kept. Why?'

'I would be interested in any papers Mr Wulf might keep there.' I watched his face. 'I need them brought to me, as well as any small personal effects of his you can conveniently carry away with you. If Wulf's away for a few days, nothing need connect you with the affair. London has as many thieves as there are lice in a beggar's hair. And no doubt the Blue Bush has its share of them.'

He drew in his breath sharply, but I held up my hand to keep him silent.

'You will be paid. When you need to communicate with me, send a message to Samuel Witherdine, care of Mistress Fawley at the sign of the Silver Crescent. Do you know it? The alehouse in the Strand near Arundel House. I shall reply to the same place, and we shall arrange a meeting.'

'Forgive me, sir, I cannot.' He was dabbing his forehead with his handkerchief. 'I would oblige you if I could, but it would be far too dangerous. If someone saw me . . .'

'Dangerous?' I tapped the fingertips of my right hand on the table, like the roll of the drum at Horse Guards.

'Dangerous? Have you considered that it might be far more dangerous to disoblige me? Forgery, remember, is a crime that is punished with the gallows.'

Johnson's eyes were huge and moist in the ruined face. I almost felt sorry for him.

'Pray allow me to advise you,' I said gently. 'You must weigh a mere possibility against a probability — nay, let us call it a certainty. Ask yourself, sir, presented with such a choice, what would Monsieur de Fermat and Monsieur Pascal decide?'

CHAPTER EIGHTEEN

M Y LORD SENT one of his own coaches, emblazoned with his arms and with glass in the windows; and Cat was glad that she had dressed in a manner appropriate to the conveyance.

At Goring House, a manservant conducted her directly to my lord. He was in a drawing room, which faced south-west. Tata was standing in a pool of watery sunlight by a window. She was playing a game with a man in an armchair, which was angled so its back was towards the rest of the room. The child's nurse stood quietly by, head bowed and hands folded in front of her. It was an unexpectedly domestic scene, and domesticity was not a quality she associated with Lord Arlington.

My lord himself was standing by the fireplace, deep in conversation with two other men. He broke off when Cat was announced and turned towards her with a very civil bow.

'Madam,' he said, 'I'm rejoiced to see you. Permit me to present these two gentlemen: Sir Thomas Clifford and Sir Richard Bellings.'

Cat curtsied. Both men were middle-aged, but younger

than Arlington. Clifford was ruddy-faced and vigorous-looking; she knew him by reputation as a prominent courtier; he had served with distinction in the last Dutch war and was now one of the Commissioners of the Treasury. She had heard nothing of Bellings, however, and gave him a quick, assessing glance. Sir Richard was a wiry, stooping man with a long chin with the wings of a dark periwig drooping on either side of it. At her entrance, he had been standing at a desk and making notes in his pocketbook.

At the far end of the room Tata squealed with laughter. Arlington glanced towards the sound, and for a moment his habitual gravity dissolved into a smile. He turned back to Cat and indicated the folder she carried.

'These are the plans for Madame's poultry house? Pray lay them out on the table over there.'

She obeyed him. Her back was to the room. No one spoke, apart from Tata, who for some reason was repeating 'Puff, puff, puff' over and over again. When Cat had arranged the plans, she turned back. All three men were looking at her. They appeared more interested in her than in the plans. Looking past them, she saw that Tata was clapping her chubby hands together.

'Tell me,' Arlington said. 'Are you proficient in the French tongue?'

'Yes, my lord – or rather I have some familiarity with it. And a lodger in my house is a Frenchman, a Huguenot whom I may apply to if I am at a loss for a word when I write the directions to accompany these plans.'

A sudden silence fell. Even Tata stopped clapping.

'You mistake my meaning. Do you speak the French?'

Cat said, 'In a word, no. Not as a Frenchwoman does. But

when I was a child, my aunts made sure that I had the rudiments of the language, enough to make myself understood in society.'

Arlington glanced at Bellings. 'Sir Richard?'

The wiry man laid down his pen and stepped forward. *'Mademoiselle, si je puis me permettre, comment êtes-vous arrivée en ce lieu aujourd'hui?'*

He had spoken in formal French, fortunately not too quickly. She answered him in the same language, stumbling over her words, and with pauses while she searched for ways to make her meaning clear with the limited vocabulary at her disposal. She had been brought in my lord's coach, she said, and they had come the Piccadilly way. The road by Whitehall and Westminster was better, but it was longer and usually more congested.

After that, he asked what commissions she had undertaken recently. While they were speaking, Tata and her playmate began another game, punctuated by enthusiastic but irregular clapping.

'Pat-a-cake, pat-a-cake, baker's man . . .'

'De quelle envergure était cet entrepôt?' Bellings asked. *'Et où se trouvait-il précisément?'*

Cat was uncertain about *envergure*, so it was best to ignore it and hope that it would not matter.

The chanting continued, a child's voice high and excited, and the man's deep murmur beneath it. 'That I will, master, fast as I can . . .'

'Par les docks, monsieur, un peu ouest de la Tour de Londres.'

Round and round went the rhyme, for repetition was part of its charm for Tata, that and the clapping. 'Pat it and prick it, and mark it with T . . .'

Cat took a chance and ventured on another sentence. '*Le monsieur qui l'a commandé vient de recevoir un lion de l'Afrique.*'

'Put it in the oven for *Tata and me*!'

Tata shrieked the last few words so loudly that everyone turned to look at her. The chair scraped back. A very tall, dark gentleman rose to his feet and took Tata by the hand. Grave-faced, he looked down at the child.

'I fear we have disturbed your father, and this lady, and these gentlemen in their conversation. We must beg their pardon, must we not?'

Cat sank into a deep curtsy and bowed her head.

'Sir,' Arlington said eagerly, 'you are too good to my daughter. You must not let her plague you.'

Tata released the King and stumbled across the room to her father. She embraced his knees and peered between them at Cat. 'Chick, chick,' she said knowingly. 'I'm a chick-chick. Look.'

She made a noise intended to resemble the crowing of a cock. Cat smiled weakly at her.

'Mistress Hakesby,' the King said. 'Pray rise.'

She obeyed, and looked up at his face. She had seen him once before, though he had not seen her. He was taller than she had realized, and swarthier. He was not a handsome man, but his height and his bearing lent him distinction. So this, she thought, is what all the fuss is about. But after all, he's only a man.

'I understand that my lord has asked you to design a poultry house for Madame my sister, and my nieces. Would you be so kind as to show me your designs?'

Cat had no reason to love Charles Stuart, but she found herself warming to the man's grave courtesy. He was already at the table, turning over the plans, holding them up to the light to see them better. He asked questions, too – sensible, practical ones such as the ideal location for such a building, the materials she would advise, and the direction the principal openings should face.

'It's most elegant,' the King said, examining the front elevation. 'It reminds me of Le Vau's pavilion for my mother's house at Colombes.' He smiled at her. 'And all this for a few fortunate birds.'

'We must house them somewhere, sir,' Cat said. 'You have your own aviary, I understand, as well as the birds in the Park.'

'I house people too. Hundreds of them. In some ways the birds are more rewarding.'

The words had a sour flavour, but he crooked his black, strongly marked eyebrows as he spoke, so perhaps it was intended as a pleasantry. He granted scores of grace-and-favour apartments at Whitehall and other palaces to his courtiers and their hangers-on. He nodded to Cat and turned back to the three gentlemen.

Arlington hastily beckoned the nurse. 'Take Mistress Tata upstairs,' he murmured.

Tata wailed, and looked piteously at the King. She was wise beyond her years and had already discovered who was the most powerful figure in her world. But the nurse swept her into her arms and curtsied to His Majesty, who appeared not to notice. Carrying the pink-faced, disgruntled child, she backed away from his presence.

The King turned to Arlington. 'Yes,' he said. 'I am sure Madame will find this entertaining, and I hope it will raise her spirits too.'

He nodded to Clifford. He smiled at Cat, who curtsied again.

Arlington left with the King, saying over his shoulder that he would return in a few minutes. A king cannot leave your house like an ordinary mortal: he must be escorted, and the due forms followed.

With their departure, the atmosphere of the drawing room changed: there was a palpable lifting of tension. Clifford and Bellings talked together in low voices, ignoring Cat. She busied herself tidying the papers and replacing them in their folder. But she could not prolong the task more than a moment. Afterwards, she went over to the window and stared at the garden.

Beyond the pleasure grounds were pastures and parkland, clearly part of Lord Arlington's demesne, which stretched almost as far as the grass-covered remains of the earthworks that Parliament had thrown up to defend London from Royalist armies that never came. My lord's London home was impressively spacious for somewhere so close to Westminster and Whitehall. If it were hers, she decided, she would tear the old house down and build a palace on the site. She toyed with the fancy of moving the house a little to the north and aligning it with the canal in St James's Park, so the windows would look down the long water to the Cockpit and Whitehall. Or would it be better to align the north-east frontage with the Mall? Then perhaps the Mall itself should be converted to roadway and form the principal approach, a straight wide avenue almost precisely aligned with Charing Cross and the Strand beyond, all the way to St Paul's and the City.

She was still contemplating the implications of this – the

rerouting of a road or two, for example, the demolition of buildings, the conversion of parkland to other uses – when Lord Arlington returned. Clifford and Bellings fell silent when he entered, but he merely nodded to them and walked over to Cat. He was smiling.

'That's most satisfactory,' he said. 'The King is sure that Madame will like it.' He rubbed the black plaster across his nose as if to relieve an itch. 'Yes, most satisfactory.'

She sensed that he was talking not only about the poultry house plans. Something had been concluded in the last few minutes, and whatever it was, it pleased him greatly.

'His Majesty,' he went on, 'has made a suggestion. Well, a suggestion from that quarter has the force of a command. He believes it would be a great advantage if you yourself were to present the plans to Madame.'

She blurted out, 'But, my lord, my work keeps me in London.'

'This is your work too, Mistress Hakesby,' he said in a sharper voice. 'And work of greater importance than any other you can possibly have. His Majesty desires you to go to France. It will not be for a few weeks yet. You will have plenty of time to arrange matters here. But you must prepare yourself, and your designs, in case Madame wishes to discuss the project herself.' He was about to turn aside but then a thought struck him. 'Perhaps you should look into the construction of a small model of the new poultry house.' He gave himself an approving smile. 'The young princess, Madame's elder daughter, is little older than my own daughter. I'm persuaded that she would be greatly diverted by a model.'

'But how will I travel?' Cat said, trying to grapple with the host of implications.

Arlington waved the question aside. 'You needn't trouble yourself about that. The arrangements will be taken care of. You will be travelling on the King's business now. Not mine.'

After dinner on Thursday, as Cat was weighing in her mind the competing claims of balancing last month's accounts and finishing the elevation on her drawing board, a servant in royal livery brought her a letter. It was from Mr Gorvin, Lord Arlington's clerk. Apologizing for the short notice, he begged that she would make it convenient to call on my lord tomorrow afternoon at four o'clock. A coach would collect her at half-past three.

Cat scribbled a reply, the only one she could reasonably make, and sent the servant away.

'Who do they think they are, these people?' Brennan grumbled. 'They whistle, and they expect you to come to them.'

'I've no choice, and you know it. One does not disoblige the King's chief minister.'

It was a measure of my lord's interest in the project that he was so impatient to see results. Cat's mind was already running ahead to tomorrow – not only to the work that needed to be done before the afternoon, but also to the selection of her clothes, and how long it would take to dress her hair. She had learned from observing Dr Wren that appearances mattered. Wren always looked the gentleman, and a prosperous one at that. If you gave the impression that you were already successful, it created a precondition for success in the future. Her late husband had never understood that. But she was different.

CHAPTER NINETEEN

IN SLAUGHTER STREET, late on Friday afternoon, Hannah passed Maria in the yard with the necessary house. 'Meet me after supper when they've gone upstairs,' the maid muttered, bobbing a clumsy curtsy for the sake of anyone who might be looking. 'In the summerhouse. You'd better come. Or I'll make you wish you'd never been born.'

Hannah went into the scullery without waiting for an answer. Thursday was the evening when the cook went to visit her widowed mother in Stepney, which meant that Hannah had more freedom of movement than usual.

Maria shut herself up in the necessary house. It was very cold. The air stank. She had never been able to rid herself of the childish idea that at night evil spirits clustered about this place and watched her at her business. She pushed up her sleeve and bit the tender flesh on the inside of her arm until she tasted blood. It distracted her, but only for a few seconds. Besides, God was watching her, she knew, even if the evil spirits weren't, because He was everywhere.

Help me, oh Lord, help me.

If only Abbott were still alive, Maria thought, if only they were still living by Temple Bar.

Since their last conversation, she had lived in dread – not merely of Hannah but of everything: every shadow leaping on the wall, every sharp word from her mother, every knock at the door, every frown on her grandfather's face. On Wednesday afternoon, when she had chanced upon Hannah talking to Uncle Van Riebeeck in the street, Maria had feared the worst, but nothing had happened. Clearly Hannah had not yet laid information against her, Maria, as a witch and a murderer. She tried to reassure herself with the thought that perhaps no one would believe it if a kitchen maid levelled a charge of witchcraft against the granddaughter of Mr Fanshawe. But they might believe it. She couldn't be sure, one way or the other. Even if they didn't believe Hannah, the accusation would cling to Maria like a bad smell for the rest of her life. After all, Abbott was dead. There was no getting away from that.

After supper, her grandfather and her mother almost always went upstairs to sit in the great chamber over the hall. Occasionally her mother read to the old man. More often, he spent the time turning over the objects in his collection. He kept many of the smaller items in the great chamber, locked away in fine cabinets of Dutch marquetry work. He gloated over them like a miser over his gold and entered their descriptions on sheets of ruled paper, which would eventually be bound in leather like an account book. He was on his third volume now. There was already an entry for Caliban, his latest acquisition.

'When the beast dies,' he'd said at dinner that day, 'there's no reason why he should leave my collection. I shall have him stuffed and mounted for posterity. He would look very fine in the hall.'

Knowing that the two of them were likely to remain in the chamber for at least an hour, Maria put on her cloak and pattens and slipped into the garden. The ground was sodden from yesterday's rain. It was very dark, with not even the light of a star overhead, but in the distance the lantern by the stable gate gave out an almost imperceptible glow. It was something to navigate by.

Feeling her way, she crept down the path. As her eyes adjusted to the absence of light, she discerned different shades in the darkness — the hedge that formed a ragged barrier to her left, and the deeper dark of the roofline of the summerhouse. The door was never locked. She slipped inside, leaving the door open, and waited for the thudding of her heart to slow.

Inside, the air was colder than outside. The summerhouse consisted of a large room at the front and a smaller one behind, where in fine weather the servants kept the wine and the sweetmeats and whatever else the company in the front room desired.

Shivering, Maria drew her cloak around her and hugged herself. Nothing was fair, she thought, why couldn't everything be pleasant again?

To her horror, she heard footsteps outside, and men's voices. They were drawing closer. She retreated, feeling her way along the wall until she reached the doorway to the back room. The door was ajar. She slipped inside. She would have liked to close the door, but she did not dare, in case the sound betrayed her.

The pavilion's heavy outer door opened with a clatter. A man swore. Maria shrank back against the wall.

'Put him down here.'

'What now, master?'

'Wait outside. Keep watch. I won't be long. I need to lock the gate.'

She recognized the first voice. The man addressed as 'master' was her uncle Van Riebeeck. The men must have come through the door in the garden wall behind the summerhouse. It gave onto an alley near the bottom of Slaughter Street, and it was usually kept locked and bolted.

The footsteps retreated. Maria was alone, but she was trapped. The second man was somewhere outside. She heard him enter the summerhouse again. He was breathing heavily as if he had exerted himself. There was a rustle, followed by a soft, dull impact, as if something had fallen on to the stone floor. And then, clearer than the other sounds, the unmistakable chink of coin.

Time passed. There was no sign of Hannah. Perhaps she was out there in the darkness. It was more likely that she had heard the sounds of movement and retreated to the house. Maria grew so cold that she was forced to stuff a fold of her cloak in her mouth to stop her teeth chattering. The fear and the cold merged with her guilt over Abbott's death: she knew God was punishing her for her sins, and that this time was a foretaste of what hell would be like, though hell would be ten thousand times worse.

She did not hear her uncle return. But she heard the voices, his and the servant's, talking in low tones which grew more distinct as they came nearer.

'Faith, he'll wake soon enough,' the other man said, his voice thickened with a brogue. 'What do we do with him then?'

'Take him down to the stables.' That was Uncle Van Riebeeck. 'That's where we'll make him talk.'

'Someone will hear us.'

'No they won't. The keeper's away, and so's his boy. They won't be back until daybreak at the earliest. There's no one else down there. They don't keep horses now, not in town. They use the livery stables.'

'What if Johnson won't open his mouth?'

Uncle Henryk laughed softly. 'I know where the keys are kept. We'll put him in with the lion. Once he sees that brute, he'll talk to us all we want.'

That evening, Margaret Witherdine called at Henrietta Street. She and her husband, Samuel, were James Marwood's servants: he housed them in his lodgings at the Savoy, he clothed them and he paid them: and in return they owed him their entire duty. But over the last few years a connection had gradually developed between Margaret and Mistress Hakesby.

The women could hardly be friends, for their respective stations did not permit such intimacy. Nor did Margaret work for Cat, or not exactly, though there were sometimes presents of money for services rendered. Curiosity played its part, however, on Margaret's side, for she had never before encountered a woman like Mistress Hakesby. Nevertheless, the relationship without a name was there, independent of all those factors, and recognized by both.

After Mr Hakesby's death nearly two years earlier, Marwood had encouraged Margaret to lend what assistance she could during the early days of Cat's widowhood, when the Drawing Office and the lodgings on the floor below were places of grief and uncertainty. At the time, Cat's maid, Jane Ash, had been barely thirteen years old, and next to useless for any but the simplest tasks. Now she was better trained, largely thanks to Margaret, and more capable, but she was still only a girl, and not a very intelligent one either. It was Margaret who remained the ultimate authority on all household matters at Henrietta Street. With calm competence, she advised on the mending of fine linen or the cleaning of carpet stains. She knew when the baker was trying to cheat them, and she had dealt with the rogue personally on Cat's behalf on more than one occasion. She was also a source of information and even guidance on certain private matters that concerned women. Margaret knew her own worth. When she allowed Cat to give her a present, in cash or kind, she received it without unseemly expressions of gratitude.

Two or three times a week, Margaret would arrive at Henrietta Street, usually in the late afternoon or the early evening, a time when her employment at the Savoy made few demands on her. Marwood was aware that Margaret visited Cat, though not perhaps how often. But he had never mentioned it to Cat, nor she to him. Cat had once asked Margaret outright whether Marwood minded her coming so often.

Margaret had shrugged. 'I do my work, mistress, and more. I make sure Sam does his, too, and young Stephen. Master knows that, and he don't ask questions unless he needs to. He's a good master.'

The answer was in its way a reproof. Margaret was loyal to Marwood and loyal to Cat. But the loyalties differed in their nature.

Cat was kept longer than she had expected at Goring House. Afterwards, she called on a prospective client in Pall Mall, which delayed her still further. It was early evening before she returned to Henrietta Street. She climbed the stairs to her lodgings, a set of apartments on the floor below the Drawing Office. As soon as she reached the landing, she heard the sound of voices in her bedchamber.

Margaret was kneeling at the end of the bed before a row of shoes that Jane had laid out for inspection like a line of soldiers on parade. She was a sturdy, red-faced woman with short legs and a head of black curls. She scrambled to her feet as Cat entered and gave her a cursory curtsy.

'The silly girl tried to brush the mud off before it was dry.' She held up a latchet shoe with a two-inch heel. 'Look at it. You'll never get that mark out of the leather. It's stained for ever.'

Jane Ash stood mutely by, her head bowed. She was on the verge of tears, which was not unusual for her.

'It doesn't matter,' Cat said. 'I never liked them much. I can't think why I bought them.'

'And these need resoling,' Margaret said, stooping to pick up a pair of sturdy, well-constructed pattens. 'Worth it, too – they'll last you a lifetime if the girl looks after them properly.' She set them down and took up a pair of shoes with pointed toes, green silk linings and three-inch heels. They were the ones that Cat had worn yesterday evening, when Van Riebeeck took her to Monsieur Grabu's concert. 'The heel's going to come off if you wear it like that again. You could break an ankle. The workmanship is shocking – they're hardly worn. You should take them back to the shoemaker's. I can't understand why you bought them.'

'They're very elegant,' Cat protested. 'Jane shall take them back and make them mend the heel. Tomorrow morning, Jane, do you hear?'

She looked wistfully at the shoes. They were so lovely. She would pack them if she had to go to France, she decided, which made mending them a matter of urgency. They would not do for travelling in, of course, but they would perhaps be useful if she was obliged to mingle in society or even if she were presented to Madame. Cat was not a vain woman but, for reasons she did not try to understand, she was particularly fond of shoes. Nothing raised one's spirits so much as the knowledge that one was wearing an attractive pair of shoes, even if nobody noticed them apart from oneself. Along with books and engravings about architecture, shoes were among the few luxuries that she allowed herself. She spent more than she could afford on them.

As a result, she possessed more pairs than she could possibly wear. Indeed, some of them were to all intents and purposes unwearable, though they looked very fine on her feet and hardly hurt at all if she did not try to walk in them. A few of her shoes were perfect in all respects. In the words of the great Roman architect Vitruvius, they combined in a few scraps of leather (and sometimes silk, that most wonderful of fabrics) the cardinal virtues of *firmitas, utilitas* and *venustas* – or, in the common tongue, strength, usefulness and beauty. If Cat were entirely honest with herself, which she rarely was on the subject of shoes, she considered that the greatest of these virtues was beauty.

She sent Jane upstairs to sweep the Drawing Office, which was empty because Brennan was working at the Fenchurch Street site. Margaret followed her into the room she used as a parlour.

'How do you do, mistress? You look pale.'

Cat turned so Margaret could remove her cloak. 'I may have to go to France soon.'

'France? For God's sake, why?'

'A matter of business.'

'Will you be alone among all those foreign devils?'

'It will be perfectly safe. I shall be escorted and looked after.'

'I hear their innkeepers cut your throat for sixpence.' Margaret sniffed. 'But what can you expect of Papists?'

She bustled away and brought Cat a bowl of water and soap to wash the grime of travel from her hands and face. She stood beside Cat, holding the towel.

'Did you see master last night?' she asked.

Cat looked up, surprised. 'Briefly, yes.'

Margaret nodded slowly. 'Thought so.'

'Why?'

'He was most particular about his clothes before he went out.' She handed Cat the towel and stood with her face averted. 'It's usually a sign.'

Neither of them spoke for a moment. They both knew that in theory Margaret was being impertinent, just as they both knew that the theory did not apply in this situation.

'He called here,' Cat said at last. 'Pheebs let him in – I was out. He was leaving as I came back. I saw him only for a moment. It was raining.'

The words were colourless, a mere statement of fact. Margaret took the towel and hung it by the fire to dry. She went away to empty the water. When she came back she said in an equally uninflected voice:

'He threw a boot at Sam when he came in. Not that he hit him.'

'Perhaps his teeth pain him again,' Cat said, wondering if Marwood had been to Vere Street before calling on her. 'Pray set some water to boil.'

Margaret went over to the fire. 'Master's sweet-natured most of the time,' she said, apparently addressing the coal scuttle. 'But this last week, it's different. He's worried.'

That meant Meg Daunt had not been kind to him. No doubt she had a string of lovers and could pick and choose whom she admitted to her bed.

Cat said, 'Why?'

'Something to do with his office.'

Cat doubted it. Meg Daunt was much more likely.

Margaret turned back to face her. 'A man he works with died the other day. Something wrong about it. Master took Stephen to look for some papers at the man's house, and the boy says there were dead rats everywhere. He's an ingenious lad, that one. He says Master thinks maybe Mr Abbott was poisoned.'

'Abbott?' Cat's irritation vanished. 'The man he works with at Whitehall?'

Margaret nodded. 'Do you know him?'

'Yes, I do,' Cat said. 'Or rather I did. Slightly. What happened?'

'He fell ill, all of a sudden. Terrible pains in the belly. He was dead in a day or so.'

'But why does Marwood think he might have been poisoned?'

Their eyes met. Margaret sighed. 'I don't know. I don't know what any of it's about. All I know is it means trouble.'

CHAPTER TWENTY

WHEN HE HAD settled Caliban for the night, Brockmore locked up and left Mr Fanshawe's stable. His son was already at home with his mother and his sisters. Thanks to the old fool who employed him, Brockmore not only had money in his pocket but he had become a welcome guest at Lambe's and other alehouses around Smithfield that catered for drovers and butchers. The lion was a foul, mangy old beast, long past its prime. But the drovers liked to hear about it, and the more intimate the details the better.

The drovers, who brought their animals from all corners of the kingdom, were hard, brutal men who did not suffer strangers gladly. But Brockmore had once been one of them, driving cattle across country from the Welsh borders. He had impregnated and then married the daughter of a bankrupt butcher, and settled in Smithfield. Sometimes he was tempted to return to his old, wild ways among the drovers on the road. It was a young man's life, however, and he was no longer young. But he still liked to drink with them and relive old memories.

It was after midnight before he left Lambe's, the alehouse at the far end of Chick Lane. When the cold air hit him, he discovered that he was drunker than he had thought. He staggered eastward in the general direction of Smithfield. The lanes and alleys were black and slippery, and they swayed inconveniently from side to side. The only light came from between the shutters of the occasional window, or from a lantern left burning above a gateway for the convenience of a latecomer.

By the sheep pens, the swaying of the darkened streets had become so violent that Brockmore was obliged to stop and steady himself. He was at the bottom of Slaughter Street, where the old stone was. He fumbled his way towards it and sank down on it. The cold seeped through his breeches, but the stone was drier than the ground, because it was a few inches above the muck. He vomited between his boots. Once purged, he felt better, though everything still had a tendency to wobble like calves'-foot jelly. He leant back and rested his hands on the slab in the hope that it would have a steadying effect on the world.

It took him a moment to realize that there was something wet on the stone, and that his left palm was resting in it. Automatically he raised the hand to his nose and gave it an experimental sniff. He smelled the sharp green smell of fresh piss. Some bastard had pissed on the stone, rather than on a wall or in someone's doorway as a Christian should.

Brockmore extended his arm. Almost at once he discovered that he had company on the Slaughter Stone. He found fingers first, then the rest of the hand, and then the arm attached to it. A drunk sleeping off his ale? For a moment he felt comfortably superior. He had been bred a drover, and drovers did

147

not let their liquor overmaster them. He followed the arm higher and higher to the shoulder and touched the coat. He felt the cloth, rubbing it between his fingers.

Worth something, that coat.

His fingertips ran over the neck of the shirt, then the man's neck, and finally reached the head.

He brushed a cheek. The skin was cold and rough with stubble. His fingers strayed into an open mouth and he jerked them away, but not before he had felt the jagged stumps of teeth. He moved up to the nose and, last of all and with a sense of gathering fear, the man's eyes. The lids were open. He touched the orb of an eye. He screamed and scrambled to his feet.

This was not a drunk on the Slaughter Stone. It was a dead man.

Shortly after midnight, the Watch patrol was shuffling the short distance from Smithfield Bar to the open space of Smithfield itself when they heard a man shouting. Appeals for earthly help mingled with prayers, wordless wails and profanities. The sounds increased in volume as they drew nearer.

The Watch advanced towards the shouting in a leisurely manner, grumbling among themselves at the thought of having to exercise their authority. When the man saw their lanterns bobbing through the darkness, he stumbled towards them, slipping and sliding in his haste. When he reached them, he tripped over the haft of a halberd. He fell so hard that for a moment he lay as silent as a stunned ox. The Watch shone their lanterns on him while one of their number prodded him with the end of his staff until he stirred and groaned.

'Drunk as a fish,' the constable said. 'Get him back to the Watch House and lock him up for the night.'

The man heaved himself up. 'God's pity, masters, there's a dead man back there.'

'Dead drunk, more like. Where?'

'On the Slaughter Stone. I felt his eyes.'

'He's raving,' said the man with the halberd. 'If he talks like that to the justice in the morning, he'll end in Bedlam.'

'Name?' the constable asked, wanting to reassert himself.

'Brockmore, sir, as anyone in Smithfield will tell you.'

'Where do you work?'

'Fanshawe's in Slaughter Street, sir. I'm his lion-keeper.'

'Fanshawe has got a lion,' the man with the halberd said uncertainly. 'That's true enough. My wife told me.'

'I've heard it roar once,' said the man whose staff had prodded Brockmore back to consciousness.

There was a silence. The lion had given Brockmore a certain respectability.

The constable said, 'Who is this dead man?'

'I don't know, master. I couldn't see him.' Brockmore gulped for air. 'I could only *feel* him.'

'You'd better show us.'

The constable gave his orders. Brockmore was hauled to his feet. With a man on either side to steady him, he was capable of walking. They made their way slowly towards the sheep pens. A few minutes later they reached the Slaughter Stone.

'His eyes are open,' Brockmore wailed. 'And he ain't breathing. And he pissed himself.'

The dim glow of the lanterns smudged the stone with light. The body had gone. Or perhaps, Brockmore thought with a sudden lurch of dismay, it had never been there in the first place. His legs gave way and he sank down on the stone. That was when he discovered that at least the piss had been real enough.

CHAPTER TWENTY-ONE

O N SATURDAY MORNING, Stephen knocked on my
bedroom door and entered with the bowl of warm
water. It was still dark and I washed my face and hands by
candlelight. My shirts — it was still cold enough for me to
wear two — were warming over the newly lit fire.

'Sam begs a word with you, master,' the boy said as he
handed me the towel.

'Tell him to wait on me in the parlour.'

Stephen opened his mouth, and for a moment I thought
he was about to say something else. But then his lips closed
in a tight line. He bowed and silently withdrew.

When I went downstairs, Sam was already there. Usually
he kept out of my way in the morning, if he possibly could,
as he often drank late. Today, however, he wished me good
morning and hobbled over to pull my chair nearer the fire.

'Well? What is it?'

He cleared his throat. 'I looked in at the Silver Crescent,
your honour, as you commanded. Mistress Fawley had something waiting for me, just as you said she might.'

He fished a letter from his pocket and gave it to me. I felt its thickness. There was an enclosure. I broke the seal. Sam was still hovering. I took out my purse and tossed him a shilling.

Deft as always, he caught it. He gave me a grin. 'Always at your service, master.'

When the door had closed behind him, I unfolded the letter. The enclosure was a smaller sheet of paper. It was much creased, as if it had originally been crumpled into a ball and later smoothed out as far as it could be. Two of its four edges were straight cut, but the others were irregular. It looked as if a paper had been torn into four, and this was one of the pieces. There was writing on both sides, though in a much a less legible hand than Johnson's. The writer had clearly been in a hurry.

I read Johnson's letter first. It lacked date, salutation and signature:

I did as you asked, at great Peril to my Self. The chamber door, tho' locked, yielded to the key of another door. W's Valise, which I have seen there with my own Eyes, is gone, and the Bed stripped to the mattress. But I took Pains in searching, nonetheless, and accordingly was rewarded, for, behind the Grate in the fireplace, I discovered a Fragment of Writing, which I enclose. The maid came within an Ace of catching me as I left but thanks be to Providence I was able to take Refuge in another chamber. I believe that concludes my Obligation to you, and that I shall therefore hear no more of the other Matter. You also said that a Reward would be payable for my Services. Pray remit this by return, care of Mistress F, as before.

I pushed the letter aside and took up the fragmentary enclosure. On one side I read, with some difficulty:

might disoblige 137, I can by no meanes advi . . .
necessity of telling 112 of the secrette now, nor indeed ti . . .
to make use of 297 towards the great business. Methink . . .
360 in 100 frindship, without knowing the reason for . . .

The left-hand margin was the original. I turned the fragment over, and deciphered the words on the other side, where the right-hand margin was complete.

. . . shall be fitt to acquainte 138 with 386 security in 152, he
 . . . must not say any thing of it in 270, and pray lett the
. . . it will infinitely discompose 269 when they meete with 334

I had no way of knowing which of the two extracts came before the other. Not that it mattered. Even without the numbers – which I assumed were some sort of code – there was not enough material for me to hazard a guess at the meaning of the complete text. But there was more than enough to unsettle me. The 'secrette', 'the great business', 'will infinitely discompose' – all this sounded ominous.

The trouble was, there were few certainties about this affair. It appeared that Wulf, alias Van Riebeeck, had left his room at the Blue Bush. Had he burned all or some of his papers before leaving? The fragment Johnson had sent me was faintly charred, so it was possible that when it had been tossed into the fire, it had missed the basket of coals and fallen into the back of the grate. It would have been hot enough there to explain the charring, but not enough to set it aflame.

I added to this what I had learned earlier. When I had dined with him at the Fountain on Thursday, Johnson had mentioned the parcels that Abbott had sometimes brought from a Westminster bookbinder for Van Riebeeck. It had struck me at the time, as Johnson sketched the outline of one of these parcels with his supple, card sharp's fingers, that the dimensions were similar to those of the files used in Arlington's office. Then again, I knew for a fact that Abbott had also taken files home with him, and concealed them under the floorboards. Another fact was that Mistress Abbott had taken these files to Fanshawe's, which suggested that she had known of Abbott's hiding place.

A third fact was, as I had discovered when I examined their contents, that two of the letters were not mentioned on Abbott's docket at the front of one of the files. Clearly they belonged elsewhere. Abbott had probably slipped them into the back of the file when he took the work home. The letters had been from our ambassador in Paris, and concerned the French invasion of the Low Countries, and negotiations between on the one hand the King and Arlington in England, and on the other Madame and Louis XIV in France. Could there be a connection between them and the scrap of paper that Johnson had sent me?

I folded the letter and its enclosure, and put it carefully in my pocketbook. I couldn't fault Johnson – he had done as I asked, and earned both his reward and my silence. But what should I do with this discovery? Perhaps it might even be best to do nothing at all.

I stood up. Hoping that a bowl of coffee might sharpen my wits, I rang the bell, and told Stephen to bring my cloak, gloves and hat.

He lingered in the doorway. 'Master . . .?'

'What?'

'When we went to that house on Monday . . .' He hesitated, looking up at my face.

'What of it? I'm pressed for time.'

Stephen winced as if I'd offered to hit him. I cursed myself. Before he came to me, the boy had lived in other households where he had not been treated well; the scars of his past were no less deep for being invisible.

I said gently, 'But I have time enough to hear what you want to say. Continue.'

'The house with the dead rats and the doll. We found a paper in the scullery, in the bin for the pigs.'

'I remember. Something had been wrapped in it.'

'The paper was marked with a pestle and mortar drawn inside half a circle or a capital letter D, sir.'

I nodded. 'An apothecary's mark, no doubt.'

'I saw it again yesterday.'

'The paper?'

'No, master.' He shifted from foot to foot. 'The mark. Mistress Margaret went to Cock Lane yesterday, and she took me to carry her shopping. I saw the same mark outside a shop there. It was an apothecary's, at the sign of the Half Moon.'

I drank a bowl of coffee and listened to the news at Will's coffee house on the corner of Bow Street and Russell Street. News of the fluctuating prices on the Exchange went in one ear and out the other. But the coffee cleared my head. By the time I left, I knew that I could not in all conscience suppress this inconvenient scrap of paper, not in the context of everything else I either knew or suspected. Abbott's death had tossed me into a nest of vipers, and I couldn't hope to escape unscathed by closing my eyes and pretending I was safe at home in my bed.

The day was dry and I walked down to Whitehall. I would have liked to discuss the whole affair with Mr Williamson. I could at least depend on his giving me a plain answer, though not necessarily one that I would want to hear. But he would not thank me for sharing the knowledge I now had. This was one of these secrets that are like a fully charged pistol with a faulty mechanism: capable of doing a good deal of damage and liable to go off in your face without warning.

If I were to confide in anyone, as I had known in my heart of hearts from the start, it had to be my lord himself. I remembered the words he had said to me on Monday, as I was leaving him: 'Remember, Marwood, a discreet servant is a good servant, and a good servant will have his reward one day. The reverse also holds true.'

I went first to my lord's office and enquired for him, only to be told he had yet not come in. I passed into the Park by the passage near the Cockpit and started down the path along the canal towards Goring House, whose tall chimneys were visible above the trees. Here I had a stroke of luck. I met my lord himself coming towards Whitehall. He was in company with Sir Thomas Clifford and another man I did not know. He ignored me, but I approached and begged the favour of a private interview.

My lord frowned at me but he told the other men he would

rejoin them in a moment. I followed him a few paces from the path. He stopped under a leafless tree and stared at the water of the canal.

'You have intelligence, I take it?' he said. 'Quickly. What is it?'

I opened my pocketbook, took out the charred fragment of writing that Johnson had sent me and gave it to him. As he looked down, his face hardened.

'Where did you get this?'

I explained as best I could, bearing in mind there was so much I did not understand myself. Arlington listened intently, his haste forgotten. I had not been so close to him before, and I found my eyes focusing on the slim black plaster across his nose. On his upper lip was a thin moustache, a copy of his master the King's, and the two black lines seemed to act in concert, twitching like a pair of clumsy caterpillars in a country dance.

Afterwards my lord stood in thought for so long that I thought he had forgotten me. He seemed not to notice how cold it was. He sighed and looked at me.

'This man Wulf,' he said, 'is clearly the key to this. You say he was introduced to you as Van Riebeeck by Mr Fanshawe. So probably Dutch, not German and Van Riebeeck is his real name.' He paused, and I had a sense that he wasn't talking to me but to himself, that his eyes were in fact fixed on something he could see in his mind. 'The probability must be that he has read and destroyed the rest of the letter – this paper, that is to say, which may have been a letter . . .'

'Could it have come from Abbott, my lord? He and Van Riebeeck used to meet at the Blue Bush, where this paper was found.'

Arlington looked surprised, as if a tree had spoken. But he didn't answer my question. Instead his voice sharpened: 'We'll put a warrant out for Van Riebeeck. Have you mentioned this to anyone else?'

'No, my lord.'

'Then not a word. This must remain between you and me alone.'

I assured him that he could depend on me. At this he dismissed me and walked away towards Whitehall. But after a few paces he stopped and looked back.

'You've done well, Marwood. I'll not forget it.'

CHAPTER TWENTY-TWO

IN MR WILLIAMSON'S office in Scotland Yard, my fellow clerks stared curiously at me when I came in. There was no sign of Williamson himself. I resumed my work, in this case copying confidential correspondence into Williamson's letter book. Usually this was drudgery to me, and increasingly irksome as my other responsibilities increased, but for once I found the work comforting. There was no need to do anything except wield a pen and transcribe what was already written. No need to worry about anything, either.

At midday, I went out to dine. At the common table in the Axe, all the talk was of a disturbance in the Strand. I kept my head down and my mouth shut. There had been a raid on the Blue Bush, people said, which had taken everyone entirely by surprise. Arlington hadn't wasted any time. The tavern was now closed, and its doors sealed. There had been several arrests.

When I returned to Scotland Yard, the door of Williamson's private room stood open. I was about to resume my own work when he appeared in his doorway and beckoned me.

'Shut the door,' he said as soon as I was inside his room. 'So you've deigned to show your face again. I've hardly had the honour of seeing you all week.'

His sarcasm was so savage that it made me flinch. 'I beg your pardon, sir. I've had no choice.'

'What's it about? Abbott, presumably. Something must have led on from his death?'

'Forgive me, my lord has commanded me not to speak of it. Even to you.'

'Devil take it,' he snapped, anger stripping his voice of its cultured veneer. 'And what's this about Fanshawe? What's he got to do with it?'

'He had a connection with Abbott, sir. Abbott's widow is staying with him now.'

'Of course he had a connection. Fanshawe's late son was Mistress Abbott's first husband, so Mistress Abbott is his daughter-in-law.'

'Yes, sir.' I had already learned this from Gorvin. 'Mr Fanshawe desired me to give you his compliments.'

'Is he under suspicion? I can't believe it.'

That was another question I couldn't answer, so I kept my mouth shut and gave him what I hoped what was an apologetic smile.

Williamson burst out, 'I hate it when my own people have secrets from me. I won't have it, Marwood, do you understand me? You and I will have to part our ways if this continues.'

I bowed. Fortunately there was a knock at the door, and a clerk brought in a letter. I was near enough to see that it was in Arlington's hand. Williamson broke the seal, scanned the letter's contents and tossed it on his desk.

'The matter is out of my hands now. It seems that I am

no longer to be your master, Marwood. My lord requests that you be sent to his office to fill Abbott's place.'

I bowed again. It was the sort of request that Williamson was not in a position to refuse.

His sarcasm returned. 'By God, I wish you joy of it.' He stared up at me. 'What are you waiting for? He wants you now.'

Once Arlington had me in his service, he did not waste time in putting me to use. An hour later, I was back in Scotland Yard again, not in Mr Williamson's office but in a modest, two-storey building near Scotland Dock. Originally, it had been a storehouse, but in Cromwell's day it had been converted into a gaol. It was used for short-stay prisoners held for questioning or before trial, usually on charges of treason. It was as secure as the Tower, but more convenient and considerably more discreet.

I knew the turnkey of old, for I had been here several times before. A former sergeant of horse, he grew fatter every year, and no doubt richer, because he received a steady stream of bribes and fees from his prisoners and their friends, as well as those who had business with them. He was a purveyor of small luxuries, too, and charged both his suppliers and his customers for the privilege of assisting them. In the privacy of my own thoughts, I called him Moonface because of his round face and his boundless appetite for silver.

He had a room by the entrance to the gaol. He greeted me as an old friend and – which I knew to be a compliment – invited me to share his fire for a moment. I had given him money more than once. It was a worthwhile investment, for a gaoler has it in his power to make everyone's life difficult if he wishes. Only a fool ignored the fact that the secret economy of both Whitehall and Scotland Yard revolved around bribes, in cash or kind, in goods or services.

I accepted a chair but declined a nip from his flask to ward off the fevers that haunt all prisons. He placed a pair of spectacles on his nose and read the warrant I had brought with me. His forefinger moved from word to word, and his lips moved silently.

'Connolly,' he said. 'The big Irish fellow they brought in this morning. I hate the Irish. Dirty brutes. Most of them Papists, too.'

'Where've you put him?'

'In the common hold.'

'It might be prudent to put him in a cell of his own.'

Moonface scratched his belly. 'Why? In case he makes mischief?'

'One way or another. And I need to talk to him in private.'

'Chains?'

'I would,' I said. 'Better safe than sorry. I'd trust him no further than I could throw a millstone.'

'Anyone want him treated gently?'

'Not that I'm aware of.'

He took up a handbell that stood at his elbow. A moment after his ring, an assistant gaoler was receiving his instructions. While we waited for them to be carried out, Moonface had several more nips from his flask, and told me more than I wished to know about the trials and tribulations of his life.

When the assistant returned, the turnkey heaved himself up from his chair and, huffing and puffing and jangling his keys, led me up a flight of stone stairs to the upper storey, where most of the single cells were. The assistant, a thin youth with a melancholy face, trailed after us. The air was very cold up here. Though there was no glass in the barred windows that lit the landing, the air was foul with smells of excrement, stale tobacco and tallow. Moonface stopped at a cell halfway down and slid back the eye-level shutter in the door.

'He looks quiet enough,' he said to me. 'Keep your distance, just in case. Bang on the door when you're done and young Nat will let you out.'

Connolly sat on a straw mattress, with his back propped against the wall opposite the door. He looked up as I entered but otherwise lay still. His hands were free. They rested on his belly, the fingers interlinked. His ankles were manacled to a ring set low on the wall beside the mattress. He had only been in the gaol for a few hours, and his complexion had not yet acquired the pallor and the grime that would soon come if he were here for long.

'Good day, your honour,' he said with a smile. 'I wish I could rise and bow.'

I stared at him. 'Where's Johnson?'

'I couldn't say, sir.'

Gorvin had given me a brief account of this morning's raid on the Blue Bush. Arlington's men had searched the tavern from top to bottom. They had found cogged dice and packs of marked cards, together with several peepholes in the walls of the private rooms. The maids had been questioned and released under surety. The men employed there had been detained, among them two who worked as dealers and were probably as honest as a couple of counterfeit shillings.

But only Connolly had merited a place in the gaol at Scotland Yard. I had been mistaken to dismiss him as the porter guarding the door. 'The tavern's in his name,' Gorvin had told me. 'He's two years into a five-year lease. But I'd lay good money on his having investors behind him.'

'Johnson lives at the Blue Bush,' I reminded Connolly. 'His bedchamber's been searched. His possessions are still up there – his clothes, his books, his portmanteaux. But where is he? Someone must know.'

'I'm not his keeper, master. We do very little business in the morning, as a rule. Perhaps he stepped out to take some air and met a friend. Or he dined with someone he knew and lingered over his wine.'

When he spoke those last words, Connolly looked directly at me. I wondered if he had had Johnson followed on Thursday, if he knew of Johnson dining with me at the Fountain. We had been careful, but it appeared not careful enough.

I said, 'If he'd dined elsewhere, he'd have been back by now.'

'Perhaps he did come back. No doubt he saw the house was closed, and thought it wiser to keep away.'

That was plausible. If I had been Johnson, and had discovered that the Blue Bush had been raided, my instinct would have been to lie low until I knew which way the wind was blowing.

'Supposing that to be true, where would he have gone? Has he family in London? Friends?'

Connolly shrugged his heavy shoulders. 'I know nothing about his life outside the Blue Bush, sir. Why should I?'

I switched my attack. 'Mr Wulf. Is he one of your investors?'

'Who?'

'Don't come the simpleton with me. Wulf was there

164

when we first met. Tall man, with a long face and a deep voice. A foreigner, man of breeding, claims to be German, from the Palatinate. Johnson told him Abbott was dead as we were coming down the stairs. And you were at the bottom, by the door. Remember?'

'Oh, Mr *Wulf*. Yes, he comes to play with us sometimes when he is in London. He has a particular fondness for backgammon.'

'That's not his real name, is it?'

'It's the only name I got for him.'

I abandoned that line of approach. 'I understand he has a room reserved for his use at the Blue Bush, and he sleeps there sometimes.'

'Is that so, your honour?'

I held on to my temper. 'It suggests a closer connection than you're admitting.'

His lips curled into a smile, but he said nothing. It was as if he realized that I couldn't seriously harm him. Without Johnson's testimony there was little we could prove against him, aside from the cogged dice and the marked cards. But in themselves they meant nothing. There were men who played with marked cards and loaded dice in Whitehall itself. The practice might touch on a man's honour but it did not make him a criminal. The prudent gamester was aware of the risk and treated it as a probable hazard of play, to be avoided if possible but accepted if not.

'Who are your backers?' I asked. 'And I ask you again, is Wulf one of them?'

'It's my establishment, master. I've no need of backers and investors.'

I didn't believe him. A place like the Blue Bush, operating

in the debatable territory between the lawful and unlawful, needed money behind it, particularly at the start, and powerful friends to protect it. The trouble was, I had hardly any leverage to use against Connolly and he knew it. A word to the turnkey could make his life difficult for the next few days. But we couldn't keep him here for ever, and there would be no advantage in doing so even if we could.

'Where's Wulf now?'

He shrugged and gave no answer. I banged the flat of my hand on the door. On the other side, I heard the assistant turnkey fumbling the key into the lock. I turned back to look at Connolly sprawling on the mattress.

'By the way,' I said 'who's your landlord at the Blue Bush? Who owns the freehold?'

Connolly sighed, as though he were growing mildly impatient with my unmannerly curiosity. But he must have known that I could easily find the answer elsewhere, so there would be no advantage in keeping silent. 'Mr Fanshawe,' he said.

'Of Slaughter Street?'

'The very same, sir. You're already acquainted with the gentleman, are you? And how convenient is that?'

CHAPTER TWENTY-THREE

NOW THERE WAS another mystery, and another reason for fear.

Early on Sunday morning, Maria had overheard her mother talking with her maid. There had been complaints about Brockmore. He had roused the Watch the other night, when he was most foully drunk, so much so he could barely stand and was seeing Bedlam visions. He had claimed, said the maid, lowering her voice to a thrilling whisper, that he had found a dead man on the Slaughter Stone, not fifty paces from this very house. But when the Watch inspected the stone, there was nothing there. It had been a phantasm conjured by Brockmore's drunken fancy.

'Does your master know?' Maria's mother demanded. 'He wouldn't want a drunken sot to look after his lion. What if it escaped and attacked us all? When was this?'

'Friday night, madam.'

Maria's insides contracted, as though squeezed by an

invisible fist. Friday night was when she had overheard her uncle talking of putting a man with the lion.

'Unfortunately,' Mr Fanshawe said, 'Van Riebeeck has been called away. Business is a hard master.' He led Cat into a hall which was dominated by a vast tapestry. 'But allow me to present my daughter-in-law, Mistress Abbott.'

Cat curtsied to the tall, angular lady who rose from a chair to greet her. She struggled to suppress the double surprise she felt. Was this Abbott's widow? Then how could she be Fanshawe's daughter-in-law? But the second surprise, which struck her while she was still dealing with the first, was still more of a shock: why did this woman have Van Riebeeck's face?

'No one could better represent him,' Fanshawe said. 'Mistress Abbott is his sister—'

'He's my half-brother, madam,' Mistress Abbott put in a toneless voice that was very like Van Riebeeck's.

Fanshawe was still speaking: '—and it has often been remarked that there is a marked resemblance between their faces. Though allowing' – with an unsteady bow – 'for the softening influence that womanly beauty brings to this lady's features.'

It was difficult to imagine a face less soft and womanly than Mistress Abbott's. A mother might have thought the face beautiful, but Cat did not. The lady was dressed in black, as befitted a widow, but her mourning clothes were not elaborate, suggesting that she had restrained her grief. She looked at least ten years older and several inches taller than her husband had been.

'And may I have the honour of presenting my daughter, Maria?' Mistress Abbott said.

A girl of about twelve, also dressed in black, had been sewing by the window and had risen when Cat was brought in. She came forward to curtsy to the visitor. She had widely spaced brown eyes that gave her a look of permanent surprise. There were vertical furrows between the strongly marked eyebrows.

'My granddaughter takes after the Fanshawes,' her grandfather said, his pride evident from his voice. 'I should have explained – my late son was Mistress Abbott's first husband. In fact we were saying only this morning that perhaps, now poor Abbott is no more, it would be proper for her to resume the name of Fanshawe, as she and Maria have returned to live with me.' He gestured at the girl's discarded sewing. 'She has been working on her sampler again, I see. Allow Maria to show it to you, madam. I'm sure she would account it a great privilege.'

Judging by her face, Maria was less enthusiastic about the proposal than her grandfather. Cat made a show of examining the sampler. It was a curious piece of work, and less skilfully executed than she had expected. Lozenges and squares, embroidered in silk, staggered across the linen backing, with a careless indifference to the customary tyranny of straight lines and symmetry. A sampler was intended to display the seamstress's mastery of embroidery, but in this case it achieved the reverse effect.

Among the geometric patterns, Maria had interspersed the occasional flower, insect or animal. These were at least unexpected, and they had a clumsy life about them. A unicorn pranced across the top left corner. It had a large, pointed pizzle together with a horn which was shaped like a parsnip and attached to the head at an acute angle that must have seriously inconvenienced its owner; it also sported a pair of yellow wings, tipped with blue. Nearby, something that might have been a spider was trapped in a tangle of black thread, presumably its own web. There was a possible mermaid with her arms waving and an object of some sort – a jewel? a vast bubo? – in her navel. A black sheep – or perhaps a dog – was standing on the mermaid's head.

'There is still much work to be done, I fear.' Mistress Abbott appeared at Cat's shoulder. 'Either it should be a unicorn, in which case it should not have wings, or it should represent Pegasus, in which case the horn is not correct.'

'But it is a *winged* unicorn,' Maria muttered, too low for her mother to hear.

'It is very interesting and most original,' Cat said diplomatically. 'Tell me, Maria – what is this to be?'

On the right of the unicorn, occupying an irregular quadrilateral at the opposite corner of the sampler and outlined in yellow silk, was a shape with four legs, a bulbous body, a head of much the same size and a very thin tail. As yet, there was nothing inside the outline.

'It is my grandfather's lion,' Maria said.

Dinner was a sombre meal. Neither Maria nor Mistress Abbott spoke much. Fanshawe steered the conversation towards the royal poultry house and its prospective owner.

'Madame's tastes are refined,' he informed her, as if this might be news to her. 'She is greatly interested in all the gracious arts. Including architecture, no doubt. More to the point, Monsieur her husband has a taste for it – perhaps the poultry house was his idea. I'm told that he has spent a fortune on remodelling the Palais Royal. It would do no harm to study it if you can, for hints about what might please him.'

Fanshawe explained Cat's profession to her for several minutes. She encouraged him to run on until he showed signs of instructing her about the three orders of classical architecture, which was equivalent to explaining the mysteries of the ABC to the Poet Laureate. Enough was enough. She led him to talk instead of his family, who had lived in the Slaughter Street house for three generations, and at Swaring, their estate in Kent for even longer. This led him by degrees to his daughter-in-law.

'Did you know that she is acquainted with my Lady Arlington? They have known each other almost since childhood. Is that not true, Anna?'

'I was one of her mother's waiting women,' Mistress Abbott said harshly, as if in accusation. Her eyes were fixed on the empty space between her father-in-law and Cat. 'And her ladyship has been gracious enough to acknowledge the connection.'

'That's how she met Abbott, in fact. When calling to pay her respects to my lady.'

Mistress Abbott said nothing. Cat sensed that she found the subject distasteful and she distracted her host by asking about his celebrated collection. Answering this question occupied him almost entirely for the rest of the meal. All the while, Maria stared at her plate. Mistress Abbott sat bolt upright on her chair, looking at Mr Fanshawe. Once or twice she stifled a discreet yawn behind her napkin.

'You must allow me to show you one or two of my favourite pieces,' Fanshawe said, rising slowly from the table. 'Then we shall step into the garden and see Caliban. I shall rearrange his dinnertime to suit us. Everyone finds the spectacle most diverting. I never tire of it myself.'

After dinner, they went up to the great chamber, and Fanshawe showed Cat a wearisome array of items, few of which seemed to her to have much intrinsic merit other than novelty. By this time, she was regretting that she had accepted the invitation to dinner. Fanshawe as a client was tolerable, but Fanshawe as a host was not.

While she smiled and nodded her head, her irritation grew. She didn't care for the collection, she decided, a mere jumble of objects, and she positively disliked Fanshawe's house. There was no evidence of his alleged interest in architecture. Despite the evidences of wealth that filled it, the house was dark, gloomy, inconvenient and old-fashioned. While her host droned on, and Mistress Abbott dropped into a light doze, Cat entertained herself in the privacy of her imagination by pulling down the entire establishment and building something altogether more attractive in its place.

At last Fanshawe rang the bell, waking Mistress Abbott, and instructed the maid to have their outdoor clothes waiting downstairs by the garden door.

'Forgive me, sir, but my head aches,' Mistress Abbott said. 'If you will allow it, I shall stay in the house. Maria will be my deputy.'

As the rest of them were leaving the house, Fanshawe beckoned his manservant. 'Mr Alink may call to see Caliban eat his dinner. I invited him and one or two other gentlemen. If they come, send them down to the stable directly, or they will miss it.'

He offered Cat his arm, and they took the path down the garden, followed by Maria. 'You must not mind my lion-keeper.

He is an uncouth fellow but the important thing is that the beast is terrified of him and wholly under his control.'

They came to the gateway that led to the stables. As they entered the yard beyond, the lion gave a roar. It was so loud, so close and above all so unexpected that Cat clutched at Fanshawe's arm.

Fanshawe gave her a delighted smile and patted her hand. 'The smell of blood excites him.'

The lion-keeper came to meet them. He was wearing a leather tunic, much stained and cut about, secured by a belt around his waist. He carried a butcher's cleaver in one hand, its blade rimmed with blood.

'Well, Brockmore?' Fanshawe said. 'Are you ready for us?'

'Aye, sir. And so is Caliban, as you heard. Will it please you to come in now?'

Fanshawe glanced through the gateway to the garden. 'Some gentlemen are due to join us. But we can't wait for ever. No, if they miss it, they must come again another day.' He smiled at Cat and Maria. 'We can't disappoint Caliban of his dinner, can we?'

'Someone coming now, master,' Brockmore said.

Two men had just come into sight, approaching along the path beside the pavilion. One of them was Fanshawe's manservant, the other a guest he was escorting.

'One of your gentlemen, sir, and just in time,' the servant said. 'Mr Marwood.'

Marwood had seen Cat. He smiled at her and bowed to the company. 'I'm here under false pretences.' He turned to Fanshawe. 'I wished to speak to you on business, sir. My Lord Arlington's business.'

'I am entertaining' – Fanshawe indicated Cat with a

courteous inclination of his head – 'and I also expect some friends to arrive at any moment.'

The servant was looking crestfallen. 'Beg your pardon, master, I thought this was one of the gentlemen from Austin Friars. And he was here the other day, and I thought—'

'The fault's mine,' Marwood said, without any hint of contrition. 'But here I am. Will you be at liberty soon? My lord's business is urgent.'

Caliban gave another roar. Marwood took a step backwards, his face filling with alarm.

Fanshawe's delight showed on his face. 'As you can hear, my lion is growing impatient. When Caliban smells blood, he waits for no man's convenience. He must have his dinner.'

'Perhaps Mr Marwood might watch,' Cat said. 'I'm sure he would find it most interesting.'

'Of course,' Fanshawe said, brightening at the prospect of increasing his audience. 'I can promise you a spectacle you will not soon forget. And it will not detain us for long. Caliban is a swift eater, though not a delicate one.'

The lion gave a third roar, louder and longer than the others.

Brockmore said, 'Master, best not keep him waiting. He smells the blood, and that makes him harder to handle.'

'Lead the way,' Fanshawe said with a wave of his hand. 'Let the entertainment begin.'

The party filed into the stable. The outer door was already open. The lion stared suspiciously at them through the bars of the inner door. Brockmore picked up a pole about six feet long with a long spike at one end, and a hook at the other.

'You will want to know how Caliban receives his dinner,' Fanshawe informed his audience. The lion roared again. In the confined space, the noise was deafening, and far more menacing than it had been outside. Fanshawe raised his voice. 'I have found a most ingenious means of doing this, as you will see. Come nearer, but not too close. When Caliban's blood is up, he can be unpredictable.'

The humans stared at the lion, and the lion stared at them. He was gaunt and mangy, his skin marked with unhealed sores. His mane was thickly matted. Then, with deliberation, he paced towards them, his tail swishing from side to side. The visitors shifted backwards, out of range of the claws. Despite Caliban's age and his poor condition, he exuded malevolence.

Caliban opened his mouth and gave another roar, allowing them to see the pink cavern of his mouth and the jagged teeth within.

Fanshawe turned to the keeper. 'Give the boy the signal.'

Brockmore rapped twice on the plank ceiling above his head. It was answered by movements in the loft above.

'Look up!' Fanshawe urged his guests, pointing through the bars. 'Look up!'

There was clatter above, as a hatch in the ceiling was lifted away. Brockmore's boy, invisible except for glimpses of hands and arms, threw down the lion's dinner, piece by piece. Bone, gristle, offal and blood rained into the cage. Caliban went berserk, seizing on the food and ripping it apart with concentrated ferocity.

'What's that?' Maria said beside her. 'Is it a handkerchief?'

The girl pointed through the bars at a crumpled piece of cloth that lay on the cobbled floor a few feet inside the enclosure. To Cat, it certainly looked like a handkerchief. The cloth had been dyed purple, and it was trimmed with lace.

'What's that, Maria? What did you say?'

She turned to her grandfather. 'A handkerchief, sir. Someone left a handkerchief in there.'

'That's impossible. What would Brockmore do with a hand-kerchief?' Then Fanshawe saw it, and a frown spread over his face. 'I suppose one of the visitors must have dropped it.' He glanced at the keeper. 'Get it out, man. It's most unsightly. Why wasn't it removed when you cleaned the cage?'

Unsightly. It was an odd word to use in the context, this foul enclosure streaked with blood and excrement, and littered with fragments of bone. And there was no sign that it had been recently cleaned. By chance, Cat's eyes met Marwood's, and she saw her own horrified amusement reflected in his face.

The keeper poked his pole, hook first, through the bars of the cage. The lion was still occupied with his dinner, crouching over it with his back to the spectators. Brockmore worked the hook into the cloth and drew it gradually back to the iron gate. When it was within his reach, he stooped and picked it up. He made as if to present it to Fanshawe, who wrinkled his nose and waved it away.

'What would I want with such a foul thing?'

'May I see it?' Marwood asked.

The question took everyone by surprise. For an instant they stared at him.

Fanshawe was the first to recover. 'But of course, sir. If you wish. But – well, it's filthy.'

He gestured to Brockmore who presented the handkerchief to Marwood. He held one corner between his gloved finger and thumb, and let it turn gently in the air.

'The lace is fine,' Marwood said slowly. 'But it's badly torn.'

'The cloth is an unusual shade,' Fanshawe said. 'What would you call it? Purple?'

Marwood looked up, and his face was intent and unreadable. 'I've heard it called mulberry.' He turned away from Caliban clawing and gnawing at his dinner. 'Would this be a convenient moment for us to withdraw and discuss our business?'

CHAPTER TWENTY-FOUR

IT WAS LATER than Cat would have liked when she returned to the sign of the Rose from Slaughter Street in a sedan. She paid the chairmen's fare, and the porter's boy admitted her. There was no sign of the porter himself.

'Where's Pheebs?' Cat asked when she was inside the house.

The boy coloured, which meant he was lying. 'In the necessary house, mistress. Terrible pains in the belly.'

Cat didn't believe a word of it. Pheebs was either asleep in his airless closet under the stairs or sitting in the alehouse in Bedford Street with a pipe in his mouth and a jug of ale at his elbow.

She began to climb the stairs. The boy cleared his throat in a meaningful way. She looked back at him.

'What is it?'

'Gentleman's waiting upstairs, mistress.'

Cat frowned. 'Who?'

'I don't know, I didn't see him. He's been here before, so Mr Pheebs thought you'd want him to go up.'

Cat nodded and continued up the stairs. She didn't like people being admitted when she wasn't there. Clients rarely called on a Sunday, but it did happen; they consulted their convenience not hers, and they would sometimes visit unannounced. The Drawing Office was locked, so the visitor must be waiting in her parlour on the floor below.

She left her muddy pattens on the landing, changed back into the shoes she had worn at Fanshawe's house, and opened the door. The parlour fire was heaped with coal and burning brightly. The room was far warmer than she would usually permit, on the grounds of economy, and the glow of the fire filled it with a dim and flickering orange light. Her maid, Jane, was staring at the occupant of the high-backed elbow chair which her husband, Mr Hakesby, had been wont to use. Jane looked terrified, which increased her already marked resemblance to a rabbit.

The chair had its back to the door, and there was a sword propped against the arm. As Cat entered, Jane curtsied to her. The maid's relief was obvious from her face.

'Mistress . . .' she said in a voice not much louder than a whisper.

A tall figure in a dark grey suit rose from the chair. It was Van Riebeeck. Unsmiling, he bowed stiffly.

'Forgive this intrusion, madam,' he said in a voice uncannily like a deeper, richer version of his half-sister's. 'But Providence led me here and who am I to question its dictates?'

'You are welcome, sir,' she said automatically, unclasping her cloak and giving it to Jane. 'I had the pleasure of seeing your sister today at Slaughter Street.'

He grunted. 'I had hoped to join you there.'

'Pray be seated.' Cat took a chair on the other side of the room. 'Can I offer you wine? Some—'

'No,' he interrupted. He threw a glance at the maid. 'I should like to speak in confidence with you.'

'Of course.' She nodded to Jane. 'Light the candles, then leave us.'

Van Riebeeck sat down, wrenching the chair round with a screech of its legs on the boards so he could look directly at her. Unsmiling, he stared at her. She felt her pulse accelerating under his gaze. Her breath seemed to come and go less naturally and quietly than usual. Neither of them spoke until Jane had left the room.

'And what do you wish to discuss, sir?'

'I've had cursed bad luck,' he said in the sort of voice he might have used to observe that the weather was a trifle milder today. 'Occasionally I amuse myself with cards or dice. I was unfortunate the other evening, and I lost far more than I'd intended. We were playing ombre, and if you know the game, you will know how easy it is to plunge more deeply than you mean to.' He waved the observation towards her with a flourish of his long fingers. 'Particularly if one is playing with wicked men who mark the cards.'

'And how does this touch me?' Cat asked, more tartly than she had intended.

Van Riebeeck transferred his stare to her. 'Because now they want to seize me for debt. I happened to be walking in Covent Garden, when I saw my principal creditor by the church. He saw me. Naturally I made haste away. I turned into Henrietta Street – and what did I see? Two of his servants approaching from the other end.' There was another wave of the fingers. 'You see my difficulty. These people are bullies and knaves. I must tell you that there is more than money involved here. The game of ombre was designed to trap me from the very start. This man has been employed by my rival in trade, and that is why he wants me ruined. Then he will attain his object — to take over my business.'

Cat nodded. She was watching the fingers, which dropped down to the chair. They moved restlessly over the end of the arm as if stroking it.

'Luckily,' the Dutchman continued, 'your porter had just opened the street door to let someone leave. And I, presuming on our acquaintance, slipped inside.' He smiled at her. 'The porter thought I had come to call on you again, and permitted me to wait.' This time he spread out both hands, and the fingers fluttered like skeletal wings. 'There you have it, madam. My entire history.'

'It's almost dark now. You can leave soon. You'll avoid Henrietta Street altogether if you leave by the back garden. There's a gate at the end into Maiden Lane, and from there it's but a step or two down to the Strand.'

He shook his head. 'No. They may have thought of that and set a watch on the back of the house as well.'

'But surely, sir, you credit them with too much—'

'You don't know them as I do, madam. I have learned that it is wise not to underestimate them. These men are devilishly cunning and they have men enough to watch half a dozen places at once. There was one outside my lodgings this morning, and I've no doubt there was another at Slaughter Street. They know of my connection with Mr Fanshawe. And of my sister.'

'Perhaps your fears make you start at shadows. You must allow that you sound—'

'I allow nothing. I merely state facts.' Van Riebeeck leant forward in the chair, his hand on his knees. 'And what I want to know is this,' he went on in a voice that was suddenly gentle, almost caressing. 'I know our acquaintance is slight. But will you do me the great kindness of helping me?'

She should send him away, Cat thought. He wasn't defenceless – he wore a sword and she was, on no evidence whatsoever, convinced that he was expert in its use and more than capable of dealing with anyone who tried to stop him.

'Well, madam? Pray let me have your answer.'

'Very well,' Cat heard herself saying. 'What do you want me to do?'

Jane was dispatched downstairs to send the porter's boy for a hackney coach. Cat supplied Van Riebeeck with a long cloak and an old-fashioned broad-brimmed hat of leather which had once belonged to the late Mr Hakesby. The cloak was long enough to conceal his sword, which he tucked under his arm.

With these clothes, Van Riebeeck said, together with a certain change in his bearing, he would look like a servant accompanying his mistress on an outing. When Cat pointed out that the one thing he could not disguise was his height, he replied with a grim twist of his lips that like all of creation he was obliged to work with what God had given him.

'But you need not trouble yourself. I have observed that a man does not see what he expects to see.'

'You speak in riddles, sir.'

'In this case, a man is on the watch for a particular gentleman. A gentleman, mark you. He sees a lady leaving her house attended by her servant. He doesn't note the servant. Why should he? He's looking for a gentleman, and a servant is merely a servant. A servant is never noteworthy in himself as long as he comports himself as befits his office.'

It was after seven o'clock before they left the house. No one was watching, as far as Cat could see. Van Riebeeck played his part with unexpected skill, hunching his shoulders and poking his head forward. He handed her into the coach with studied servility. She heard him directing the coachman and settling the fare. 'My mistress desires to be set down by Somerset House.'

In the coach, Van Riebeeck sat opposite her, and his long legs collided briefly with hers. Neither of them spoke. It did not take them long to reach Somerset House in the Strand. He paid the fare, took her arm and led her over the road to the hackney rank by the Maypole.

'I'm deeply sensible of your kindness, madam,' he said, looking down at her, his face filled with sudden warmth. 'I shall go to Austin Friars now. I shall be quite safe there, and Mr Alink will look after me. I will drop you off in Henrietta Street on my way.'

'I hope you resolve your difficulties soon.'

Van Riebeeck shrugged them away. 'May I ask for your discretion in this matter?'

'Of course.'

His grip tightened on her arm, and his voice sounded even deeper and richer than ever. 'And now I have another favour to ask. May I hope that we shall meet again soon? Perhaps you will sup with me one evening?'

Cat swallowed. 'I believe, sir . . . I believe you may hope.'

He kissed her hand, bowed and handed her into a coach.

CHAPTER TWENTY-FIVE

'I WANT IT,' Hannah said.

She had waylaid Maria in the yard. It was Monday morning, and still early, barely light, and Maria had been on the way to the necessary house. Her need to be there increased when Hannah appeared in the doorway of the coal shed, looming pale and insubstantial against the greater darkness within.

'Want what?' Maria said, wishing she had the strength of will to pretend she hadn't heard.

'That handkerchief they gave you. The purple one with the lace.'

Mulberry, thought Maria. She said, 'I haven't got it. My mother says it has to be washed and pressed, and then she'll think about whether I can have it. She says perhaps the owner will ask for it back.'

'I want it,' Hannah repeated, stepping out of the shadows. 'You know what will happen if you don't let me have it.'

The maid's hair was loose and uncombed, as if she had only just dragged herself from her bed. She wore a shawl over the clothes she worked in. She clutched the shawl around her neck with both hands. The fingers were red and raw from scrubbing.

'Otherwise,' Hannah went on, 'they'll hang you by the neck until you're dead. And old Fanshawe will have your body thrown on a dunghill. You know that, don't you?'

'If they give me the handkerchief, I swear you can have it.'

Hannah considered. 'On your father's grave?'

'On my father's grave.' Maria hopped from foot to foot. Her need for the necessary house had grown acute but she remembered to cross her fingers behind her back, just in case. 'And if they give me money, you can have that too.'

'It's only right,' Hannah burst out, as if driven by a sudden need to justify herself. 'A girl like me has to look after herself. No one else will do it, will they? And you said I could be your maid. You *promised*.'

'You can,' Maria wailed. 'You will be. When I'm older and they let me have a maid of my own.'

'I'll want a woman to work under me as well.'

'What?'

'Why not? Someone to wash your linen and iron your lace and empty your pot. You don't think I want to do it, do you?'

'But . . . would not the expense of it . . .?'

'Expense!' Hannah hissed, taking a step closer, her face flushing as red as her hands. 'You're rich. Or you will be. Everyone says so.'

'I won't.'

'Who else is the old fool going to leave his money to? You're his granddaughter, you're a Fanshawe. He's got no one else, except your mother, and she's not his own blood.'

'He'll live for years.' Maria stuck her chin in the air and added tremulously, 'I hope.'

'Are you sure? It depends. Sometimes people die.' Hannah came another step closer and laid a hand on Maria's arm. 'You know that, don't you, you saw it happen with Abbott. Maybe master will die, sooner than everyone thinks.'

Hannah's eyes were pale blue, flecked strangely with green. They locked onto Maria's as a magnet locks onto an iron nail.

'What then?' Hannah whispered.

Maria parted her lips to reply, though she had no idea what she could say. She was trembling, and she could not stop. Warm liquid trickled down the inside of her leg.

The door to the house opened with a crack of the latch and a scrape of wood against stone, and the cook came outside. Hannah sprang back, lowering her head, and bobbing down into an awkward curtsy, as a lowly kitchen maid might do if she chanced to encounter her master's granddaughter.

Maria turned and fled to the safety of the necessary house.

It was Monday morning, and I was back in my lord's office by the Privy Gallery.

'I understand we are . . .' Gorvin hesitated as if searching for the right word '. . . colleagues now.'

'Not by my choice,' I said.

He shrugged and gave me a wry smile. I could tell he didn't believe me. He thought I was trying to better myself. At Whitehall a man was defined by his master's importance. Arlington was more important than Williamson so therefore it was preferable to work for my lord.

'He left word that you're to go to him directly. I warn you, he's not best pleased this morning.'

I was about to leave but he stopped me with a gesture. 'Shall we go to the theatre this evening?' Gorvin swallowed, and suddenly his polished manner deserted him. 'I thought perhaps Mistress Daunt might take a late supper with us.'

'I regret I'm engaged.'

I knocked on my lord's door and went in. He scowled at me. 'The rogue's been released.'

I stared at Arlington in a most unmannerly way. 'Connolly? I don't understand.'

'It's Fanshawe's doing. He spoke to the Duke of Buckingham, who spoke to the King and told him there was no evidence to hold Connolly and thereby deprive scores of gamesters of their lawful amusements. Connolly's back at the Blue Bush, and the place will be open for business again by evening.'

Buckingham lacked Arlington's power but he had the King's ear, a plausible tongue and many supporters. He could be a bad enemy, as I knew to my cost. I pushed my luck and asked, 'What is Fanshawe to His Grace, my lord?'

'Fanshawe's a wealthy man and he has many friends in the City. He's shown his support for the Duke before, and the Duke is grateful. Fanshawe's probably lent him money, too.' Arlington rubbed his plaster so savagely I thought it might come away. 'Besides, His Grace always finds it amusing to obstruct other people's business. That's reason enough for him.' He shuffled the papers on his desk. 'What did you learn from Connolly? Anything at all?'

I was prepared for this and I gave him a succinct account of my unsatisfactory interview. 'As we know, my lord, Mr Wulf is an alias for Mr Van Riebeeck, a Dutch merchant who moves between here and Amsterdam. Connolly pretends he is merely an occasional patron with a particular fondness for backgammon, which is nonsense. We've tried to lay hands on him but failed. I understand that he was seen yesterday evening in Covent Garden, but he escaped before he could be apprehended. The one man who might be able to tell us more is Johnson. He's a gamester at the Blue Bush, and he lodges there as well. But he's disappeared too.'

I paused. But Arlington's face was impassive. He motioned me to continue.

'Yesterday I went to Fanshawe's house in hopes of finding Van Riebeeck or learning more about him. He and Fanshawe do much business together, and they are friendly. But Fanshawe told me nothing of any use. He swore he hadn't seen Van Riebeeck for days. He made no bones about owning the freehold of the Blue Bush – he claimed it's purely an investment for him, and he plays no part in its management and he's never even met Connolly. But when I pressed him, Fanshawe admitted that Van Riebeeck might sometimes visit the tavern.'

Arlington drummed his fingers on the desktop. 'Everything comes back to Fanshawe. Fanshawe and Van Riebeeck.'

Yes, I thought, everything came back to them, and everyone: including Cat.

'Was Abbott murdered?' Arlington said suddenly.

'It's likely he was poisoned, probably because he threatened to confess to you that he had been taking documents from your office. I met Abbott on the day they had dined together, and he was very drunk. Looking back, I believe he was racked with conscience, and desperate to find a way out. It's possible that he had already been poisoned.' The alternative was that Mistress Abbott had poisoned him shortly afterwards, but I did not mention that. 'But nothing can be proved.'

'How long had Abbott been at this knavery? And why was it not uncovered sooner?' The words came out as a snarl: Arlington's rage came out of nowhere, and its ferocity took me by surprise. 'In God's name, am I surrounded by fools and incompetents, as well as rogues? First a spy at work in my own office, and then murder – and no one notices?'

I bowed my head and let the storm pass over. Arlington himself bore some of the responsibility for this. It was he who had brought Abbott into the office, and he who was ultimately responsible for the security of his own papers. He also knew, as I did, that we had reached an impasse. We had no evidence against Fanshawe, who had a powerful friend in Buckingham. Van Riebeeck had vanished. Abbott's death was suspicious and might well have been murder, but there was no evidence there, either. The one fact that could not be ignored was the fragment of charred paper that Johnson had given me, with what looked like a number cipher scattered among words in plain text: meaningless to me but clearly of great moment to Arlington. It struck me as significant that he had not mentioned it to me now.

'We'll put a watch on Fanshawe's house,' he said at last, in a calmer voice. 'That's the one thing we can do. Gorvin will arrange it.'

'There are other things, my lord. We might try to find Johnson, for one. His job was to put Abbott so far in debt that he was vulnerable to blackmail. And he was there on that last day before Abbott fell ill, when he dined with Van Riebeeck at the Blue Bush and got so drunk.'

'Very well. Do as you think fit. But be warned: if you

prove yourself an incompetent fool like the rest, you won't last long in my service or Mr Williamson's.' He lowered his head over his papers. 'Send Gorvin in as you go. Good day.'

It was still early in the morning. I walked along Whitehall in the direction of Charing Cross. I had much to occupy my mind, not least Arlington's veiled threat. He was reputed to be ruthless with his inferiors. I did not give much for my future prospects if I failed to produce some results worth having. Williamson valued me but only up to a point. Forced to make a choice, he would not jeopardize his own position with Arlington for my sake.

As I walked, I made a list in my head. In truth I had little enough to go on. One dead man, Abbott, and five dead rats, all displaying the same symptoms, of vomiting and voided bowels. An apothecary's mark on a wrapper discarded in a bin of pig waste. Stephen's discovery that there was an apothecary with that mark who had hung up his sign in Cock Lane, a stone's throw from Smithfield. A scrap of paper from a professional gambler. A mulberry-coloured handkerchief abandoned in the cage of a mangy lion in Slaughter Street, also within a stone's throw of Smithfield.

When I turned into the Strand I glanced across the street at Blue Bush Alley. The tavern's shutters had been removed. The door stood open and I glimpsed a maid sweeping the entry passage within. Three men were unloading a dray and rolling barrels up the alley. Connolly hadn't wasted much time since his release.

The Blue Bush set my thoughts chasing off in a different direction. Abbott had ruined himself there. Johnson had vanished from there after speaking to me. Van Riebeeck had had a room there and was possibly a shareholder of the tavern as well. Fanshawe owned the freehold. Van Riebeeck, who had so inconveniently evaded capture, was a family connection and business partner of Fanshawe's.

Van Riebeeck appeared to be on such friendly terms with Cat Hakesby. I had dreamed about the pair of them more than once, and my sleeping brain had pictured myself opening a door and finding them in the chamber within, fondling each other and so wrapped up in what they were doing that they did not even notice me.

Van Riebeeck and Cat. The very notion of them together was a canker that gnawed within me, waking and sleeping.

CHAPTER TWENTY-SIX

LATER THAT MORNING, I went to Cock Lane with Stephen. The boy was right about the apothecary's shop. The sign was identical to the mark we had found on the paper in the bin at the Abbotts' lodgings. I entered and asked for the apothecary himself, Mr Thrumbull.

'Do you stock powdered unicorn horn?' I asked.

'Powdered unicorn horn, sir? I wish I could oblige you, indeed I do. If wishes were horses, I should keep it in stock at all times. But the demand is too great and the supply too scarce.'

'When do you expect some more?'

The apothecary spread his hands wide and turned down the corners of his mouth. He was a brown-faced man, much wizened and shrunk into himself; his skin was like a walnut shell bleached in the sun. 'That I cannot tell. I buy from a gentleman who imports it from Amsterdam. Originally it comes from the East Indies. Even there, I understand, the noble beast is becoming harder to find than ever. May I ask what you wanted it for? I might be able to recommend an alternative.'

'I want it as a prophylactic against the plague,' I said. 'A physician tells me we are due for another bad outbreak in the summer.'

'Very likely, sir. And you are wise: it pays to plan ahead. Unicorn powder has been a tried and trusted remedy since the time of the ancients. Once the plague returns you will not be able to find it for love or money the length and breadth of London. Why, I remember when I was a young man, in the old king's time . . .'

I let Mr Thrumbull ramble on. I had chosen to ask for unicorn horn because every reputable apothecary liked to talk about the substance but was unlikely to have it in stock. It could hardly be otherwise since it was so rare, so peculiarly and widely efficacious, and above all so profitable. I smiled and nodded and looked about me, trying to get a sense of the man and his establishment.

The shop was on the ground floor at the sign of the Half Moon. It was divided by a wooden counter with a pair of scales at one end and a brass mortar and pestle at the other. Behind the counter, shelves stretched up to the ceiling. They were lined with ceramic jars and wooden boxes, with flasks and tiny pillboxes. The air smelled musty and faintly spicy, but there was no sign of dust, and the brass gleamed from recent polishing.

'. . . but I am fortunate, nonetheless, in that whenever Mr Fanshawe receives a consignment, he puts some by for me. So if you leave me your name and direction, I could—'

'Fanshawe?' I interrupted. 'Did you say Fanshawe, sir?'

'Yes – I had the pleasure of wishing him good day at church, only yesterday. We have a longstanding connection.'

'That's Mr Fanshawe of Slaughter Street?'

'Faith, yes, the very man. We are practically neighbours – Slaughter Street is barely two minutes' walk from this end of Cock Lane if you take Cow Lane up to the sheep pens.'

'What an agreeable coincidence,' I said. 'I'm acquainted with the gentleman. In fact I was there only yesterday. He was showing me his lion.'

'A magnificent animal.' Thrumbull beamed at me, exposing wooden teeth the colour of his complexion. 'I had the honour of making up a purging electuary for it. Its bowels were blocked when it arrived in this country. Tell me, has its application been efficacious?'

I remembered the smell of Fanshawe's stable and the piles of dung in Caliban's enclosure. 'It's done its job to great effect. I've seen the evidence with my own eyes.'

'I rejoice to hear it. I hope the lion is thriving. There are some who say that with Brockmore as its keeper, the poor beast is to be pitied.'

'Why? Is he a cruel man?'

The apothecary shrugged. 'No more than necessary, as far as I know. But the fellow's a drunken, quarrelsome sot, far gone in his debauchery. Why, sir, he even sees visions now. I have it on the authority of my nephew, a young man of unimpeachable veracity. He is at present doing duty in the Watch, and last week – in the middle of the night, sir, when respectable folk were all abed – they found Brockmore raving like a madman in the middle of Smithfield. He claimed there was a dead man lying on the Slaughter Stone, but when—'

'The what?' I interrupted. 'The Slaughter Stone?'

'Your pardon, sir.' Thrumbull looked condescendingly at

me. 'I forget you're not familiar with the neighbourhood. It's the name the common people give to a stone slab at the bottom of Slaughter Street. No doubt in past times they slaughtered animals there. But, as I was saying, when the Watch inspected the stone, there was nothing there. It was nothing but a vision conjured up by Mistress Lambe's ale.'

'I wonder Mr Fanshawe still employs him.'

'Brockmore does his job well enough when he is sober. Besides, they say his son does most of the work.'

I nodded gravely. 'Let's hope they keep the lion secure. After all, there's a child in the house, little Mistress Fanshawe.'

Thrumbull smiled indulgently. 'A sweet-natured girl. I saw her in church with her grandfather.'

'I don't suppose you knew a connection of theirs – the late Mr Abbott? I was acquainted with him. He recommended you to me.'

'How very obliging – though I never had the honour of meeting the gentleman, sir. His wife is another matter, of course.'

'Ah,' I said. 'Perhaps it was her then. You know Mistress Abbott?'

'I did when she was Mistress Fanshawe, married to Mr Fanshawe's son. I haven't seen her for years. I hear she's returned to live in Slaughter Street, and they say that she's gone back to her former name. She's Mistress Fanshawe again.'

Stephen was waiting for me outside the apothecary's shop. For a moment he did not notice me. With an air of grave concentration he was studying the blue-and-white plaque set

195

in the wall by the door. It bore the arms of the Society of Apothecaries.

His expression rapt and almost childlike, the boy ran his finger over the shield, tracing the figure of horned Apollo with his bow and arrow, with the vanquished serpent coiled around his ankles. The shield was supported by unicorns, and the crest above took the form of a rhinoceros, and these animals seemed to have a particular fascination for him. Perhaps, I thought, as an infant in Africa, he had seen the unicorn and the rhinoceros roaming his native plains and jungles.

At the sound of the door closing, he gave a start and turned towards me. His face might have been carved in some dark substance, harder than any wood. I had the foolish, fleeting thought that behind this mask lay hatred for me. That was clearly nonsense. Had I not saved his life? Did I not give him the food on his plate, the clothes on his back and the roof over his head? Had I not encouraged him to learn his letters? Did I not intend to give him his freedom when I judged the time had come? He had every reason to love me.

Stephen bowed to me and took the package I handed to him. It contained a small flask of extremely expensive distilled wine in which a long list of ingredients had been steeped. I could not remember them all, but among them were rue, angelica, mugwort, pimpernel and agrimony. According to Mr Thrumbull, it was a reliable prophylactic against the plague. At the first sign of a new outbreak, I should take a small glass of the wine on rising every day. This would protect me until he was able to send me some powdered unicorn horn, whose prophylactic powers were even more assured.

It was already past midday. With Stephen trailing behind me, I walked along Cock Lane in the direction of Holborn Bridge. Cow Lane was only a few paces away, running northwards.

A beggar was sitting at the corner, his hands stretched out, palms upwards, muttering prayers or imprecations at the passers-by. His hands, inadequately covered with rags, were frost-bitten. He had lost an eye. I paused beside him, and at once he redoubled his whining, raising its volume and leaning towards me as if he wanted to claw my legs into his embrace. I took a step backwards and showed him my stick, at which he cowered.

I drew closer again. 'I mean you no harm, fellow, and perhaps I shall do you good.'

'A penny, master, love of Christ, pray, sir—'

'Is there a tavern nearby called Lambe's?'

'There's Mistress Lambe's alehouse,' he mumbled. 'Chick Lane, master, but a penny, or two for the—'

'Here.'

I dropped a newly-minted sixpence — far too much, a ha'penny would have been generous — onto the man's palm. It rolled off and fell with a tinkle to the cobbles. He scrabbled wildly for it.

I left him to it. We walked up Cow Lane until we reached the sheep pens on the west side of Smithfield. Instead of turning left into Chick Lane, I lingered at the foot of Slaughter Street, examining the large stone at the corner. The Slaughter Stone was raised a few inches above the surrounding roadway, and it was certainly large enough to hold a man's body. I wondered that it had been suffered to remain there, for it must have been a considerable hindrance to traffic. The stone's surface was fissured with cuts and indentations, and a deep, moss-filled crack ran across one corner. I crouched and ran a finger along one of the worn channels that had been cut to drain away the blood.

I glanced up the street. I could be at Fanshawe's door in a moment or two. Arlington had told me he would have Gorvin put a watch on the house, but there was no sign of it. That did not surprise me. Our lords and masters consider a thing done once they have ordered it, and done perfectly, but often there is a considerable delay, during which the urgency of the matter gradually diminishes.

I turned and looked at the lane at right angles. A high wall ran along the side. I calculated that it must belong to Fanshawe's garden. As I had discovered yesterday, the garden stretched from the house to the stables where I had seen Caliban. I made out the roof of the disused coach house at the end of the lane. Halfway along the wall, there was a gate, which must lead into the garden itself.

It was bitterly cold at the corner, for the wind blew from the north, down Slaughter Street. Huddled in his cloak, Stephen was shivering. Despite his years in England, his blood had still not adapted to these climes.

'Come, lad. Chick Lane.'

He did not reply. His teeth were chattering. We would both be the better for a bowl of soup, I thought, and once we had seen Brockmore, the next thing we would do was find our dinner.

We turned into Chick Lane. The alehouse was near the far end. I stopped outside. Two things were immediately obvious. The place was doing a roaring trade, and Mistress Lambe was not over-particular about the manners of her customers. Even with the door closed, I could hear the shouting and singing inside, drowned of a sudden by a wave of raucous laughter.

I judged it better to send Stephen inside to ask for Brockmore. I told him to tell the lion-keeper that a gentleman wished to hear about the beast in his charge and would pay generously for the privilege. While I waited, I leant against the wall opposite the alehouse, tapping my iron-shod stick on the stones at my feet. The neighbourhood was not a pleasant one. I was an obvious target for thieves and ruffians, even in broad daylight. One by one, men and even boys drifted along the lane towards me. They kept a safe distance. They did not look at me, let alone talk to me, but I knew I was the focus of their attention.

I turned my head at the sound of the alehouse door. Stephen came out, followed by Brockmore, who blinked at the light after the gloom inside. He wore a drover's sleeveless leather jerkin, much stained and scratched, with a long knife in his belt.

'Brockmore,' I said. 'You remember me from Sunday, I daresay. When you showed us your lion having his dinner at Mr Fanshawe's.'

He nodded and tilted his head to see me better. 'He's like a second son to me, that lion.' He hawked and spat.

'Does he ever attack you?'

Brockmore considered me. His neck was short. His head perched on it like the upper half of an egg, narrowing as it rose to the eyes and even more at the forehead. I sighed and produced a shilling. The crowd dispersed. Stephen and I were, in a manner of speaking, under the lion-keeper's protection.

His stubby fingers wrapped themselves around the coin. 'When the mood's upon him. But if you can deal with a bull, you can deal with a lion.'

I was feeling my way into this conversation. 'And when is the mood upon him?'

'If he feels threatened. If he's hungry.' Brockmore made an obscene gesture with his hands and chuckled, making a sound like water running out of an underground cistern. 'Or if he wants *that* and he can't have it.'

'Would he attack someone who went into his cage?'

'Depends. He's like your mother's cat, sir. If he's got a full belly and he's sleepy, he'll take no notice of you, if you don't go too close. But you never know with Caliban.'

'Do you go in there yourself?'

He shrugged. 'When Master says the smell's too bad, I have to clean the place somehow.'

'And he attacks even you, his keeper, who gives him his food?'

'He's no more fond of me than I am of him.' Brockmore spat again, and glanced back at the door of the alehouse. 'Yes, he's gone for me. I don't take chances.' He took a step away, clearly anxious to get back to his ale. My time was running out. 'When I go in, I take that pole you saw me with, the one with the iron tip, and I have my son standing by, with a whip and a torch of flaming pitch. The beast can't abide fire.'

I produced another shilling. 'I am curious about another matter. I hear you found a body on the Slaughter Stone the other night.'

'Who told you that?' he snapped, snatching the shilling from between my fingers.

I waved in the general direction of Smithfield. 'It's common talk.'

He tilted his head and thrust his chin towards me as though he had it in mind to poke me with it. 'It was true. There was a body. Anyone who says otherwise is the devil-born spawn of a draggle-arse, pox-ridden punk.'

'No doubt. You actually saw it?'

'How could I? It was black as the Devil's arsehole that night. I didn't see him. I felt him.' He lifted his right hand, palm outwards, the fingers splayed like loose sausages on a butcher's stall. 'I sat down on the stone to catch my breath – and I felt him lying there. I touched his hand, his arm. Then his face. His cheeks were as clammy as death. I felt his mouth. His teeth, what was left of them. His open eyes. I touched his *blood*.'

Brockmore was an artist in his way. He was watching me, studying the effects of his words.

'I know it was blood,' he went on. 'I smelled it first. Then I tasted to make sure.'

I winced at the thought. 'Are you certain the man was dead?'

'If you've been a drover, master, you know what a dead animal feels like, night or day.'

I considered. 'Then you prudently summoned the Watch, as any good citizen would,' I said. 'But when they came with their lanterns, they found the body was gone? Is that right?'

'Numbskulls.' He spat once more for emphasis. 'They said I'd imagined it all. I told them, it's plain enough what happened. The killer came and took the body away. They wouldn't believe me, the fools. Even next day when I gave them proof of it. I showed them my hand. There was blood on it, on the one I touched the body with.'

'And what did they say to that?'

'They laughed in my face, master. Said I was handling meat all day to feed that damned beast, so of course there was blood on my hands.'

'Cruel,' I said, shaking my head.

'They laughed like a pack of monkeys, sir. But I know there was a dead man on that stone. And he was a gentleman, too.'

'How do you know that?'

'His suit. My uncle was a clothier, and he taught me to feel with my fingers. It was good broadcloth, not kersey, and I'd lay any man a pound that the shirt was Holland cloth.'

Clothes like that were expensive, even second-hand. Neither of us spoke for a moment. I took out another shilling, the last I had on me. I wrapped it in my fist.

'Do you remember yesterday?' I said. 'How young Mistress Fanshawe saw a handkerchief in Caliban's cage, and begged to have it?'

'Aye, master.' He frowned, and I knew he was grappling with the implication of my words. 'Purple, it was. Or maybe red.'

Mulberry, I thought, not red, not purple. 'How long had it been there? Do you know?'

He shrugged.

'Let me put it another way,' I said. 'When did you last clean out the cage? If it was there, you'd have noticed it, wouldn't you?'

Brockmore's eyes met mine. He might be a drunken sot but he wasn't altogether a fool. He said, 'Friday, maybe?'

I tossed him the last shilling. He had found the body on the Slaughter Stone on Friday night.

'I don't want nothing to do with it, master,' he said suddenly. 'Any of it. It's nothing but trouble.'

He turned and stumbled across the lane and into the sanctuary of Mistress Lambe's alehouse.

CHAPTER TWENTY-SEVEN

THAT EVENING I got drunk.

I had changed my mind and gone to the theatre with Gorvin after all. From the stage, Meg Daunt had displayed her charms for all she was worth. She was not a beauty in the usual sense, but she had a quick wit, an unexpectedly sweet smile, and a talent for displaying her charms to best advantage. Gorvin was enchanted by her performance. Afterwards he dragged me to her dressing room, where several gallants were already waiting on her.

In his everyday life, Gorvin's polished manners and smooth tongue rarely deserted him. But Gorvin in love was a different matter. His speech stumbled, his complexion grew red and his movements clumsy. That was why he needed me. I made everything easier. I chatted to Meg Daunt – she was indeed good company – and by degrees brought Gorvin more and more into the conversation. Slowly his awkwardness would drop away.

At my urging, she invited us back to her lodging in Vere Street. Two of the gallants accompanied us. Once there,

Gorvin sent out for wine as usual. His boldness increased with every glass he tossed back. I engaged the gallants to the best of my ability and Gorvin laid siege to Mistress Daunt.

We ordered supper – again at Gorvin's expense – from Chatelin's in Covent Garden. When it arrived, I merely picked at it, ignoring the gurgles and giggles at the other end of the table. Afterwards, the gallants admitted defeat and staggered down the stairs, one of them pausing to vomit long and loudly in the hallway below.

This was my signal to slip away, leaving Gorvin to what I hoped would be bliss. By now it was past midnight. It was only when I came out into the night air that I realized I was drunk. Fortunately two chairmen were setting down a fare in Clare Market, and I hired them to carry me down to the Savoy.

When I reached Infirmary Close, I banged on my door until Sam let me in. He was already wearing his nightcap.

'Damn it,' I said, though he hadn't spoken. 'You're my servant.'

'Yes, master,' he muttered, 'I know.' He set to barring and bolting the door again.

As I said, I was drunk. Not the sort of drunk that means a man falls over in the street like poor Abbott, or slurs his words, or laughs immoderately at a funeral. No, that evening I was the sort of drunk whose world is larger than life, more thickly populated with joys and sorrows. I was also the sort of drunk who wants to make the world a little better for someone if not for himself. In other words, the sort who makes foolish gestures.

'Sam? Rouse Margaret and Stephen directly. I want all three of you in the parlour.'

'Now, your honour? Can't it wait?'

'No, you knave,' I roared. 'It cannot. Get them in there. I'll join you in a moment. Hurry, man.'

He hobbled off, thumping his crutch more loudly than usual to express his disapproval. I went up to my bedchamber and into my closet for a moment or two. When I came down to the parlour, all three of them were waiting, sullen-faced, their cloaks flung over their night clothes. The fire was out. The only light came from two candles. I set down the papers I had brought with me, together with a box containing pen, ink and a sander. I sat down, facing my servants, who were standing in a line on the other side of the table.

'Stephen. Come here.'

The boy obeyed. I held up one of the candles to see his face better.

'I've decided to free you,' I said.

His face did not change. But Margaret gave a muffled squawk. Sam cleared his throat, and I guessed he wanted to spit.

'It means you can leave my service at any time you want. Should you wish to.'

Stephen's silence surprised me. I put it down to shock at the unexpected nature of my news. The idea of freeing him had been in my mind all afternoon and evening, though it had taken a few bottles of wine this evening before I was ready to translate idea into deed. The possibility that he might not like being my slave had struck me from the blue when we were outside Mr Thrumbull's shop in Cock Lane. It was a notion that had not previously occurred to me. After all, I told myself, I had shown myself a good master to him. But – leaving that aside – would it not be a noble gesture on my

206

part if I made Stephen a present of his freedom? In the last two years, he had given me no cause for complaint. Besides, I already thought of him as a servant, not a slave. The only practical difference of altering his status would be that I would have to pay him a wage which, for a footboy, would cost me next to nothing.

'I shall now draw up this document that grants you your freedom,' I announced grandly. 'These other papers confirm my ownership of you, but I shall cancel them and hereby disclaim all title to you.'

Warmed by my generosity, I sat down and wrote a certificate granting Stephen his freedom. I signed it with a flourish and told Sam and Margaret to approach the table where I sat.

'You've seen me sign. You must sign here or make your mark as witnesses.'

I turned the paper towards them and slid it across the table. Margaret went first. She could write her name and many other words with tolerable ease. Sam added his cross together with a spatter of ink drops to represent his name, underneath which his wife printed SAMUEL WITHERDINE in wavering letters.

All this time, Stephen stood in silence, barely visible in the gloom. When we were done, I beckoned him over and presented him with the papers.

'There,' I said, leaning back in my chair. 'Now you are as free as anyone in England.'

He took the papers, bowed and took three steps backwards, still facing me, as though I were the King's Majesty himself. I wondered that he still made no expression of gratitude. It irritated me. And why were the Witherdines still standing there like a pair of wooden blocks? All three of them were watching me, their outlines quivering in the two flames between us.

'Go away,' I said. 'All of you.'

The mingled warmth of wine and generosity had drained away from me. I was cold and tired. I missed Cat.

CHAPTER TWENTY-EIGHT

THE WORST OF it was that Maria had no one to confide in.

At least in the old days, when they had lodged at the sign of the Black Boy in Fleet Street, she and Hannah had been allies of a sort, united in their hatred of Abbott and his tyrannies. It was so unjust, Maria thought, that when Abbott was only a memory, and all should have been well, she felt even more unhappy, even more fearful than ever before.

True, she ate better food now, and she wore better clothes, and slept in a better bed than she had when Abbott was alive. But she also started at every shadow, in case it was Hannah's, or a constable's, or a justice's. Scratching her fear like a scab, she had asked Uncle Van Riebeeck if he knew where they hanged witches, but he had shrugged and told her not to waste her time, for time was a gift from God and should be cherished and husbanded. It should not be frittered away with idle fancies and foolish questions.

That was before last Friday, when she had waited for Hannah in the garden pavilion, and Hannah hadn't come.

Maria had heard her uncle talking in the dark to that man with the uncouth thickness in his voice. They were going to put another man with the lion to make him speak to them. She hadn't said a word to her uncle since then, and nor did she want to. To her relief, Van Riebeeck had not been back to Slaughter Street since Saturday.

It was now Tuesday, and Maria dared to hope that her uncle had gone away again, back to Amsterdam or even further. Neither her grandfather nor her mother had mentioned him.

That morning, her mother had given her the washed and pressed handkerchief – the mulberry-coloured handkerchief, as the strange gentleman had called it on Sunday.

'You might as well have it,' her mother had said. 'But if the owner asks for it you will have to give it back. It must have been a gentleman's, and a careless one at that. There's a burn near the corner – see? – it's probably his foul tobacco – and the lace is so badly torn on one side that it's beyond mending.'

'Thank you, madam.'

'You're looking pale,' her mother said accusingly as Maria was looking at the handkerchief and wondering who it had belonged to. 'What have you been doing to yourself?'

'Nothing.'

'Where's your appetite gone? You hardly ate anything yesterday. God didn't put food on your plate for you to waste it. We should be grateful for His blessings, not spurn them.'

Maria bowed her head. 'I'm sorry. I wasn't hungry.'

Even Mr Fanshawe noticed that Maria was not herself. When they met downstairs, he chucked her painfully under the chin and said, 'Why so pale and sad, little mistress? This will never do.'

But you could not discard a trouble so easily, by saying it wouldn't do.

'Perhaps we should send you down to Swaring, hey? Country air, country food.'

Her grandfather wandered away. Perhaps it would be good to go down to Swaring after all, despite the cold and the mud. But only if Hannah stayed in Slaughter Street.

After Maria had broken her fast, she went into the parlour to do her hour's work on the sampler, which was part of the regimen her mother prescribed for her. Instead of working on the lion, who was still skimpy and insubstantial and wholly uninteresting, she took out the handkerchief. She examined it with a pleasure tinged with melancholy, because it would soon be hers no longer.

An idea struck her. She laid the handkerchief on the table beside her basket of silks. To her delight, she found a thread that was an almost exact match for the handkerchief's shade of purple. She threaded it through her needle and began to sew, choosing a vacant spot between the unicorn's foremost hoof and the lion's upraised paw. A tiny blob of thread grew larger, and attained a more or less square shape.

Here it is, Maria thought, here is my own mulberry handkerchief. I shall lend it to the unicorn if he should need it, but not to the lion.

On Tuesday morning, Cat received a letter from Mr Alink, begging her to visit Austin Friars as soon as possible and hinting that Van Riebeeck was in low spirits. The note enclosed an even shorter one, unsealed and unsigned, which said in a bold, upright hand: *Pray come at once*. Alink's manservant, a taciturn Dutchman in late middle age who appeared to have no English at his command, waited to escort her or to receive her reply.

She was not averse to meeting Van Riebeeck again – quite the reverse if the truth were known. But she was determined to do it at her own convenience. Before she left, she took her time discussing the day's work with Brennan and changing her clothes. Afterwards, the servant conducted her to the hackney he had kept waiting at considerable expense to his master.

At Austin Friars, however, the man did not take her to the Alinks' house, but begged her to follow him through a small door in a stone wall some fifty yards away. In ancient times, there had been a friary attached to what was now the Dutch church, and this wall had once marked the boundary of the site. Some of the friary's buildings remained, scattered among the houses, tenements and gardens.

'Where are you taking me?' Cat demanded as he was unlocking the gate.

The servant bowed and said, 'Through here, mistress. Please to follow.'

He locked the gate behind them and set out across a courtyard with a shuttered house and a long, overgrown garden on the other. To the left was another wall, beyond which Cat saw the roofs and chimneys of Mr Alink's house.

'Please to follow,' the man repeated.

He led her down a path strewn with the remains of last year's weeds. The hedges had once been trimmed into the forms of columns and outlandish animals. They were now bushy and overgrown, sprouting into monstrous shapes beyond the reach of imagination. They rounded a corner and a cottage appeared. It slumped against the garden wall as if weary. It was fashioned from bricks and stones filched from the ruins. The tiled roof dipped and buckled, and ivy had thrown a green curtain across the small window.

Van Riebeeck was sitting on a bench by the door, his long legs stretched in front of him. He was wearing an old coat, and smoking a long-stemmed pipe. For an instant, she took him for a gardener or watchman.

'There you are,' he said when he saw her. He rose to his feet and bowed. 'You've taken your time. I have been counting the moments.'

The servant bowed. 'I'll wait at the gate, mistress,' he said, and left them alone.

It was the first time that Cat had seen Van Riebeeck without a peruke. Its absence made his face seem even longer and bonier than before. But even in such mean attire, he retained an air of distinction.

'Are you living here?' she said. 'Here?'

'Why not?'

There were a thousand reasons. 'But how do you eat?'

'The servant brings my meals from the house, and anything else I need.' He smiled. 'Including you, madam.'

Cat was surprised that his precautions against arrest were so extreme. Why didn't he stay in the comfort of the Alinks' house? It was unlikely that any creditor or business rival would reach Van Riebeeck in so secluded and private a place.

'Pray walk with me,' he said.

He laid down his pipe, took up a stick that was leaning against the wall, and offered her his arm. He marched her briskly down the path. He whistled to himself and marked time by slashing his stick at the weeds and bushes.

'I'm pleased that your spirits have recovered so quickly,' Cat said. 'How are you?'

He ignored the question. 'Why didn't you come sooner?'

'I came as soon as I could,' Cat said. 'Though it was not convenient. I have a client to see and much else to do today.'

'Is the business to do with my lord's new poultry house?'

'Partly. I can't stay here long. Mr Alink wrote that you were in low spirits, but you seem quite cheerful to me.'

He beheaded a decaying thistle with a grunt of satisfaction. 'That's because you're here.'

'But why do you really want to see me?'

He swung his stick again, this time at a straying bramble sucker that resisted him. 'When do you go to France with your poultry house?'

'I don't know. Probably next week.'

'I shall count the days of your absence,' he announced. 'Naturally.'

'I doubt it, sir,' Cat said primly. 'Anyway, there's no point. I shall come back when I can, and not before then.'

'You must tell me when you are to go, as soon as they tell you. Yes? Write to Alink.'

She moistened her lips. She was puzzled by this sudden interest in her work. 'Very well. If you wish it.'

'I do wish it.' He gripped her arm tightly, as if fearing she might run away. 'But why the delay in going to France? Why not go at once?'

'Brennan and I have to draw up a set of plans to present to Madame. And my lord wants a model to be made as well. There's no urgency.'

They walked in silence. After a moment or two, she said, 'What will you do? You can't stay here for ever. Can you satisfy your creditors?'

Van Riebeeck snapped the fingers of his free hand. 'A fig for my creditors. I shall contrive a settlement.'

'You make light of your debts now, but the other evening you seemed at your wits' end.'

He stopped abruptly. 'The other evening it was a subterfuge because I wanted you to help me, and it was obliging of you to do so. I wonder, will you consent to be my wife?'

'You jest, sir.' She tore her hand away from his arm. 'And at my expense.'

Van Riebeeck's tone had not changed with the subject. Cat stared at him. He stared back. Neither of them spoke. She felt simultaneously angry, tremulous, happy and embarrassed. And then angry again, for he was clearly mocking her.

'Well?' he said. 'Will you?'

'Be damned to you.'

She turned and walked away in the direction of the waiting servant at the gate. She expected Van Riebeeck to run after her, to say something, anything. But there was only silence behind her.

CHAPTER TWENTY-NINE

CAT TOOK A coach from Austin Friars. On the way to Whitehall, she conducted an inconclusive argument with herself. Perhaps Van Riebeeck had meant what he said and his attachment to her, though strangely sudden, was genuine. In that case, the proposal was a compliment, even if the manner of it left much to be desired.

On the other hand, what was this nonsensical story he had given her about his creditors? If they existed, and he was in real difficulties, he was therefore a fool and a liar to pretend otherwise. If they did not, or if they did not pose a serious threat to him, then he was not only a liar but he was making a fool of her. And if he truly wished to marry her, he should not have let her leave without trying to plead his case.

Not that she would ever have agreed, even if he had meant his proposal. She had had enough of marriage and what it entailed. She preferred her life as it was, answerable to no one other than herself. What made it all more complicated, though, was that she had a traitor within: something inside her responded almost against her will to the sound of his voice and the way he moved.

She went first to Scotland Yard. As she passed under the archway into the first court, she glanced up at the windows of Mr Williamson's office, where Marwood had worked for the last four years. She wouldn't know what to say to him, how to act. It seemed that Van Riebeeck had invaded her life and unsettled every part of it, including her friendship with Marwood.

The workshop of the royal cabinetmaker was next door to the clock house in the northern courtyard. It was a cheerful place that smelled of varnish and wood shavings. The cabinetmaker himself bustled towards her and bowed. 'Mistress Hakesby, good day to you. You're come to inspect the work? I believe we are nearly done.'

The poultry house model was standing on a table underneath a window near the back of the workshop. It was about twenty inches square in area, and eleven inches high at its apex, which was the pediment that formed the central gable above the doors. In the middle of the pediment was a delicately carved cartouche.

'Madame's arms will be painted there tomorrow. My lord has engaged the services of Mr Cooper, who is skilled at working in miniature.'

Cat ran her finger along the front of the model. 'The base is too thick, isn't it? It should have been thinner than this. May I have a ruler and a sight of the measurements?'

The cabinetmaker's air of good humour was growing strained. 'Madam, I had these dimensions from my lord's office. I discussed them with Mr Gorvin at some length. He made the point that the base must be substantial because it must fold to form a box when the model is transported. There-fore it has to be extraordinarily robust to withstand the rigours of travel. See – I have reinforced the corners with brass. I've also caused handles to be fixed at either end. A man will be able to lift the model with ease, whether it's open or closed.'

Cat gripped the handles and lifted the model a few inches above the table. 'Or even a woman.'

The greater a man or woman, the longer they make you wait on their convenience. The candles had been lit by the time Gorvin, spreading apologies before her like flowers, con-ducted her to his lordship's private office off the Privy Gallery. Arlington did her the courtesy of half-rising as she entered.

'Mistress Hakesby, good afternoon.' He waved her to a chair as she rose from her curtsy. 'You've inspected the model of our poultry house?'

'I have, my lord, and it's very fine.'

'I understand it will be ready tomorrow.'

'The painting of it will be complete by then. But it will then need varnishing, perhaps more than one coat. And varnish can't be hurried if you want it to be durable.'

Arlington drummed his fingers on the desk, as if accom-panying inaudible dance music. 'Today is Tuesday.' He stared down at his dancing fingers. 'Tomorrow is Wednesday.' Another flourish of the fingers. 'Thursday, Friday.' The fingers became still. He looked at up at her. 'Let's say Saturday. Will that suit you?'

'In what way, my lord?'

'To set out for France.' He frowned at her. 'What else do you think I could mean?'

'My draughtsman and I still need to make fair copies of the plans and elevations. That could take—'

'Can you be ready by Saturday?'

Cat swallowed. A presentation folder of drawings fit for a princess was not something that could be put together in a few hours. The fingers resumed their damned drumming, more quickly and more urgently than before.

'It can be done, my lord.'

The fingers stopped. 'Then that's settled.'

'How am I to travel?'

'You will travel under the protection of a clergyman, Mr Hobell, and his wife. It will all be perfectly respectable and safe. Mr Gorvin will notify you of the details.' The heavy head lowered itself over the papers on the desk, and the hand picked up the pen and dipped it in the inkwell. 'Good day to you, Mistress Hakesby.'

When Cat returned to Henrietta Street, she found Margaret there. She was trying patiently to teach Jane Ash to turn an old sheet. 'There's at least another year in it, probably two,' she was saying as Cat came into the parlour.

The two servants rose like startled birds when Cat entered. Jane took her cloak from her.

'Is Mr Brennan here still?'

'No, mistress. He went to Fenchurch Street after dinner and said he wouldn't be back until the morning.'

Cat sat down. 'Go to the cookshop. Bring me a pie, beef if you can. One of the small ones. And be quick about it.'

Margaret took up her sewing.

'How is your master?' Cat said when they were alone.

'Sour as a bowl of whey.' Margaret laid the sewing aside.

'He went to the theatre. It was nearly one o'clock by the time he came home, and he was in his cups. You ain't seen him lately?'

'Only for a moment, and that by chance. At someone's house. Is he – is he well?'

'He may be well enough, mistress, but he ain't happy. Something's going on at his office, I think.'

'I'm to go to France on Saturday,' Cat burst out, her own concerns overwhelming her. 'To Paris. I'll go to court, probably. I may be presented to Madame – the Duchess of Orléans herself. I may have to *talk* to her.' She paused. 'What should I wear?' She paused again, as the full horror of her situation presented itself. 'Margaret, which shoes should I take?'

'Your pattens, and the new boots for travelling,' Margaret said in a matter-of-fact voice. 'The shoes you're wearing now will do very well for everyday, once you're there. If Her Highness summons you, it had best be those ones with the three-inch heels and the green silk lining. As long as you've had them mended. You spent enough on them, mistress, so you'll want to give them some use, I daresay, and they're very fine. But mind you don't break an ankle.'

'Pointed toes are quite *à la mode* at Whitehall. But that probably means they are already old-fashioned in France.'

Margaret threaded her needle again. 'You can only make the best of what you have. Same as everyone.'

CHAPTER THIRTY

THE WEATHER CHANGED as the week went on. By Friday, the morning sky was clean and cloudless. In the kitchen yard, a low, pale sun gave off a faint but perceptible warmth, a foretaste of spring.

Maria picked her way among the puddles and patches of mud to the necessary house. She settled there for longer than she needed, feeling the draughts curling around her legs and watching the yellow outlines of light between door and frame. She felt almost happy for the first time in days, if not weeks.

But when she came out, Hannah was waiting. Beside her on the ground were two buckets of kitchen waste for the pigs.

'You been hiding from me?'

'No,' said Maria. The sunlight gave her a flimsy sort of courage. She had known this meeting would come sooner or later and she was tired of being scared all the time. 'I can't come looking for you. You know that.'

'It's three days since I seen you. Have you got it?'

Maria took the mulberry handkerchief from her pocket. She dropped it into Hannah's outstretched palm. The thought of touching Hannah's skin repulsed her. It would be like touching a snake or a toad.

She watched Hannah stroking the handkerchief as if it were a kitten. It was a beautiful thing, even in its torn state. The sunlight picked out its brave colour. The cloth was so soft, the lace so delicate, and you hardly noticed the burn mark or the tear. Now it was worthless, soiled for ever by Hannah's touch.

Maria's eyes filled with tears. She started back to the house.

'Stop.'

She turned slowly.

Hannah stuffed the handkerchief into her skirt. 'Something else for you to do.'

Maria said, 'I can't make you my maid, not for years and years. But if they give me some money, I'll—'

'It's that lion.'

'What about it?'

'I hate it.'

'Why? What's it done to you?'

'It eats better than me, for a start. And it stinks, and it roars fit to wake the dead. I want you to kill it.'

'Hannah, pray don't be foolish. I can't do that.'

'Who are you calling foolish? Say it again, and you'll wish you hadn't.'

Maria said, 'But how could I kill a lion? It's impossible.'

'No, it's not. It's easy.' Hannah's eyes were paler than the sky. 'And it'll be good practice for you.'

'For what?' Maria stared at Hannah's face, which was smudged with soot. 'Practice for what?'

Hannah didn't answer. She picked up the pails and slouched through the archway towards the pigsty. A cloud had appeared from nowhere and swallowed the sun. There were goose pimples on Maria's arm, and she felt sick. She hurried into the house.

On Friday morning, I lay in bed, enclosed in the comfortable, stuffy darkness by the curtains. It was my sanctuary, and I fought against the need to leave it. In the distance, I heard the morning sounds of my house. My people downstairs would be waiting for me to stir. I would have liked to fall asleep again, but my restless thoughts would not let me alone. Round and round they went, swaying and staggering like a child's top on uneven ground.

I was as sure as a man reasonably can be that Jeremiah Johnson had been murdered, probably at or near Fanshawe's house in Slaughter Street. I couldn't prove it. But the handkerchief that Maria Fanshawe had found in the lion's enclosure supported the notion. According to Brockmore, it hadn't been there during the day on Friday last week.

Then, on the evening of that very day, there was Brockmore's story about the body on the Slaughter Stone. The story was so far-fetched, and it reflected so badly on him, that I was inclined to give it credence. The detail about the corpse's clothing was particularly revealing. Johnson's suit, though well-worn and far from clean, had been of unexpectedly good quality.

Fanshawe had a business interest in the Blue Bush, but perhaps that was all it was. It was significant that he had shown no sign of recognizing the handkerchief, and no sign of a guilty conscience either. He might be more of a dupe than a knave.

Van Riebeeck himself was in a different category. I had no difficulty in believing him capable of murder. And he was the obvious link between Slaughter Street and Johnson's base at the Blue Bush. There had been a warrant out for him since last Saturday. It was now Friday. He had disappeared since the brief sighting in Covent Garden – either he had gone into hiding or he had left London altogether.

An idea occurred to me. Covent Garden was at the eastern end of Henrietta Street. The Drawing Office at the sign of the Rose was not above five minutes' walk from where Van Riebeeck had last been seen. I myself had seen him there one evening last week, when he had brought Cat back from some mysterious excursion and I had come close to an open quarrel with him. What if he had taken refuge there?

All I had to do was ask. Once I had clothed the idea in words, I realized how strange it was that I had not thought of it before. It was almost as if I found the possibility so disturbing that I had not even been able to entertain it.

Margaret had told me that Cat was leaving for France tomorrow. With sudden, desperate urgency, I flung back the curtains, swung my bare legs out of the bed and shouted for Sam.

At the sign of the Rose, Pheebs opened the door to me. He ducked his head in a show of respect that was as convincing as a whore's compliment on a customer's manhood.

'Is Mistress Hakesby above?'

'Yes, your honour.' His eyes drifted towards Stephen at my side. 'Will you go straight up or shall I send my boy to enquire if it's convenient?'

Pheebs and I had come to an understanding two years ago,

around the time of Mr Hakesby's death. Nowadays he did his best to oblige me, within limits. I took care to keep him sweet with a present of money every now and then. He was scared of me, which helped, partly because I had encouraged him to think that I was considerably more important at Whitehall than I was.

'No need to announce me,' I said. 'I know the way. But first, a word in your ear.' I motioned him to withdraw, so we were out of Stephen's earshot. 'Do you remember when I last saw you?'

'About a week ago, sir, wasn't it?' Pheebs avoided my eyes. 'That evening you called but Mistress Hakesby was abroad with the tall gentleman, and you chanced to meet her as you were leaving. A wet night, as I remember.'

It was a bland and diplomatic summary. 'Tell me,' I said, 'have you seen that gentleman again since then?'

Pheebs frowned, as if trying to remember. 'Foreigner, wasn't he?'

'Have you seen him?' I rapped out. 'Yes or no.' I saw the flash of fear in his eyes. 'Don't waste my time.'

'Your pardon, master. I . . . I was trying to fix the day in my mind . . . Sunday, I think, this Sunday just gone.'

'What time?'

'Around three or four of the clock. He was out of breath. I marked it most particular.'

It fitted. Van Riebeeck had given Gorvin's men the slip in Covent Garden on Sunday afternoon. My guess had been right – he had found refuge here.

'And he went up to Mistress Hakesby?'

'Mistress was out.'

Of course she had been out. That was the day I had

encountered her in Slaughter Street, and she had still been there when I left the house after my unsatisfactory interview with Fanshawe.

'But I let the gentleman go up,' Pheebs went on, 'as he'd called before, and I knew that Mistress Hakesby would want it. I hope I did right, sir. Her maid was there, so I thought there could be no harm in it.'

There must have been a present of money. Or Pheebs wouldn't have let Van Riebeeck go upstairs, not on so slender an acquaintance. But the bribe hadn't been big enough to outweigh my influence.

I extracted the rest of the story in less than a moment. Later, Pheebs had provided Van Riebeeck with a cloak and a hat. 'I hope I did nothing wrong, master, but Mistress Hakesby wished it so I thought it must be all right.' Cat had ordered him to send the boy for a hackney, in which she left the house with Van Riebeeck shortly afterwards.

'When was this?'

'Must have been after seven by then. Getting dark already.'

I made a rapid calculation: Van Riebeeck had been upstairs for at least three hours.

'He looked like her servant when he left, your honour. That's what she wanted, you see, she said it was for a wager. He was bowing and scraping for all he was worth. And he walked different, too, bent over – made him look smaller. He told me to come out to the hackney with him, and we were to pretend to jest with each other. Like we were both servants.'

'How long was Mistress Hakesby gone?' I asked. 'And where did they go?'

'I don't know where they went. She came back alone in another hackney, about half an hour or so later.'

I probed a little more but I got nothing else from Pheebs. I gave him some money and told him that if he breathed a word of having talked to me about this, I'd make sure he was out of his job and into a pillory before he could say the Lord's Prayer.

Then I went upstairs.

There was a sour atmosphere in the Drawing Office.

Brennan had the sullens because Cat had made him work on the plans for the presentation folder. She argued that he had a lighter touch with the fine detail than she had. In return, he reminded her that this illustrious commission hadn't earned them a penny yet, while it had already cost them dear.

She suspected that his mood wasn't improved by the fact that he would have sole charge of the office while she was away. Responsibility weighed heavily on him. To make matters worse, the folder itself, which was of fine calf leather and stamped with Madame's monogram, should have been delivered yesterday but it had not yet arrived.

Cat had sought refuge in her own apartments on the floor below, only to find them in chaos. The bed was piled with clothes that should already have been packed in the big valise, and the shoes – Cat had decided that she could not reasonably be expected to manage without five pairs as well as those for travelling – were lying in a jumbled heap on the carpet. Jane was watering these with her tears.

'What is it?' Cat said, restraining her temper with difficulty.

'A drop of wax,' Jane wailed, holding up a shoe. 'Look. Oh, mistress, I'm sorry.'

Cat took it from her. It was the left-hand one of a dark-blue pair decorated with silver-gilt thread. A small smear of wax sat on the toe, clearly visible against the blue. It was obvious that Jane had tried to remove it, for the wax was cracked and smeared, making the mark twice the size it had been.

'These are quite ruined,' Cat said, ominously calm.

'Perhaps Margaret—'

'Margaret isn't here. And even if she were . . .'

Jane credited Margaret with almost supernatural powers in anything relating to housekeeping. But this mark would challenge even her skill.

There was a knock at the outer door. 'Make them go away,' Cat said between clenched teeth. 'Whoever it is.' Jane scurried away.

'Is your mistress within?'

Cat knew the voice, this voice, all too well. Devil take it, she thought, not now, for God's sake. If only Jane had the sense to say her mistress was indisposed.

But it was too late. Marwood was already in the parlour, with Jane bleating helplessly and incoherently at his elbow. He had caught sight of her through the open bedroom door – and he must also be able to see the heap of clothes on the bed and the pile of shoes on the floor. He bowed. Cat went out to meet him, closing the door behind her.

'I'm afraid, sir,' she said, 'I'm pressed for time, and I can't receive you.'

'You're preparing for France, I suppose. Margaret told me. I hope you have a safe journey, and everything falls out as you would hope.'

It was a civil speech, but all Cat could say was, 'We shall see. But as I say, I can't spare a—'

Marwood interrupted, 'I must speak to you alone, madam.'

Without risking gossip, Cat realized, there was no easy way to get rid of him. 'Go up to the Drawing Office,' she told Jane, 'and clean the windows. But don't disturb Mr Brennan while you work.'

When she and Marwood were alone, she abandoned any lingering trace of politeness. 'This is not at all convenient, sir. I've too much to do, and I'm not sure we have much to say to each other at present.'

'This won't take long. It concerns Mr Van Riebeeck.'

'What of him?'

'I understand he called here on Sunday afternoon.'

'Pheebs can't keep his mouth shut. A porter who blabs one's business to all and sundry is worse than useless. I'll see he's dismissed if it happens again.'

'He stayed for several hours, and—'

'My visitors are nothing to do with you. Good day, sir.'

She turned, meaning to take refuge in the bedroom – he would hardly dare follow her there – and leave him to show himself out. But Marwood seized her arm.

Shock and rage coursed through her, robbing her of prudence and leaving blind anger behind. She swung round and slapped him as hard as she could.

He dropped her arm. His hand went up to his left cheek. A red stain was spreading across the skin, throwing the white of his scars into high relief.

'You should not dare to touch me, sir,' she snapped. She felt in her pocket for the knife. 'You know that as well as anyone.'

'I'm sorry,' he said, letting his hand fall to his side. 'This is important. I don't ask about Van Riebeeck for my own interest. There's a warrant for his arrest.'

229

'What of it?' She dismissed it with a wave of her hand. 'Any man can find himself embarrassed for money. Let his creditors wait.'

'This warrant has nothing to do with debt. My Lord Arlington authorized it, and it bears the King's signature.'

The fight went out of her. 'I don't understand.'

'There's certain evidence against him. He must answer for it.'

She wondered if Van Riebeeck had lied to her. Perversely, that rekindled her anger with Marwood. 'You don't like him, do you? I believe you're jealous.' The thought of Meg Daunt, all curves and simpers, came unbidden into her mind. 'Though God knows, you have no right.'

'What I feel doesn't matter.' Marwood's voice was as hostile as hers. 'He was up here until about seven o'clock. He dressed himself up to look like a servant. That means he knew someone was after him, and so did you. You took a hackney together. Where did you go?'

'Why should I tell you?'

'Because if you don't, you will leave me no choice. I'll inform my lord that you're aiding and abetting a fugitive.'

'You really are jealous,' she spat, repeating the accusation for the pleasure of seeing him wince again. 'That's rich.'

'Where did you go, madam?'

'Somerset House, if you must know. He took another hackney at the Maypole.'

'Where?'

'God knows. Now, sir. We've said all we can say. In fact, you've said more than enough. Leave me.'

They stared at each other. Marwood's cheek was still flushed from her slap. She felt the anger radiating from him like heat from a fire, mingling with her own. He bowed stiffly and left the parlour without another word.

Cat heard his steps descending the stairs. She was briefly tempted to rush out onto the landing and call him back. Instead she shut the door with a clatter. It was only then that she realized that she was still holding the wax-spattered shoe in her left hand. She flung it away from her. It bounced off the wall and fell into the coal scuttle.

She told herself that she had acted reasonably and fairly. Marwood was plainly maddened with jealousy. She wasn't even sure that she believed this story of a warrant. In any case, he had no right to interrogate her, or to be jealous for that matter – the very notion was absurd.

She herself had nothing to be ashamed of. She had acted with the utmost propriety. She had not even lied to Marwood. She had said that God knew where Van Riebeeck had gone after they had left the first hackney at the Maypole, which was no more than the truth. Marwood hadn't asked whether she knew as well as God, which meant she had not uttered a falsehood. She had simply failed to mention something, which was not at all the same thing.

And now she felt miserable as well as angry, and it was all Marwood's fault.

Pheebs was waiting in the hall when I came down the stairs from Cat's parlour. I wondered if the imprint of her hand was visible on my cheek.

'Sir,' he said. 'You know my boy?'

I paused on the last flight of stairs. 'What?' I snarled.

'Josh?' Pheebs called. 'Come here.'

I had seen the porter's boy about the place for years,

without giving him much attention. He was a young, under-nourished lad who never seemed to grow any larger. He might be Pheebs's son or just a boy he had picked up somewhere and allowed to sleep on the floor in return for running errands and doing the dirty jobs of the house.

'He knows something about that night, about the foreigner.'

I looked at Joshua directly, perhaps for the first time. There was a smudge of soft dark hair on his upper lip. He was older than I had assumed.

'Stand still, boy, and tell the gentleman.'

The boy looked attentively at the floor, as if help lay there. 'It was a different coach from before, master.' His voice wobbled from high to low. 'The one that dropped the mistress off, I mean. And I know the coachman.'

'How?'

'My aunt lives up near Bishopsgate, and I seen him there, more than once. I think he lives off Broad Street. Sir, there was someone else in that coach. I saw a hand draw back the curtain. But he didn't get out, even to help the mistress down.'

'He?'

'Aye, sir. I only saw his hand. But it was a man's hand.'

'What time was this?' I asked.

The lad wrinkled his nose. 'Not long after she left with the foreigner. Half an hour?'

'Do you know this coachman's name? His hackney number?'

'No, master. But you can't miss him – he's got a big swelling on his neck. He's often down the Maypole, waiting for a hire.'

Pheebs nudged the boy with his elbow. 'And? Eh?'

'And he's the one who brought the mistress back the other night too.'

'When?'

'Last week. That was with the foreign gentleman. You was here when they came back, master, you was just leaving. Remember?'

'Oh yes,' I said, as the facts and possibilities swirled together and made a pattern in my mind. The first hackney had been a ruse. Van Riebeeck had found another at the Maypole and doubled back to his real destination, dropping off Cat on the way. 'I remember.'

CHAPTER THIRTY-ONE

O N FRIDAY MORNING, the two girls were standing behind the summerhouse, where the overhanging roof sheltered them from the rain.

The arsenic was in the form of coarse white powder – not a clean, pure white but a white tinged with dingy grey, like linen worn too long without washing; the sort of white that will never be truly white again.

'Where did you get it?' Maria asked.

Hannah didn't answer. She refolded the paper, hiding the arsenic from sight. She drew nearer, bringing with her the smell of sweat and rancid fat. She held out her hand with the arsenic cupped in the palm. 'Here. You know what to do.'

'No I don't,' Maria said.

'Take it, you little doddypoll.'

Maria's fingers closed around the packet. She stuffed it into her pocket.

'You put some on the lion's food,' Hannah went on. 'It's a greedy devil, and it won't notice.'

'But *why?*' Maria said.

'Because,' Hannah said. 'Because I say so.'

She stared at Maria with accusing eyes, as empty of the feeling as the sky. They both knew the reason, because Hannah had already made it clear. The lion was practice for Mr Fanshawe. Practice for Maria.

Practice for Hannah, too. The habit of power was like a muscle: the more you exercised it, the stronger it grew.

Bishopsgate and Broad Street. Austin Friars was in that part of the City, its precincts nuzzling against London Wall. It was the obvious place for Van Riebeeck to find refuge.

The Dutch church was in Austin Friars, and many of the Dutch community lived nearby. Londoners hated foreigners, so they tended to cling together. The Dutch were better than the French, in the opinion of most of my fellow citizens. But that didn't alter the fact that they were foreigners, which made it impossible for a true-blooded Englishman to like or trust them. Fanshawe was an exception to the rule. His business depended on the Dutch. Last Sunday, in Slaughter Street, his servant had assumed that I was one of the gentlemen from Austin Friars, come to see the lion being fed.

I walked quickly to the Savoy and picked up Stephen. We went first to the Maypole in the Strand. I recognized one of the coachmen waiting there.

'Do you know a hackney man with a growth on his neck?' I asked. 'He comes from around Bishopsgate, I fancy.'

'Rattigan, master? Big fellow, wears an old beaver with half the brim missing?'

'Could be. A friend of mine left her glove in his coach the other night when he brought her back from Austin Friars. Is he here today?'

'I ain't seen him. When he's up by Bishopsgate, he usually looks in at the Fox in Broad Street. Do you know it, sir?'

'I will when you take me there,' I said.

Stephen and I settled inside the coach and we lumbered towards the City. The sun chose that moment to emerge from behind the clouds. I took it as a good omen. Our road went through the City, past the blackened hulk of St Paul's and into Cheapside. I lifted aside the leather curtain and looked out. It was extraordinary to see how many shops and businesses had sprung up among the ruins since the Fire nearly four years earlier. Though the main thoroughfares were thriving, they were not as busy as they had been five years earlier, and one did not have to go far from them to find the ashes and weeds and squalor that the great conflagration had left behind. It was noticeable that many citizens whom the flames had driven from the City were showing no desire to return.

We turned into Poultry and thence to Broad Street, which ran north to Bishopsgate. There were older buildings here, because this part of town had narrowly escaped the Fire. The Fox was an old alehouse next to a livery stable. Both buildings had clearly been built in the time of the old friary that had covered so much of this area. Our coachman, scenting a bigger tip than usual, escorted us inside the alehouse and conferred on our behalf with the landlord. As luck would have it, Rattigan was within.

Once found, he was happy to talk after a few coins had changed hands. Yes, he remembered the gentleman he had brought here on Sunday evening, a tall fellow whom he had seen before. He was a regular visitor at Mr Alink's house, a big old place in Austin Friars. He'd seen the young lady with him before, as well. He had dropped her off near Covent Garden, he thought, in Henrietta Street. Mr Alink was Dutch, but despite that he and his wife were well liked in the neighbourhood. They were open-handed people who treated their servants well and paid their bills on time.

'Give me a Dutchman any day,' Rattigan said, scratching the goitre on his neck. 'One of them's worth a score of them Frenchies.'

My good fortune continued. At the Alinks' house, I left Stephen in the court by the gate and instructed him to keep his eyes and ears open. Servants lived in a different world from ours, a more fluid one perhaps, and they picked up far more information about their betters than their betters realized.

I knocked on the door, gave my name and requested an interview with the master of the house. Mr Alink did not keep me waiting long, though I doubted he knew my name from Adam's. He received me in his counting house. He was a man in middle life, on the plump side and clearly prosperous. Though he was dressed soberly, in the way of Calvinists, his manner was brisk and he had a ready smile.

The smile slipped when I showed him the warrant for the arrest of Henryk Van Riebeeck. He read it slowly and then sat back in his chair. 'What's this, sir?' he said. 'I've known Van Riebeeck since he was scarcely more than a boy. I'd put my hand on that Bible over there and swear he's as upright and law-abiding as any in this city.'

'How do you know him?'

'He came to London with a letter of introduction from Mr de Witt himself.'

I hoped my surprise didn't show in my face. 'The Grand

Pensionary?' Johannes de Witt was the most powerful man in the Dutch Republic, and no friend to England.

'The same. He was an intimate friend of Van Riebeeck's late father.' Alink smiled placidly. 'But why is there a warrant for his arrest?'

I said, 'Forgive me, sir, but I can't discuss the details.' I folded the warrant and put it back in my pocket. 'You'll have to ask my Lord Arlington.'

Alink glanced shrewdly at me, trying to assess how important I was, how much I was likely to know. I returned his stare until he dropped his eyes. He was in a difficult position. His home was in London, and his business was here. He could not afford to alienate the authorities.

'I haven't seen Van Riebeeck for more than a week, I believe.' Alink frowned, giving a good impression of a man trying his hardest to oblige. 'Yes, I remember – it must have been Wednesday – the third day of the month, was it? We sometimes have a supper party with music here on Wednesdays, you see, and he came to our last one. It was an occasion of some note – we had Monsieur Grabu himself. You know him, perhaps – the Master of the King's Music? He gave us a private recital with a few of his musicians. We were quite ravished.' He shook his head slowly, as if still enraptured by the music. 'In fact' – his eyes met mine again – 'now I come to think of it, it was my Lady Arlington who forwarded my invitation to Monsieur Grabu. I am honoured to provide my lady with silks and one or two other trifles on occasion.'

It was neatly managed, these mentions of Monsieur Grabu and my Lady Arlington: Alink was warning me that he was not without friends at court; yet it was so delicately done, almost as if he were doing me a favour, that I could not take offence.

'Have you come across the Blue Bush?' I asked.

He took the sudden change of subject in his stride. 'I don't think I have. What is it? A tavern?'

'No matter. You've no idea where I might find Mr Van Riebeeck now?'

'If he's not at his lodgings – I assume you will have been there already? – then you might try Mr Fanshawe's in Slaughter Street by Smithfield. There's a family connection between them.'

'Is there? How?'

'Mr Fanshawe's late son was married to Van Riebeeck's sister. Or half-sister, I should say.'

'Mistress Abbott?' My head reeled. That explained why her face had seemed familiar to me. I had only seen her once, briefly and in poor light, when I brought Abbott home. I had mistaken her for a servant.

'Perhaps you are acquainted with the unfortunate lady?' Alink was saying. 'Abbott was her second husband, but he too has died. Van Riebeeck told me that his sister and her daughter have gone back to live under Mr Fanshawe's roof. So you might enquire after him there.'

'He's not there,' I said.

'Can you be sure that he's still in London? He goes between here and Amsterdam, you know, or even further afield. Often at short notice, if business calls unexpectedly or a passage in a ship becomes available.'

Alink might very well be right. Arlington had belatedly ordered a watch on the ports, but Van Riebeeck might have slipped through, or left beforehand.

'Was he alone when you last saw him?' I asked carelessly. 'At this recital?'

'No – he brought a charming English lady with him, a widow named Mistress Hakesby.' If Alink thought the question strange, he gave no sign of it. He chuckled. 'You'll be amused to hear that the lady follows the profession of architect and surveyor. It was her husband's business, and no doubt the journeymen do the actual work. Van Riebeeck met her through Mr Fanshawe, who is a client.'

I rose from my chair and made my farewells. I knew from Rattigan that he had brought Van Riebeeck to this house on Sunday night, which meant that Alink had lied to me. But there was nothing to be gained by confronting him with this, or not yet. I needed to discuss the next step with Arlington and receive his commands. There might be a case for searching the house, but that would need another warrant, and a group of officers to carry it out.

When I was shown out of the house, I could not see Stephen at first. I walked towards the gate and, halfway across the court, saw him talking to a gardener's boy who had been cleaning out the weeds from between the flagstones with a broken knife when we arrived. The two of them were leaning against the wall, sheltered from observation from the house by a pair of crumbling buttresses, and taking advantage of a patch of sunshine. When Stephen saw me, he broke away and came to meet me.

'There's a man staying nearby,' he murmured. 'Not here, master, he's in a cottage in the neighbour's garden at the side, beyond that wall. A tall man, quite young. He dresses like a servant, but their master visits him after dark.' He glanced back at the gardener's boy, who was still lounging against the wall. 'Yesterday he found Dick near the cottage. He buffeted him most cruelly round the ears for spying on him, but he was only looking for kindling.'

We passed through the gateway and into the street. I couldn't see much of the house next door because of the wall, a continuation of the one that separated Alink's house from the street. It was a smaller building, with tiles missing from the roof. No smoke was rising from the chimneys. Its gate was oak, hard as iron and half as old as time. It looked as if no one had opened it since the departure of the friars.

I went back to the Fox, where Rattigan was still communing with a jug of ale. I ordered him another and sat down opposite.

'God bless you, master,' he said, peering blearily at me. 'Did you find your friend, sir?'

'Not exactly. I've another question though. Do you know the house next door to Mr Alink's? It looks like no one's living there now.'

He nodded solemnly. 'Ah. Poor Mr Purser.'

'What happened to him?'

'The plague last summer. That's what did for him. And his family, and his servants. Been shut up since then.'

'Why?' Even now, houses within the City walls were at a premium since the Fire. 'There can't be any risk of infection, surely?'

Rattigan held up two stubby fingers with blackened nails. 'Item,' he intoned, touching the first finger, 'there are the ghosts . . . there are many reports of mysterious noises and lights. Item' – touching the second finger – 'Mr Purser's estate is in the hands of the lawyers, who argue which heir should have what. Item, in the meantime, the place goes to wrack and ruin. Ah, master, what fools we mortals be.'

He frowned at his fingers, as if wondering what they were doing there, used them to scratch his goitre, and then returned to his ale.

'Even lawyers must conclude their business sometime,' I said. 'As it happens, I am looking for a house in the neighbourhood on behalf of a friend. I wonder if this place would suit him? But I don't want to waste his time. Is there a way I might look more closely at it without troubling anyone? Only from the outside, and the garden.'

At this point, the goitre required another scratch, which I was beginning to recognize as a symptom of thought. 'You might try the tower, sir. Ain't been up there since I was a boy, but there used to be a fine prospect from the top.'

'What tower?'

'It's by the Dutch church. Ask for the sexton there. He'll let you have the key.'

Here it is again, I thought smugly, another instance of Providence granting me a special favour.

CHAPTER THIRTY-TWO

O N FRIDAY, CAT ordered her dinner from the cook-shop in Bedford Street. A little after midday, the porter's boy brought up the dishes to her. She was not in the Drawing Office but in her own apartments, struggling to pack her belongings. There was a letter propped against one of the dishes.

'What's this?'

'A boy brought it, mistress,' Josh said. 'He's below, waiting for an answer.'

Cat tore the letter open. The writing was unfamiliar to her.

Madam

Forgive me if, in the urgency of my passion when we last met, I spoke too bluntly for a lady's ear. I could not restrain myself. I am a plain man, and I fear I lack the graces of a lover. But you must not doubt my sincerity or my devotion. My dearest hope is that you will allow me to plead my suit anew on your return to these shores. Pray send word of your route so that I may write to you.

There was no signature. None was needed. While Cat's dinner cooled on the tray, she scribbled a few lines in reply, sealed it up, and handed the note to Josh with sixpence for his pains. When at last she sat down to her dinner, she found that her appetite had deserted her. She toyed with the food on her plate and afterwards would have been hard-pressed to remember what she had eaten.

The tower was not attached to the church but to a building in a ruinous state nearby. It was not much of a tower, but I judged it high enough for my purpose. Only the shell of the outer walls remained, with a turret attached to one corner. The internal floors had long since been removed. But a stone spiral staircase still wound its way upwards within the turret.

I mounted the steps with Stephen at my heels. We passed two empty doorways giving on to the vacancy inside the tower. There was a third at the top, where the roof had been, and where perhaps, on fine evenings, the ancient inhabitants of this place had once strolled on the leads.

The roof itself was gone, but a stone-floored ledge ran from corner to corner around the top of the tower. The neighbouring house and garden lay on the far side, though from here I could see only the tops of its chimneys. To have a better view, I would have to cross to the other side of the tower. I looked with distaste at the ledge. It was about two feet wide. Although irregular in places, where the masonry had crumbled, it seemed perfectly solid. On one side ran a parapet topped with battlements.

I glanced down, into the empty spaces below. The ground seemed very far away – unexpectedly so, the tower had looked stumpy when I had looked up at it from the ground, hardly worth calling a tower at all. A tangle of dead weeds filled the space at the bottom. I shivered involuntarily. One night, nearly four years ago, I had climbed the ruined tower of St Paul's a few weeks after the Great Fire had gutted the cathedral. My experiences there had left me with a dislike of heights that sometimes amounted to terror. I fought to bring my fear under control, telling myself I was quite safe up here.

Coward that I am, I clung to the parapet and said to Stephen as casually as I could, 'Walk over there and tell me what you see.'

He glanced up at me. His face was unreadable, as it always was, to me at least. 'On the other side of the wall?'

I nodded, and waved him off. He walked along the ledge, as surefooted as if he had been on a gravel path in St James's Park. He stopped on the far side and leant over the parapet. He turned back to me.

'I can't see anyone, master,' he said. 'There's a big garden, all overgrown, and the house over towards the street.'

'Can you see a cottage in the garden?'

He turned again. A moment later, he looked back at me. 'Yes, sir, against the garden wall beyond the house. Next to Mr Alink's. But you can hardly see it — the bushes and trees around are grown so big.'

He turned back and suddenly crouched down, bringing his head below the level of the parapet wall. He peered through the embrasure, keeping well back.

'What's up?' I said.

'Someone's down there, master. Just come out of the cottage.'

'What's he like?'

'Tall man. Like a gardener.' Stephen ventured another

245

look and then drew back again. He stared across the void that lay between us. He turned to the embrasure, and then back to me. 'Except he's got a sword. He's lunging, and parrying. He's . . . he's fighting a duel with the air.'

Bidding Stephen to lie low and keep watch on the cottage, I returned to the safety of Mother Earth. I found a hackney and commanded the coachman to drive to Whitehall. I promised the driver a double fare if he went like the wind.

Even with that inducement, the journey took me the better part of an hour. We were caught up in traffic in the Strand, where we eventually came to a complete stop. I abandoned the hackney and hurried the rest of the way to Whitehall on foot. I went straight to my Lord Arlington's office. On my way in, I met Gorvin on his way out to a late dinner. I caught his sleeve.

'Is my lord within?'

He stared curiously at me. 'What have you been doing with yourself? You look as if the hounds of hell are after you.'

'Where is he?'

'You're out of luck. He left half an hour ago. He's dining with Sir Thomas Clifford.'

'Where?'

Gorvin shrugged. 'No idea. But he should be back here by two. Why don't you come and dine with me while you wait?' He put his head on one side. 'What is all this, anyway? Why are you in such a pother? Something to do with Van Riebeeck and Fanshawe?'

I shrugged in return. I knew better than to allow Gorvin to extract a confidence from me. But he was right: there was no point in starving myself while I waited. So the two of us went off to the Axe. I didn't enjoy my dinner. It wasn't just the danger that Van Riebeeck might slip through our fingers. The thought of Stephen on top of that tower nagged at my conscience and lessened my appetite. Meanwhile Gorvin prated about the perfections of Meg Daunt.

I left my pie unfinished and went back to wait at the office, in case my lord returned early. As it happened, it was nearly three o'clock before Arlington appeared. When he entered a room, he had a way of conducting a rapid survey of it, his heavy-lidded eyes flickering from one side to the other. He saw me standing by Gorvin's desk. I executed a hasty bow in his direction. He crooked his finger at me and proceeded in a stately, though slightly wavering manner to the door of his private room. He sat down heavily in the chair behind the desk.

'My lord,' I said, 'I believe I've found Van Riebeeck. After he evaded arrest in Covent Garden, he lay low for a few hours and then went to Austin Friars.'

'Found shelter among his own kind, eh?'

'Yes, my lord. With a Mr Alink.'

Arlington frowned. 'Alink? I know the name. I believe my lady has had dealings with him.'

'Yes, my lord. He was at pains to mention that. He makes no attempt to conceal his acquaintance with Van Riebeeck. And he told me this: Van Riebeeck is the half-brother of Abbott's wife.'

My lord took an ivory toothpick and set to probing his teeth. All the while he stared at me.

'Mr Alink claims he's not seen him since last week,' I went on. 'I know that to be a lie. Moreover, he is concealing someone in a cottage in the garden of the empty house next door. This man is tall. He's dressed as a labourer or a gardener, but he carries a sword. Indeed, he was engaged in fencing exercises at midday.'

'Have you seen him with your own eyes?'

'No – but my footboy has. He's entirely reliable.'

'Has he met Van Riebeeck before?'

'No, my lord.'

Arlington grunted. 'Pity. If you had seen him yourself, the identification would be quite certain.'

I felt myself grow warm with the thought of my cowardice, my fear of heights. 'I didn't want to risk discovery.'

He caressed his chin, which was small and rounded, with rolls of fat along the sides of his jaw, and a baggy dewlap beneath. He pointed the toothpick at me. 'You shall go back with a warrant and two or three men. Send Gorvin to me, and we shall arrange it.'

To draw up a warrant and have it signed is not something that can be done in a moment. It also took a little time to summon three soldiers from the Foot Guards House in the Tiltyard to accompany me. And yet more time to set the horses to one of the government coaches kept in Scotland Yard and have it brought round to the Great Gate. In the end, it was nearly five o'clock before we left Whitehall.

It was growing colder. I cursed myself for leaving Stephen on top of the tower without considering how long I might be gone. I hoped he had had the sense to come down and find shelter somewhere.

We made better time than my hackney had done. At Austin Friars, I told the coachman to wait by the church, and the soldiers to stay inside the coach and not show themselves. I didn't want to lose the element of surprise.

First, though, I went through the churchyard and found my way back to the ruined building with its low tower. I called Stephen's name as I passed through the doorway to the spiral staircase. There was no answer.

I took the steps two at a time. The light was poor, and shadows gathered around every turn of the stairs. At the top, I stopped and looked around the parapet. It was empty. I looked again, as if my wishing hard enough to see Stephen might miraculously make him appear. But there was no one there.

Clinging to the jamb of the doorway, I lowered my head and stared into the vacant interior of the tower. At last I saw the boy. He was lying on his back, his arms and legs spread out. In the gloom of this place, I could not be sure but I fancied I could make out the whites of his eyes.

'Stephen,' I called. Then louder: 'Stephen.'

There was no answer.

CHAPTER THIRTY-THREE

O N SUNDAY, THE family at Slaughter Street attended divine service at St Bartholomew the Less because Mr Fanshawe was more comfortable with his surroundings there than at St Bartholomew the Great. Like Mr Fanshawe himself, the incumbent at St Bartholomew the Less was Presbyterian by inclination but, for reasons of convenience and material advantage, Anglican in terms of outward conformity.

The kitchen servants did not go to church at this time, for they were engaged with the preparations for dinner. For Maria, this meant two hours during which there was no possibility of Hannah's path crossing with hers. Despite the tedium of the sermon and the disapproving presence of her mother beside her in the pew, this was usually one of her favourite times in the week.

But not this week. Hannah had lain in wait for her yesterday evening. She had said nothing as Maria came in from the yard. But she had drawn a finger across her throat as Maria passed her, and her meaning had been clear enough. The lion must die.

On their way back to Slaughter Street, her grandfather offered her mother his arm. Maria followed behind with her mother's maid, who had been waiting for them in the church porch.

'My dear,' Mr Fanshawe said to Maria's mother, 'have you had word from your brother?'

'No, sir.'

'It's very strange, isn't it? I know he has some problem with the authorities at present, but surely he could have let us know where he is?'

'Henryk probably thought it prudent to leave London until this foolish business is resolved,' Mistress Abbott said. 'I believe he has a dispute with the Customs over the duty payable on some spices.'

'Perhaps my Lord Arlington might be able to smooth matters out. Could you write to my lady?'

'I'd rather not trouble them at present, sir. All this will blow over soon enough. Henryk may well be back in Holland by now.'

At that moment, as they were passing the Slaughter Stone, they heard the unmistakable sound of a roar.

Mr Fanshawe cocked his head. 'Ah,' he said fondly, 'Caliban grows hungry for his dinner. And so do I.' He glanced over his shoulder to Maria. 'We shall go and watch him eat, my love, when we have had our own dinner. Would you like that?'

She smiled and said, 'Yes indeed, sir.'

On Sunday afternoon, the Reverend Mr Hobell insisted on stopping the coach four miles outside Dover.

'You'll not regret it, madam,' he said to Cat, leaning towards her and treading on her toe again, while his wife looked on disapprovingly. 'Indeed, you will see once again the benefit of having a seasoned traveller as your guide. We shall descend for a moment and admire the prospect.'

They had just passed through a dank and dripping wood. Cat was cold, and her limbs ached. Beside her, his massive thigh pressing against her leg, was the Hobells' manservant, a large man with a small forehead and an unconquerable need to scratch himself at least once a minute.

'Put down the steps, Merriman,' Hobell ordered. 'Be quick about it.'

The servant clambered down. He and the coachman held a muttered conversation. There was a rattle as the steps were lowered. Hobell climbed out and held out his hand to assist Cat.

'Will you join us, my dear?' he asked his wife.

'No,' she snapped. 'I will not.'

'Look!' cried Hobell, waving his arm. 'There is the castle on its steep eminence overlooking the harbour. The key to England, they call it. And there is the sea. You mark that ruinous tower standing alone in the outer enclosure? Follow my finger, madam, it is the one by the sea. That is a great curiosity, the Pharos, which means—'

'The lighthouse, sir. The Romans most obligingly left it for us.'

'Indeed.' Hobell looked disappointed but recovered quickly. 'What a pity the weather is so cloudy today. On a clear day, towards evening, a man may easily see the French coast and the towers of Calais.'

Cat stared at the view, an uninviting study in shades of grey. The castle, sprawling on the flank of a hill beside the sea, was vast and uninviting. Beyond it, the sea and sky blurred into one amorphous mass without beginning or end.

'We shall see more than enough of France before we are done,' said Mistress Hobell behind them. 'There's no need to anticipate.'

'No matter.' Hobell assisted Cat into the coach. 'Perhaps we shall see it later. One can never tell – sometimes a break in the clouds will cast a temporary illumination over the scene. At least you have now seen something more of Kent. Any experienced traveller would advise you to pause now and then in your journey and look about you. It is always profitable to take a wider prospect of the country one travels through.'

They scrambled back to their seats. This was Cat's second day on the road with the Hobells. They were connected in an unspecified way with Mr Gorvin, who had arranged the passports for the whole party and a coach to take them to Dover. Mr Hobell had been invited to discuss certain theological matters of great importance with a group of Swiss divines in Lausanne, and their route would take them through Paris, where they had friends.

'You need have no qualms about placing yourself under my protection, madam,' he had assured Cat. 'I have made the journey many times before, and my wife and I will do all we can to lessen its inconveniences.'

They had left London early on Saturday morning, trundling over London Bridge in a fine drizzle. The weather had not been kind. They had spent the first night in Sittingbourne. They should have been in Dover by now, but one of the horses had cast a shoe as they were going over Barham Down.

With a jerk, the coach moved off again. When at last they

253

reached Dover, Cat was not impressed by what she saw of the town. It seemed a mean little place, lashed by the weather blowing off the sea, and fit only for fishermen and seamen. Seen at closer quarters, the castle was weatherbeaten and partly ruinous. But it was full of activity. A line of waggons stretched up the hill from the town, waiting to enter the main gate. Scaffolding masked one face of the keep, and workmen were swarming over it like seamen on a ship's rigging.

Mr Hobell had written ahead to bespeak two chambers at the Ship Inn. On their arrival, they found that one of these had been taken already by a foreign gentleman. The other was a tiny garret barely fit for a servant.

After a three-cornered negotiation between Mr and Mistress Hobell and the landlord, it was settled that Hobell and Merriman would share a bed in the chamber that already contained the foreigner, a German gentleman, while Mistress Hobell and Cat would make the best of the narrow truckle bed and a straw palliasse in the garret. Hobell ordered the luggage of the entire party to be taken upstairs.

'Stop, Merriman,' Mistress Hobell said. 'I'll have my portmanteau and box in the chamber where Mistress Hakesby and I are to sleep.'

'There's not much room up there, mistress,' the landlord said.

'I've no intention of being separated from my own belongings.' She turned to Cat and added unsmilingly, 'I'd do the same if I were you.'

They stood in silence, watching the heavily laden Merriman staggering up the stairs. Cat's luggage included the box containing the wooden model of Madame's poultry house, newly painted, gilded and varnished, as well as the calf-leather folder of plans and elevations. Cat tucked them out of sight behind the bedhead, and covered them with her travelling cloak.

The mishap on the road had meant they had missed their dinner by several hours. Mistress Hobell had an early supper sent in for them. She pronounced it execrable, but Mr Hobell reminded them that it was probably their last chance to eat good English fare for months to come.

'Believe me, madam,' he warned Cat, 'French cooking would be inedible even without the garlic they insist on using. Their inns are more uncomfortable than ours, and riddled with lice and plagued with thieves. We must make the most of our last night on our native soil.'

Mr Gorvin had arranged their passage to Calais the following morning. The party went to bed early, for they would have to rise before dawn in order to catch the morning tide. The two women climbed up the narrow stairs to the garret. It was so small that, with the palliasse on the floor and their luggage piled up against the door, Cat could only stand to her full height in the centre of the room.

Without a word being spoken, Mistress Hobell had made it clear that she was to have the truckle bed, and Cat the mattress on the floor. Neither of them undressed fully. Mistress Hobell knelt on her bed, as there was no space for her on the floor, and prayed aloud for nearly ten minutes in a quiet, determined voice that must have warned God that He would be unwise not to oblige her in whatever she asked. Afterwards she read her Bible by the light of the single candle for about twenty minutes. At the end of this, she closed the book with a bang, blew out the candle and appeared instantly to fall asleep.

The straw mattress was uncomfortable, and Cat had expected to spend a wakeful night. In the event, she fell asleep almost at once. She was only aware of this, however, when she was dragged from a deep and dreamless pit by a loud and continuous banging below, mingled with shouting. She heard Mistress Hobell stirring.

'What do you think it is?' Cat whispered.

'I've no idea,' Mistress Hobell replied. 'Some folly or other.'

She fumbled for the tinderbox and lit the candle. She struggled out of bed, opened her valise and took out what looked like a short, thick stick. She weighed it in her hand.

'I never travel without this,' she said. 'It's weighted with lead. I broke a man's arm with it in Lyons once.'

'Do you mean to go and see what's happening?' Cat said.

'No. Let the men try to sort it out themselves.'

Unfortunately the men proved incapable of doing that. About ten minutes later, as the noise below was subsiding, there were hurried footsteps on the attic stairs and a frenzied knocking on the door.

'Who is it?' Mistress Hobell said.

'My dear, it is I,' said Mr Hobell. 'Open the door! We have been attacked and robbed!'

The story poured out of him. He and Merriman had fallen asleep before the arrival of the German with whom they were to share the chamber. The reverend had been rudely awakened to find a dagger at his throat. The foreigner had tied up and gagged both Hobell and Merriman, and set to rifling through their possessions. When the man had gone, Merriman had worked his gag free and shouted for help.

'Two men overwhelmed by one, and that one a foreigner to boot?' his wife said.

'He was very strong, my love, very strong indeed, and most ruthless. He threatened to cut both our throats if we did not lie still. God be thanked, he didn't take my papers for Lausanne. I would have lost months of work.'

'But what about the money?' his wife demanded. 'The passports? The letters of exchange?'

'Fortunately, I'd taken your advice and put them in the belt you gave me. It was around my waist, and the thief did not discover it.'

'That's one mercy. Then what did he take?'

'I can't be sure, but not a great deal. My two cambric shirts are gone. And Merriman lost his purse with a few shillings in it. God has tempered the wind to the shorn lamb.'

With difficulty, Mistress Hobell persuaded her husband that there was nothing to be gained from pursuing the matter further now. Their best course was to return to their beds and get what sleep they could.

When they were left alone, the two women returned to their beds. As she lay in the dark, listening to the other woman's slow and regular breathing, Cat wondered about the robbery. The foreigner who had claimed the other bed in the room had done so before the Hobells' coach arrived in Dover. Had it always been his intention to prey upon whatever travellers chanced to join him in the chamber? If so, he had had a poor return for the risks he had run.

As Cat reached the verge of unconsciousness, she thought she heard Mistress Hobell muttering something, but so quietly it barely disturbed the air between them. Perhaps she was talking in her sleep. It was hard to be sure, but Cat thought the words were:

'Seasoned traveller? Then so is mine arse.'

CHAPTER THIRTY-FOUR

ON SUNDAY EVENING, Maria chose her time with care. Her mother and grandfather were at supper, and the servants were making everything ready for tomorrow. She unlocked the garden door and slipped outside. She stood on the step for a moment to allow her eyes to acclimatize. The night was clear. The moon was in its first quarter, its crescent sinking towards the western horizon. A sprinkling of stars pierced the darkness. In the house behind her, shutters were closed and curtains drawn.

The dog had already been let out. It came to investigate, sniffing her hand, and then the meat in her pocket, for its smell oozed through the layers of material that covered it. For a moment or two, Maria worried that the dog wouldn't leave her alone. But it was well-trained. It knew that Maria belonged here, and that it must not interfere with her, however tempting she smelt. It slipped away into the darkness, attracted by some other sound, and was soon invisible again.

'Take your time,' Maria whispered to herself, wishing that the words came from a guardian angel, standing reassuringly close just out of sight behind her. 'Nothing will go wrong if you're careful.'

Slowly the outlines of roof and walls revealed themselves. The paved path along the side of the garden was a fractionally paler shade of black than the hedges on either side. She tightened her cloak around her and took her first step, then her second, then her third. The further she went from the house, the easier it became. She passed the pavilion and continued down towards the stables at the end. The gate that led into the yard was barred. The bolts were cold to the touch and so heavy that at first she feared she would not be able to move them. She worked them loose and slowly moved them across.

Nothing moved in the stable yard beyond. The Brockmores, father and son, had long since left for the night. Maria crept across the cobbles to the door of the old stable. It was kept locked, but the whole household knew that a spare key was concealed above the lintel. Maria had to stand on tiptoe to reach it. She turned the key in the lock, lifted the latch and opened the door. The stench of the lion rolled out to her like a foul tide. She retched. She scrabbled in her pocket for a handkerchief and covered her mouth and nose.

The interior of the stable was almost entirely black. Caliban stirred when she went inside. She stopped and waited for a moment. Had it been like this the other night, nearly a fortnight ago, when Uncle Henryk had brought a man here and shown him the lion? A man with a torn handkerchief? Her mind shied away from the thought.

She stretched out one hand in front of her and took a tentative step into the dark. Step by step, she inched across the floor. She stumbled into a gutter that ran across the floor and almost fell. The lion stirred again. This time he did not settle. She could hear him moving.

Maria felt her way along the partition to the left of the door, sweeping her hand up and down in a zigzag pattern four or five feet above the ground. She felt the outline of the sliding shutter. It was such a small opening, designed for the eyes of a single spectator, that it wasn't even bolted into place. She eased it back.

Caliban was an invisible presence in the darkness beyond. She felt in her pocket for the package at the bottom. She had wrapped a piece of her own dinner, a large, fat-rimmed slice of this year's spring lamb, in a table napkin. The gravy had seeped through the cloth. It had probably left its mark not only on the pocket but on her shift as well; there would be a reckoning for that when her mother discovered the stain.

The thought of Hannah stiffened her resolve. She pushed the napkin through the opening, shook it out, and whipped her hand back to safety. Careless of the noise, she slid the shutter across to its closed position.

There was a frenzied scuffle on the other side of the partition, followed by the gobbling sound that Caliban made when he ate. God be thanked. Maria was already blundering towards the dark grey rectangle of the open doorway and the stableyard beyond, longing desperately for the warmth and safety of her own bed.

On Monday morning, the ship was underway before it was light.

Cat and Mistress Hobell had the advantage of being ill in private. The captain's cabin had already been taken by a baronet and his wife, but the two ladies had been able to secure the master gunner's for their exclusive use, albeit at a cost of ten shillings. (Mr Hobell had assumed that he would be admitted as well, but his wife had soon disabused him of this notion.)

As well as the crew, there were forty-five passengers, and most of them did not have the luxury of a cabin. The master gunner's was not large, which made intimacy a matter of necessity rather than choice, even more so than in their cramped accommodation at the inn. The ladies' boxes were lowered into the hold, but they kept their portmanteaus with them, as well as the box with the model, the Hobells' money and papers.

Mistress Hobell said they should be thankful for small mercies. Thanks to Mr Gorvin, they were on a king's ship, a fifty-ton pink with a broad upper deck to accommodate the quarter guns that formed part of its armament. Had they travelled on one of the packet-boats that plied to and fro across the Channel, or even a merchantman, they would have been far more uncomfortable and had even less space at their disposal, assuming they had been fortunate enough to secure a cabin.

The seasickness struck them both almost as soon as the ship left the protection of the harbour. Mr Hobell had assured them beforehand that, according to the captain, the weather conditions were ideal, and he had every hope that they would make a swift, smooth passage. When the swell began to toss the ship from side to side, Mistress Hobell was the first to succumb. Her example encouraged Cat to follow almost at once.

'Is it always as bad as this?' Cat gasped as the first paroxysms subsided.

'Usually it's worse. Why, once in the Bay of—'

Mistress Hobell broke off and snatched the bowl again.

After about two hours, which resembled two eternities, their seasickness abated a little, first Cat's and then Mistress Hobell's. They went up on deck, painfully and slowly. They were not troubled by their fellow passengers, most of whom were in an even worse condition than theirs.

It was better in the fresh air. For one thing, they no longer had to suffer the stench below deck. Occasionally they retched companionably over the side. There is nothing like prolonged vomiting into the same bowl to create an atmosphere of mutual confidence.

'Face towards the bows,' Mistress Hobell advised, 'and stare at the horizon. It seems to help.'

As time went by, she produced from her pocket a variety of alleged remedies that could be smelled or sucked. There were cloves, root of angelica, rosemary and even a shrivelled orange, which she shared with Cat, segment by precious segment. Afterwards both ladies were obliged to turn aside to vomit downwind, but there was little to bring up and somehow the business was more manageable in the open air.

According to a passing sailor, their passage should take between four or five hours if the wind did not change. When they were about halfway across the Channel by Mrs Hobell's calculations, her husband joined them on deck. He looked paler than usual, and his manner was more subdued.

'I was talking just now with one of the ship's officers,' he said after they had enquired after one another's health. 'He dined at the Ship yesterday. He chanced to be there when the foreigner arrived yesterday afternoon – the German thief who had the other bed in our chamber.'

'Could he describe him?' Mistress Hobell asked.

'He was very tall. An ugly rogue. He had the bearing of a gentleman, but he looked as if he'd come down in the world. The landlord told him there were no beds to be had, but the fellow was pressing, and at last the landlord agreed to set up another bed in our chamber.'

'Pressing?' Mistress Hobell snorted. 'You mean that money changed hands, I take it?'

'No doubt it did.' Her husband was looking puzzled. 'There was an odd circumstance. The man enquired who had taken the chamber first. The landlord said it was for us, Mr Hobell and party. And the stranger gave a laugh and said that in that case he would sleep more easily, knowing that he shared a chamber with a clergyman.'

'What is so odd about that?'

'The landlord hadn't mentioned that I was in orders. So how did this fellow know?'

When the Brockmores arrived at first light on Monday morning, they found their charge in a pitiable state. Caliban was lying on his side in the far corner of his enclosure. He was whimpering, and his eyes were dull and unfocused. Around him lay pools of dried vomit and loose faeces. The stench was so foul that even young Brockmore gagged.

His father sent the boy up to the house with the news. A quarter of an hour later, early as it was, Mr Fanshawe himself came down to the stable. In his haste, he had not even taken the time to dress himself fully. Holding his nose, he peered through the bars at the lion.

'Will he die?' he demanded.

'It's in God's hands, master,' Brockmore said, clasping his own hands as if on the verge of uttering an extempore prayer.

'This could hardly be worse timed.'

There were footsteps behind them. The men turned. Maria was in the doorway, wrapped in a cloak.

'Child, what are you doing here?' Fanshawe said.

Her face was very pale against the darkness of her cloak. 'What's amiss, sir?'

'Caliban's very ill, like to die. And my Lord Brouncker dines with us tomorrow. I asked him expressly to see the lion.'

Maria drew closer, with a handkerchief pressed to her face, covering her nose and mouth. Her eyes were huge and frightened. She stared through the bars. The lion's flanks were heaving up and down. His eyes flickered. She fancied he was staring directly at her from the depths of his agony, blaming her for his plight.

'Is — is he in great pain, sir?'

'I fear so.' Fanshawe glanced down at her, and his face softened. 'But animals have no souls. Which means they do not feel pain as we do.'

'Why — why is he ill?'

'Because Providence has decreed it, my love. We'll send for the apothecary. Thrumbull is a good man, and he may be able to help.'

Caliban gave a long, low moan.

'But I fear he may die,' Fanshawe said, shaking his head sadly. 'In which case, I shall have him stuffed, of course. But it won't be the same.'

CHAPTER THIRTY-FIVE

I LAY AWAKE in the long, small hours of Monday morning, just as I had done the day before, and the day before that. Each night I went to sleep easily enough — wine helped and, on the Saturday evening, the juice of the poppy. Each morning I woke with a headache and a dry, foul mouth in the stuffy darkness of my bed. However hard I tried, I could not fall asleep again. My thoughts took hold of me and whisked me around and around in their unhappy dance.

The Witherdines had hardly addressed a word to me since Friday evening. Margaret did not sing as she went about her work in the kitchen. Sam thumped his crutch on the floor as he walked, as if he were trying to hammer something to death. They heard my commands with apparent respect and they obeyed them with an uncharacteristic lack of discussion or complaint. They did not look me in the face. It was as if they feared that I might somehow blight their lives if they met my eyes, just as I had blighted Stephen's.

During the four years of their service with me, Margaret had never been with child. Insofar as I had marked the circumstance at all, I had assumed that she was barren or that Sam's seed was faulty. This had been convenient for me, in that a child would have disrupted the smooth running of my establishment.

It was only now, as I lay in the dark of my bed, that I realized that of course they had had a child of their own, and I had simply failed to notice. For the last two years, they had loved Stephen as a son. And now he was dead.

Less than three days earlier, at some point on Friday afternoon, Stephen had fallen from the top of the ruined tower at Austin Friars and landed on the rubble within its walls. It was I who had left him there to watch, who had left him there for hours. It was I who had known how dangerous Van Riebeeck could be, and I who should have known that Stephen was vulnerable in that place. The boy was sure-footed, careful and intelligent, the last person I would have expected to lose his footing.

Dear God. Why had I not taken him with me when I went to Whitehall? Van Riebeeck knew that I had a blackamoor for a footboy. When I had met the Dutchman for the first time, outside the Duke's Theatre with Cat, Stephen had been waiting for us to light us back to Henrietta Street.

Gorvin told me that there had been nothing to show that Stephen's death was not an accident. The rubble was littered with bricks and stones. It was thought that these had been responsible for the two wounds in his skull, one of which had probably caused his death.

'My lord himself has considered the matter,' Gorvin told me. 'He considers there is nothing to be gained by treating the boy's death as murder, and given the lack of evidence it would prejudice future relations with the Dutch community at Austin Friars.' He cleared his throat and looked pityingly at me. 'You do not know everything, Marwood. You should study to remember that. As the prophet says, there is a wheel in the middle of a wheel.'

Gorvin could quote the Prophet Ezekiel at me for all eternity but he wouldn't change my mind about the manner of Stephen's death. I was convinced that Van Riebeeck had seen the boy watching from the tower. He had decided to shut his mouth for ever to prevent his reporting to me. In my mind I saw the Dutchman throwing the boy from the tower and running back down the stone stairs. I saw him kneeling beside Stephen and crushing any remaining life from him with a stone or a brick. I saw the murder so vividly that I might have been hovering over them like a dark angel when the deed was done.

Unlike Gorvin, I had actually examined the body. I had seen Stephen lying on his back, his arms and legs spread out, on a bed of dead and dying weeds at the bottom of the tower. I had noted the marks on Stephen's neck and examined the back of his skull. Someone had taken him by the neck and hammered his head against a stone or a brick until it had cracked like the shell of an egg. You don't do that to a boy who is already dead.

In the long hours of darkness, night after night, I rehearsed this sequence of events again and again, as though it were performed before me on the brightly lit stage of the Duke's Theatre. So I hated Van Riebeeck with every bone of my body. And I hated myself too.

In the gathering gloom of Friday evening, I had discovered that the sexton at the Dutch church held a key that fitted the gate to the empty house next to the Alinks'. Once inside, the three soldiers and I searched the house itself, the overgrown garden and the cottage. In the latter, there were signs that someone had been staying there recently – tumbled blankets on a straw mattress; half a loaf of stale bread; a pitcher of small beer; and a broad-brimmed hat made of leather.

But there had been no sign of Van Riebeeck. The soldiers and I went next door to the Alinks' house. He denied all knowledge of Van Riebeeck sheltering in the cottage. I asked for Dick, the gardener's boy who had talked to Stephen, and Alink denied the lad's existence altogether.

He also did his best to stop me looking over his property, including his garden. He said that my warrant was not valid. I told him that these three soldiers were all the warrant I required, and if he did not cooperate with me, I would put him up against the wall of his own great chamber and have him shot in front of his wife and servants. I saw the terror leaping into his eyes. God's body, I even frightened myself almost to death.

But in the end I found no evidence to suggest that the Alinks had hidden Van Riebeeck in the cottage, and indeed nothing that showed that Van Riebeeck had ever been there at all.

The following morning, Saturday, I was at Goring House by eight o'clock, but Lord Arlington would not see me until after he had dined. He listened coldly to my account of the previous day's events. He showed no surprise. I guessed that the news had already reached him from another source.

'In sum, then,' he said afterwards, 'you have failed to find Van Riebeeck, let alone arrest him. You have caused Mr Alink a great deal of unnecessary trouble, and threatened him in his own home.'

'But he's been sheltering Van Riebeeck.'

'Sheltering him? Prove it. Alink would sue you for slander if you made that claim in public. He is a most respectable man in every way.'

'Even now he almost certainly knows where to find him.'

Arlington sighed. 'Alink is a man with many friends, and I've no desire to upset the Dutch community for no good reason. You didn't even see Van Riebeeck there with your own eyes. The whole matter rests on the word of your footboy. Who is dead.'

'My lord, the boy was murdered.' To my horror, I felt tears welling in my eyes.

'So you tell me.' He drummed his fingertips on the arm of his chair. 'But you have not a tittle of evidence to support the claim. But the boy doesn't matter. We need to lay hands on Van Riebeeck.'

'But my footboy—'

'There will have to be an inquest, I suppose,' Arlington interrupted. 'I'll see that Gorvin has a word with the coroner, and he'll make the arrangements for the burial, too. It will probably come out as accidental death. I advise you to put it out of your mind. Boys are like monkeys, Marwood. Sometimes they climb too high in the trees for their own good, and then they fall to their ruin.'

Even Stephen's body had been snatched away from the three of us who cared for him: Sam, Margaret and me.

CHAPTER THIRTY-SIX

CAT TRAVELLED WITH Mr Hobell and his party to Paris. The journey took them the better part of three days. At last even Mr Hobell fell silent, his spirits so depressed that he declined into a state of lethargic melancholy that prevented him from lecturing the ladies in his charge about the country through which they passed.

'If I were you,' Mistress Hobell advised Cat, 'I should try to sleep. You won't succeed most of the time, but at least it gives one a goal in life.'

The roads were bad. The hired coach lumbered uncomfortably through the mud, jolting over the ruts, while the travellers listened to the rain drumming on the roof. There were unexpected delays – once when the coach canted sideways into a ditch, and again when one of the traces broke. The only relief came when they stopped at the inns that lined the road, to eat, change horses and try to sleep. But there was an air of penny-pinching about the arrangements for the journey, which made it more arduous than it need have been.

'Mr Hobell prides himself on his economical habits,' his

wife told Cat. 'He says the Lord God abhors a profligate, and that the pursuit of luxury is an abomination.'

Her words were framed as an explanation, but they were the closest Mistress Hobell was able to come to apologizing for her husband.

On the road, there was more than enough time for thinking about the tall man, with the bearing of a decayed gentleman, with an accent that might have been German. The man who had robbed them at Dover.

The thief had known beforehand that Mr Hobell was a clergyman.

If Cat's letter had reached Henryk Van Riebeeck at Austin Friars on Friday, he would have known only that she was leaving for France on Saturday with the Reverend Mr Hobell and his wife. She had not told him anything about the plans for the journey. He would not have known that she was sailing from Dover or that they would be putting up at the Ship beforehand. But he might have guessed that the Dover route was by far the most likely. If he had reached the town an hour or so before them, a few enquiries would have brought him to the Ship. But that was nonsense. Why would he have followed her, if not to renew his suit?

'That robbery in Dover,' Mistress Hobell said out of the blue as they were preparing for bed on their second night in France. 'A curious business. It's as if the thief intended to rob us from the start. As if we were always his mark.'

As the journey continued, Cat found herself wishing that she could consult Marwood, despite his intolerable behaviour with that poxy little whore from the Duke's Theatre. He was a blockhead for much of the time, but he was no fool in matters of this sort. Perhaps, she thought, she had treated him too harshly recently. (On the other hand he had richly deserved it.) Nevertheless, he had helped her a great deal over the years, and he had put himself in danger for her too. However tiresome and foolish he could be, she owed him something for that.

On the morning of the third day, Mistress Hobell poked Cat's arm with her finger. 'Are you weeping?' she said sternly. 'I believe you are.'

'No, madam.' Cat sat up and sniffed vigorously. 'It's the dust. It makes my eyes water sometimes.'

They reached Paris on Thursday 27 March by French reckoning. It was raining, and the city looked dreary and tired.

'It's the seventeenth of March by rights,' Mr Hobell said, who clung as a matter of national pride to the Julian calendar still in use in England rather than the new and much more accurate calendar in use on the Continent. 'I cannot understand why the French should make matters so complicated for the rest of us.'

That same day, Mr Hobell wrote to Mr Montagu, the English ambassador, to advise them of his arrival. The latter's secretary wrote back on the ambassador's behalf to say that a coach would collect Cat from their inn at eleven o'clock in the morning and convey her to St Germain, where the court was in residence.

To Cat's regret, there would be no time for her to see the great buildings of Paris before she left. She was also sorry to see the last of Mistress Hobell.

'May I beg a favour, madam?' she asked as she was making her farewells. 'Would you send this letter for me? It may not be easy for me to arrange it in St Germain.'

'Very well.' Mistress Hobell glanced at the name and direction. 'Mr Marwood, at the Savoy. In fact we dine with a friend tomorrow who is returning to England. I'll entrust it to him to give to Mr Marwood.'

'Thank you. Allow me to defray any expenses he may have.'

Mistress Hobell took the money Cat offered her, counted it, and slipped it into her pocket. 'Don't trust anyone,' she said. 'These flouncing monsieurs are a heartless lot. They either want a woman's money or her favours, usually both.'

Her voice was harsh, and her face was stern, but she embraced Cat with unexpected warmth.

'You're a sensible woman. I'm sure you'll do very well. You must call on us when we are all back in London.' She looked directly at Cat with her sharp little eyes. 'And don't worry about that letter. God willing it will reach your Mr Marwood.'

The scale and the magnificence of Château de St-Germain-en-Laye took Cat's breath away. She was accustomed to the palaces of England: but in comparison with St Germain, Whitehall, St James and Hampton Court were no more than rambling redbrick cottages with endless unplanned extensions and unfortunate delusions of grandeur.

In fact, St Germain was not one but two palaces: an old, which reared up on the footprint of an ancient castle; and a new, a splendidly regular building which had been erected in the last century, and from which a series of terraces descended like the steps of a broad and splendid staircase to the River Seine below.

The secretary had sent a clerk to escort Cat. He was a

273

lanky, taciturn young man who toyed with the curls of his periwig and stared at anyone and anything to avoid looking at Cat. The journey of about twelve miles took them the better part of three hours, for the roads were busy, and there were many stops. Much of them took them through the forested country that lay over the invisible land like a bright green coverlet.

At St Germain, the clerk proved his worth as a guide, for the palace was vast, sprawling and unfriendly to strangers. He conducted her to Madame's apartments in the Château Neuf.

'And Monsieur her husband?' Cat asked. 'Is he in residence as well?'

'Yes.' Unexpectedly, the clerk continued without prompting. 'But you won't see much of him. He has other interests. And Monsieur and Madame do not care for each other.' For the first time he looked directly at her. 'I'd steer well clear of him if you can.'

On her arrival, Cat was shown to an apartment on the second floor of Château Neuf, with a view of the river below. It was a large chamber, though relatively modest in comparison with others in the palace. A maid had been assigned to attend her, and instructions had been left about where and when she should take her meals.

There was also a letter desiring her to wait for a summons to attend the Princess later in the day. In the meantime, Cat washed off the dust of the journey, changed her clothes and agonized over which shoes to wear. When at last that was settled, she examined the model of the poultry house to make sure nothing had gone amiss with it. She went through the folder of plans, placing the enclosures into the best order for an orderly exposition.

The afternoon had slipped into evening before a servant knocked at the door to say that she was awaited below. She went downstairs, where a stout middle-aged woman, attended by a footman, introduced herself as Madame des Bordes.

'I am Madame's waiting woman,' she announced. 'And I shall take you to her directly. But she is tired, and she may not be strong enough to see you. Good – you have brought the model. She is anxious to see it.' She indicated the footman. 'He will carry it for you.'

'Pray tell him to be careful,' Cat said. 'And I'll carry the folder myself.'

Madame des Bordes returned and led her to another part of the château, and then through a suite of three lofty apartments to a doorway, which framed a room full of people beyond. At this point, to Cat's relief, the footman surrendered the model to her. A high-backed armchair had been drawn up to face the open window. Around it, half a dozen ladies fluttered like gorgeously feathered birds in an aviary. An abbé was reading a book, his lips moving silently with the words and his beringed fingers toying with a rosary.

Madame des Bordes approached the chair, turned to face it, curtsied low and murmured a few words. She curtsied again, backed away and ordered two servants to set up a table behind the chair. Then she beckoned Cat to approach.

'Madame wishes you to place the model on the table, so she may look at it when she is at leisure.'

Cat obeyed. She placed the box on the table and opened it up. A lady standing nearby gave an involuntary gasp when she saw the model in all its glory. For an instant her distantly respectful expression slipped, and her mouth opened, as a child's does, when she sees something both unexpected and delightful.

A hand appeared over the arm of the chair. It was thin, white and long-fingered. It fluttered in the air, like the wings of a moth nearing the end of its strength. Madame des Bordes curtsied again and came back to Cat, who was still beside the table.

'You are to withdraw now,' she whispered.

'I'm not to be presented?'

'No. It is not convenient.'

CHAPTER THIRTY-SEVEN

MONDAY WAS THE third morning after Stephen's death. Unhappiness, anger and guilt can skew a man's judgement, but that morning it seemed to me that I had nothing left to lose. I summoned Sam to the parlour. He stood surly-faced in the doorway, coming no nearer than necessary in case I might infect him with something.

'We're going out,' I told him. 'I don't expect trouble, but bring your pistol. Keep it hid under your cloak. And fetch my heavy stick, and the larger dagger from the closet.'

His head snapped up. For the first time in three days, he looked directly at me. 'What's this, master? Trouble?'

'I don't expect trouble,' I said. 'It's a precaution.'

Half an hour later, when we left the Savoy, I didn't turn towards Whitehall, though my failure to appear at the office would be yet another black mark against me. But what did it matter now? My employment with Lord Arlington was already hanging by a thread. He did not forgive failure, and I expected him to dismiss me, which would probably mean I would lose my place with Mr Williamson as well, and also my sinecure as Clerk of the Board of Red Cloth. Whitehall is a marketplace for transactions of power; it places ever-shifting valuations on those who go there; and I was now damaged goods.

It was a brisk, bright day with gusts of wind blowing off the river, and a hint of spring in the air. The fine weather felt like an insult. In the Strand, I picked up a hackney. When I ordered the coachman to take us to Austin Friars, Sam muttered something under his breath. In the coach we sat opposite each other. I leant forward, so I could make him hear me without having to raise my voice over the din outside.

'I think Stephen was murdered,' I said. 'But I can't prove it.'

In the gloom, Sam's features seemed to swirl and reshape themselves into a different, crueller face. 'Who? Give me the devil's name.'

'I'll give you nothing ever again if you don't mind your manners.'

'Your pardon, master.' His voice was strained; he was clinging to his self-control. 'But who was it?'

'A Dutchman named Van Riebeeck,' I said. 'Though I can't be sure. Not quite. Not yet.'

'Do we find him then, and make ourselves sure?'

'I wish we could. But he's on the run. He gave me the slip on Friday. That's when . . .'

Sam made an inarticulate sound, half-snarl, half-sob.

'Many Dutch folk live in Austin Friars,' I said. 'One of them was sheltering Van Riebeeck. Stephen saw him there. I left him on watch, and went for help. But it took longer than I'd hoped. And when I got back . . .'

Neither of us spoke for a moment. The coach jolted noisily over the stones of the road.

'Foreigners,' Sam muttered. He drew his finger across his throat. 'That's what they need.'

The sexton at Austin Friars was an old Englishman, married to a Dutchwoman. My warrant from Arlington had been withdrawn, but he didn't ask to see it again. I asked him to lend me his key to the empty house next to the ruins in the churchyard. He went to fetch it.

'Sorry about the boy, your honour,' he said when he came back.

I nodded, dropping a coin into his waiting palm. 'You didn't hear anything over the wall, did you?'

'Not when it happened.'

His voice alerted me. 'But at other times?'

'There's been coming and going next door. Before and afterwards.'

'Who?'

'I don't know, master. I've heard voices over the wall two or three times recently. Last time was yesterday dinnertime.'

'English voices? Dutch?'

He shrugged. 'Couldn't hear. But Mr Alink's people go over there sometimes. He's got a key too.' As I was turning away, he eyed Sam's leg and the stump at the end of it. 'Land or sea?'

'Sea.' Sam patted his truncated right leg. 'Lowestoft. 'Sixty-five.'

The sexton grinned at him and raised his right hand, which had lost two of its fingers. 'Cádiz,' he said. ''Fifty-six.'

I moved aside the key. I pretended to be studying a note in my pocketbook.

The sexton lowered his voice. 'Watch yourself over there. I've nothing against the Dutch, but Alink's not a good man

279

to cross. Two of his servants fought in Flanders, and they're handy in a fight.'

'Poxy foreigners,' Sam said. 'They're all the same. Saving your wife, sir, of course.'

At first I thought the empty house was as we had left it on Friday evening after our fruitless search for Van Riebeeck. Then I noticed that someone had boarded up the side door, which the soldiers had broken down to allow us entry.

Sam and I made our way slowly through the abandoned garden in the direction of the cottage. The path was uneven and puddled with yesterday's rain. The air smelled dank and even the weeds looked dispirited, as if spring had been postponed in Austin Friars.

I had already searched the cottage on Friday. But the evening had been creeping on, and I wanted to examine it in broad daylight. It was a mean, single-storey building. The low door was not locked. Beyond it was a single chamber with an earthen floor, which lacked even a ceiling. The light came from the doorway and a small window covered in ivy. The only furnishing was a straw mattress and a crudely made three-legged stool. The fireplace was in the middle of the room. There was no chimney, merely a hole in the roof framed with smoke-blackened timbers.

While I was poking about among the rafters, Sam announced that he had a pressing need to void his bowels. I told him to find somewhere in the garden and to be quick about it.

He was longer than I had expected. Without warning, panic washed over me. I could not be responsible for another death among my servants. I took up my stick and went outside. To my relief, I saw him at once. He was hobbling rapidly towards me. But my relief gave way to alarm when I saw his face.

'Master, you'd better come.'

Without a word Sam turned. I followed him into what must once have been a kitchen garden. A tangle of fruit bushes filled one corner. There was ample evidence that Sam had already relieved himself between the bushes and the wall.

'Behind them bushes,' he said. 'Look.'

He hopped over the still steaming pile of shit. I followed. The bushes did not fill the entire corner. Behind it was a patch of waste ground in the angle of the walls, perhaps six feet by four. Some of the space was filled by yellowing cuttings from the previous autumn. But not all of it.

'Do you see, sir?' He pointed. 'Down there.'

The earth had been recently disturbed. I kicked aside some of the cuttings. The soil had been freshly turned.

'Not there. *There*.'

At last I saw what Sam wanted me to see. Something was poking out of the earth. At first I thought it was a stick.

I crouched. It was part of a hand, including a thumb and forefinger. The nails needed trimming, and they were rimmed with black. There were small toothmarks on the finger, and the skin was broken. A creature of the night had been here before us.

I swallowed back the vomit rising in my throat. I used the tip of my stick to scrape away more of the earth. The entire hand came into view, followed by the wrist that was attached to it.

Not just the wrist. There was also a grimy coat cuff, sodden with moisture. I swallowed once more. A dark coat. Purple? Dark blue, even?

Then, with a sense of history repeating itself, I said aloud, 'Mulberry.'

Sam looked blankly at me. We hadn't found Van Riebeeck but we had found Johnson.

'Dead?' Lord Arlington said to me three hours later. He frowned as though he took the news as a personal affront. 'This business goes from bad to worse.'

He and I were walking in the Privy Garden at Whitehall. He broke wind; he had come from dinner with the Duke of York, and his face was flushed with wine. He took the tooth-pick from his pocket.

'How did he die?' he asked.

'There's no mark on Johnson that I can see, my lord. His face was contorted but there was nothing to show how he was killed. His purse was gone and his pockets were empty, but whoever did it left him his clothes.'

Except, I thought, the mulberry-coloured handkerchief in the lion's enclosure.

Which suggested that Johnson had been in the house, or rather the stables, at Slaughter Street. And that tied in with the body that Brockmore claimed to have found on the Slaughter Stone on the night of the fourth of March, ten days ago. About thirty-six hours before that, I had dined with Johnson and persuaded him to search Van Riebeeck's chamber at the Blue Bush. It looked as if I had been respons-ible for his death as well as Stephen's.

'Someone took the trouble to bury him,' Arlington said. 'Why?'

We walked in silence for a moment or two.

'It must have been convenient for someone that Johnson's

body should not be found,' I said. 'It was better that he should simply disappear off the face of the earth.'

'Which brings us to Van Riebeeck.' Arlington paused by the sundial and stared at me with his protuberant eyes. 'Who else could have wanted Johnson out of the way? Everything comes back to that damned Dutchman.'

My lord jabbed the toothpick into his mouth and spat out a shred of meat. He was a man who habitually masked his feelings. But for once his control over his face had slipped. He looked desperately anxious.

'You must find Van Riebeeck,' he said. 'I cannot tell you how important this is.'

'And how is Caliban today, sir?' Maria's mother asked.

'A little better, I fancy, God be thanked,' Mr Fanshawe said, warming his hands at the parlour fire. He had just returned from the stables. 'Or at least no worse than yesterday.'

'I rejoice to hear it.'

'But his appetite remains pitiful, madam. You should have seen him pick at his meat today. It would have moved the sternest heart to tears. Brockmore brought him some pieces of young lamb for his dinner. All he could manage was a few mouthfuls.'

She looked up at him imploringly. 'Would it — would it be wrong to include him in our prayers this evening, sir?'

Mr Fanshawe smiled down at her. 'Your kind heart does you credit. Perhaps I will say something, if it would not be theologically improper.'

'How can it be wrong to pray for the relief of suffering? We are suffering too, after all.'

'A good point, well made.'

Maria's mother smiled at him and inclined her head on its long neck, as if to thank him for the compliment. Maria, sitting unregarded by the window with her head bowed over the cursed and interminable sampler, watched and listened. Her mother was habitually stern to her daughter and her servants, though in an impersonal way as if she felt it was for their own good; as if too much kindness might spoil them, and lead them into mischief, even put them at risk of damnation. But she could soften her manner and be obliging enough if she wished. She had doted on Abbott, for example, in their first few weeks together, before his shortcomings had become so painfully obvious. She loved her brother, Uncle Van Riebeeck. And she always behaved with the utmost kindness and consideration to Mr Fanshawe.

There was guile in this, Maria knew, because she and her mother were now wholly dependent on Mr Fanshawe's support. In private, Mistress Fanshawe, as she now called herself again, sometimes addressed him as 'Father'. She made sure that his house was run with exemplary efficiency. She served him the choicest morsels at table, and placed his personal comfort above everything else. She would listen by the hour, and with every sign of interest, to Mr Fanshawe's disquisitions on his collection and the state of the world, however often she had heard them before.

'Father,' she said after a moment. 'Pray, may I beg a favour of you?'

He raised his eyebrows. 'What favour?'

Mistress Fanshawe moistened her lips. 'It concerns Swaring.'

'You wish to send Maria there? I've had the same thought now and then, as you know. It's a very healthy spot.'

'Not Maria, sir. Or not at present. My brother.'

'Your *brother?*' The placid expression vanished abruptly from Fanshawe's face. 'My dear Anna, there's still a warrant out for him.'

'Yes, sir, but it's only some trumped-up affair over a debt or two. But it makes it hard for him to take ship to the Continent at present, or to stay in London. But if he could rest a while at Swaring, which is quite retired, and no one knew where he was to be found – why, that would be another matter. His affairs would arrange themselves in due course. All he needs is a little time.'

CHAPTER THIRTY-EIGHT

THE DAYS SLIPPED by without a summons.

Madame was surrounded by scores of servants, by ladies-in-waiting and maids of honour, by priests, clerks and doctors, and by numberless men and women whose purpose was mysterious. Somewhere at the heart of all this activity was Princess Henriette Anne, Duchess of Orléans, the second lady of France after the Queen. On two occasions, Cat glimpsed her from afar. She looked like a small, thin doll decked out in magnificent clothing; more a plaything than a woman.

Yet Madame was clearly no cipher in her own household or at Court. Her people were fiercely loyal to her. The King himself was said to have been Madame's lover at one time, though she could not be said to conform to the usual standards of beauty that were admired at Court. He was now her close and loyal friend; everyone knew that he valued her opinion highly on affairs of state; he had given her an apartment close to his own in the Vieux Château because he regularly took counsel with her there.

The Princess's popularity was a mystery to Cat, who as time passed felt increasingly irritated by her lack of interest in the poultry house. On the third day, she begged the favour of an interview with Madame des Bordes. In the afternoon, they walked along one of the terraces below the Château Neuf.

'Tell me, madame,' Cat said in her careful French, 'when will Madame find it convenient to receive me?'

Madame des Bordes shrugged her heavy shoulders. 'That I cannot say. Or even whether she will desire to see you. Madame has not been well. Also, she has many calls on her time. At present the King sees her almost every day. He wants her to go to England, to conclude some business for him with the King her brother. And . . .'

'Yes?' Cat prompted, pausing by the stone balustrade at the head of the flight of steps. She stared out over the river.

There was another shrug. 'And Monsieur her husband desires her company more than usual, often when it is not convenient.' A third shrug. 'But what Monsieur wants, Monsieur gets.'

They turned and made their way slowly back along the terrace. Madame des Bordes asked Cat about the Court at Whitehall — was it really such a shabby, old-fashioned place as people said? Did King Charles really force his poor wife to take his mistresses as her ladies-in-waiting? Had the whole city been razed to the ground by the Great Fire?

Gossip is a great leveller. As they talked, Madame des Bordes lost some of her stately mannerisms. Her plain, creased face grew animated. Once she even gave Cat's arm a playful tap with her hand. When they parted a quarter of an hour later, she acknowledged Cat's curtsy with a smile and an inclination of her head.

'Take comfort, my dear,' she said as she was leaving. 'Madame keeps the model of your *maison de volaille* close to hand. And I have seen her looking over the folder of plans you left for her. You are not forgotten.'

There were no letters from England to lighten the tedium. Nothing from Brennan, nothing from Marwood, nothing from Van Riebeeck.

At night, Cat dreamed twice of Van Riebeeck, of encountering him unexpectedly, and in situations where there was no way to avoid him; and on both occasions she woke with a start and found her heart racing uncomfortably. At night, when her powers of reason were at their weakest, Cat even wondered whether Henryk Van Riebeeck had paid a witch to lay a spell on her.

One morning, Cat went up to her bedchamber and took out her notebook. Sitting by the window, she sketched out the ground plan of a mansion, the lines of ink flowing easily and rapidly over the paper. She drew the four facades of the house, and made separate drawings of the architraves of the doors and windows.

The bell rang downstairs, the signal for dinner. Only then did she realize that she had been at work for nearly three hours. After dinner, she came back and started work on a church, a stately affair with a dome at its crossing.

She slept better that night, and for the first time since coming to France, she did not dream of Van Riebeeck or wake with him in her thoughts.

The following day, she drew the plan of an entire city

along the banks of a broad river that curved around one side of it like a sheltering arm. What it must be, she thought, to have a free hand on a site where no one had ever built before. In the Americas, she knew, there were vast, virgin territories where no one had ever put a spade into the earth. Here, she thought, architects would be able to create future cities untrammelled by those of the past.

In the morning of Monday, 7 April, the tenth day after Cat's arrival, a page in the Orléans livery brought Cat a note from Madame des Bordes. She was to present herself at eleven o'clock at the door leading to the Princess's private apartments here in the Château Neuf.

Cat was before her time. She had been expecting to have to wait, quite possibly for hours, or even to be sent away without seeing Madame at all. But the guard marked her name on a list and immediately summoned a footman, who had clearly been sent to escort her. She was led through an enfilade of enormous and gorgeously decorated rooms which outdid in splendour anything she had yet seen in France.

Madame des Bordes was waiting in an anteroom. Behind her, two footmen stood, one on each side of a doorway. She held her finger to her lips.

'Madame slept badly last night, and she's in pain again as well. But she commanded me to bring you to her as soon as you came.'

The footmen noiselessly opened the leaves of the door. Madame des Bordes glided forward and stopped in the doorway.

'Entrez.'

The voice was soft and low, the words almost inaudible.

Cat followed Madame des Bordes. She found herself in a bedchamber the size of a small church. There was a great bed set on a low platform within an alcove. Beside it was a crucifix and a prie-dieu. At the foot of the bed, below the platform, cushions had been piled up beside a richly decorated marquetry table. The poultry house sat on the table, and Madame sat, swathed in silks, on the cushions. She looked like a potentate in an Arabian tale.

Cat and Madame des Bordes curtsied. Cat made a swift survey. The three of them were alone in the room.

The cushions billowed around Madame; they seemed in danger of swallowing her up. 'Madam Hakesby. I am glad to see you. I hope you have not found the delay too tedious.'

'No, Madame,' Cat lied. 'Not at all.'

'I am sure that's untrue. But a polite untruth, so it's forgiven.' The Princess smiled up at her, her lips parting to reveal her own teeth, which were small and well-formed. 'Your poultry house is delightful. Lord Arlington writes that you have already designed one for his daughter.'

'Yes, Madame. Though yours, if it is built, will be twice the size, and . . . and suitable for a princess of the blood. Naturally.'

The Princess laughed, though not maliciously. 'Very nicely put. But let us talk in English now. My English is very bad, but I have a particular desire to practise it, as I shall go to England soon. Besides, it's my native tongue, when all is said and done, and I should speak it more. My brother tells me that my letters to him should be in English, for that reason.' Her lips twisted and then curled up into a smile. 'He is very strict with me.'

Cat found that she was smiling back. 'As you wish.'

'To be frank, I was curious to see you. I have encountered many architects, but never one who was a woman. Are there many like you in England?'

'If there are, Madame, I haven't met them. But there are certainly women in England who have an interest in architecture. My aunt was one. She and my uncle travelled much in France and Italy when they were younger . . . And then my husband was an architect; he had worked with Inigo Jones in his youth . . . but forgive me, Madame, my tongue runs away with me.'

'I shall tell you when you need to rein it in. For the present you do very well as you are. You're a widow, yes? That's sad in one so young. If I may hazard a guess, when your husband died, you decided to continue his business on your own account?'

'Yes.'

'Will you marry again, do you think?'

'I have no desire to do that at present, Madame.'

This earned a quick, assessing glance. The Princess's eyes were small but very blue, like chips of sky. She raised her hand, and Madame des Bordes rushed forward to help her rise. Silk shawls fell away from her as she rose. When she was on her feet, she steadied herself for a moment, holding the other woman's arm for support. The lines on the long, narrow face had deepened. She drew in her breath sharply.

'Madame . . .?'

'I am perfectly all right.' The Princess pushed away the protective arm of Madame des Bordes. One of her shoulders was higher than the other. She turned to Cat.

'We shall look at the plans together. I have an idea for the facade to the south. Pray set them out for me there.'

She indicated a second table, larger than the one on which the model stood, that was at right angles to a window. Cat carried the folder to it, and laid out the plans and drawings.

Leaning on the arm of her lady-in-waiting, Madame approached the table. Her hair was tied up, but the ribbon restraining it had come loose, releasing a rich, chestnut-coloured strand of hair that swung as she moved. She was wearing a belted bedgown over what looked like a shift; there were slippers on her feet. In such informal attire, Cat thought, she would not have received an architect who was a man.

Madame rested her hand on the table, partly for support, and drew the drawing of the south facade towards her. 'I have in mind a particular spot at Saint-Cloud. You know this château? It is outside Paris, and on the Seine. Monsieur my husband . . .' She paused and swallowed. 'Monsieur has many plans for it. But I have a private garden, with a wall around it, where my daughter – my elder daughter, that is – takes exercise with her nurse. I shall build our poultry house at the end of that, on the far side of a stream. It has a grassy bank beside it. My daughters can sit there and watch the fowls go about their business.'

'I'm sure they will find it diverting. I know my Lord Arlington's daughter does.'

'So.' Madame tapped the sketch of the north elevation, which was where the main entrance was. 'That will look over the stream, towards the bank where my daughters will be. What if we added a loggia, with columns supporting the roof, running east from the main building? Not so very high . . . A yard above the ground, shall we say? Perhaps the poultry will entertain themselves there if the weather is inclement, or take the air in its shade when the sun is hot.'

'A loggia would be both decorative and practical,' Cat said diplomatically. It would also run counter to any notion of symmetry and create a strikingly eccentric addition to a building that had previously been chastely elegant. 'Would you permit me to sketch it in my notebook now? And then, if it is agreeable to you, I will work up a more detailed design.'

'Do so.' The fingers fluttered. 'I'm weary now. I shall take your arm.' Supported by Madame des Bordes on one side and Cat on the other, she returned to the heap of cushions, where she subsided gracefully. 'Pray turn the model round so it faces me. Then we can see where this loggia will go.'

Cat rotated the model through ninety degrees. It was only then she noticed that the base had been damaged. Or rather that it had come apart: it seemed to be formed of two separate layers. She gripped the lower layer and tugged gently. It slid out easily, as if on runners. A shallow, rectangular depression had been cut into the thickness of the wood. It was less than half an inch deep.

At that moment she recalled the evasive manner of the cabinetmaker in Scotland Yard. She had accused him of making the base of the model too thick. He had insisted that he had followed the measurements given him by Mr Gorvin.

Measurements? Or instructions to make a secret compartment in the base?

'Show me where the loggia will be,' Madame said.

Cat indicated the line and shape of the loggia.

'Draw it for me. There's pen and ink on the desk.'

She took out her notebook and made a rapid sketch of the outline.

'Show me! Show me!' Madame beckoned her to approach.

293

'Yes, that's perfect. You are quick with a pen, are you not? May I look at your other designs?'

Cat had no choice but to surrender the notebook. Madame turned the pages slowly, examining the imaginary city, the church with the dome and the mansion.

When she was done, she closed the book and handed it back to Cat. 'I wonder . . .' She looked up, and she was frowning again. 'Did you mind my looking at that? Perhaps – for an architect, like you – such things are private? Like thoughts sometimes are: they are half-formed things, not ready to be turned into words.'

Cat had minded. 'Not in the slightest, Madame.' But as she spoke, she found that she no longer did mind. If anything, in fact, she was flattered.

'I want you to design something else for me,' Madame said. 'Something larger. By far.'

CHAPTER THIRTY-NINE

NOW THAT SPRING was here, the smells of blood and excrement were much stronger. The livestock market was now fully open after the lean winter months. When the wind was from the east, it carried not only the smells but the sounds of Smithfield towards the windows of Mr Fanshawe's house. It brought the cracking of whips and the grinding of waggon wheels into the great chamber and the kitchen, as well as to the garden and the old stable. It brought the neighing of horses, the groaning and bellowing of cattle, and the grating protests of numberless sheep.

Maria thought that the din sounded for all the world like a great battle. This year there was a new voice to be heard among the others. Caliban would stagger to his feet. He paced about his enclosure, sniffing the air. Sometimes he lifted his head and roared. His sickness had passed, but he was listless.

After the beasts were sold, some were driven off on behalf of their new masters. Others were killed and disembowelled on the spot. Rain or shine, the stones of Smithfield were slippery with blood. The entrails of the slaughtered beasts were cast into the gutters, where they provided a feast for dogs and birds and rats and all the vermin under heaven. Brockmore's son sometimes brought back a bucket or two of the more edible refuse for the lion.

Nowadays, whatever had been the case in the past, Slaughter Street itself was blessedly free of this traffic of the living and the dead. But the smells remained, and the noises of the market. And the smell of fresh blood still had the power to work its dark magic on Caliban.

'Now what would happen, I wonder,' Mr Fanshawe mused in a spirit of philosophical enquiry, 'if Caliban broke free and ran amok through the market? Now that would be a sight to see.'

'But he might kill us, sir,' Maria pointed out.

It was a fine, brisk April morning. She and her grandfather were standing in the stable, looking through the iron gate at Caliban, who was lying along the wall opposite them. His hollow flank slowly rose and fell. He watched them with sad, dull eyes. The wind was from the west, and without the sounds and smells of the market to goad him into action, he was lethargic.

'I believe he knows us to be his friends,' Mr Fanshawe said. 'He would not attack us. After all, we feed him and house him. But I wish he were stronger. Thrumbull swore by his physic but it has not answered. His vital powers decline.'

The apothecary had mixed another purging electuary, with the addition of aqua mirabilis, efficacious for almost all maladies, and a mixture that included white henbane, cassia lignea and opium against the pain. Thrumbull had recommended bleeding the lion as well, but no one was prepared to undertake this task. The purging had certainly been effective as far as it went. But afterwards, Mr Fanshawe observed, the electuary appeared to have left Caliban even weaker than before.

He was deeply touched by Maria's interest in his lion. He had been fond of his granddaughter before, mainly because she was the only person of his own blood left alive. But her concern for Caliban's health had increased his affection for her. This pleased Maria's mother, because their future prosperity depended on Mr Fanshawe's goodwill.

Hannah said the dose of arsenic had been too small to do the job properly. She didn't ask Maria to try again. Perhaps she had run out of arsenic and not been able to steal any more.

'I wonder,' Mr Fanshawe said. 'If I offered to double his fee, would Thrumbull come and bleed him?'

'I fear it might not help, sir.'

Footsteps entered the yard behind them. Mr Fanshawe's manservant appeared in the doorway of the stable.

'What is it now?' Fanshawe said peevishly.

'Your pardon, master. Mr Marwood's called again. He begs the favour of a word.'

'Tell him I'm not at leisure.'

The servant cleared his throat. 'He – he's most pressing, sir, and comes from my Lord Arlington. I said you were engaged, and he said he would wait. He's in the hall.'

Mr Fanshawe sighed so loudly that Caliban raised his head to stare.

Maria accompanied her grandfather back to the house. She waited until she heard him entering the hall. She slipped down the passage and climbed the short flight of stairs up to the gallery. In the room below she heard her grandfather's voice, speaking in a slow and stately drone, as he often did to impress, particularly with strangers and with those he did not care for.

Crouching, Maria edged towards the front of the gallery.

'Forgive me if I sound unwelcoming, sir,' Mr Fanshawe was saying with a marked lack of conviction, 'but I've many urgent calls on my time this morning. Pray be brief.'

'My lord sent me to enquire again if you have had news of your kinsman, Van Riebeeck.'

'Sir, I have told you before, he is not my kinsman. He is the half-brother of my daughter-in-law.'

'Your kinsman by marriage then, sir.' Marwood sounded exasperated. 'Well? Have you seen him? Or heard anything from him, or about him? Has Mistress Abbott?'

'She prefers to be called Mistress Fanshawe again, sir, now she has returned to live in my house. I regret that I cannot help you, and she will not be able to either.'

'Where do you think he might be?'

'How should I know? I'm not his keeper, sir, any more than you are mine.'

Marwood said, so softly that Maria had to strain to hear his words: 'May I remind you that there is a warrant for Van Riebeeck's arrest, and I come here with the King's authority? His Majesty himself is most concerned in this matter.'

'I'm sure it's some foolish misunderstanding.' Mr Fanshawe sounded less stately now. 'Mr Van Riebeeck will no doubt explain all when he returns.'

'It's difficult to explain away murder.'

'Murder? You jest, sir.'

'I fear not.'

'Why would he murder anyone? And who?'

'I'd like to ask him that myself, sir,' Marwood said. 'Good day to you.'

CHAPTER FORTY

ONE OF MADAME'S secretaries took down a list of Cat's requirements. ('Ask for whatever you need,' Madame des Bordes advised. 'If Madame wishes something to be done, she does not mind a little expense.')

Madame desired Cat to design her a palace. She called it a palace, but Cat was wise enough to realize that what was expected was no more like a palace than a Dissenters' chapel is like Canterbury Cathedral.

The morning after her meeting with Madame, Cat was conducted to an apartment in the Château Neuf which had been set aside for her to work on the designs undisturbed. It was larger than the Drawing Office in Henrietta Street. North-facing windows flooded it with light. It had already been equipped with two drawing slopes, together with tables, stools and chairs, with presses and shelves. Paper of all sizes and qualities had been provided for her, together with all the implements an architect could desire for the pursuit of her profession. She was to send down to the librarian if she wished to consult any books.

There were servants on call, too: a boy to mix the inks, trim the candles, run errands and keep the fire burning; a maidservant to sweep the floor, empty the pot in the closet, and bring food and drink from the kitchens; and even a draughtsman who stood before her, hat in hand, and begged to know how he might be of assistance.

Cat sent away the draughtsman, saying that she would call him when she required his services. She told the maid to come every morning, before breakfast, and make the place clean. She kept on the boy, who made himself useful when he was needed and made himself scarce when he was not.

The building took shape in her mind. Madame had a location in mind for it, an estate the King had given her, not far from St Cloud. The house was to stand on an eminence, a platform that would be at least partly manmade if nature did not oblige them completely. It would take the form of a hollow square. On the south side, there would be a broad terrace, below which the formal gardens would gradually descend, with four fountains, arranged in pairs, each leading the eye to a pavilion.

One day after dinner, Madame des Bordes arrived. She stood in the doorway and looked about her. She shrugged, managing to convey that some things are beyond human understanding. Then she smiled, which made her look more like a concerned aunt than a stately lady-in-waiting.

'Madame sent me,' she said. 'She asked me to make sure you are content with this.'

'Thank you, yes.'

'You are already at work, I see.'

'I have all I need, so there's nothing to hinder me.' Cat

gestured around the room. 'It was provided so quickly. It's a miracle.'

'Madame sometimes has the power to do miracles. But she must not be kept waiting.'

'When will I see her again?'

A shadow passed over the face of Madame des Bordes. 'I don't know.'

Cat looked up, alerted by something in the older woman's voice. 'Is Madame ill?'

Another shrug. 'She's never been strong. The birth of her second daughter set her back last summer. And there have been other pregnancies.' There was a pause. 'She has much to bear.'

When Cat was left alone, her pen resumed its journeys across the paper clipped to the drawing board. Minutes turned to hours, and hours into days.

'Monsieur went with the army to Flanders last year,' Madame des Bordes said. 'Not that he had time to do much fighting. He and his beloved friend the Chevalier were too busy choosing the best chandelier for his tent.'

There was a sour expression on her face, which nature had designed for smiling. She had taken to visiting Cat on most days, usually after dinner, ostensibly to enquire about progress and to ask if there was anything she required for her work. Sometimes she lingered to talk, or even to sit quietly by the window. She desperately needed a confidante, Cat realized, someone who did not matter, someone who did not belong at Court and who would not be there for long.

It was no secret that Monsieur loved his intimate friend the Chevalier de Lorraine above all things and above all people, including Madame. According to Madame des Bordes, the Chevalier was a monster whom God had seen fit to give the face of an angel. He persecuted Madame relentlessly. True, the King had exiled him, after an episode in which the Chevalier's spite had outrun his prudence. But even from afar, he exercised his baleful influence on Monsieur and nursed his hatred of Madame.

'Take this question of England,' Madame des Bordes said. 'Madame longs to see her brother again. It's her heart's desire. The King wants her to go, for reasons of state and brotherly love for a fellow monarch. But Monsieur her husband forbade it. Purely to spite her.'

'So she won't go to England?' Cat was making a copy in ink of a triumphal arch that at present existed only as the merest sketch. 'Because of her husband?'

Madame des Bordes shrugged. 'His Majesty has overruled Monsieur. At last. But then what does Monsieur do? He comes to lie with Madame every night. The King can do nothing about that. Even he cannot prevent a man from lying with his wife.'

'But why, if he hates her so much?'

'In the hope of making her with child again.'

'Ah. In which case she couldn't go to England?'

'But Madame hasn't recovered from her last confinement,' Madame des Bordes wailed. 'She's not strong. Monsieur is a brute, and has been for years. But Madame bears it all with the fortitude of a saint.' She crossed herself, and then whispered, 'I know it's a sin, but I wish someone would take a dagger and plunge it into his breast. Because that's the only way this will stop.'

Cat looked up, surprised by this lurch into tragedy. 'Surely

303

not. Monsieur can't be spiteful for ever. For one thing he won't want to offend his brother.'

'You don't know Monsieur,' Madame des Bordes said. 'Believe me, unless he is lying in his grave, one way or another he will be the death of Madame.' Her face twisted with anxiety. 'I swear to you, he will kill her.'

CHAPTER FORTY-ONE

I T WAS SUCH a fine morning that Pheebs opened the
street door. He stood on the step and leant against the wall.
The sun was warm on his face. He scratched himself with
languid satisfaction while the world passed up and down
Henrietta Street. Soon it would be time to leave the door in
the charge of the boy and slip away to the alehouse in Half
Moon Passage.

He recognized a face he knew approaching from the direction of Bedford Street. It was Mistress Witherdine, Marwood's
servant. He eyed her up and down with qualified approval.
Broad in the beam, and not much in the way of a pretty face.
But a fine pair of eyes, nonetheless, a high colour, a spring
to her step, and breasts to make a man weep with joy. He
would happily take a turn or two with her between the sheets
if she were not also such a shrew.

'Well, then.' She had drawn herself in front of him. 'Are
you going to step aside and let me pass or not?'

Pheebs moved to give her room, but only just, leaving a
sporting chance that a passing breast would brush against his

arm. She stared up at him in silence until he stepped further away.

'That's better, sirrah.'

Margaret walked briskly upstairs. She had a low opinion of men in general, her husband included, but God had ordained that there should be degrees in this, as in all things. Pheebs was the lowest of the low.

Mistress Hakesby had asked her to visit her apartments occasionally while she was away in France. Brennan was coming into the Drawing Office every day, but the private chambers were on the floor below and he went there only by invitation. Jane Ash, who had been sent to live with her mother in Cat's absence, was supposed to come in every day to air the place and to mend and clean the summer hangings and bed curtains.

Usually Margaret came after dinner, in the afternoon lull when the main work of her day had been done. Today, however, she was early. As she approached the door of the parlour, she heard slow, clumping footsteps within. She paused on the landing to listen. First the steps went one way. Then they stopped. Then they resumed. It was as if the person inside were walking from one side of the room to the other, and pausing occasionally for refreshment.

Margaret opened the door and flung it wide. Jane Ash was in the middle of the room, frozen in mid-step. She was wearing one of her mistress's bodices, which compressed her small, scrawny body even further than it was already. On her feet was a pair of Cat's shoes, made of soft open-work leather lined with silk, with sharply tapering heels. The shoes were too large for Jane. At her neck, covering that place where her breasts would have been if nature had yet seen fit to provide them, was a kerchief edged with a broad band of lace.

'And what do you think you're doing?' Margaret said softly.

Jane stared at her. She opened her mouth. No words came out. She closed it again, and the colour flooded her pale cheeks, blotting out the freckles.

Margaret advanced, her hand raised. Both of them knew that while she was away Mistress Hakesby had lent her authority to Margaret. It was in her power to give Jane a beating, or even to discharge her.

As she drew closer, the kerchief caught Margaret's eye. Or rather the lace that bordered it. You had only to step down to the Strand and into the New Exchange to see how inadequate that simple word, lace, was to describe the range and quality that the word embraced. Margaret saw at a glance that this lace was exceptionally fine, probably Flanders work, made as a single piece from the most delicate linen. It was not the sort of lace that should be worn by an honest fifteen-year-old servant girl who earned, at best, three pounds a year in wages, most of which went to her mother.

'And where did you get that, you thieving baggage?'

'I – it was a present,' Jane wailed, her hand flying to her chest as if to protect the lace. She stumbled backwards, leaving the shoes behind, one on its side. 'I didn't steal it, God's my witness.'

'Who would give a girl like you something like that? What did it cost? Ten shillings? A pound, even?'

'I don't know . . . but he gave it to me.'

'Who did?'

'The Dutchman.'

Margaret's hand shot out. She seized Jane by the neck and shook her violently. 'What Dutchman?'

Jane's legs gave way. She crumpled to the floor, where she lay sobbing with her face in the carpet, a quivering huddle of borrowed silk and whalebone, leather and lace.

After my fruitless visit to Slaughter Street this morning, I had business on my lord's behalf with the captain of a merchantman lately returned from Russia; he had intelligence of Dutch warships manoeuvring in the German Ocean, about ten miles east of Lowestoft. Believing me to be of more importance than I was, he gave me a very good dinner at Lockett's, by Charing Cross.

Afterwards, rather later than I had intended, I called at my house to collect some papers I had left there. Sam opened the door at my knock. To my surprise, Margaret was waiting in the hall with him.

'Thank God you're here, master,' she blurted out.

She rushed towards me with such enthusiasm that I had the odd notion that she was about to embrace me. Since Stephen's death, nearly a month ago, she had barely said a word to me except in answer to a direct question. She stopped abruptly about a yard away from me.

I looked from one to the other. Both their faces were unnaturally grave.

'It's that Dutchman,' Margaret said. 'The arrant devil.'

'Who? Van Riebeeck?'

Hands on hips, Margaret told me what she had learned from Jane Ash. I was aware that Margaret occasionally went to Henrietta Street to advise Cat on matters of housekeeping but I had not realized the regularity of these visits, or that

Margaret was acting as a caretaker of the apartments in Cat's absence. It disconcerted me and, on another occasion, it might well have angered me, for the Witherdines were my servants and they owed their duty to me alone.

But all that flew out of the window now. Despite her cold anger, Margaret was clear enough in what she said. Van Riebeeck had intercepted Jane in Covent Garden as she was walking to Henrietta Street from her mother's lodging in a yard off Bread Street Hill in the City. She knew him as the friend of her mistress and therefore had no reason to distrust him. Van Riebeeck could be charming enough to a woman if he wanted to be, as I knew to my cost. That, and a most extravagant present of lace, had made Jane his creature. He told her that Mistress Hakesby had given him her itinerary before she left for France, so that he might write to her, but he had mislaid the paper. No doubt she had left a copy of the itinerary at Henrietta Street, and he begged to have a sight of it.

'Jane meant no harm, I'm sure, but she has no more wit in her head than a Bethlem halfwit.'

'What is this itinerary? Do you have it?'

Margaret had anticipated this. She produced a grubby paper from her pocket and gave it to me. When I saw Cat's writing, it took me unawares; it was like unexpectedly catching sight of a friend's face in a crowd of strangers.

Here was information she had seen fit to share with Margaret and Jane Ash, but not with me – though why should she have done? I learned from the paper that she was travelling to Paris in company with the Reverend Mr Hobell, his wife and manservant, and that Mr Hobell had written ahead to reserve rooms for himself and his party at the Lion

309

in Sittingbourne and the Ship in Dover. Their accommodation on the road in France could not be booked ahead, as the time of their crossing was dependent on the weather, which was particularly uncertain at this time of year. Any letters to her should be addressed to Mr Dodington, at Mr Montagu's house in Paris, who would know where to forward them; Montagu was the English ambassador, and Dodington his secretary.

'When did Jane let him see this?' I asked.

'Just after Mistress Hakesby left, sir. The very day.'

Mr Hobell and his party would have travelled by coach to Dover. If Van Riebeeck had gone after them, he would have had plenty of time to overtake them on the road. Or to send word ahead that they were expected.

The question was, why had he taken the risk of approaching Jane Ash in a public place like Covent Garden? He knew there was a warrant for his arrest. Looked at another way, the fact that he had been prepared to run the risk argued that he had a pressing need to discover Cat's whereabouts. My jealous mind ascribed that to a lover's passion. But I retained enough wit to realize that Van Riebeeck was not the sort of man who allows himself to be ruled by his lusts. He had been playing a different game, one of sufficient importance to him to make it worth his while to commit two, possibly three murders.

'There's more,' Margaret said.

I looked sharply at her. 'She's seen him again?'

'Yes, master. Just once. It was when she was going back to her mother's house a few days later. Jane saw him by Puddle Wharf. He'd landed at the stairs, and he went into a house by St Andrew Wardrobe churchyard. On the side nearest the river, she said. There was an old sail over part of the roof. And a pig in the yard in front.'

'Very well.' Anger boiled inside me, and my words seemed to spurt like pus from a squeezed spot. 'Bring my old cloak. And the weighted stick, and the big dagger.'

'If you're going, master,' Sam said, 'I'm going as well.'

I nodded. 'With your pistol. And your cutlass.'

Margaret looked at me and then at her husband. She was a prudent, cautious, law-abiding woman, fiercely protective of her husband. 'If you find that Dutch devil,' she said, 'make the wretch suffer.'

CHAPTER FORTY-TWO

HOWEVER MUCH I tried to ignore it, my upbringing among Dissenters, and in particular my father, had bred within me an inconvenient habit of self-examination.

I had time enough to contemplate my actions, past and future, as we were rowed down the river from the Savoy Stairs. Part of me was horrified by my own folly. The sun was bouncing off the water and making it sparkle. The sky was a clear, fresh blue, with a chain of small clouds sailing northwards like a fleet in search of new worlds to conquer. Sam had turned his head away and was staring at the Surrey side of the river.

I should have gone directly to Henrietta Street and questioned Jane Ash myself. I should then have gone to Whitehall to lay this new information before my Lord Arlington, for him to do with it as he thought fit. Instead my crippled servant and I had set off like a pair of impetuous children on a forbidden jaunt. But impetuous children do not usually hope to kill a man.

God alone knew what my lord would do if he learned what

I was about. His business – which was probably the King's business too – had something to do with that fragment of paper with the ciphered letter on it, and with the files that Richard Abbott had taken home with him. Van Riebeeck was at the heart of this mystery. Whatever it was, I knew it must be an affair of state, and one of great moment. It had almost certainly cost Jeremiah Johnson and Richard Abbott their lives. But to Sam and myself, Van Riebeeck was the man who had killed Stephen.

And there was also this – Van Riebeeck was the man who was in his own strange way paying court to Cat Hakesby. Had that swayed my judgement too?

I was not the same man I had been two or three years ago. The life I led at Whitehall had changed me. The deeper I looked into my own heart, the less I saw clearly there, and the darker it seemed, and growing ever darker.

The waterman glanced over his shoulder and began to scull the boat towards the shore. 'Puddle Stairs, master.'

The steps were slippery, forcing Sam to take my arm for support. Puddle Wharf was south-west of St Paul's, near the remains of Baynard's Castle, where the King's Wardrobe had been kept. The area had been badly damaged by the Fire. But it was an important location, and by now most of it had been redeveloped or at least made habitable.

The house we sought was immediately recognizable. It looked weary of life, a small, sagging building partly of one storey, partly of two. The gable wall of the lower part bowed out into the churchyard. Blackened tiles covered this part of the roof, together with what looked like a patched mainsail attached to the house by a tangle of ropes. The two-storey end was equally dilapidated but appeared more weathertight.

Its windows overlooked a yard with a stye where a small hairy hog was rooting aimlessly in the dirt.

The house seemed a very unlikely place to house a man like Van Riebeeck. Perhaps Jane Ash had been mistaken. Or I was acting the fool again.

'If the Dutchman's there, master?' Sam said softly.

'We hold him. I question him.'

Sam looked disappointed. 'And then?'

I glanced at him but said nothing. Stephen's murder had unlocked something within us both. But it was best left to itself in the darkness and not put into words, even between ourselves.

The hog looked up at us as we passed, its snout smeared with mud and its small eyes gleaming with intelligence. I rapped on the door with the head of my stick. Sam adjusted his cloak so he could reach the pistol in his belt.

'Who are you? What do you want?'

The woman's voice seemed to drift down from heaven. There was a lilt to it, and the words sounded only half-formed, as if she had something uncomfortably hot in her mouth that impeded her speech. We looked up. Immediately above us was a projecting lattice casement, which was a few inches open. If I had stood on tiptoes, I would have been able to touch the sill. An old woman was looking down on us. She had a thin, lined face. When she opened her mouth I saw three brown teeth randomly scattered along her gums.

'I'll break the door down if you want, sir,' Sam whispered. 'Just say the word.'

I ignored him. 'The parish clerk sent me, mistress. I'm a surveyor. We need to have a look at your roof and the gable wall from within the house. There's a danger of it falling into the churchyard.'

'I can't have it mended,' the woman said. It was the paucity of teeth that made her speech so strange, together with a thick brogue. The window began to close. 'No money. No nothing.'

'One moment, pray. The parish will pay for any work deemed necessary.'

The window opened again, more widely this time. 'Parish? You sure, master?'

'Of course I'm sure. Do you think I give my labours for free? I am informed that a parishioner has established a charitable fund for the repairs.'

'Wait there, master, if you please.' Her head withdrew and the window closed.

I whispered to Sam, 'Do nothing unless I tell you.'

I heard her unchaining and unbarring the door. She opened it a crack and looked out at us. Her face was still wary. I took out a paper from my pocket – the notes I had made when I was dining with the captain earlier today.

'Quick, woman, I haven't all day. Here is my warrant from the churchwardens.'

It was a safe bet that she couldn't read, but the sight of the paper soothed her doubts. The sight of words on paper often has a magical effect on those who cannot read. She opened the door fully and we entered the house.

The interior was neater and cleaner than I had expected. I told her we were required to inspect the entire property before I could authorize the work. She led us first into a kitchen, which had a scullery and yard beyond.

The kitchen had a box bed recessed into the gable wall,

with a curtain hanging in front of it. This was the wall that was leaning into the churchyard on the other side. In the scullery, I looked up and saw blackened roof timbers and a hole in the tiles where part of the roof had fallen in. This was covered by the sail, which pulsed up and down with every motion of the wind outside.

'And the rest of the house?' I said.

'But why do you want to see that, your honour? It's the other end from the churchyard.'

'Do you set yourself as a judge of a surveyor's business?' I demanded. 'Leave such matters to your betters, woman, and do as I bid. It is important that I examine the whole. Unless you want the house to fall down when we start the repairs.'

She quailed before my expertise, and led us down a passage to another door, which she unlocked from a key she had hanging from a cord around her waist. As soon as this door opened, my hopes began to rise. The room beyond was gloomy, for its windows were small and the panes of glass thick and grimy. It was furnished with a table, three high-backed chairs, a long chest and a press. Against the far wall was a narrow staircase, almost a ladder, to a chamber above.

At a glance from me, Sam backed against the door, blocking our hostess's line of retreat. I looked about me. There were ashes heaped in the grate. The air smelled faintly of tobacco, with a hint of beeswax beneath. A pair of neatly trimmed candles, wax not tallow, stood in pewter holders on the table. Between them was an open book. I picked up the book and carried it to the nearest window.

'What – what are you doing?' she asked.

'Peace, woman,' I said, turning the pages.

The book was in Dutch. From what I could make out, it was a record of a voyage to the East Indies. We were on the right scent. I closed the book with a bang and tossed it on to the table.

'Who does this belong to?'

She said nothing. She had begun to shake. She clung to the back of the chair.

'Sit down, mistress,' I said. 'We mean you no harm. Answer me.'

She sat down and laid her hands on the table to steady them. 'A man who sometimes lodges here.'

'A Dutchman?'

She nodded.

'Name?'

She shrugged. 'I don't know.'

I pointed up towards the chamber above our heads. 'Is he here now?'

She shook her head violently. I couldn't be sure that she was telling the truth. I was in no mood to take chances.

'Keep her there,' I said to Sam. 'I'm going to look upstairs. If it turns out she's lying, you can hack her head off for all I care.'

Sam ripped the cutlass out of its sheath, and the woman gave a squeal. He laid the naked blade on the table. He took out his pistol, cocked it, reversed it and held it out to me. 'It's a light trigger, master. Watch how you go.'

The woman was watching his every move, her mouth open. 'I swear there's no one,' she muttered almost inaudibly, crossing herself. 'Oh Jesus, Mary and all the saints save me.'

I climbed the stairs, stick in one hand and the pistol in the other. There was no one lurking in the low-ceilinged chamber above. It was scantily furnished with a bed, whose curtains were tied back, a night table and another press, which was empty. One of the two windows was above the house door, and it was still unlatched. On the floor was a pile of dirty sheets. The old woman must have been changing the bed linen when we knocked.

I went back downstairs. Sam and the woman hadn't moved. They were staring fixedly at each other, as children do, each willing the other to be the first to drop their eyes.

I opened the other press. I found pewter mugs and plates, two or three glasses, and more books, some in English, some in Dutch. There were three unopened bottles of wine, and a squat corked flask made of earthenware. I had been hoping for better – letters, perhaps, or other papers.

Next I tried the chest, which was longer than the average coffin and made of oak. It was not locked. Inside, wrapped in a cloak, were two swords. There was a suit of broadcloth beneath, as well as more shirts and other items of clothing. I took out the coat and held it against me. It belonged to a tall man, broad in the shoulders. A man like Van Riebeeck.

I heard something chink. I patted the coat until I found a secret pocket concealed under the flap at the front and secured by a tie. I tore it open and removed two coins, both gold. They winked up at me from the palm of my hand.

On one side of each coin was stamped the figure of an armoured man holding a sword in one hand and a sheaf of arrows in the other. Dutch ducats. I dropped them on the table, one by one.

'Where is he?' I said to the woman.

'I don't know.'

'When did you last see him?'

'I don't know . . . last week?'

'What name did he give you?'

'Mr . . . Smith.'

I was sure she was lying. 'When did he start coming here?'
She shrugged. 'A month ago?'

That would tie in with Van Riebeeck escaping from the
cottage at Austin Friars.

'He'd heard I had apartments to let,' she went on. 'I don't
know where . . . he paid me for them, two months down,
without board.' She squinted up at me, measuring the effect
of her words. 'He's hardly ever here. I send out if he wants
to dine or sup here, and he pays for that too. It's good money,
master, and on the nail.'

I didn't believe her. It was all too neat. Van Riebeeck had
apparently lost one refuge and immediately found another
– and then effortlessly furnished it with his own possessions.
But I could prove nothing, and I had failed in my main
purpose in coming here, finding Van Riebeeck. There was
nothing left for me to do except report what I had discovered
to my lord and Gorvin.

Sam looked at me and raised his eyebrows, wordlessly
asking for orders.

'We'll take the books,' I said, 'and make another search in
case there are—'

At that moment the street door opened, and a man's voice
called out 'Mam? Where are you?'

Sam reacted faster than I did. He lunged forward and
clamped a hand over the old woman's mouth, contriving to
pin her to the chair with his elbow. His other hand stretched
towards the pistol, which was on the table. I edged behind
the door of the room and raised my stick.

319

There were hurried but heavy footsteps outside. The old woman twisted her body in the chair, struggling to escape Sam's grip.

'I've told you before. You mustn't leave the door unbarred.'

The door opened and a big man came in, still speaking. He stopped just over the threshold, staring at the tableau before him.

His hand snaked towards the hilt of his sword. I swung the weighted stick against the side of his head as hard as I could in the confined space. He half-turned. In the split second before the blow hit him, I recognized him and he recognized me. His hat absorbed some of the force, but enough remained to fling him sideways against the wall. Dazed, he fell to his knees.

The old woman made a loud, keening noise and she writhed like a landed fish. But Sam did not let her escape.

I stepped away from the wall and raised the stick again. I held it with both hands. This time I had the space around me to lift it above my head. I swung it down with all the force in my body on his right arm, his sword arm.

The impact almost jolted the stick from my hands. I heard a crack. He screamed and clutched his arm, his face contorted in agony. The stick had caught his upper arm just beneath the ball of the shoulder. What made it worse was that his hand was on the floor, for he had been in the act of levering himself up. His own weight fixed the arm in place, which meant there was nowhere for it to go when the blow landed on it. Shouting with pain, he clamped his other hand over the injured arm.

'Hush now, Mr Connolly,' I said, the bile within me rising like sap in the spring. 'Or you'll disturb the dead next door.'

CHAPTER FORTY-THREE

LATER, SOMEWHERE OUTSIDE the little hell of this house, a church clock began to strike. I counted the strokes. Six o'clock.

The weather was changing. Squalls of rain and gusts of wind rattled the windows and doors.

Connolly and his mother were sitting at either end of the table. Sam, whose talent as a maker of knots verged on the supernatural, had lashed their legs to the legs of the chairs on which they sat, using Connolly's belt and neckcloth. He himself had pushed a chair back to the wall and now sat watching them, with the pistol lying close to hand on the chest and the naked blade of the cutlass lying across his legs.

The old woman was muttering under her breath, moving from prayers to curses to prayers again in one continuous stream. Connolly was clutching his arm and moaning. He had fainted briefly when we moved him to the chair, and vomited from the pain when he came to his senses. Now his face was corpse-white and covered with a sheen of sweat. I almost found it in my heart to feel sorry for him.

It wasn't only the pain that was making his life hell. It was the fact that his mother was here too, tethered like a goat on the other side of the table. Even in his agony he had managed to ask her how she did, and whether we had harmed her.

'Connolly,' I said. 'You're in trouble.'

Anger flared in his face, but he controlled it. 'For pity's sake, sir, let my mother go for a surgeon to bind me up. And give me something for the pain.'

'Not yet.'

'You English devil,' his mother shrieked at me, pounding her fists on the table. 'May you dance in hell.'

Sam growled at her.

'Peace, woman.' I raised my voice to make myself heard above the racket and rapped my stick on the floor for emphasis. 'The last time we talked, Connolly, was in Scotland Yard. If you want something for the pain, you must be more frank with me than you were then. If not, we'll have to break your other shoulder, and then where will you be?'

His head bowed over the table. I opened the press and took out a pewter cup. I uncorked the earthenware flask and sniffed its contents. It was the strong, coarse spirit that they use for keeping out the damp in the Low Countries.

'Speak freely,' I said, 'and I'll see that you're released. But if you don't, why then—' I broke off and glanced at his mother. 'In that case, your mother will see her son on the gallows.' I poured a half-measure into the cup. 'Where's Van Riebeeck? Or Wulf or whatever you call him.'

'I don't know.' Connolly looked imploringly at me. 'I swear.'

'When did you last see him?

'Last week, sir. Here. I haven't seen him since.'

I took the cup over to him. He snatched it up and drank.

He coughed and spluttered, but most of it went down his throat. He glanced at his mother and muttered something in the Irish tongue. She began to reply but I cut her off.

'English. Speak English, both of you.'

Connolly groaned, clutching himself with his good arm. 'I was asking her when he left. She says it was Saturday.'

'He was here a week, this time,' she put in. 'Ten days maybe. I don't know where he went—'

'Nor me, sir,' interrupted Connolly, 'on my oath. But last time—' He broke off, and seized the cup. He drank the rest of its contents. 'For God's sake, sir, more.'

I slid the empty cup away from him, keeping my distance, and taking care not to block Sam's line of fire. Even injured and hobbled, Connolly was not a man to underestimate. I gave him another inch or so. I set down the cup on the table, a few inches beyond his reach.

'Last time?' I prompted him.

'About a month ago . . . he'd been somewhere else for a while, because of the warrant out for him. But he didn't stay more than a night . . .'

'One night,' his mother said, nodding her head vigorously.

'He was going to keep close here but something changed his mind. He went out that first morning, and when he came back here, he'd settled on going to Kent. He asked what the roads to Canterbury were like, and whether I could hire him a good horse. Oh pray, Mr Marwood, give me that cup.'

It fitted. I put the pieces together in my head. Dover was only a few miles from Canterbury. After Stephen's death, Van Riebeeck had come to this house on Friday evening, directly from Austin Friars. On Saturday morning he had waylaid Jane Ash in Covent Garden and persuaded her to give him a sight of Cat's itinerary. Then he had returned here and immediately made preparations to go to Kent. Clearly he intended to pursue her.

'For pity's sake, master,' the old woman said. 'Let him have it now.'

I pushed the cup within Connolly's reach and watched him drink. Van Riebeeck had gone after Cat, despite the dangers of showing himself in public. But why? Because he lusted after her? No, Van Riebeeck had not struck me as a man who would let lust be his master, particularly when his own life was in danger.

'Does Fanshawe know why he went to Kent?'

'Fanshawe knows nothing.' Connolly wrenched the words out of himself. 'He's a windy fool. A useful one, Van Riebeeck says, but no more.'

'Did he ever mention a woman to you?' I said, touching the cup with my fingertips.

'There was someone he'd met, someone who could be useful. I don't know who. I only know what he wanted me to know, sir. I wasn't privy to his secrets. I only saw him here and the Blue Bush.'

'How long has Van Riebeeck been here?'

'In this house? Or in London?'

'Both.'

'He came to London in January. Old Fanshawe brought him to me at the tavern, said he was a friend, needed lodgings.' The words emerged by fits and starts. At one point Connolly seemed on the verge of fainting again. 'I gave him the chamber there, and a few weeks later he said he wanted somewhere else as well.'

'You must have thought that strange,' I said.

He tried to shrug, which made him howl with pain. When he could speak again, he said, 'If a gentleman pays, it's not my business to think.'

'My last lodger left at the end of January,' the old woman said, suddenly loquacious. 'And my son thought of me. He's a good boy.'

'Where's Van Riebeeck gone now?' I asked.

'Back to the Low Countries, maybe?' She looked slyly at me. 'Could I go for a surgeon, master? Just to bind him up. I know a man who'd keep his mouth shut.'

'No,' I said.

'More . . .' Connolly moaned.

I took the cup but made no move to refill it. I didn't want him to get so drunk he became incoherent. Nor did I want the pain to overwhelm him and deprive him of consciousness again.

'Who killed Johnson?'

He licked parched lips. His eyes were on the bottle. 'Perhaps . . . perhaps it was an accident.'

I poured a thin stream of liquid into the cup. I looked up. 'Perhaps.'

'Perhaps . . . he died of fright when he was being asked a few questions . . . If he saw something that terrified him, and . . . remember, sir, his constitution was already enfeebled.'

I remembered the mulberry handkerchief. 'Where might that have happened?'

'I don't rightly know, sir.'

I pushed the cup an inch across the table towards him. 'And I don't rightly know if this cup will ever reach you.'

He swallowed and winced. Momentarily he closed his eyes. 'Mr Fanshawe has a lion in Slaughter Street. Did you know?'

I said nothing.

'If a man was to see a beast like that, and think – quite wrongly of course – that he might be the beast's dinner . . . why, sir, that might cause him to be fearful . . .'

'Fearful unto death?' I said.

'Aye, master. Fearful unto death.'

'And then you and Van Riebeeck had to get rid of the body?'

Connolly nodded, biting his lower lip against the pain.

'Austin Friars?'

He nodded. I pushed the cup towards him and watched him drink.

'And now,' I said, 'tell me about Abbott.'

But it was too late. Connolly put down the cup so clumsily it fell over. He had emptied it. For a moment he stared at me with glassy eyes. Then his head fell forward with a crash on the table.

CHAPTER FORTY-FOUR

THE FOLLOWING MORNING I tried to see Lord Arlington. Gorvin told me it was impossible today, but that he would send word to my lord that I desired to lay fresh intelligence before him.

I was unwilling to trust Gorvin himself with the details of all my discoveries but I told him that Connolly and his mother had sheltered Van Riebeeck in the latter's house near the Wardrobe, by Puddle Wharf. I had called there with Sam on my way to Whitehall this morning. Connolly had been lying in a stupor, for his mother had given him too much laudanum last night to ease the pain.

Gorvin was about to go back to his desk. I feigned a casual air and enquired if there was news of Mistress Hakesby in France.

He gave me a quizzical glance. 'Ah. Your architect friend. I hear she's with the French court at St Germain.'

'Does her business with Madame prosper?'

'As far as I know. Why?'

I shrugged. 'I had some slight acquaintance with her late

husband. And Van Riebeeck has shown an interest in her. She met him with Fanshawe at the theatre in February. Fanshawe is one of her clients.'

'Interesting.' Gorvin's lips twitched as if he were restraining a smile. 'But no doubt there's a perfectly innocent and obvious reason why a man like Van Riebeeck might show an interest in Mistress Hakesby. I believe that even these cold-blooded Dutchmen are occasionally prey to lusts of the flesh.'

Half an hour later, I was approached by a footman in the King's livery, who told me that His Majesty desired me to attend him at once. I knew the summons must have to do with my message to Lord Arlington. If the King had such a pressing interest in the matter, it must mean that it was even more important than I had thought.

The footman escorted me to the back stairs of the Royal Apartments, when another servant led me to the office of Mr Chiffinch, the Keeper of the King's Privy Closet. Chiffinch guarded the private access to his master, and his discretion was legendary. He and I had had dealings before, and he did not much care for me, nor I him. But we were obliged to tolerate each other.

'What's this about, Marwood?' he demanded. 'What trouble are you in this time?'

'I regret I am not at liberty to say, sir.'

He scowled. 'Come along.'

I followed him up another flight of stairs, through a doorway past two guards, and into a passage where even the air smelled different, more perfumed and somehow richer, than on the other side of the door. We had entered the King's private apartments. Chiffinch tapped on a door and, without waiting for an answer, pushed it open.

'Mr Marwood, Your Majesty.'

The King turned from the window. I made my reverence to him, while a small, fluffy spaniel ran about my legs, barking impartially at Chiffinch and me.

'Peace, Dido.'

The dog scampered over to her master, her feathery tail waving. I glanced about me. We were in a large closet, one of several by the King's private bedchamber. Arlington was standing by the fire, warming the backs of his legs. He gave me a nod in answer to my bow.

The King dismissed Chiffinch and flung himself into an armchair. 'I can't spare more than a moment.'

Nonetheless he fell silent, and no one spoke for at least thirty seconds. Dido lay down on the carpet and rested her head on a royal foot. The King looked older than he had when I had last had a private interview with him – his face more lined, the bags under his eyes more pronounced. I calculated he must be almost forty now. He looked upright and hale enough, but it was probable that grey hairs were sprouting among the dark ones underneath the black periwig.

He stared at me, the brown eyes weary beneath the heavy brows. 'My lord has told me about the affair with the Dutchman,' he said suddenly. 'Van Riebeeck. The matter of the stolen papers. These two deaths – of my lord's clerk, Mr Abbott, and that gamester from the Blue Bush—' He broke off and glanced at Arlington, raising his eyebrows.

'Johnson, sir. Jeremiah Johnson. Sent down from the University for cheating and immorality.'

329

The King nodded impatiently. 'Quite so. These two deaths—'

I cleared my throat. He looked at me, his eyebrows knitting together into a frown.

'Three deaths, Your Majesty. I believe Van Riebeeck threw my footboy from a height and then beat him to death.'

He waved his hand. 'Three then. This Dutchman, Van Riebeeck, has a half-sister, who was married to Abbott, and before that to the dead son of a Mr Fanshawe, a merchant who has a house near Smithfield and trades a good deal with the Dutch. Yes?'

'Yes, sir,' I said, for he seemed to require my confirmation of these details.

'Van Riebeeck is much esteemed in his native country,' the King went on. 'My lord has corresponded with our embassy there. They say he's in the confidence of the Grand Pensionary himself, with whom he no doubt shares a firm attachment to republican principles.'

His nostrils flared slightly as he spoke the last two words. He glanced at Arlington, who smoothly took up the summary.

'The father was a Dutch gentleman who served in their navy, and the mother a French Huguenot whose parents were forced into exile. Van Riebeeck was bred to hate the Papists and the King of France. His father was killed in the first Dutch war, and his elder brother in the second. He maintains that his brother was shot after his ship had struck its flag and surrendered. I believe he intends to do us harm by any means he can.'

'The question is, how.' The King glanced at the clock on the mantlepiece. 'Marwood? Where's he been since the warrant went out for his arrest?'

'He hid in an empty house in Austin Friars, sir, with the help of some of the Dutch community. When I discovered him, he fled to another house, this one in the City, where he lodged with the mother of a man named Connolly, the landlord of the Blue Bush. Van Riebeeck left the place last week and hasn't been seen since. However, he had previously made a journey into Kent, possibly in pursuit of Mistress Hakesby on her way to France.' I hesitated. 'I don't know why.'

The King looked at Arlington, and Arlington looked at the King. The King nodded slightly. I guessed that this last piece of information had not come as a surprise. He rose from the chair, dislodging Dido, who scratched herself vigorously. I hurried to open the door for him.

'I want you to go to Dover,' he said to me. 'My lord will tell you all you need to know.'

Arlington stirred. 'Perhaps Gorvin would be better than Marwood, sir. He is a man of much experience and considerable penetration. And also—'

'No. Send Marwood, and you may tell him why.' The King paused in the doorway, and looked down at me from his great height. 'You've done me good service in the past. I know you will do so again. And you will not regret it.'

He smiled, and his charm briefly enveloped me like a warm cloud of nothingness. I watched his tall figure receding down the passage, with the dog pattering after him.

Only a fool would rely on the goodwill of Charles Stuart. But the dog did, and so did I. A little kindness makes fools of us all.

The King went one way towards the Privy Stairs and the river, and Lord Arlington and I the other. My lord preceded me, and it was most unfortunate that he placed his foot on a small but well-formed turd in the passage. Arlington skidded; he swore softly, losing for once his stately self-control.

'My lord?'

The King had turned to see what was amiss.

'It's nothing, sir,' Arlington said smoothly. 'I chanced to slip.'

The King's eyes were sharp. 'I fear Dido should crave your pardon for inconveniencing you. Ah! She looks at you most meltingly, my lord. You will forgive her, I know.'

'With all my heart, sir.'

'We all make mistakes sometimes, my lord, even Dido.' The King seemed no longer in such a hurry to be gone. His voice acquired an edge. 'But there must be no mistakes in this other matter. No betrayals. You understand me? Or I can't answer for the consequences.'

I was suddenly unsure who the words were meant for. The King's eyes seemed fixed on a spot somewhere between me and Arlington.

The King turned and sauntered away. I followed my lord to his private room. He scraped the sole of his shoe on the rim of the coal scuttle. He sat down at his desk, unlocked a drawer and took out a paper.

'There are discussions in train between ourselves and France,' he said quietly. 'They are most highly confidential. Their purpose will be ruined if even the fact of the negotiations becomes known. If all goes well, a certain agreement will be signed at Dover by the representatives of the two kings, ours and the French. Thanks to Abbott's folly, Van Riebeeck has caught wind of this, and now he would ruin it all if he could. That's why this is so important. He must be stopped.' Arlington paused and gave a sniff. Irritation burst from him like molten rock erupting from a volcano. 'God damn that stinking dog.'

On the last Sunday in April Mr Fanshawe took his daughter-in-law and granddaughter to watch Caliban devour his dinner. It was a cold, grey afternoon. It had rained all morning, and there were puddles on the path.

The lion was healthier than he had been. He had not quite regained all his former strength, but his appetite had returned with a vengeance, and his roar now had a vigour that delighted his owner.

'That is most gratifying,' Mr Fanshawe said, as they were walking back to the house. 'I would not care to leave Caliban while he was lying ill.'

'Leave him, sir?' Maria's mother looked startled. 'You intend to go on a journey?'

'All of us might go. In less than three weeks, the whole world will be in Dover. Perhaps we should be there too.'

'Dover, sir?' Mistress Fanshawe's face was framed by the hood of her cloak, and her nose was pink with cold. 'But why?'

'Not to lodge there, Anna. The town will be full to over-flowing. But to visit, to see the Court and the Princess. That would be another matter.' Mr Fanshawe was warming to his theme. 'We would stay at Swaring, where we would be perfectly comfortable and among our own people. It's only a few miles up the road. And—' He broke off, turning to look at his daughter-in-law '—and you could see Henryk. He is still there, I believe, leading a retired life. What could be more pleasant?'

'You are too good, sir, always studying how to do a kindness to us. But consider – would there be space enough for all of us in Swaring? Would you be comfortable enough there? It's not a large house, and there are the servants to be considered. And then there is the weather . . .'

He smiled benignly at her. 'It's dreary enough now, but you'll see – it will be a different matter in a week or two. The weather in Kent is always better than here, and the air so much purer.'

They walked on, Mr Fanshawe's mind running ahead to the projected expedition. It would be good for Maria to observe the forms and manners of the great world. Anna would surely enjoy the opportunity to study the latest French fashions at first hand. He himself would be able to show himself to gentlemen he did business with, and perhaps meet new ones. And he would also be glad of an opportunity to see how his new bailiff was doing at Swaring. It was so easy for one's people in the country to grow slack when their master was away in London.

'Besides,' he said, 'Maria is looking as thin as a shadow these days. As my old father used to say, a change of pasture makes fat calves.'

CHAPTER FORTY-FIVE

HIGH ABOVE THEM, a buzzard circled, calm and watchful above the ant-like activity below. It floated between earth and heaven, describing lazy ellipses against the low, grey sky. It had no apparent interest, Cat thought, in the affairs of men, however grand they believed themselves to be. It was looking for its dinner.

Below the buzzard, the greatest king in Europe, perhaps the world, was making a progress across his domain, with an appropriate retinue to reflect his glory and guard his sacred person. He was on his way to inspect his newly acquired domains in the Spanish Netherlands. The Queen was with him, in whose name the King had claimed the province, and so was his brother Monsieur, the Duke of Orléans, and his brother's wife, Madame. Monsieur had failed: Madame was not with child, so she could go to England. She had commanded that Cat should accompany her, together with the plans for her new mansion near St Cloud.

The entire Court had left St Germain with the royal family on the 28 April, escorted by an army of 30,000 men. With

335

them went the great officers of state and a host of ecclesiastical dignitaries. The planning had taken months. There were hundreds of coaches, including the great state coach. There were splendid horses, richly dressed noblemen, the finest troops that France could muster, and legions of servants. Behind them trailed convoys of waggons, laden with enough goods to supply the whole of Paris. Among their loads were furniture, tapestries, and gold and silver plate, for Their Majesties were to be served on the journey as if they were in one of their own palaces. Last of all swarmed the ragged crowd of camp followers, persistent as flies.

Unfortunately, like the buzzard, the weather did not appreciate the splendour of the occasion. Rain made roads muddy, clothes wet, horses slip and tempers short. It made rivers burst their banks and fields turn to marshland. It made tents leak and cooking fires fizzle feebly and die. The food was appalling, despite all the preparations, and there were never enough fresh eggs, milk or butter.

The French Court at this moment reminded Cat of the refugees streaming in their thousands from London during the Great Fire, or even of the braying, lowing, mooing herds driven through the narrow streets to Smithfield towards their deaths. There seemed no end to this journey. Time lost its familiar forms and divisions, with nothing but degrees of discomfort to distinguish one day from the next. Cat would have almost preferred to be seasick in the middle of the English Channel.

She herself was relatively fortunate, in that the worst of the weather did not affect her. She was travelling in an old-fashioned coach with two physicians, a fat priest, a seamstress, and a woman who dressed the hair of one of Madame's ladies, talked incessantly and gave herself airs. The coach was draughty and the roof leaked. The seamstress was flatulent, the priest had bad breath, and one of the physicians had wandering hands.

One afternoon, when they had stopped to dine on watery soup and stale bread, a horseman in the Orléans livery struggled through the crowd with a note from Madame des Bordes. Madame had summoned Cat; she was to accompany the bearer of the letter.

Her spirits rose, partly because she welcomed any variation that broke the monotony of the journey. The messenger took her up behind him, and rode back up the column. The great royal coach was about three miles ahead, heavily guarded and marooned in the middle of a ploughed field. She was handed over to Madame des Bordes, who escorted her through the soldiers and servants to the side of the coach. Both doors were open. Inside, reclining against red silk cushions, were Madame and Queen Marie-Thérèse, whose broad, awkward body dwarfed her sister-in-law's slender figure.

There was a sudden stir among the bystanders, and Madame des Bordes placed a restraining hand on Cat's arm. Monsieur himself was approaching the other side of the coach, his elegant figure cleaving through the crowd and throwing them to either side of him like the bow wave of a ship.

He bowed – low to the Queen, and almost imperceptibly to his wife. 'It is intolerable,' he said in his clipped, carrying voice. 'I am served by fools. Do you know what they've done now? They've lost the case with my cosmetics.' He passed his hand over his delicate features, which were as elegantly perfect as ever. 'I cannot be seen in public anywhere until they are found.'

337

Monsieur seemed oblivious of the fact that twenty or thirty people were seeing him now. The Queen made a soothing remark about how often what was lost would turn up when one least expected it. Madame said nothing. She stared down at her long white hands.

'It was foretold,' Monsieur went on, his nostrils twitching. 'I saw an astrologer the other day. He said I should take care lest a great disaster befall me while I was on this journey. What do you say to that?'

'Very interesting,' said the Queen placidly.

'And you, Madame?' her husband said, his voice rising in pitch. 'Have you nothing to say for yourself? Or are you too ill to speak again?' He sniffed and added in a deeply sarcastic voice. 'I'm *so* sorry you are unwell.' He smiled at the Queen. 'But it reminds me of something else that the astrologer told me. He predicted I should have several wives!' He took a step closer and tilted his head. 'Evidently Madame will not live long,' he said to the Queen, 'so the prediction seems likely to be fulfilled.'

The Queen gasped, her hand flying to her mouth. Monsieur smiled, glancing over his shoulder to assess the effect of his words. Their meaning ran through the people within earshot. Only Madame did not react. Still she sat, rigid in her misery, staring at her hands.

'Monsieur,' said the Queen at last, 'you cannot mean . . . pray, you must . . .'

Madame des Bordes pulled Cat aside, away from the open door of the coach. Neither of them spoke until they had reached the road.

'Madame won't see you now,' Madame des Bordes said. 'Go back to your coach. Try to forget this.'

Cat said, 'He cannot mean to be so cruel, surely?'

'Monsieur says and does just what he wants. Sometimes even the King cannot control him.'

The days passed. The journey continued, and so did the rain. Near Landrecies, close to the Flanders border, with their destination almost within reach, the royal progress came to the River Sambre. Unfortunately, the river was in flood, and the bridge had been destroyed. There were fords, but they were now completely impassable.

Military engineers were brought up to deal with the problem. No one knew how long they would be forced to wait here. Within Cat's coach, tempers soured still further.

Then came a second letter from Madame des Bordes, summoning Cat to attend the Princess. One of the Orléans servants escorted her through the sprawling encampment. For want of anything better, the royal party had commandeered a small farmhouse not far from the bridge. It was little more than a cottage surrounded by barns. It stood a few fields away from the swollen river.

'They're all in there,' the servant said in answer to Cat's question. 'The King, the Queen, Monsieur and Madame. Squeezed in that filthy hovel like a bunch of peasants. There are only two rooms.' He was too well-trained for his face to betray his emotions, but Cat thought she detected a hint of amusement in his voice. 'All they could find for their dinner was two or three scrawny chickens. Imagine, madame! Not an hour earlier those hens were running around the yard and pecking at the dirt.'

The farmyard stank. The servant escorted her past the sentries to the doorway of the house. Somewhere a woman was shrieking, her voice swooping up and down. Inside, in a narrow hallway, a number of gentlemen were standing, studiously ignoring the racket. Cat was taken to a tent which had been erected in the yard. It was full of ladies-in-waiting with pinched faces and damp clothes. They stared suspiciously at Cat. In a moment, Madame des Bordes appeared and drew her aside.

'Madame says you are to wait on her outside,' she said, speaking into Cat's ear to make herself heard. 'In this weather! She'll be soaked to the skin if she's not careful, and catch her death of cold. She's had nothing but milk for days. *Elle est maigre comme un clou.*'

Her face creased with concern, Madame des Bordes took Cat outside again and led her round the corner of the house to a herb garden. It was smaller in area than Cat's chamber at St Germain.

The shrieking was audible even outside.

'Who is it?' Cat said.

'The Queen. And who can wonder at it? To be Queen of France and forced to shelter in a hovel like this. The King says they must all sleep together on mattresses in one room, ten or twelve ladies, and the King and Monsieur. It is so unseemly. It is against all that is right and proper. Come – over here.'

On this side of the house there was a lean-to built against the wall, against which a few logs had been stacked. The roof leaked, and drops of water dribbled down into a puddle. Beside it, Madame sat on a folding chair. Madame des Bordes and Cat dropped into curtsies.

'Leave me with Mistress Hakesby,' the Princess said.

'But the rain . . .'

'It's only a little water. I shan't drown.'

Madame was swathed in a dark cloak, its hood framing her face. She looked even thinner and frailer than before. She waited until the door had closed behind Madame des Bordes.

'This is like a comedy in the theatre,' she said, and her face broke into a smile, that briefly flooded her face with vitality. 'All of us packed together in this horrible place.' She hesitated, and her voice dropped to a whisper. 'May I entrust something to you?'

For a moment, Cat thought that she must have misheard. 'But of course, Madame.'

'There are . . . there are those in this country who wish me ill. I cannot be sure . . . quite sure . . . of people.' The voice stopped. The blue eyes searched Cat's face. 'My brother says you are to be trusted. I have a letter for him. Take it for me, and give it to him when you are back in England. To him, mark you. To no one else.' She fumbled in her cloak and held out a letter. 'Unless I ask for it back beforehand.'

'But surely you yourself will see His Majesty in a few days?' Cat said as she took it.

'I hope and pray that I shall,' Madame said. 'But it will be as God wishes. This letter is in case He does not permit me to see my brother again in this life.'

Before she left the farmhouse, Cat saw Madame des Bordes again.

'How did she seem to you?'

'The journey fatigues her, I think,' Cat said, choosing her words with care. She had been shaken by the Princess's appearance, by her fatalism, by what had seemed to be her premonition of death.

'It's more than fatigue. You saw what Monsieur was like

the other day. He could not have been crueller. And to speak so before the Queen and her ladies and God knows who else.'

The servant was approaching, ready to escort Cat back to her coach.

'But I forget,' Madame des Bordes said in a rush, as if anxious to change the subject. 'I have a letter for you.'

Confused, Cat stared at her. Her mind was still on the letter which Madame had given her, the letter that was now in her pocket.

'The courier brought the postbags yesterday afternoon,' Madame des Bordes went on. 'It was the greatest good fortune that the letter for you was directed to Madame's household, and I happened to catch sight of it.'

Cat glanced at the address on the outside, hoping it might be a reply from Marwood or even something from Van Riebeeck. But the writing was unfamiliar. With a murmured apology, she broke the seal and unfolded it. Her eyes went straight to the signature.

I remain your servant, Madam, M. Hobell.

When she had said goodbye to the Hobells in Paris, she had not expected to hear from them again until they were all back in London, if then. After the conventional enquiries about Cat's health, Mistress Hobell regretted that the letter to Mr Marwood had gone astray. The gentleman carrying it, she wrote, had been set upon and robbed on the road near Rouen. Cat's letter had vanished along with the rest of his possessions. Mr Hobell begged to send his compliments to her. Mistress Hobell added that her husband wished to remind her that the robbery was yet more evidence that the French were a nation of rogues.

*   *   *

When the royal party crossed the River Sambre, the atmosphere changed. Everyone felt it, even the camp followers. Shortly afterwards, the King entered Courtrai as a conquering hero. English envoys were waiting for them there. King Charles was already at Dover. His fleet was waiting for Madame at Dunkirk.

Dunkirk was barely fifty miles to the north-west. Monsieur, however, was still sulking, though his box of cosmetics had now been found. He made a final attempt to thwart Madame's departure. But the King overrode him; the visit, he reminded his brother, was a matter of state, as well as a courtesy to a fellow monarch. Nevertheless, Monsieur insisted that his wife should stay no longer than three days in Dover.

Madame looked as waif-like as ever, but there was now a strange vitality about her that Cat had not seen before.

'That is what she used to be like,' Madame des Bordes said fondly. 'So full of life. I fear there will be a price to pay.'

At dawn on the 25 May, though it was a Sunday, Madame and her suite left Courtrai with an escort of six hundred horse. With them went Cat. The French and the English envoys accompanied the party. There was a new sense of urgency, with Madame constantly urging her coachman to go faster. She was determined to reach Dunkirk within a day.

'Madame is in such a hurry,' Madame des Bordes told Cat. 'She would grow wings if she could.' A frown creased her forehead. 'But it's hardly right for her to travel with such a small *suite d'honneur*.'

Dover was a modest town, Cat pointed out, barely more than a large village. It could not accommodate many people of quality, even in far poorer accommodation than they were accustomed to. Besides, she thought but did not say,

Madame's *suite d'honneur* was not small by any normal standards. Together with the rest of her household, she was crossing the Channel with 237 persons, including five maids of honour, hairdressers and priests, doctors, musicians and cooks – and Cat.

It was after sunset by the time the party reached Dunkirk. Everyone was travel-stained and weary. But Madame insisted that they should embark without delay, so that they could catch the ebbing tide in the early hours of the morning. She was determined not to waste a moment of this precious time with her brother.

The fleet was underway during the night. Cat, who was not travelling on the flagship with Madame, dozed off for half an hour until the sounds and smells of seasickness wrenched her back to consciousness. The cries and moans of the women who shared her cabin filled the air. Her stomach heaved. She reached for the nearest bowl.

Later, Cat went up on deck and tried to follow Mistress Hobell's advice. *Face towards the bows and stare at the horizon.*

The morning was dreary, and the sea choppy. The rain fell steadily, with the occasional squally gust whose viciousness took the breath away. Light poured slowly into the world like milk into a bowl. There was a grey shimmer on the horizon. An officer said it was the white cliffs of Dover, and a ripple of relief ran through the passengers on deck.

Cat's spirits rose, and her seasickness began to diminish. She thought briefly of Marwood, wondering if he would be in Dover. She thought more about Van Riebeeck, who if he had any sense was back in his native country. But most of all, she thought about the Drawing Office in Henrietta Street. She had been away too long.

The approaching fleet had been seen from Dover. A number of craft had put out to sea to greet the returning princess. One outpaced all the others: a barge whose oars rose rapidly up and down to the muffled beat of a drum. The Royal Standard flapped stiffly in the wind. Like Madame his sister, the King did not mean to waste time.

CHAPTER FORTY-SIX

O N THEIR FIRST evening at Swaring, Maria was sent
to bed while it was still light.

'Don't whine or you'll have a whipping in the morning,'
her mother told her. 'You are tired from the journey. Say
goodnight to your grandfather.'

Maria made her curtsies and retired. There had been only
the three of them at supper. Her uncle had not yet returned
from Dover.

Swaring was old and dark. The house lay in a hollow,
protected by a stand of trees. It seemed smaller than before,
its rooms mean and low-ceilinged, and its furnishings shabby
and old-fashioned. During the day, the smells and sounds of
the farmyard, which was inconveniently close, filled the air.

Maria had been very young when she had last come here.
It was long before her mother's marriage to Abbott. Her
nurse, an old countrywoman, had terrified her with stories
of the apparitions and phantoms that inhabited the house.
One evening, Maria was convinced that she heard a ghost
moving about the landing place. She had fled screaming

towards the warmth and light below. In her haste, she had slipped and fallen on the stairs. She had broken her arm, which still tingled in damp weather, a ghost pain to remind her of Swaring.

Her bedchamber was a closet even smaller than the one she had occupied in Abbott's lodgings in Fleet Street. It opened out of her mother's room, where a small fire burned, sullen and low, in the grate. Maria left the closet door ajar, to steal what warmth she could from her mother.

The light was fading from the sky and the first stars were already appearing. Even now, in the half-light of the evening, Swaring was an unsettling house, a place of creaking floors and unexpected shadows. Today was Friday the thirteenth. Everyone knew that was a doubly unlucky day. It wasn't over yet, and the worst time was always after dark.

Maria pulled back the coverlet on the truckle bed that had been brought in from her mother's room. The sheets felt damp. There was ominous scratching behind the panelling.

She bit her lip and tried to remind herself of the advantages of her situation. Swaring wasn't as bad as Abbott's lodging had been. Caliban was in London, which meant that Maria could have a holiday from the unpleasant spectacle of his dinner. Best of all, Hannah was still at Slaughter Street, with a low fever added to her toothache.

Something would have to be done about Hannah. The realization had been creeping over Maria for weeks, growing steadily in strength. Otherwise there was no end in sight to the maid's tyranny.

Maria drew the curtains and made herself ready for bed. She was in the act of using the pot when she heard footsteps. They were heavy and deliberate, not like her mother's, which were rapid and light, or Grandfather's, which were slow, and often shuffling.

A servant? She hurriedly stood up, pulling down her shift. A *ghost*?

To her horror, she heard the clack of the latch on the door of her mother's chamber. The footsteps were louder now. Her candle was still alight, her door still open. There was nowhere to hide.

The closet door was flung open. Maria opened her mouth to scream but no sound emerged. Standing on the threshold was an enormous man, dressed all in black, with a tall black periwig that shaded his dark face. It was the Devil, Maria thought with the cold lucidity that fear sometimes brings, the Devil come to take her away for using witchcraft to murder Abbott.

'Ach, it's you,' the Devil said.

A warm tide of relief flooded over her. 'Uncle?'

'Who else did you think it was, you foolish girl?'

'You took me by surprise, sir, and then . . .'

'I came up the backstairs so as not to disturb your grandfather and your mother at supper. I must wash the journey away and change my clothes before I see them.' Van Riebeeck raised his candle to examine her better. 'You look half-dead with fear, child. Why?'

'I . . . took you for someone else.'

'Because of the suit and the black wig, eh? My other wig is in your mother's press. That's why I came in here. I don't want to frighten them downstairs.'

It was, she realized, intended as a joke. Emboldened, she peered up at him. His stern face had a blessed familiarity. 'And . . . your skin looks darker, sir.'

'Walnut juice.' He smiled. 'All to the good. My creditors are pursuing me, as you may know. I want to be taken for someone else.'

When the French party arrived, on the 16 May by our reckoning and the 26 May by theirs, I had been in Dover for nearly four weeks; and that was far too long. I was heartily tired of the place.

At first my orders had been to search for Van Riebeeck. Within a few hours of my arrival, I had established that he had almost certainly been in the town at the same time as Cat and her party had passed through on their way to France. The Hobells had put up at the Ship before embarking, and there had been an attempted robbery that night. Nothing of importance had been taken, and the thief had not inconvenienced Cat.

According to the innkeeper and the constable, the criminal had been a foreigner, a tall man who had shared a bedchamber with Mr Hobell, the clergyman escorting Cat. The thief had disappeared immediately afterwards. I reported these meagre details to Lord Arlington. The scent was already three weeks old, I wrote, and all the indications were that Van Riebeeck had long since left the town. Gorvin replied that my lord had heard of the robbery from Mr Hobell. He urged me to pursue my enquiries further.

There was clearly more to this than met the eye. Cat and her poultry house somehow had a bearing on the forthcoming negotiations at Dover. I conducted a search of the entire neighbourhood, and drew another blank. I made a second report, three days after the first. I expected my lord to order me back to London. Instead, Gorvin wrote that I was now to remain in Dover until the royal visit was over. He enclosed a new warrant for me, signed by the King himself. Not only was I to watch out for Van Riebeeck, I was to take careful note of all who came and went, particularly any foreigners. I was also to familiarize myself with the preparations for the royal visitors at the castle, and report immediately anything that might indicate foreign interference.

There was an urgency about these commands that suggested that my commission was more than a routine precaution. I knew enough of the matter to understand the reasoning behind this. A French treaty would negate our existing treaty obligations with the Dutch, with whom the French were at war. The French army was the most powerful in Europe, but its navy was weak. On the other hand, the English navy was formidable, and at the very least could do great damage to the Dutch fleet. The Grand Pensionary and the rest of the Dutch government knew that an Anglo-French alliance had the potential to defeat the Dutch both by land and by sea.

But the treaty hadn't yet been signed. And Van Riebeeck was still at large.

The one thing you could say in favour of Dover Castle was that it was big. That was just as well, given the hundreds of people who were about to descend on it.

It was clear that the ancient builders of the place had little interest in the comfort of its inhabitants. The strongest part – the keep, together with the inner ward in which it stood – was set on a windswept headland above the town. Around it, and vastly larger, was the outer ward, a long loop of stone, punctuated by square towers, which began and ended with the steep cliffs. Many of the buildings within the outer ward were in poor condition but some had been patched up, and there was space for the erection of temporary shelters. There was also accommodation for senior courtiers in the Keep Yard, as the inner ward was known, a cheerless place which high walls and towers made gloomy even at midday. The keep itself was reserved for the royal family and their intimates.

From my point of view, the castle was at least secure. The King had ordered the guard to be doubled.

Whitehall was flocking to Dover. The King, the Duke of York, the Duke of Monmouth and Prince Rupert would be there to greet Madame and the French envoys, and so would an army of courtiers and their servants. The royal family would occupy the massive keep at the heart of the castle. Their more important followers would be accommodated nearby, in varying degrees of comfort. Everyone else would be billeted in the town.

'It sounds simple enough on paper,' Mr Naunton said, not for the first time. There were two guttering candles on the table, and his face wavered between them, seemingly about to disintegrate into the darkness. He was a senior clerk in the Lord Steward's office, which controlled the household below stairs, and he had been sent down from Whitehall to make preparations for the impending visit. 'But most of the castle hasn't been habitable for decades. The town stinks of fish and the houses are no better than pigsties.'

'They can hardly blame you for that,' I said, though I suspected that they would.

'Mark my words, we'll have peers of the realm lying on the floors of alehouses, and their ladies sleeping three-to-a bed in garrets. Somehow we have to house and feed them all. And then there are the horses . . . Meanwhile Smirke talks endlessly of precedence and presence chambers and the Lord knows what.' Naunton threw up his hands in the air. 'What's a man to do, sir?'

'You make the royal party as comfortable as you can,' I said. 'And you let the rest go hang. Including Smirke.'

'Exactly. It's the only possible plan. Let's have a bottle and drink a toast to it.'

Naunton bellowed to his servant to bring wine. I felt sorry for him. It hadn't taken him long to realize that Dover was grossly inadequate for the purpose of a royal occasion of this magnitude. There were never enough craftsmen, artisans or labourers, let alone enough money to pay them. How was he even to find in this small corner of Kent sufficient quantities of food and drink to feed the visitors?

To make matters worse, he had to deal with Smirke, the Lord Chamberlain's man. The latter's responsibilities were the rooms of state – the presence chamber, the privy chamber, the chapel royal and so on, fixed since time immemorial as the sovereign's public apartments, and replicated as far as possible wherever His Majesty was.

Somehow Naunton was expected to work miracles. It was now Saturday 14 May. He had only two more days before Madame arrived.

He and I shared lodgings in the outer bailey of the castle, along with several other officials who had been sent down from Whitehall to make preparations for the royal visit. As well as the Lord Chamberlain, the Master of Horse had sent his representative, and so had the Groom of the Stool, the Master of the Robes and the Lord Almoner. All of the main departments of the royal household were in open competition for the scanty resources available.

'By the way,' I said with elaborate carelessness, 'do you happen to have a Mistress Hakesby on any of your lists?'

'Hakesby?' Naunton scrabbled among a sheaf of papers at his elbow. 'I don't remember the name offhand. English, I assume. Who's she with?'

'If she's here, I think she'll be with Madame's party.'

He ran his finger down the columns. 'Can't see her. But not everyone has a name to himself. I've got "Two Pastry Cooks", for example. Or "Monseigneur de Croissy's Man". Is she with anyone in particular?'

'Not as far as I know,' I said.

'Someone's waiting woman, perhaps? I've got about a score of those.'

'No. She's an architect.'

Naunton stared at me. 'How odd. An *architect*?' He contrived to wiggle his eyebrows in a manner intended to be salacious. 'A beauty, too? A rich widow? Or both?'

Fortunately the servant returned with the bottle at this moment, distracting him. In silence, we watched the wine streaming into our glasses, full of golden promise. We had supped together, and Naunton was halfway to being drunk.

'I believe I could bear everything,' he said, his mind reverting to the former subject, 'if it wasn't for Smirke.'

I raised my glass. 'Let's drink confusion to him then.'

We drank, and the servant poured again. I liked Naunton, a tubby, competent man who gave himself no airs. He drank too much but he wasn't alone in that. Smirke was another matter. If ever a name was a misnomer, his was. He was a thin, unsmiling gentleman, with manners so elaborate that they rivalled Lord Arlington's and an almost puritanical distaste for wine, a strange quality in such a devoted Royalist. He took care to remind those he met that his maternal grandfather had been an earl who died fighting for the King at Naseby.

When Smirke was obliged to dine with the rest of us, as he had today, he made it quite clear that he shared our company from duty, not by choice. He was convinced that the proper maintenance of the rooms of state was, if anything, even more important than the proper maintenance of the sovereign. He reminded everyone who would listen to him that Madame was, after all, coming on a state visit, and that she was representing the King of France. The Lord Chamberlain was determined that the visit should be ceremonially perfect for the honour of the King of England.

'Do you know what Smirke wants now?' Naunton said. 'A bedchamber for a Frog who's coming early. All to himself, if you please, and as close to Madame as possible. Which means somewhere in the Keep Yard. And it's a matter of urgency, because he's the Duke of Orléans' man, and Smirke wants to oblige him.'

'What's his job?'

'He's been sent to advise on questions of poxy precedence from the French side. Always full of pitfalls, apparently, a royal visit of this kind. A diplomatic quagmire. A slightest slip, Smirke says, and we'll all drown in the mud and never be heard of again.'

'Why isn't he coming with Madame, like the rest of them?'

'Because Monsieur and Madame don't see eye to eye, and she wouldn't let him join her party.' Naunton reached for the

bottle. 'If you ask me, this Frog is Monsieur's spy. The Duke
wants to know what his wife gets up to when she slips the
leash.'

I took another glass to keep him company. 'When does
he arrive?'

'He's here already.'

'In the castle?'

Naunton shook his head. 'He's coming on Saturday. But
I met him this morning. Smirke brought him in. He's some
sort of secretary to the Duke. His name's Jolliet but don't
let that fool you. He's about as jolly as a funeral. All in black,
a long, pompous face like a frowning donkey.'

I laughed. Naunton thought of himself as a wit. His witticisms were rarely very amusing, but I knew it was his way
of coping. That and the wine.

'Catholic, of course, like Smirke. They stick together, those
Papists. Which reminds me. I thought of something droll to
cheer us up. Why are Papist priests like pox sores?'

'I don't know,' I said.

'However much you try to get rid of them, they keep
coming back.'

Naunton laughed so hard that he almost fell off his chair.

I said, 'Will you find him somewhere to lodge?'

'I have to, or I'll have the Lord Chamberlain down on me.
Smirke said he'd report me if I didn't oblige him.' He
chuckled. 'But I'll teach the Frenchman a lesson. I have a
chamber in mind for him. It's downwind from the privies.
And the ceiling is very low. Ha!' He looked at me, as if for
approbation.

I made a face. 'A man must take his pleasures where he
can find them.'

355

'In this case, Marwood, my pleasure is to give him a sore head. Jolliet's as tall as a steeple. You know what Francis Bacon said? Wise Nature did never put her precious jewels into a garret four storeys high: and therefore that exceeding tall men have ever very empty heads. It's because all the brains have been knocked out of them. Ha! That last part was me. All the brains knocked out of them. A rich jest, eh?'

He burst out laughing and called for another bottle.

CHAPTER FORTY-SEVEN

THE FRENCH ARRIVED on Monday, 16 May. Despite the rain and the cold, the streets of the squalid little town seethed with activity. Some people had been up at dawn, watching for the lanterns and topsails of the approaching fleet.

'There's nothing I can do now,' Naunton said as we stood shivering in our cloaks among the crowd that lined the quayside. 'It's all in God's hands.'

His appearance of saintly resignation was so droll that I snorted with laughter. He looked offended. For once he hadn't intended the words as a joke. Then he smiled. 'Damn me, but I'll be glad to be back in Whitehall.'

The royal barge was the first to land its passengers. We watched the King hand out the Princess. He was a tall man, and she looked no larger than a child beside him. He gave her his arm, and led her to the waiting coach, with the bowing and curtsying crowd parting on either side. Madame's pale, dishevelled ladies clustered behind them like a flock of weary sheep. I had been long enough in Dover to observe that the sea is cruelly democratic: it treats all alike, usually badly.

At the coach, the Yeomen of the Guard pushed back the bystanders. For a moment, as the King was helping his sister into the coach, I saw their faces. He was looking down at her, his face full of a grave kindness I had never seen there before. She was looking up at him as if she could not believe the evidence of her eyes.

'Faith,' Naunton said, sounding surprised, 'she looks as if she's seen the Blessed Virgin Mary.'

I turned away and stared at the disembarking passengers. I was searching for Cat. I knew she had not returned to London, for I had ordered Margaret to send word if she did.

I couldn't see her. But as I scanned the crowd I caught sight of someone else. Towering among the bystanders who had come to watch the French arrive was the tall figure of Mr Fanshawe. I made my way towards him. Such was the press of people, it took me several minutes, and he was already moving away, in the direction of the town. He had Mistress Abbott – or Mistress Fanshawe as she now called herself once more – on one arm, and his granddaughter on the other.

'Mr Fanshawe,' I said, as I drew level with them, 'your servant, sir.'

I bowed to him and the ladies. The old man looked at me and compressed his lips. 'Mr Marwood,' he said without any sign of pleasure. 'What are you doing here?'

'I'm on the King's business, sir. And you?'

He glanced back at the harbour. 'Why, the world is here, come to see the King and the Princess.'

'You have come a long way. Do you lodge in Dover?'

'As it happens, I have an estate nearby. I am often here in the spring.'

'Where exactly?'

He frowned, for I had spoken bluntly. For a moment I thought he wouldn't answer, but he must have realized how easily I could find out by other means. 'A place called Swaring. It lies to the south of Canterbury. And now' – he glanced to either side of him – 'the ladies are growing fatigued, and we must leave you.'

The granddaughter was staring at me with wide, frightened eyes. I wondered, fleetingly, why she always looked scared. As for her mother, if her expression was any guide, she would cheerfully stick a dagger in my side. I looked more closely at her. Her features were pinched by the cold, which increased her resemblance to her half-brother.

'One moment, sir, if you please. Have you had news of Mr Van Riebeeck?'

'No,' Mistress Fanshawe burst out. Colour stained her pale cheeks. 'None at all.'

'I fancy he's returned to Holland,' Fanshawe said.

He gave me a curt nod. I watched them walking away. The sweet-faced child looked over her shoulder at me. She was frowning. They turned a corner and were gone.

For the next few hours, both the castle and the town were a ferment of activity. The air was full of horrified French voices. The newcomers were looking for their lodgings; they were tired, miserable, cold, wet, and in many cases still suffering from seasickness.

The rain fell relentlessly on bedraggled courtiers and their servants. Every now and then, I glimpsed Naunton: he seemed to be everywhere, plodding through the mud in the outer bailey and dealing with crisis after crisis with every appearance of imperturbable efficiency.

359

Now that the King, Madame and the rest of them were safely in the keep, their safety was the responsibility of the royal guards. In theory, my job had come to an end. I wrote a note to Lord Arlington about Fanshawe and Swaring, suggesting that we should have the place inspected in case Van Riebeeck was hiding there. There was no harm in being careful. Besides, I had not forgotten what he had done to Stephen.

Afterwards I patrolled the familiar streets of the town and the paths that criss-crossed the outer bailey of the castle, partly out of habit but more (if I am honest) in the hope of catching sight of Cat.

In the early evening, I made my way back up the hill towards my lodging. I heard Naunton call my name as I was passing the door of the guardroom at the main gate of the outer bailey. He beckoned me inside. He had been warming himself at the fire and talking to the officer in charge.

'What was the name of that rich widow of yours? Hayter? Haines?'

'Hakesby,' I said, aware that the officer was listening with interest. 'But she's not rich and she's not mine.'

'So you say.' Naunton gave a throaty chuckle, took out his wad of papers and waved it at me. 'I'm sure I've seen her somewhere here. The name caught my eye, and I said to myself, Aha, pound to a penny that's Marwood's mistress.'

'She's not my mistress,' I snapped.

He ignored my tone. 'Here we are.' He moistened his thumb and extracted one of the papers from the sheaf. 'The temporary passes for the inner bailey. Look – there.'

The Keep Yard was guarded far more strictly than the outer bailey, and by the King's own guards. Visitors were required to apply for a pass, and their names were recorded on a list, together with the purpose of their visit.

Cat's name was two-thirds of the way down. *Mistress Catherine Hakesby.* When I saw it, something twisted in my chest.

'Do you know where she's lodged?' I asked.

'Yes – it says.' Naunton stabbed his forefinger at a number beside her name. 'Thirty-four. That's the old wooden building below the Pharos and that ruined church on the headland. It's on the chilly side out there, I'm afraid, exposed to all the winds. She's sharing with some of the French maids.'

'Is she there now?'

'How do I know?' He looked at the list again. 'She wanted to see someone called Madame des Bordes. One of the Princess's ladies.' He grinned and gave me a friendly punch on the arm. 'Why don't you see if your mistress is back at her lodging? Head towards the Pharos. Number thirty-four is on the landward side. You can't miss it.'

'He's in the right of it, sir,' said the officer, who had been following the conversation with interest. 'It can't harm your chances with the lady, and fortune always favours the bold. Believe me, a lady likes an ardent lover, who *thrusts* himself on her attention.'

'Enough,' I growled. I cleared my throat. 'Anyway, she's not my lover.'

I heard them laughing as I left the guardroom.

CHAPTER FORTY-EIGHT

THEY HAD BEEN at Swaring for four days. The weather was bad and the house was damp. After the first evening, Maria saw little of Uncle Henryk. His movements were unpredictable, and he spent much time on business of his own in Dover. Even when he was at Swaring, he rarely joined them. Mr Fanshawe was not best pleased.

'He was here yesterday evening, you know,' he said at dinner. 'Why didn't he sup with us? I know for a fact he supped with Baines and his brother instead. Why the devil would he want to do that when he could have been with us?'

Baines was the bailiff. He lodged on the other side of the orchard. His brother, who worked in Dover, was a regular visitor.

'I'm sure there must have been a good reason,' Mistress Fanshawe said.

'Baines is too fond of his ale.' Fanshawe picked at the bread on his plate. 'I've been going over the accounts of the farm. The yields were down quite considerably last year. I fear I shall have to find another bailiff. Such a tiresome business.'

'Indeed, sir, it's too bad.'

'He's a coarse fellow too, and his brother's even worse. I cannot understand why Van Riebeeck seeks out their company.'

Cat curtsied.

Madame beckoned her to approach. She was seated at her dressing table, which had been placed close to the fire in her private closet. This was part of the suite of rooms set apart for her above the great chamber in the keep. The only other person in the room was Madame des Bordes, who was standing by the door, with her hands folded in front of her.

The Princess smiled. Her eyes were bright, and there was colour in her cheeks. She had undergone a mysterious transformation since Cat had last seen her, outside the wretched farmhouse near the border with Flanders.

'I wondered if you might be too ill to come,' she said. 'Were you seasick yesterday?'

'Yes, Madame. But it was better when I came up on deck.'

'I found that too. And now we are both safely here, and everything is well. You may return the letter.'

Cat held out the letter which had been entrusted to her at the farmhouse.

Madame glanced at it. 'Turn it over.'

Puzzled, Cat obeyed. Then she understood. Madame was making sure that the seal had not been tampered with.

'Good. Now put it on the fire.'

Cat crouched and dropped the letter onto the bed of burning coals. They watched a flame sprout from a corner. It ran around the letter until the paper blackened and curled.

'Use the poker now, if you please.'

In a few seconds, there was nothing left of the letter.

'You have been a faithful letter carrier for both my brother and me, Mistress Hakesby.'

'For . . . the King too?' Cat hesitated. 'You mean – in the poultry house model?'

The Princess smiled. 'You guessed? Yes – there were confidential papers concealed in it. My brother ordered a compartment to be made in the base. He has a taste for intrigue in these matters. Perhaps he's right to be cautious. He learned that lesson in a hard school. Not everyone can be trusted.'

There was a pause. The coals shifted in the fire. Cat wondered what had been inside Madame's letter. A word of farewell to her brother? An accusation of murder against her husband, Monsieur?

'I wish to show the King your designs for my new house,' Madame said, her voice strong and cheerful again. 'Bring them to me tomorrow morning, and he and I will look over them, and you will answer any questions we have.'

'But Madame,' Madame des Bordes said, 'Tomorrow is Wednesday. His Majesty has other plans.'

A look of understanding passed between the two women. Madame turned her head back to Cat. 'Mistress Hakesby, we must look over your designs another time. I shall send word.'

'Of course, Madame.'

Cat curtsied again, and the meeting was over.

As Cat hurried back to her lodging, the rain swooped on her. The weather matched her mood. Madame had been charm itself, but the brief meeting had served to remind Cat of her own unimportance. There was nothing for her to do except wait for Madame to summon her. Quite possibly the call would never come, for clearly both the King and his sister had more important things to do with their time.

At St Germain, Cat had at least been able to work. But there was nothing for her to do in Dover. She was trapped in this unpleasant, uncomfortable place with time on her hands. Brennan was probably at his wits' end in Henrietta Street. She felt a stab of longing, as acute as a needle, for the shabby surroundings of the Drawing Office.

Her lodging was in what the French called a *barraque*, a building mainly of wood, originally designed to house soldiers. It was near the crumbling Pharos and the dilapidated church, standing below them on the headland. The structure had been intended to be temporary but no one had bothered to remove it. In the last month or so, there had been a half-hearted attempt to make it habitable. On a day like this, it was one of the dreariest places imaginable, exposed to every freak of the weather.

The door was unlocked. It led to a long room open to the rafters, with a small chamber meant for an officer on one side, which had been appropriated by a large, grim-faced woman named Madame Goffre. All the walls had been newly white-washed. The main room had been temporarily divided with a series of partitions to give the occupants an illusion of privacy. The section nearest the door served as a vestibule.

The air was full of the chatter of women and the smell of damp clothes and stale perfume. Cat felt as if she had nothing in common with them but her sex. She lingered in the vestibule to remove her cloak, listening to the screeches of laughter within. Her spirits sank still further. There was nowhere to go in this town, nowhere to find refuge. Even if there had been, both she and these women were trapped by the weather.

Their only hope of diversion was a summons from one of the great ones that they served.

Madame Goffre, a woman whose skill at dressing a lady's hair was supposed to verge on the miraculous, was standing in the doorway of her chamber. She looked up as Cat entered the main room.

'Madame Hakesby! A gentleman called to see you.'

The chatter and the laughter diminished rapidly, and then stopped altogether.

'Indeed,' Cat said.

Madame Goffre made a moue. 'An English gentleman, I'm afraid, and perhaps not so very much of a gentleman. But still. We must make allowances, eh?'

Someone tittered. Madame Goffre had come to dominate the party by force of personality, and her witticisms were treated with respect.

'Did the gentleman leave a name?'

But Madame Goffre was not to be hurried. 'Moreover, perhaps they do things differently on this island. You must advise us, Madame Hakesby. Certainly this castle is not the sort of royal residence we are accustomed to visit in France.'

'A name?' Cat repeated.

'Ah, no. The monsieur did not think fit to leave a name with me, or a message. He was a man of middling height. Not old. His command of the French language was no better than a child's.' Madame Goffre shrugged and looked around her audience, as if for inspiration. 'What more can one say about him? Ah. His face. It was strangely scarred on the left side.' She opened her eyes very wide. 'But perhaps that too is not unusual in England.'

There was another titter.

'That was Mr Marwood, I believe,' Cat said. She was not pleased with Marwood but she did not care to have him insulted by others for no good reason. 'As you say, appearances may mislead. If I were you, I should have a care if you encounter him again. He has the ear of the King, and of the King's chief minister. In this country, only a fool would venture to offend him.'

She turned on her heel, took up her cloak and went outside into the rain and the wind.

With her head down, Cat splashed through the mud and puddles. She had no destination in mind, but she could not bear to be in the same room as Madame Goffre and her sycophants for much longer.

If anything, the rain was falling harder than before. But Cat had reached the point where she no longer cared much about the weather. She walked away from the Pharos and the church towards the high, grey walls of the inner ward. There she allowed the flow of people to bear her along like a twig in the current towards the Constable's Gateway. She did not pass through it. That would have brought her out onto the road that led down the hill to the town and the harbour. She had already seen more than enough of Dover.

Instead she walked aimlessly along the range of buildings that abutted the gateway, passing under the shelter of a covered walkway that ran along the front of a long storehouse. The space was crowded with men staring out at the rain. The press of people was so great that she was forced to wait with her back against the wall until she could pass on. She could not help overhearing the conversation of two gentlemen who were talking in French a few paces away.

'. . . I am desolated, Monsieur Jolliet.'

'Desolation is all very well. But what can you do about it? That is the question.'

'I shall talk to my colleague directly.' The speaker was facing Cat. He was a slim, fussily dressed man with a narrow face. 'I cannot think how it was allowed to happen.'

'Monsieur may choose to take it as an insult to his honour when he hears.' Jolliet had his back to Cat. He was tall, and made even taller by an enormous black periwig. 'As indeed it is. The chamber smells like a privy. I cannot even stand up to my full height. I must have somewhere more fitting.'

His voice was familiar. It was something to do with its timbre, she thought idly. Perhaps she had overheard the gentleman at St Germain.

'On my honour, sir, I would count it a tragedy if Monsieur should hear of this foolish mistake,' the other man said.

'I can't be sure he won't hear of it from someone, Monsieur Smirke, even if I don't tell him. I fear that you English are not so respectful of the due forms and ceremonies as we are in France. Your colleague forgets that I am the accredited representative of the Duke of Orléans. An insult to me is an insult to him.'

'An insult? No, sir, pray—'

'But as it happens, I have fixed on alternative accommodation that will answer my requirements and . . .'

Jolliet's voice died away. As he was speaking, he had turned his head and caught sight of Cat. They stared at one another. Jolliet was dressed with sombre elegance in the French style. His long face was powdered. The darkness of his wig enhanced his pallor. And he had Van Riebeeck's pale, searching eyes.

Cat turned and pushed through the crowd. She hurried away, slipping and sliding in the mud, careless of appearances. She heard footsteps behind her, and Van Riebeeck's voice saying her name. She turned abruptly and faced him. In his haste, the rain had fallen on his cheeks and made tracks through the powder.

'Madam—'

'What are you doing here?' she burst out. 'And why are you dressed like this? Why are you pretending to be a Frenchman?'

'Forgive me.' Van Riebeeck had switched to English. 'I will explain everything.' He glanced back at Smirke. 'But I can't speak now.'

'I don't understand – and what's this nonsense about Jolliet? And Monsieur? Was everything you said to me a pack of lies?'

'No.' He screwed up his face as if in sudden pain. 'I'll tell you everything, madam, and then you will understand. I swear it.' He touched her arm. 'But you must trust me. My feelings for you are as they ever were, and my motives are honourable. On my word as a gentleman.'

'Monsieur Jolliet?' Smirke called from the shelter of the walkway. 'Time is of the essence if we're to find you better quarters.'

Van Riebeeck ignored him. 'Quick. Tell me where I can send word.'

'I lodge in the building below the Pharos and the old church. With the number thirty-four on the door. But that does not mean I—'

'Promise me, madam.' He stooped over her, and his black cloak flapped in the wind as if it wanted to embrace her.

369

'Promise on your honour that you will come when I send word. And for the love of God be discreet.'

She said, with a spurt of anger, 'Why should I?'

'Please.' His voice was gentler than she had ever heard it. 'Please come. I cannot tell you what a joy it is to see your face.'

'I may come,' she said. 'If it pleases me.'

On Tuesday, the second day of the French visit, I hardly saw Naunton. He had been busy before, but now Madame's suite had arrived he was never still. 'I shall go mad,' he said when we met by chance in the town. 'The wretches complain about everything.'

He stumbled back to our lodgings in the evening as I was finishing a late supper. He rang for the servant and sank into a chair.

'By God, sir, I hate French courtiers even more than I hate our own. Pass the wine.'

I had already lifted the bottle to pour. After he had drunk two or three glasses he gnawed on the leg of a fowl.

'But I tell you this, Marwood.' He waved the half-eaten leg at me. 'If I were to rank everyone I hate in order, there's one man who would take the first place by a mile. That odious, mealy-mouthed, oily-tongued, two-faced Smirke.'

'What's he done now?'

Naunton growled. He watched the servant opening another bottle. 'It's like a lute,' he said, sweeping his left arm out and fluttering the fingers on his right hand to mime the actions of a musician. 'My job is like a lute. If one string is out of tune – a single string, mark you – then everything sounds out of tune.'

'And your meaning, sir?'

'Isn't it plain enough? Smirke is that untuned string. My arrangements in Dover were finely balanced and perfectly tuned. But Smirke insists on changing one thing, and that puts the whole at risk. That damned Jolliet's behind it. I knew he would be trouble.'

'Ah. The man near the privies.'

'Exactly. And he complains about his lodging to Smirke. More than that, he insists on having another chamber, also in the Keep Yard, where space is hardest to find, and where the most important courtiers are lodged. The one he wants has the Chevalier de this and that in it. So out goes the Chevalier, and into the room by the privies. But then the Chevalier complains and I must find him somewhere else. Which means I must eject a third person, who will then complain in turn. And so on, and on, and on. All the while, Smirke rubs his hands together and says it's a matter of the appropriate ceremony, which the Lord Chamberlain commands us to follow with a particular degree of nicety when it concerns members of the French suite.' He snorted. 'Why, sir, the next thing I know they'll make me give up my own bed to this mincing Frog.'

I held up my glass. 'Damnation to the mincing Frog.'

Afterwards, Naunton refilled our glasses. 'Should we drink to your mistress? Did you contrive to see her?'

'No,' I said. 'I called at her lodging but she was not there. And she's not my mistress.'

Naunton crowed with laughter. 'I have you, sir! I have touched you on a tender spot, eh? A toast to her! What is her name again?'

I didn't want to talk about Cat. 'We should drink damnation to the mincing Frog again. Just to make sure.'

We drained our glasses again.

'Though,' he said, a trifle owlishly because the wine was beginning to have its effect on him, 'to be accurate, it should be the mincing horse.'

I looked blankly at him. I feared that Naunton was going to produce another of his droll remarks. 'What horse?'

'Jolliet,' he said. 'Not a frog. A horse. I told you.'

'Told me what?'

'That Jolliet looks like a horse.'

'A donkey, sir, surely. I distinctly remember that you said he looked like a donkey.'

Naunton spread out his hands. 'A horse – a donkey – it's all one, Marwood. God made very little distinction between the two faces, and who are we to question His wisdom? Anyway, on my honour, Jolliet looks like a mincing horse in a black wig, and we should drink to his damnation.'

So we did. More than once.

'A witty phrase, Marwood, you must agree. Perhaps I should leave Whitehall and write plays instead. Mincing horse, ha!'

Naunton's words lingered in my mind. Later that evening, as I was sinking into sleep, I thought of them again, and they had acquired an unexpected familiarity: or rather, they bounced back like a faint and distorted echo from my memory.

A horse in a wig.

CHAPTER FORTY-NINE

IT WAS STILL raining the following day, Wednesday. There was nothing for Cat to do except wait — for a summons to attend Madame or for Van Riebeeck to send word. Madame Goffre had been called away early in the morning to work her customary miracles with her mistress's hair. Otherwise Cat could not have answered for the consequences.

She sat on a stool and tried to read. It was one thing to be kept waiting by a princess of the blood, but quite another to be kept waiting by Henryk Van Riebeeck. Cat was reluctant to leave the lodging for long in case she missed a message. She was furious with herself for waiting, and furious with him for keeping her waiting.

It was difficult to think of any honest reason for his disguising himself as a Frenchman. On the other hand, he had been so urgent in his pleas to see her, so sincere in his manner, and so much the anxious lover, that she should at least allow him to defend himself.

A man like Marwood, she thought as she turned another

unread page, one could read like a book. If Van Riebeeck were a book, it would be one written in a language nobody could understand.

It was not until the sun was setting that a French pageboy brought her a note. It was written in English.

Madam
If you will be so kind, the bearer of this will conduct you to my lodging, where I shall have the honour of unburdening myself of what I have previously been obliged to conceal. I have had your name set down on the guards' list at the Palace Gate, so there will be no difficulty about admitting you to the inner ward.

There was no signature. While the boy stood by, his eyes discreetly lowered, Cat read the note again and tried to squeeze more meaning from it. She told him to wait outside while she found her cloak and put on her overshoes. Van Riebeeck had not tried to cajole her. He had not told her to be discreet, though that went without saying.

She was not obliged to go. But it was still light outside, and the Keep Yard was always full of people. Someone must always be within earshot. There could be no danger in it, except perhaps to her reputation if she were careless. But the risk of that was small in comparison with what she might gain: the solution to the mystery of Van Riebeeck's motives.

Then there was that other matter, that abrupt and discourteous offer of marriage. At the time, in the ruined garden at Austin Friars, he had seemed deadly serious and entirely sane. Marriage? And to a man like that? Even if Van Riebeeck had spoken the truth that day, the very idea of marriage to him or anyone was absurd.

She shivered involuntarily, a ripple of sensation wavering between fear and desire. She wondered what it would be like to be married to a vigorous man in the prime of life rather than to a cantankerous old man more than twice her age.

The boy led her to the Palace Gate, where a guard ticked her name on his list and permitted her to go through to the Keep Yard. The tang of burning pitch caught the back of Cat's throat and made her cough. The torches had recently been lit, their flames flaring against the darkness of the stone and glinting on the flints embedded in the masonry. Thanks to the height of the walls, it was darker here than in the outer ward. It was as if the guards were keeping so strict a watch that even twilight was forbidden entry.

'This way, mistress,' said the boy.

A pentice linked the main entrance of the keep to a substantial range of buildings set against the curtain wall to the right. The boy led her up a flight of steps and along the covered way to the largest of these lodgings. It was arranged on the plan of a capital E, with three projecting gables.

The boy navigated their course through a crowded anteroom into an even more crowded hall, where people were talking loudly in English and French. After a passage, a staircase, and a suite of public rooms, he opened a door and stood back, waiting for Cat to pass through. The doorway led to a spiral staircase.

'Monsieur says you're to go up. His chamber's the door at the top, before you get to the leads.'

As she climbed the stairs, Cat heard the door closing behind her, cutting off the bustle and chatter in the rooms below. Rushlights stood at intervals in embrasures cut through the thickness of the wall, giving a faint murky glow that brightened as Cat's eyes adjusted to them. She passed two doors, both closed, and mounted higher until she came to a third. The stairs continued upwards to another, smaller door, which she guessed gave access to the roof.

She knocked on the third door and waited. The door remained closed. In a while, she knocked again, more loudly and for longer. Still there was no answer. Losing patience, she twisted the ring of the handle and pushed. The door swung silently inwards.

Cat stepped inside the room and looked about her. It contained a small bed, its curtains tied back, two chairs and an oak chest. The only light came from two candles standing on the chest. There was no fireplace, and the air was chilly.

There was a dark, formless animal crouching at the foot of the bed. Her heart leapt into her mouth. The animal dissolved into a black periwig on a stand.

A cloak and a hat lay on the bed. A valise stood in the shadows beyond the chest, with a sword propped against the wall beside it.

'Madam.'

Cat spun round. Van Riebeeck was standing in a second doorway, which was set in the wall behind the door from the stairs. It was so low that he had to stoop to avoid hitting his head on the lintel.

'I rejoice to see you.' He was in the room now, standing to his full height and towering above her. 'Pray keep your voice low.'

'Why are you calling yourself Jolliet?' she said. 'Why are you pretending to be French?'

He sighed. 'My mother was French, as it happens. Her father was a Huguenot from La Rochelle.'

'But you're Dutch. And your name is Van Riebeeck. Unless that's a lie too.'

'It's not a lie. But in this place, my name is Jolliet.'

'Because of your creditors?'

'I have no creditors. I was obliged to tell you an untruth.'

'Only one?' Cat said. 'Perhaps everything you said to me was a pack of lies.'

'No. I said I wanted you to be my wife. That was true. In some ways, I wish it were not so, but a man cannot always choose for himself in these matters. Providence has a mind of its own, I find, and it has led me to you.'

Cat took a step backwards, closer to the door, which was still open. 'Wouldn't it be truer to say that you wanted my help and so you said whatever was necessary to get it?'

He shrugged. 'It is possible for two things to be true at once. I do want you to be my wife. There's—'

'Were you the thief at the inn? When I passed through Dover before?'

'Later.' He held a finger to his lips. 'We haven't time for this now. Come with me. And you must be very quiet.'

Without waiting for a reply, he turned and ducked into the second doorway. Cat followed. His lack of doubt and absence of hesitation had something to do with that. But there was more: something pulled her towards him, whether she would or not, as an undercurrent sucks a swimmer from her course.

She found herself in a passage in the thickness of the wall. Five yards ahead, Van Riebeeck was passing an alcove, where

377

a candle burned in a bracket. The passage made a sharp right turn. Cat glanced into the alcove as she passed it, making out a wooden seat of a privy set into a stone bench. She turned the corner and almost collided with him. He swung round and, with a casual assumption of ownership, put his arm around her shoulders and his hand over her mouth.

'Listen,' he whispered. 'And learn.'

They stood together in a parody of embracing lovers. His hand smelled of perfume and smoke. At first Cat thought the passage had come to a dead end. Then, as her eyes adjusted, she made out a faint and irregular line of light that made a rectangle from floor to ceiling. There were voices on the other side, low-pitched and urgent. A few seconds later, she realized that the rectangle marked a doorway, and that the privy behind her had originally been intended to serve more than one chamber.

Gradually her ears adjusted to the voices. She could make out the occasional word, then phrases and even entire sentences. One speaker in particular had a deep, deliberate voice that was more audible than the rest. It was also a voice that Cat knew.

Lord Arlington's.

She tried to pull away from Van Riebeeck, but his grip tightened, and she couldn't move.

'. . . but if it becomes known . . .'

'It won't be, my lord.' The second voice was familiar too. Sir Richard Bellings, the man who had examined her command of the French language in Goring House, while the King was playing with Tata a few yards away.

'Very well. But consider. When he announces his conversion, as he is sworn to do, then . . .'

Van Riebeeck pulled her back. She allowed him to draw her down the passage, back to his chamber. He closed the door quietly and turned to face her. The only light in the room, which came from the two candles on the chest, was behind him.

'You're eavesdropping,' Cat said.

'Yes.' He ignored the condemnation in her voice. 'I listen to them going to and fro over the same ground. Like a pack of hounds that can't find the scent.'

'Who?'

'My Lords Arlington and Arundell, Sir Thomas Clifford and Sir Richard Bellings. They use the room as their privy council chamber.'

'Are they plotting something?'

'In a way. They are negotiating a treaty with the French on behalf of the King. They have been discussing the day's business and preparing their arguments for when they meet the French again in the morning. Fortunately for me, the castle's office of works were meant to brick up the doorway to the privy as part of the preparations for the King's visit. But they didn't. They were rushed, and they merely fixed a wooden screen over it. There's a hanging on the other side that masks it. Those men don't know the doorway is there.'

'But you do.'

'Naturally. I had made thorough preparations. There is an English official – you saw me with him yesterday – who believes that I am the accredited servant of the Duke of Orléans. He let slip to me that Lord Arlington and the other negotiators were meeting there. But I already knew that the workmen had skimped the task.'

'How could you know that?'

'You remember Mr Fanshawe?'

'Of course I do.'

'He has a house and land between here and Canterbury. His bailiff's brother is the foreman of the constable's office of works at the castle. He's a foolish man who talks too much when he drinks. Before Madame had even landed, I knew more about the castle than most of its inhabitants ever do.'

'I don't understand what you're about,' Cat said. 'But I do know I've no reason to trust you.'

Van Riebeeck moved, putting himself between her and the door to the stairs. He lowered his voice still further. 'Madam, your king is about to sign a treaty with the King of France against Holland. They will attack us by land and sea. The English want revenge on our navy for their defeat at our hands, and they want to steal our trade from us. The French want the Low Countries, and they would gobble us up entirely, as well as the Spanish Netherlands, if only they could. That's why Madame has been permitted to come to England. She has been acting as a go-between for the two kings. Thanks to her, they have been able to avoid the usual diplomatic channels and therefore the risk of betrayal. The treaty is to be signed here, at Dover, perhaps in that very chamber, by the representatives of England and France.'

'Then there's nothing you can do about it,' Cat said. 'Except tell your masters what the whole world will know soon enough.'

'Do you think I don't know that?' Van Riebeeck's voice was still quiet, but his tone was savage. 'Tell me, would you want this country to have a Catholic king? A Papist on the throne of England again?'

'Of course not.' Cat paused, her mind filling with childhood nightmares of the Inquisition combing the country for heretics, of Godly men and women being burned at the stake in Smithfield, of Jesuits sauntering through the streets of London and lording it over the kingdom. She had grown up in a family who took for granted the fact that the machinations of Papists were equivalent to those of the Devil, and that the subjection of England was the Pope's dearest ambition. She said, 'There would be another civil war if the King went over to Rome and tried to convert the country.'

'Indeed. He would be a traitor to his own country. They would cut off his head, if they could, as they did his father's.'

'But this is an alliance between England and France. Agreed, that's bad enough, but not—'

'I haven't finished.' Van Riebeeck gripped her forearm. 'Listen. This treaty will contain a secret article. The King of France undertakes to pay your king a generous pension. The money will lessen the power of Parliament over him, perhaps allow him to dispense with it altogether. And in return, when the time is right, your king will declare war on Holland. At the same time he will also declare himself a Catholic and work to return this country to Rome.'

Cat shook her head. 'That's impossible.'

'Is it? You heard them talking, Lord Arlington and the others. My lord does what the King tells him to do. Sir Thomas is as devoted to the King as a dog to his master, and he himself already warps towards Rome though he has not yet declared himself. Arundell and Bellings are Papists, and they are desperate for England to return to Rome. Did you know that Bellings is the Queen's secretary? The Queen prays night and day that her husband will be received into the Roman church. They are desperate to have that secret clause, even

Arlington, for if the King becomes more powerful, then so do they. But the world will tumble about their ears if the clause becomes known before the King is ready to declare for Rome. And they know it.'

'Assuming that's true,' Cat said slowly, 'what do you intend to do about it?'

Van Riebeeck was still holding her arm. 'Lay my information before the Grand Pensionary. These negotiations have been in train for months. Thanks to that fool Abbott, I have acquired copies of many of the preliminary letters and memoranda. And now' – he gestured towards the chamber on the other side of the passage – 'I know the final form that the secret clause will take. I have proof. De Witt will know how best to use the ammunition I give him. If he wishes, he will be able to undermine this alliance before it has started.'

'This is treason.'

'Is it? Or does your king propose to commit treason against his people, as his father did?' His voice softened. 'In the long run, madam, you English will thank us. Apart from a few malcontents.'

His argument struck home. The monarchy already had its enemies. A Catholic king on the throne would increase them tenfold. Perhaps, Cat thought, it would be better to nip this treaty in the bud. She was a regicide's child, after all, and she had no love of kings for their own sake. She had no taste for republics, either, not in themselves. The best anyone could hope for was a government which brought peace and prosperity, and which guaranteed the safety of the people it ruled. A Catholic king would do neither.

'Time is of the essence,' Van Riebeeck was saying. 'I shall

leave tomorrow.' He tugged her arm with sudden force. 'And you must come with me.'

'No,' Cat said, her voice loud with shock.

He swung round. He was now gripping both her upper arms. 'You want to. Don't you? I know you do.'

She thought of the Drawing Office then, of her slope standing by the window with a fresh sheet of paper on it. Of Brennan waiting for her to tell him what to do. Even of Marwood—

Van Riebeeck pulled her closer. He lowered his lips to her forehead. A tremor ran through her.

'No,' she said again, more quietly this time. She tried to pull away but Van Riebeeck drew her closer. Part of her stood aside from all this and marvelled at her own helplessness, at her inability to resist.

'I've trusted you, madam, and now you must trust me.'

'Must I?' She felt her treacherous body soften against his. 'Must I?'

CHAPTER FIFTY

IT WASN'T UNTIL after six o'clock that I heard Naunton's footsteps stumbling up the stairs to our lodgings. He flung open the door and saw me sitting at the table.

'Thank God,' he said piously. 'Praise the Lord to the highest, Marwood. The day's work is done, and it's time to drink a bottle of sack.'

'In a moment,' I said.

Naunton stopped, his hand on the bell rope. 'What? Why the delay?'

'Would you do me a favour? And then we shall order two bottles, sir, and they will be set down to my account.'

He stuck out his lower lip, like a child asked to defer a treat. 'What favour?'

'Smirke's Frenchman. Jolliet.'

'What about him? I haven't heard a word from either of them all day, or seen them, and I'd like to keep it that way.'

'I want you to call on Monsieur Jolliet now, and take me with you. You could say you wanted to make sure he was comfortable in his new lodging. He would see it as a mark of respect.'

'I leave flattery to Smirke.' Naunton lifted the candle so he could see my face more clearly. 'What's this about?'

He sounded more sober now. He was no fool, so I decided to take him at least partly into my confidence.

'Jolliet is very tall. He's got a face like a horse.'

'More like a donkey——'

'And he did not travel here with the rest of Madame's suite.'

'Yes, yes,' he said impatiently. 'Stop talking in riddles. Your point?'

'My Lord Arlington has commanded me to be on the alert for a man of that description. If it's Jolliet, I don't want to alarm him. If it isn't, I don't want to upset him more than he already is. But if you were to call on him, which in the circumstances would be entirely natural——'

'Not to me.'

'——then I could hang back in the shadows and see his face without his remarking it.' I smiled at him. 'Come, sir, what have you to lose? If Jolliet is who he says he is, you gain two bottles of wine. And if he's not, you earn my lord's gratitude, as well as the wine.'

The wind from the sea was still whipping the rain into spiteful flurries. Naunton grumbled as we splashed through the puddles and climbed the slope that led to the Palace Gate. At the guardhouse, they waved us into the Keep Yard. The officer of the guard that evening was Naunton's friend, the man who had taken it upon himself to offer me unwanted advice.

'Found your mistress yet, sir?' he said to me.

'Not yet.'

'Remember what I told you.' He thrust out his pelvis in an unmistakably obscene gesture. 'Fortune favours the brave.'

'I shall bear that in mind, sir,' I said, and hurried after Naunton.

He had put on a spurt to reach the shelter of the pentice across the yard. Even at this time, and in this weather, it was crowded. People lingered there to hear the gossip, and to speculate about what the great ones were doing in the keep.

'This way,' Naunton said, leading me to the right in the direction of an old building with lighted windows. 'It's through Arthur's Hall.'

As we were threading our way through the crowd, my sword entangled itself with a gentleman's legs. I apologized profusely, and fortunately he did not take offence. That was the trouble with swords – you were more at risk from tripping over your own or someone else's than you were from being run through with a blade. Naunton glanced back at me.

'Why the devil did you bother to wear a sword?' He was growing tetchy, wanting his wine. 'Trying to impress the Frog?' He paused at the bottom of a dimly lit spiral staircase. 'His chamber would be at the top, wouldn't it? I should have held out for three bottles.'

'Why did he want that one in particular?' I asked.

'God knows. The French are full of fantastic quirks. I've come to expect them now, as a sailor expects to find weevils in his biscuit.' He snorted with laughter at his own wit.

'Try to let the light fall on his face,' I whispered as we climbed. 'But not on mine.'

Naunton shrugged and smiled, as if humouring an idiot. 'He probably won't be there. I wager he'll be with Smirke somewhere. I expect they're talking about how deeply you should bow to the bastard son of the Bey of Algiers.' He turned his head and grinned at me. 'Or how tenderly Monsieur's groom of the closet should wipe his master's arse.'

On the landing at the top, he paused at the door to catch his breath. I stood a pace or two behind him. 'Don't knock,' I whispered as forcefully as I could. 'Try the door.'

He twisted the handle. I heard the click of the latch on the other side. The door swung inwards.

A man and a woman were standing in a close embrace at the foot of the bed. Their shadows wavered on the bare boards of the floor as they turned towards us. The man was very tall. He was not wearing a wig, and his head was long and narrow. The candles were behind him, and the lamps on the stairs were too faint for their light to penetrate the room.

'What is this?' the man said. 'Get out at once.'

I could not see the couple's faces. But I knew the man's voice.

'A thousand pardons, Monsieur Jolliet,' Naunton said. 'I wouldn't have inconvenienced you at such a time for the world.'

'Van Riebeeck,' I said, pushing past Naunton and laying a hand on the hilt of my sword. 'I've a warrant for your arrest.'

The woman in his arms turned her head. It was Cat. I could not move, could not speak, could not think. I was powerless, as incapable of motion as one struck by a petrifying palsy.

'Marwood—'

She broke off as Van Riebeeck pulled her towards a chest

on which two candles were standing. He snatched a sword that had been leaning against it. He gripped its sheath with the hand of the arm holding Cat, and ripped out the blade.

'This is a plot against me, madam,' he said to Cat.

I couldn't understand why she did not struggle to escape. 'Cat, get away from him. He's a Dutch spy.'

Naunton swore under his breath. He and I advanced into the room. The light had now fallen on Cat's face. She was frowning. To my consternation, I realized that my words had not come as a surprise to her.

Van Riebeeck scowled at me. 'Have done with this nonsense, Marwood.'

'He bribed your maid to have a sight of your itinerary,' I went on, staring intently at Cat. 'He tried to intercept you at Dover. But he's worse than a spy. Much worse.'

Cat looked dazed. At last she spoke. 'I don't understand. What do you mean?'

'He's a murderer.'

'That is a lie,' Van Riebeeck said. 'Not a word is true. Why would I kill anyone?' He glanced down at Cat. 'My love, you know why Marwood says these things, don't you? He hates me because he wants you for himself. The fool is jealous.'

The endearment was like a blow to the heart.

'Damned if I understand what this about,' Naunton said briskly. He nodded to Van Riebeeck. 'But you, sir – you're here under a false name, that's clear enough, and Mr Marwood says you're a spy. He's my Lord Arlington's man, and I'll take his word against yours. Let this lady go, and we'll discuss what's to be done.'

Without warning, Van Riebeeck glided forward, dragging Cat with him. The point of his blade caught Naunton in the chest. He cried out and dropped his stick. He slumped to his knees, both hands clutching his wound, and fell sideways with a thud on the floor.

I tugged out my own sword. Van Riebeeck drew back. Cat was struggling to free herself, but he held her close.

'Let her go,' I said. 'You damned scarecrow.'

Even as I was speaking, he lunged again. I tried to avoid the blade but he was too fast. There was a sharp, intolerable pain in my right hand. My sword clattered on the floor. I cried out.

Cat was trying to claw herself from Van Riebeeck's embrace. But he had her crushed against his body, with her arms pinned to her sides. She kicked at his legs but could do little damage because he had drawn her so closely to himself.

'Let her go,' I said again, and blundered towards them.

Naunton groaned. 'Marwood,' he croaked. 'Help me.'

Without thinking I looked down at him. Only for a second, but it was enough for Van Riebeeck to lunge again. I leapt back, but too late. The blade caught me in the throat, pinning me to the wall. I squirmed. The tip nicked my skin.

I said, 'Cat—'

The blade dropped away. He must have relaxed his grip on Cat when he lunged, for she was wriggling, a blur of motion. She gave a sudden cry – indeed, it was more accurately a howl of rage, a sound barely human. He reared backward. She tore herself away from him.

Van Riebeeck dropped his sword on the floor and clasped his throat with both hands. Blood spurted between his fingers. He staggered to the chest and slumped onto it, oversetting one of the candles. It fell to the floor, and its light died.

I kicked Van Riebeeck's sword away and picked up my own. Only then did I look at Cat.

She was leaning against the wall and breathing heavily. She raised her head and looked at me. The room was lit only by one candle. Its flame caught the edge of the blade of her knife. Reflections of the flame filled her eyes with golden sparks.

CHAPTER FIFTY-ONE

IT WAS FORTUNATE that the officer of the guard knew me.

'What's this, sir?' he said in surprise. 'Is your hand bleeding? We must find you something to bind the wound.'

He sent a soldier to bring a dressing. I drew him aside from the guardroom fire. He looked curiously at me.

'How did you do that?'

I told him that one of the foreigners had drawn his sword on our friend Naunton and left him gravely injured.

'And the foreigner?'

'Dead by my hand.'

He whistled silently. 'A private quarrel, sir? That's not wise, especially not here.'

'Not a quarrel,' I said. 'This is a matter of state. I must send to Lord Arlington at once. He will want us to act with the utmost discretion. But first, pray send for a surgeon.'

'And what do we say to him?'

'If we must say something, call it a duel over a gambling debt. If possible, let Naunton be removed to our lodgings.'

'And this foreigner?'

'Leave him where he is. I've covered the body with blankets. My lord will make known his commands in due course. No doubt he'll speak to you.'

'We'll need a litter for Naunton. With curtains.' The officer was no fool, fortunately, despite his taste for talking bawdy.

'An excellent plan.' I took the key from my pocket. For Naunton's sake, I had to trust him. 'If the surgeon comes before I return, take him up to Naunton. The door of the chamber is locked. Apart from Naunton, nothing must be disturbed in there, including the body, and the door must not be left unlocked. I give you my lord's authority to leave your post and accompany them yourself. Your men must be sworn to secrecy, and they must touch nothing. Tell them they will not regret it if they keep their mouths shut.'

He took a moment to think. Then he nodded. 'I understand, sir.'

'And now I need pen and paper. I must write a line to my lord.'

At that moment, over his shoulder, I saw Cat passing the open door of the Palace Gate guardroom and slipping out of the Keep Yard.

Half an hour later, my lord received me in his lodging, a set of apartments on the first floor of Arthur's Hall. I gave him a carefully edited version of the truth. I was sharing a lodging with Mr Naunton, I told him, the Lord Steward's man, and he had mentioned to me that a Frenchman, a Monsieur Jolliet, had made a fuss about his accommodation; he had demanded to be given a certain chamber at the top of Arthur's Hall.

'His description of the man had some faint similarity to

Van Riebeeck, my lord. And Jolliet's behaviour was strange. I asked Mr Naunton to call on him this evening and take me with him – in case it was Van Riebeeck. When we entered the bedchamber, I knew him at once. And he knew me, as well. He went for his sword. Poor Naunton went down in the struggle, with a wound in his chest. A surgeon is seeing him now. But Van Riebeeck is dead. His body is still up there for the present.'

'Who killed him?' Arlington looked curiously at me. 'You?'

I looked steadily at him. 'Yes, my lord. A lucky thrust indeed – I'm no swordsman. Indeed, I scarcely know how it happened. By that time, you see, the candles had been knocked over, and we were in the dark.'

'Where precisely is this chamber?'

'In the same wing as this. At the very top. You reach it by a spiral stair at the eastern end.'

He brooded for a moment. 'Did you say the surgeon's there now?'

'Yes, my lord. And two soldiers who will carry Naunton down to a litter when the surgeon's finished his examination, together with the officer of the guard from the Palace Gate.'

'Then what are you doing here, Marwood?' Arlington demanded angrily. 'Go back at once. Make sure nothing is touched. As soon as the wounded man is fit to move, get rid of them all. Then search the place. And the body.'

I had little sleep that night.

After Lord Arlington dismissed me, saying that he would confer with me later, I returned to the bedchamber in Arthur's Hall. At least Cat had escaped. There was a good chance that no one would ever know that she had been there.

There had been blood on her clothes, but fortunately her cloak covered it.

But why had she been in this room in the first place? How much did she know? And what had there been between her and Van Riebeeck? I could not rid my mind of seeing her in his embrace.

I found the surgeon examining poor Naunton, who was now on the bed, his shirt open, whimpering as the surgeon's fingers explored the wound. The soldiers were on either side, each with a candle. Van Riebeeck's body lay against one wall, shrouded in blankets. Nothing, so far as I could see, had been disturbed.

'How does he do?' I asked the surgeon.

'The thrust missed the heart and the lungs,' he said without looking up. 'If the wound's not infected, he should live.'

'Thank God,' I said. 'Is he well enough to move?'

The surgeon snorted. 'He was calling for wine a moment ago.'

He straightened up and turned aside to wipe his hands on a cloth. The soldiers backed away from the bed. I sat beside Naunton and took his hand.

'You'll soon be back to health,' I said in a bright voice. I bent closer, bringing my mouth close to his ear and murmured, 'Don't mention there was a woman here.'

The whimpering stopped. I stood up and said, 'I've not forgotten, sir, I owe you some sack. Or was it three bottles? No, I believe it was four. I shall help you drink them as soon as you are yourself again.'

I saw a flash of teeth in the gloom of the bed. Naunton was grinning at me.

* * *

394

It took some time before the arrangements for removing Naunton were in place. At last the two soldiers linked their hands and made a chair of their arms. They staggered down the spiral staircase with their burden. I heard the poor man's groans fading in the distance. A litter was waiting at the door downstairs, and the surgeon would see him settled in his own bed. There was talk of a dose of laudanum.

I was alone with Van Riebeeck's body. The room was brighter now, with half a dozen candles. In the last hour or so, I had grown very cold, even tremulous, as a man sometimes does after he has been in peril or labouring under great anxiety; and I had suffered both. The lack of a fire made it worse. Indeed I was shaking so much that I tugged the two blankets from the body and wrapped them around my shoulders.

It was only then that I noticed the existence of the second door, for it had been obscured by the opening of the door to the stairs. This one was smaller. It opened into a narrow passage, which led to a privy in the thickness of the wall. But it continued beyond until it came to a dead end. I held up my candle and by its light saw a partition made of planks, fresh from trimming by the adze. There had once been a door here – the iron pintles of the hinges were still embedded on the wall.

A hole had been bored in the partition a few inches above my eyes. It had been made recently, for there was a sprinkling of sawdust on the ground below it. A peephole? It was too high for me to look through without a stool, but Van Riebeeck had had the advantage of me in that respect.

There was one mystery solved: the reason for Van Riebeeck's desire to be moved to this bedchamber. He had needed to see and hear what was going on beyond the partition. I retraced my steps to the room where the body lay. My shivering had lessened, though I was still very cold. I worked my way around the chamber, starting with the bed, which I stripped, in case Van Riebeeck had concealed anything in the mattress. Next came the chest, which was empty, apart from a black, broad-brimmed hat.

A valise was on the floor beside the chest. I lifted it onto the bed, unfastened the straps and upended it. Shirts, neck-cloths and stockings cascaded over the mattress. So did a pistol in a wooden box, which also contained a mould for making bullets and a supply of gunpowder. At the bottom of the valise, tucked discreetly into a pocket that had been sewn onto the side, was a bundle of papers tied with a ribbon.

I untied the ribbon and laid the papers on the chest. Most were in Dutch. They looked as if they might be letters or memoranda. One mentioned the name of Mr Alink of Austin Friars, and also certain sums of money. Two documents were in French, and were letters of accreditation in the name of Monsieur Jolliet, signed by an illegible representative of the Duke of Orléans. They had been fastened with large imposing seals, presumably forgeries.

There were no other papers in the valise. I was relieved. I had feared that I might find incriminating letters from Cat.

All that remained to search was the body itself. I had no taste for the task but it had to be done. I knelt down. Van Riebeeck lay on his back. His muscles had relaxed in death, and the breeches stank. The eyes were open. In the light of the candle, they looked blank and cloudy. I touched the skin of the cheek, which was already cold. The mouth was open. He had shaved recently, presumably in case his fair stubble betrayed his change of colouring. Without his wig, it was easy to see how he had darkened the skin of the face.

Five minutes later, I sat back on my heels and surveyed my haul. A knife with an ivory handle and a leather case. A purse containing silver and two pieces of gold. Nothing else.

I emptied out the coins. I was surprised not to find more. The gold pieces were Dutch ducats, like those in Mrs Connolly's house by Puddle Wharf.

There was something else in the purse, a crumpled scrap of paper at the bottom, lodged in the seam and probably concealed by the purse's contents. I picked it out and unfolded it. It had been torn roughly from a larger paper. In the corner there was a design, a tradesman's mark. I held it to the side of the candle to examine it. I saw the familiar pestle and mortar, drawn by hand in ink and enclosed in the outline of a wavering semicircle. It was the mark of Mr Thrumbull, the apothecary of Cock Lane.

Had Van Riebeeck gone there? For arsenic?

I turned the paper over. There was something on the back — a small sketch, scribbled so hastily that the ink had smudged. At the top was the letter C, and at the bottom the letter D. A wavering line connected them. To the right of this line, nearer the C than the D, was the letter S, linked by a short horizontal line to the vertical one.

The candle flame wavered in the draught. The letters blurred and danced as if under moving water. C, I thought. D and S. My tired mind drifted away, and by some mysterious process returned with three names and the memory of meeting Fanshawe on Monday at Dover harbour.

Canterbury. Dover. Swaring.

Swaring. The name of Fanshawe's estate in the country.

CHAPTER FIFTY-TWO

MARIA WOKE SHORTLY after dawn. She lay on her back and listened to the familiar noises of the farmyard below until hunger drove her from the warmth of her bed.

By daylight, Swaring and its noises held no terrors. She rose, dressed herself and tiptoed across her mother's room. Enclosed by the bed curtains, her mother was invisible, but her snores were regular and loud. They did not falter at the opening of the door. Maria tiptoed across the landing and descended the creaking stairs.

The kitchen was empty, but the door to the yard was ajar. The maid had gone to fill the jug with the new milk. The fire was already lit and there was a pat of butter on the table and a hunk of yesterday's bread in the larder.

Maria perched on the edge of the table and ate, swinging her legs to and fro. The food had the flavour of forbidden fruit. Eating at this hour was not allowed, particularly in such a slovenly manner. But the kitchen maid at Swaring was an ally, as Hannah had once been in the Fleet Street house. Maria heard the girl talking in the yard to the cowman who, she had confided to Maria, might one day become her sweetheart if God willed it. Maria kept her mouth shut about the cowman, and the maidservant kept her mouth shut about the food.

Gradually, as Maria chewed, another sound reached her attention. Horses were on the lane from the high road, approaching at a fast trot. The voices in the yard fell silent. The maid came running into the kitchen. She was wide-eyed and pink-cheeked with news.

'There's soldiers coming.'

Maria crammed the last crust into her mouth and slid from the table. She left the kitchen and stood listening at the foot of the stairs. The horsemen were now very close. She saw them through the tall window beyond the staircase. They had come through the gate from the lane. They were making for the main door, which was rarely used except when there was company at Swaring.

'Maria!'

Startled, she looked upstairs. Her mother was standing on the landing, beckoning her to come up. She was in her shift still, without even a gown to cover her. Her feet were bare. She had lost her nightcap. Her hair, streaked with grey and tangled from sleep, flowed over her shoulders.

Someone hammered on the door.

'Quickly, Maria.'

Maria ran upstairs. Her mother's appearance alarmed her almost as much as the soldiers. 'Why are they here?'

The words were drowned by another burst of knocking. Her grandfather was on the landing now, wild-eyed and frail, his thin body wrapped in a furred gown.

'Take this.'

399

Her mother thrust a small leather pouch towards her. It was heavier than it looked, and it chinked when Maria took it.

'Hide it outside,' her mother hissed. Her face was white, and despite the morning chill it was shiny with sweat. 'They're in the kitchen yard too – go by the side door. Fast as you can to the woods. For the love of God say nothing about your uncle. You've not seen him since London.'

Maria ran back downstairs. The side door opened into the small garden where they grew herbs for the house. Maria let herself outside. She crouched and ran beside a wall that stretched from the house up the slope towards the orchard at the top, with the roof of the bailiff's cottage beyond. In the orchard, the pigs were rooting contentedly and paid her no attention. She scrambled over the low gate at the far end, which brought her to the belt of woodland that stretched along one side of the lane from the high road.

The ground sloped down from the lane to a stream. It was boggy underfoot. Maria was wearing flimsy slippers, and these were already soaked. She stumbled along a narrow, twisting path made by fox or badger. Fresh undergrowth was springing up beneath birch and sycamore saplings, stunted ash and rowan trees, and mixing with the remains of last year's weeds. A brown bramble sucker tripped her, and she measured her length on the ground. The fall drove the air from her lungs, but Maria did not let go of the pouch.

Blood began to ooze from her grazed knuckles. She licked it away. There were no sounds of pursuit. No sounds at all, apart from the farm dogs barking in the distance. Even the birds had stopped their singing, as if holding their breath to see what would happen next.

A flutter of wings made her start. A robin landed on a branch nearby. It put its head on one side and looked at her. The branch had fallen from a beech, which must once have dwarfed everything around it. The tree had been struck by lightning several years earlier, and most of it was now blackened and dead.

Maria struggled to her feet. She scrambled onto the branch, startling the robin, who flew away to a neighbouring tree and watched. The branch was still partly attached to the tree. When it had fallen, it had scooped out a shallow hollow from its parent trunk. Maria half-climbed, half-dragged herself up the branch towards the trunk. Stretching on tiptoe, she dropped the pouch into the hollow.

She slithered down. With a twig, she scuffed the marks she had left in the soft ground around the tree. She walked on, deeper in the wood. She was tiring, and her skirts were sodden and muddy, clinging clammily to her legs. Her slippers were falling apart, more of a hindrance than a help to walking. Somehow she had cut her left foot.

After a while she abandoned the slippers and went on bare feet, wincing with pain at every step. She made a wide circuit and limped back to the house as directly as she could.

The first person to see her was a soldier posted by the open front door. He called into the house, and another soldier came out. He marched towards Maria, seized her arm and dragged her inside.

'Let her go,' a man said sharply as he came downstairs. 'She won't run away again.'

The soldier released her arm. Maria knew the newcomer at once – it was Marwood, the man with the scarred face who had come to Slaughter Street twice, the first time with the black boy. On the second visit, he had been alone, and he had come down to the stables, where her grandfather had been showing them Caliban at his dinner. Her mother and her grandfather disliked and perhaps feared him, but she did not know why. He had once worked with her stepfather, Abbott. Perhaps that was the reason, because everyone still hated Abbott even now he was dead.

'Maria Fanshawe?' Marwood demanded.

'Yes, sir.' She sketched a curtsy as well as she could in her bedraggled state.

'Where have you been?'

'Outside, sir.'

'Why?'

'I . . . I was taking the air.'

'Don't jest, child. Where did you go and why? How did you get in that state?'

The soldier who had been posted at the door took a step forward. 'She came up from that wood, sir.'

Maria took refuge in silence, staring mulishly at Marwood. She hugged herself, for she was still trembling from the cold.

'God's teeth. Someone find her a blanket or a cloak.'

'She's done nothing, sir,' her grandfather said, his voice shaking. 'On my honour.' Still in his furred gown, he was at the head of the stairs, with another soldier beside him. He seemed to have shrunk since Maria had last seen him. 'Pray, sir, pray do not be rough with her.'

'The soldiers frightened her,' her mother said, appearing beside Mr Fanshawe. She looked even more like a madwoman than before. 'So of course she ran away. Is it any wonder, with you breaking into the house at the crack of dawn?'

'If I were you, madam,' Marwood said, 'I would want to find her some dry clothes.'

He and the soldiers were there for another two hours. They shut the family and servants in the kitchen and ransacked the house. The kitchen maid was allowed upstairs under escort, to find Maria a change of clothes. When at last Marwood and the soldiers rode away, they took with them Uncle Van Riebeeck's possessions, as well as certain papers belonging to Maria's mother and grandfather.

Mr Fanshawe slumped in his chair. 'God be thanked they've gone.'

'Marwood will be back. Here or in London.' Anna Fanshawe seized Maria's arm and lowered her voice. 'Where did you put it?'

'In the woods, madam.'

At that moment, her mother's long face was very like her brother's. 'Take me there.'

'But Anna,' Mr Fanshawe bleated, 'the child is weary. And I need you here. We must put the house to rights. And I'm faint with hunger.'

'Later, sir.'

Maria had never heard her mother speak so curtly to her grandfather. They left him sitting at the kitchen table, with his head bowed. They put on cloaks, shoes and hats and went out by the side door. Her mother walked rapidly, holding Maria's arm and urging her to go faster.

'Madam, what did those men want with us?'

'They didn't want us. They wanted your uncle.'

'Where is he?'

'I don't know.' Her mother's face twisted with anguish. 'I only wish I did.'

In the woods, Maria cast about, searching for the ruined beech tree with the fallen branch. Her mother grew increasingly agitated. Without warning, she boxed Maria's ears.

'Hurry, you little fool.'

By the time that Maria found the beech, she was weeping. She retrieved the pouch and dropped it into her mother's waiting hands. Mistress Fanshawe tore it open and looked inside.

'The Lord is merciful,' she murmured.

Without another word she set off towards the house, walking as fast as she could. Maria ran after her. As they were crossing the open ground between the trees and the house, two figures appeared in the gateway to the lane, Marwood and one of the soldiers. The men were both on foot, and the soldier had unslung his carbine.

Her mother looked wildly about, as if in search of rescue or a way of escape.

'There's no point,' Marwood said wearily, advancing towards them, with the soldier plodding beside him. 'Give me what the girl hid in those trees. Otherwise I'll take it.'

'Don't you lay a hand on me, sir.' Her mother drew herself up to her full height and clutched the pouch to her breast. 'You wouldn't dare.'

'Believe me, I would.'

'It's not mine to give you. It's my brother's property.'

'It's no use to him now,' Marwood said.

'What? Why?'

'Because he's dead.'

CHAPTER FIFTY-THREE

LATE ON THURSDAY afternoon, less than four-and-twenty hours after Van Riebeeck's death, Marwood sent Cat an invitation to sup with him at eight o'clock that evening. He proposed to send someone to escort her. After the events of yesterday evening, it was such a dry, bloodless and unfeeling note that for a moment Cat hated him. She told the boy who had brought the message to inform his master that she would be there.

Apart from dinner at midday, a necessity rather than a pleasure, there had been nothing else to distract her. She could not leave the castle in case she was summoned to attend Madame. She was dependent on her patron's whim, and her patron had other matters on her mind.

Every time she tried to read or sketch or write letters, the memory of Van Riebeeck's death flooded over her. It was as if she were standing outside herself and watching what had happened, again and again, while simultaneously being aware of every sensation, every impulse, every feeling. The way the knife – the knife that was in her hands now as she cleaned her fingernails – had slid so easily into the soft skin beneath Van Riebeeck's chin; the gasp he had given; the clatter of the sword falling to the bare boards of the floor; how he clutched his throat; and, most of all, how his blood, almost black in the half-light of the candles, had oozed through his fingers.

She had too much time to think. Had Van Riebeeck really wanted to marry her, or had his overtures of love been a matter of policy to win her cooperation? Or even a malicious tease?

She had killed a man for Marwood, she thought, and she would never be free of that knowledge. What made it worse was that it had not been any man: it had been a man she desired, though God alone knew why. Now the desire had lost its object; but it was still there, unsatisfied, an itch unscratched. There was also the niggling possibility that Van Riebeeck had after all been right, that in the long run it would have been better for England if the truth about this treaty could be known to the world. And better for her if Van Riebeeck had lived.

She would never know now. It was Marwood's fault. He had made her choose. Marwood or Van Riebeeck.

In the event, Marwood was more considerate than Cat had expected. He sent a chair for her, rather than merely a boy with a torch. As well as the two bearers, there was also a pair of linkmen to light them on their way. It couldn't have been easy for him to find either the chair or the linkmen – because of the royal visit, they were much in demand, with prices to match.

His lodgings were near the Constable's Tower. When Cat arrived, she was both drier and in better humour than she had been all day. She paused in the porch to change from her galoshes into her best shoes, the ones with pointed toes, green silk linings and three-inch heels. She was not wearing them for Marwood's sake, she told herself, but because she liked them, and besides the shoes had cost so much that it was her duty to have as much use from them as possible.

He was waiting for her, his back to the fire. He started forward when she was announced and bowed. He looked tired and pale.

She handed her cloak to the servant. 'You are better lodged than I am,' she said, looking about her. It was a good-sized room, low-ceilinged and square in shape. 'Clearly you're in favour.'

'I had nothing to do with it.' Marwood led her to the table and pulled out the chair nearest the fire. 'I share this set of rooms with poor Naunton. He's the Lord Steward's man. He arranged the accommodation in Dover for everyone, including himself.'

'Naunton? Is that . . .?'

'The man I was with last night? Yes.'

'How is he?'

'The physician removed him to his own chamber last night. In case there were complications.'

'Will he live?'

Marwood sat down opposite her. 'When I saw him an hour ago, he was calling for a bottle of sack.'

After a pause, she said, 'Thank you for sending a chair. I am obliged to you, on such a night especially.'

'All nights here are like this, I think. Rain and wind and cold. Will you take wine? They'll bring supper in half an hour or so.'

She watched him filling the glasses. The room was warm, and she felt very tired.

'First, I must thank you,' Marwood said. 'You saved my life.' He raised his glass and drank to her. 'You knew that Van Riebeeck was a spy?'

'He told me. He said the King was making an alliance with France against the Dutch. And . . .'

'And what?'

Cat hesitated. 'He told me something else. That there was to be a secret clause to this treaty. That the French would give the King a pension, and in return he promised to turn Catholic and work for the reconversion of England.'

Marwood laughed, throwing back his head. 'He was trying to gull you.' He was still smiling as he refilled their glasses. 'Between ourselves, the treaty is true enough. They mean to sign here, in the castle. But not this other thing. The King has many faults but he's not a fool. He would never consent to a clause like that. The alliance with the French is going to be unpopular enough as it is. But to turn Papist in return for French gold — that's nonsense. Why, it would lose him the throne.'

It was a relief to hear Marwood dismiss the idea so robustly. He was right. The very idea of such a clause was fantastical. Van Riebeeck must have put a spell on her last night; he had warped her judgement.

'I knew nothing of this spying until last night,' she said, reaching for her glass. 'On my honour. In London, he told me he was fleeing from his creditors, and that was why he had to hide himself away.'

'He was worse than a spy.' Marwood's voice had become suddenly harsh. The firelight flickered on the scars on the left side of his face, making them look angrier than they were.

'You said last night he was a murderer. Who did he kill?'

'Three people, probably, to my knowledge. Abbott — you recall him? — Lord Arlington's clerk, who was stealing information for him. That was arsenic, I believe. The second was a man called Johnson, a gamester who fleeced Abbott so Van Riebeeck could blackmail him. Johnson was killed to stop him talking to me. I think they frightened him to death with the help of Fanshawe's lion. They buried him afterwards in Austin Friars.'

Marwood stopped. He drained his glass, set it carefully down on the table and refilled it. There was a spot of wine on the table and he rubbed it with his fingertip.

'That's two,' Cat said. 'Who was the third?'

He looked up. 'Stephen.'

'Stephen? *Stephen?* Your footboy?'

They sat in silence for a moment. Marwood stirred in his chair.

'He and I discovered Van Riebeeck's hiding place in Austin Friars. I left him there to keep watch. I was longer than I meant to be. When I returned, Stephen was dead. Lying on his back with his skull beaten in.'

Cat cried out. Her hand jerked up to her mouth, knocking over her glass. Wine flooded onto the table and trickled to the floor.

'And now I'm in your debt, madam,' Marwood said. 'If I'd had the chance, I would have killed Van Riebeeck myself.'

CHAPTER FIFTY-FOUR

THAT NIGHT, CAT slept fitfully and dreamed of dead children. At intervals she came awake and listened to the snores and snuffling of the women around her.

In life, Stephen had been almost invisible to her, a small shadow coming and going in Marwood's wake. But Margaret Witherdine had doted on the boy, for all her rough tongue, and Sam had felt much the same. As for Marwood, when he had been talking about Stephen's murder last night, she had seen something in his face that scared her.

In the morning, a footman in the Orléans livery brought a note from Madame des Bordes. Cat was to wait on Madame at eleven o'clock. It was possible that the King himself might graciously inspect the plans for the new mansion. Cat made her preparations mechanically. She had longed for this invitation, for the opportunity to show her royal patron what she could do. But now the chance had come, it seemed as worthless as fairy gold.

Madame received her in the same chamber as before. The King was already there, lounging in a chair by the fire. A spaniel lay beside him, its head resting on its master's foot. A large table had been brought in and placed under the window. Madame des Bordes lingered, her eyes rarely straying from the face of her mistress.

At Madame's command, Cat set out the plans on the table. Brother and sister examined them, the King bending down so that his head was very close to his sister's. Both of them threw questions at her over their shoulders. Cat replied, fluently enough for she knew her subject intimately.

But part of her was simultaneously wondering whether Madame had heard Mass this morning in a private chapel within the keep, and whether her brother had knelt with her to receive the Host. Perhaps Van Riebeeck had told her the truth. Perhaps the King was already privately a Catholic, despite the fact he was by law the Supreme Governor of the Church of England, and perhaps he was already plotting to restore England to the Holy See. It was difficult to equate such devious behaviour with the man before her: good-humoured, considerate, and so obviously adored by his sister and his dog.

'Remarkable,' the King said. 'Mistress Hakesby, I congratulate you. This is quite a different matter from a mere poultry house, however grand, and on a very different scale. Dr Wren tells me he has encouraged you, and I can see why. You have made an apt pupil.'

Cat curtsied. The King meant well, though she would have liked to point out that she herself deserved some credit for her own talent and her own hard work.

Shortly afterward, he left them, the dog snuffling at his heels. Cat tidied away the papers. Madame took her brother's chair by the fire.

'I return to France soon,' she said. 'Send copies of your designs after me, will you, as soon as you can.'

'Yes, Madame.' That would mean at least a week's work. Cat wondered when she would be paid for any of it, and also what Brennan would say.

'Come here. Where I can see you.'

Cat put down her notebook and obeyed.

'Will you come to France again, later in the summer perhaps, and inspect the site for me?'

Cat curtsied. 'As you wish.'

Madame stared up at her. 'Are you quite well? You look pale.'

'Forgive me.' Despite herself, Cat was touched by the Princess's concern, which seemed so natural that it was difficult to believe it could merely be politeness. 'I've much on my mind. But I should not have let it show.'

'Easy to say, harder to do.' Madame was frowning slightly. 'What worries you?'

A man killed, Cat thought, a man I once thought I loved. Another man, a man I killed for, but don't understand. She said, 'I've been away for weeks. I worry about money.'

'I wish all our sorrows were so easily cured.' Madame glanced towards Madame des Bordes. 'Tell them to prepare a draft for — let's say — a hundred pounds for Mistress Hakesby, and bring it to me to sign this afternoon.'

Cat curtsied, hoping that the money would turn out to be more than a promise. 'You're very kind.' She took a deep breath. 'May I also have your permission to leave Dover? In London I will be able to work on your designs. But here I can do nothing.'

Madame smiled at her. 'That would never do. You may go

back to London. It will be arranged. Go now, Mistress Hakesby.'

Madame des Bordes rose from her chair. The audience was over.

On Friday morning, I passed through the Palace Gate and into the Keep Yard. Cat was waiting for admission among the crowd that always gathered outside the entrance to the royal apartments. She was carrying a folder and she did not see me.

Lord Arlington received me in the council chamber at the top of Arthur's Hall. Its modest size surprised me – the dimensions were the same as those of Van Riebeeck's bedchamber, which lay at the other end of the privy passage connecting them. The partition that had blocked off the passage from the council chamber had been removed, and a door reinstalled instead.

Unlike Van Riebeeck's, however, this room had a fireplace. Arlington was sitting beside it, annotating a sheaf of papers that lay before him on a small table.

'Stand there where I can see you,' he said, pointing to the other side of the table, where the window was. He laid down his pen. 'How did you fare at Fanshawe's house?'

'Van Riebeeck had been hiding there for weeks, my lord. He'd told Mr Fanshawe that his debtors were pursuing him.'

'Are you sure? And if he did, did Fanshawe believe him?'

I shrugged. 'I think Fanshawe believed what he wanted to believe.'

'An old fool rather than an old traitor?'

'Exactly so. Van Riebeeck's half-sister was there too.'

'Abbott's widow?'

'Yes. She did her best to conceal evidence. But it was

413

obvious that her brother had been there. Van Riebeeck's belongings were all over one of the bedchambers. Just before we reached the house, she gave her daughter a pouch of his. She tried to hide it outside.'

He studied me. 'Did she know her brother's dead?'

'She does now, my lord. She was like a madwoman.'

'A pity. But there it is.'

He looked mildly irritated. Since Mistress Fanshawe, as Abbott's widow now called herself, had once been part of Lady Arlington's household before her marriage, her status in the matter was more delicate than it would otherwise have been.

I laid the pouch on the table, but Arlington made no move to take it.

'What's inside?' he asked.

'I thought it best not to open it, my lord.' I wasn't sure whether he believed me.

'Open it for me now.'

I untied the pouch and put it back on the table, nearer to him. First, he took out a purse and upended it. Gold coins rattled on to the table, forming a glittering pile with a few outliers. One of these rolled over the edge and fell to the floor.

I picked it up. A Dutch ducat, with the familiar man in old-fashioned armour. I turned it over. The mintmark was Utrecht. The piece was identical to those at the Connollys' house at Puddle Wharf, and those I had found on Van Riebeeck's body on Wednesday night. I dropped it on the pile.

Arlington pushed his hand into the pouch and brought out a bundle of documents. He glanced through them, holding the papers at an angle that prevented me from overlooking them. Not that I needed to. I had already examined them yesterday evening before Cat arrived. They were in Dutch, French and English. Those in Abbott's hand were copies of letters and memoranda that had passed through my lord's private office. Some included numbers scattered among the text, presumably part of the same code I had seen on the charred fragments that poor Johnson sent me just before he disappeared.

There was a knock at the door, and Gorvin slipped into the room. He bowed, murmured something in Arlington's ear and handed him a letter. My lord tore it open. He read it quickly and stood up.

'The King desires to see me.' He turned to allow Gorvin to lay his cloak across his shoulders. 'And you, Marwood.'

On the north turret of the keep, the Royal Standard was rippling in the wind. It was cold but for once it was not raining, and pale sunshine was finding a way through the clouds. The leads of the roof shone with recent rain.

The King and Madame were standing in the shelter of the south turret. Before them was the grey, gently heaving sea that separated us from France. Diagonally opposite, by the south turret, were their attendants. One of them was Mr Chiffinch, the Keeper of the King's Privy Closet and many of his master's secrets. When he saw us, he broke away and approached.

He bowed to Arlington, and allowed his eyes to flicker over me. 'My lord, His Majesty will see you now.'

I followed Arlington along the walkway. Chiffinch didn't call me back, so I assumed that I was included in the invitation. As we neared the King, a spaniel detached itself and rushed barking towards us.

415

'Peace, Dido,' the King roared. 'Come here.'

Duty done, Dido ran back to her master, wagging her tail. Madame bent down and patted the dog's head.

Arlington and I bowed.

'I wanted to show Madame something,' the King said. 'And now you shall see as well.'

'I beg your pardon, sir.' For once Arlington sounded at a loss. 'I don't quite—'

'Look.'

The King stood back, pointing down at the sloping leads. There were marks roughly incised on them, as if with the tip of a dagger, the lines thrown into relief by the sun. Standing at my lord's elbow, I looked more closely. There were about a dozen shapes, with something written within each of them.

'The outlines of shoes, sir?' Arlington said, hazarding a guess. 'And . . . names within them.'

I coughed. I pointed at the highest outline, which was also the largest. 'Look, my lord.'

There wasn't a name inside that one. Only two initials: CR.

'Ten years ago, when I returned to take my throne,' the King said, 'we landed at Dover. Some of us left marks of our passage.' He smiled at his sister and then turned towards us. 'I've no intention of leaving this country again. Whatever happens. Whatever I do.'

Madame and Arlington were looking fixedly at him. I sensed that all three were aware that there was more to this remark than I understood.

'Now.' The King's voice was suddenly sharper. 'Van Riebeeck. Is there any possibility that he was able to send word about anything he might have learned here?'

416

'No, Your Majesty,' Arlington said. 'We have prevented that. Before he came to Dover, he was hiding at Mr Fanshawe's house near Canterbury. Marwood went there yesterday at first light and brought back his papers. He searched the house while he was there.'

'Had Van Riebeeck confided in anyone? His sister? Fanshawe?'

'Not to our knowledge. Marwood thinks that Fanshawe knew nothing of this, and I'm inclined to agree. We believe his sister helped him, but she may not have known what he was about.'

The King glanced at Madame. 'But they were close, weren't they? You must make sure she knows nothing of . . . of what has been discussed. There may be something at the London house – so have that searched too. And as soon as possible. Even if there's nothing to find, it will remind them that we are not to be trifled with.'

Arlington bowed.

The King stared out to sea. 'And the Dutch?'

'According to our information, Van Riebeeck worked for the Grand Pensionary alone. There was a private connection between them, and he reported directly to him. Mr Alink, the Dutch merchant, was ordered to assist him in London. He advanced funds and provided other help. He sheltered Van Riebeeck at Austin Friars when we had a warrant out for him. But Alink seems not to have been in on the secret himself. Mr Marwood has also dealt with an Irish tavern keeper who assisted Van Riebeeck in return for money. But he was a mere instrument – he knew nothing of what his master was about.'

'I don't understand.' A crease appeared between Madame's

eyebrows. 'How did Van Riebeeck contrive to be here in the Keep Yard? Convincing everyone he was a French gentleman?'

Arlington threw me a glance. 'Your Royal Highness,' I said, 'I'm told that he was half-French. His credentials as Monsieur Jolliet were prepared in Amsterdam. And his story was . . . plausible.'

I was stopped abruptly, for I was edging towards delicate territory. The story was plausible because the Duke of Orléans was well known to be fiercely protective of his own exalted position as a Son of France. He was also well known to be fanatically jealous of his wife, despite the fact he loathed every bone in her body.

'The forgeries were excellent,' Arlington said smoothly, like the polished courtier he was. 'Good enough to fool the Lord Chamberlain's man.'

'Smirke, was it?' said the King. 'I fancy fooling him wasn't a difficult task.' He glanced at me again. 'And the body?'

'Already in hand, sir. A burial at sea, with a double-weighted shroud. It seemed best for all concerned. The ship went out with the morning tide. We told the captain that it's a servant who died of the plague, one of Madame's party. To counter any risk of infection.'

The King stared out to sea, as if looking for the ship that bore Van Riebeeck's body.

'All's well that ends well,' Madame said cheerfully. She touched her brother's arm. They were standing very close together. 'You've been well served, sir.'

He turned and smiled at her, and then at us, at me. 'I know. I shall not forget.'

The words might well prove valueless. Nevertheless I was

418

grateful, as the spaniel was grateful for the slightest caress from her master.

'One thing puzzles me,' he said, still smiling. 'I talked to the surgeon who examined Van Riebeeck's body yesterday.'

'Yourself, sir?' For once Arlington looked surprised. 'I – I had no idea.'

The King looked at me and raised his eyebrows. 'He told me that the wound that killed the Dutchman was a thrust under the chin and up towards the brain.'

'Yes, Your Majesty. He and I were fighting at close quarters, and the candles had been knocked over. I was beyond fortunate.' I tried to look modest. 'As I told my lord, I'm no swordsman.'

'Not that it matters, but the doctor was surprised to hear that it was a sword. By the width and shape of the wound, he thought it had been made by a dagger. A small one.'

'How strange, sir. The sword – it has a mighty thin blade . . .'

Arlington yelped with irritation. Dido was squatting down on the leads at his feet. A puddle of urine was spreading around my lord's shoes.

Madame gave a crow of laughter, as merry as a child's.

'Dido,' the King said chidingly. 'You naughty girl. That's the second time you've been discourteous to my lord. Come here.'

He bent to scratch the dog's head, but his eyes lingered on me. I thought the corners of his mouth twitched slightly. As if I had told him a good joke but his breeding obliged him to moderate the signs of his amusement.

*   *   *

Later that day, in the evening, my lord summoned me again – this time to his private apartments. I found him alone, writing at his travelling desk.

'You are to leave for London in the morning,' he said. 'A packet boat will take you round to the Medway, and then you'll travel by post to London. It will be faster than the road after this rain. If all goes well, you'll be there by evening.'

'Yes, my lord.' My mind was already running over what I needed to do over the next few hours. 'And the name of the packet?'

He pushed a paper towards me. 'Gorvin made the arrangements this afternoon. It's all there.' He skimmed another paper over the desk like a gamester distributing a card. 'Your warrant for travel.' A third paper followed. 'And the warrant for Slaughter Street.

'His Majesty is most concerned that nothing should escape us there,' my lord went on. 'Take as many men as you want. Herd the people of the house together and have them watched while you search. Including Fanshawe and his family if they've returned.' He pursed his lips. 'But I suppose I don't need to tell you how to do your job.'

He dismissed me. But when I had my hand on the door latch, he called me back.

'One more thing. You are to escort a lady to London. Mistress Hakesby. You're acquainted, I think? Madame is anxious you should treat her with the utmost consideration.' He hesitated. 'And at present we are all particularly anxious to oblige Madame.'

CHAPTER FIFTY-FIVE

ON SATURDAY AFTERNOON, the Fanshawes' hired coach and four turned with difficulty in Slaughter Street, grazing a wheel against the great stone at the corner. It came to a halt outside Mr Fanshawe's house. Even travelling post, with no expense spared, the journey from Swaring had taken them the better part of two days. The postilion dismounted and knocked on the door with the butt of his whip.

'Damn them,' Mr Fanshawe muttered, climbing stiffly down from the coach and looking up at his house. 'Knock again. Lazy rogues! What do I pay them for?'

There was a rattle of chains on the other side of the door. Fanshawe turned back to the coach to help first his daughter-in-law alight and then her maid. Mistress Fanshawe was wearing a vizard to protect herself from the dust and dirt of the journey, and to hide her grief from the world. Fanshawe took her arm and they went side by side into the house. Finally, Maria jumped down without any help at all just as the house door opened. The manservant appeared, buttoning his coat, as she followed the others inside.

'Forgive me, master. We had no warning . . . most of the fires aren't lit, and cook hasn't—'

'Light the fires,' Fanshawe interrupted. 'Prepare Mistress Fanshawe's chamber. She's not well.' He touched Maria's shoulder. 'Go with your mother, child. Tend to her.'

Maria curtsied and followed the two women up the stairs. In her room, her mother stripped off her vizard and let her cloak drop to the floor. She turned and saw Maria standing in the doorway. Her haggard face was almost unrecognizable.

'Leave me,' she screamed, opening her mouth wide. 'Let me alone.'

For want of anything better to do, Maria went downstairs, let herself out of the house and set off down the garden. Her grandfather had gone down to see Caliban. In the stable yard, he was berating Brockmore, whom he had found asleep in the old coach house with an empty jug of ale beside him. The lion's enclosure was fouler than usual, and Caliban himself was thinner and mangier than before.

'Wretch!' cried Fanshawe, thrashing Brockmore with his stick. 'Scoundrel! Blockhead! You've drunk the money I gave you, eh?'

Brockmore cowered, his arms over his head.

'Give him some meat now! Or by God I'll have you fed to him.'

Late that afternoon, Maria went out to the privy in the yard. As she turned the corner into the place where the privy stood, she saw Hannah standing by the wall and staring intently at it. She heard Maria's footsteps and spun round.

'What are you doing?' she demanded, her face blazing with anger. 'Sneaking about like a thief.'

'I wasn't. Truly. I need the privy.'

Maria had hoped, even prayed, that something would have happened to Hannah while the family were in Kent. That she had run away, perhaps, or even that the low fever had proved fatal.

'Wait.' Hannah folded her arms. 'I'm still here. Still waiting to be your maid.'

'I – I don't want to talk now.'

'Don't you, madam? But I'm going to talk to you.'

'I told you again and again – they won't let me have you as my maid.' Maria was weary with repetition. 'We must wait till I'm older.'

'The longer we wait, the worse it will be.' Hannah smiled. She had lost one of her front teeth while Maria had been in Kent. 'Let's hurry things up. Come here after supper.' She pushed past Maria, her shoulder driving the younger girl against the privy door. 'At ten o'clock.'

Maria went into the privy and bolted the door. She sat inside, waiting for the trembling to stop. Her head was hurting and full of a buzzing sound. It was as if someone had cut it open with an axe and a swarm of bees had rushed inside.

A thought struck her. Why had Hannah been standing at the side of the privy? Why had she been looking so intently at the wall?

Maria went outside and stood in the spot where Hannah had been. The privy shielded her completely from the windows of the house. You couldn't be seen from the yard, either, unless someone was almost at the privy door. Maria faced the wall. It was made of old bricks and rubble. The mortar was in poor condition. Maria poked it with her finger and yellow dust trickled to the ground. She followed it with her eyes and saw there was already a larger pile of dust on the ground not twelve inches away from the one that she had just made. She trailed her hand up the wall in a vertical line that rose above the second pile.

About a yard above the ground, a brick shifted slightly under her fingers as they passed over it. She found it again. The brick wobbled at her touch. Crouching down, she brought her eyes level with it and worked her fingers around its edges.

She eased the brick from the wall and laid it on the ground. She pushed her hand into the cavity. It went back further than the brick had done. The wall swallowed the hand and then the wrist.

Her fingertips touched something soft. Something dead? No, cloth. She pinched it between finger and thumb, and tugged it gently towards her.

Maria knew almost at once that there was something else, that this was not merely a piece of cloth. She could tell by the weight of it, and by the way it moved, snagging on obstacles. She lifted it out and laid it on the ground.

It was a stained rag, perhaps a dishcloth from the kitchen. Its four corners had been knotted roughly together. She untied them with fingers that were suddenly clumsy. The first thing she saw was her purple handkerchief, trimmed with lace, the one that Maria had found in Caliban's cage. Wrapped inside was a gold coin, a shilling piece, three farthings, and a small paper package.

Carefully, Maria unfolded the paper. Inside was a heap of white powder, slightly clogged with damp.

Arsenic.

Maria went inside the privy again and bolted the door. She sat down. Was God looking down on her? She hoped not. Her head was hurting worse than ever. She shook it gently from side to side in the hope of dislodging the pain. It didn't work.

On the floor beside her was the box containing scraps of paper and parchment, rubbish from the old hospital at St Bartholomew's on the other side of Smithfield. Mistress Fanshawe had bought a couple of barrowloads for the outdoor privy, as they tended to be drier, and gentler on the skin than rags; cheaper too. Maria took one at random. Breathing heavily, she slid some of the powder onto it, about a quarter of the amount. She made a parcel and slipped it into her pocket.

She folded up Hannah's paper, with the bulk of the arsenic inside, and wrapped it with the handkerchief and the coins in the dishcloth. She knotted the corners together. Her movements were no longer clumsy. They had a strange, dreamlike precision, which she watched and wondered at. It was as if she were somewhere outside herself, perhaps clinging like a bat to one of the rafters above her head.

Afterwards the bundle looked much the same as before. Maria unbolted the door and went outside. No one was waiting to use the privy, and the yard beyond was empty. A moment later, the cloth and its contents were pushed into the hole in the wall, and the brick was back in place. She scuffed away the second pile of dust with the toe of her shoe.

The bees were still buzzing painfully inside her skull,

jumbling her thoughts until they looked unfamiliar, as if they now belonged to someone else.

Mr Fanshawe had not dined to his liking on the road, and he was therefore unusually hungry in the evening. In consequence, supper was a substantial meal, with the dishes sent in from outside. Cook, aware like all the servants that their master was displeased with the meagre welcome they had given him, exerted herself and prepared an Italian pudding, one of his favourite dishes, to go with the rest of the meal.

In old age, Mr Fanshawe had acquired a sweet tooth that demanded more and more sweetening as time went by. He had a particular fondness for Italian pudding, made with fine wheaten bread and beef suet, both diced small and then mixed with cloves, mace, minced dates, raisins of the sun, marrow, rosewater, eggs, cream and a great deal of sugar.

Because Mistress Fanshawe was indisposed, it was Maria who went down to the kitchen to discuss the arrangements for supper with the cook. As cook explained, all you need to do for Italian pudding was to put the ingredients in a buttered dish and bake it. It would be ready in less than an hour. It was important not to leave it too long in the oven, for the master liked it moist, almost runny inside because his teeth troubled him. Finally it was necessary to scatter even more sugar on top – for the master's tooth had grown very sweet indeed in the last year or so – and then the pudding could be carried up to the table.

On the first evening back in Slaughter Street, supper was at eight o'clock. Mistress Fanshawe was still in her bedchamber. Her wails could be heard in much of the house, but fortunately not in the dining room. Mr Fanshawe sent word up to her that supper was waiting, but her maid brought the news that her mistress would not be coming down. Nor did Mistress Fanshawe want food sent up to her, for she could not eat a morsel.

As a result, Maria sat alone with her grandfather at table. They had little conversation at first, for Mr Fanshawe liked to concentrate on his food while eating; he was not a man who was able to hold two ideas in his mind at the same time. Food improved his mood, and the Italian pudding made him almost cheerful. He pressed another helping on Maria, who did not really want it.

'Take some more, my love,' her grandfather said. 'It is too delicious to leave for the kitchen.'

'Sir, I cannot take more than a spoonful.'

'Your poor mother then. If anything might tempt her appetite, it is this. Prepare a bowl and take it up to her. Try to make sure she eats it.'

Maria filled a bowl with the pudding.

'More,' urged her grandfather. 'Stay, let me put a little sugar over it.' He upended the caster over the bowl and shook it vigorously. 'Sugar is an excellent specific against black bile. It will help regulate your mother's humours. It may help to ease her grief.'

It was a kindly thought in its way. Maria carried the bowl and a spoon carefully upstairs and knocked on the door of her mother's bedchamber. The maid let her in. The curtains were drawn to shut out the fading daylight. Her mother was lying on the bed, face down, sobbing into her pillow, more quietly than before.

'My grandfather sent me up with this. It's Italian pudding.'

The maid shook her head. 'You're wasting your time. Madam won't eat it. She won't take a thing.'

'Go away!' howled the figure on the bed with a sudden burst of energy. 'Go away!'

The maid grimaced. 'You see? You'd better leave.'

By now, less than a month away from midsummer, it was still light outside at ten o'clock in the evening. The church bells had only just finished their tolling of the hour when Maria walked slowly down the yard, holding the bowl in both hands.

Hannah was waiting beside the privy. 'What you got there?'

'For you.' Maria held out the bowl.

'Is that the pudding that cook made?'

'Yes. My mother didn't want it, so . . .'

'So you brought it for me?' Hannah's mouth twisted. 'A present, is it? Make me sweet? Make me kind?'

Maria came a step closer, bringing the bowl nearer, letting the pudding do its work.

The tip of Hannah's tongue appeared. 'I might as well have it. Now it's here.'

She took the spoon and then the bowl. She ate with ferocious speed and with savage attention to the task at hand. She reminded Maria of Caliban at his dinner. When the bowl was empty, scraped and licked, Hannah handed it back.

'I got something for you, little mistress.' She licked her fingers and fumbled among the folds of her skirt. She brought out a twist of paper. 'Here. For the old man. All of it. I want him dead.'

Hannah pushed past Maria and walked away to the house. Maria went into the privy. She knelt down in front of one of the holes and was violently sick into the foulness beneath.

428

Later, in her bedchamber, she took the twist of paper from her pocket and opened it. She estimated that Hannah had given her about half of the arsenic that was left. She hesitated, wondering whether to go downstairs and throw it on the fire. Better to wait until tomorrow. Someone would notice if she went downstairs at this late hour.

With trembling hands, Maria opened her work basket and lifted out the unfinished sampler, that botched and hideous thing which made her cringe every time she saw it afresh. The basket was lined, but at the bottom the seam had gone. She tucked the twist of paper through the hole, replaced the tapestry and closed the lid of the basket.

There was no hurry. She would decide tomorrow.

CHAPTER FIFTY-SIX

'PAST TWO OF the clock,' cried the bellman in the Strand in his wavering voice. 'A fine, clear Sunday morning.' He staggered along the pavement, occasionally ringing his cracked bell. 'Past two of the clock . . .'

'Shall I set you down by the Savoy?' Cat said.

Marwood stirred. He was facing her in the rattling darkness of the coach. 'I'll see you to your house first.'

'There's no need,' Cat said as a matter of form, though she was glad to have his company. London at night was not a safe place for an unaccompanied woman.

They had not exchanged a word for some time. They were both bone-weary. The day had lasted too long. First, at crack of dawn, the packet from Dover, around the coast and into the Medway estuary as far up as Rochester. They had disembarked and dined there. Then the thirty miles to London, travelling post. Then this other coach, hired at vast expense at the posting inn to bring them over London Bridge.

The coach turned up towards Covent Garden. Even at this

hour there were people about in the piazza, mainly men bargaining with the whores in the arcades. Somewhere out of sight, a woman was singing a ballad of love abandoned. She had an unsteady, tuneless voice that was loud enough to be heard over the grating of the coach wheels and the hooves of the horse.

Henrietta Street was in darkness, apart from lines of light between a few of the shutters. The coach came to a halt at the sign of the Rose. Marwood climbed down and knocked hard on the door with the head of his stick. Cat joined him on the pavement. After nearly a minute of knocking, the sliding hatch slid back, and Pheebs's boy asked anxiously who was there.

'Open the door, Josh,' Cat commanded. 'Quick as you can.'

They listened to the familiar rattle of chains on the other side of the door. Marwood shivered, and then so did Cat. The night was not particularly cold, but they were both exhausted.

'I'd better come in with you and make sure all is well,' Marwood said.

'There's no need,' Cat said again.

He ignored her. He turned away and told the coachman to wait.

The door opened at last. Josh stood back, bowing awkwardly.

By rights, Pheebs should have opened the door. Cat heard the porter's muffled snores emanating from the airless closet under the stairs that he had appropriated for his own.

'Fetch our baggage,' she told the boy. Then, over her shoulder to Marwood: 'If you're coming in, you'd better stay for the night. Your servants won't thank you for rousing them so late, even if you can make them hear you. There's a bed in the closet.'

There was a pause. The hall was lit by a single candle. She turned to look at Marwood, who was standing in the doorway. The candle flame wavered, and so did the shadows that filled the hollows of his face.

'Very well,' he said, as if she had suggested nothing more remarkable than another turn about the Park on a sunny afternoon. 'I'll pay the fare.'

There was no more conversation. When the door was closed and barred again, Josh lit their way upstairs. It was with a sense of relief that Cat unlocked the door of her own apartments. But the air inside was seemingly colder and damper even than in the street. She had expected her lodgings to embrace her with their familiarity. In her absence they had become strange and unfriendly.

While Marwood helped Josh bring their luggage, Cat went from room to room, lighting candles. The parlour smelled musty but it was tidy enough. The coal scuttle was almost empty, however, and there was no kindling. Next door, the summer hangings were spread over the bed. A pair of curtains had spilled onto the floor. The lid of the sewing basket was open. Cat swore under her breath.

'What is it?' Marwood said behind her.

'My maid was told to come and air the chambers every day and mend the curtains. They should have been ready for hanging by now. I don't think she's even started.' Cat's eyes filled with the easy tears of tiredness. 'Margaret said she'd keep Jane to the mark. But I could hardly expect her to come in every day. She's your servant, not mine.'

'It will look better in the morning, madam,' he said gently. 'Everything will.'

The kindness in his voice made her want to cry. 'We can't even light the fire.' Her voice was almost a wail. 'There's no kindling and hardly any coal.'

'I'll call the boy back if you want a fire.'

'It's not worth it. I'm so weary I could sleep on my feet.' She swept the hangings from the bed. 'Thank God. The bed's made up. I'll show you the closet.'

The closet opened off the bedchamber. During her husband's lifetime, it had largely been reserved for his use. His big chest was still there, as well as the truckle bed where Jane Ash usually slept. It had been arranged for her to spend her nights with her mother during Cat's absence.

Cat opened the closet door and held up the candle. The unmade bed was placed along the window wall. There was a sheen of water on the floor between it and the door. 'Oh devil take it. That wretch. You'd think she'd take more care after her folly in blabbing to Van Riebeeck.'

The closet window had been left open, probably some time ago. Cat felt the mattress. It was soaked with rain. She pulled the window shut so violently that for a moment she thought the handle might come off in her hand.

'I'm sorry,' she said, turning back to Marwood. 'You can't sleep in here.'

'It doesn't matter,' he said. 'I'll walk to my house. Or find a hackney.'

'A hackney? At this time? Don't be foolish. You're here now, and with your bags. You might as well stay.'

'Then the parlour will do me very well. If you give me a blanket or two, I'll sleep on the table. Or the floor.'

433

'You can't sleep on the floor. The table's not long enough. Have the bed. I'll have the table.'

'No. The bed's yours.'

'You're stubborn as a block.' Suddenly she was shouting at him. 'You'll have the bed.'

'And you're wilful as a pig, madam,' he said, raising his voice to match hers. 'You'll be neither driven nor led. I'll have the floor.'

'Sir, you will not! Otherwise I'll turn you out of the house! For all I care you can take yourself off and find a ready-warmed bed in Vere Street.'

'What?' His jaw dropped. 'Vere Street? What's this?'

'Where that Daunt woman is.'

'Cat, you think I . . .?'

'Well? You go there often enough. When you're not ogling the little whore on stage.'

Marwood said in a gentler voice. 'Meg Daunt isn't my mistress. She's Gorvin's. Or he'd like her to be. His alone.'

'You can't cozen me.' She hesitated.

'But it's true.'

'I don't understand.'

'He's a bashful lover. You wouldn't think it, but he is. He asked me to come with him to – well, to give him countenance, I suppose. And draw away his rivals. She has a regiment at her disposal.'

'Oh.'

Marwood grinned. Cat started to laugh, and after a moment Marwood joined in. The laughter was brittle and uncertain. They stopped at the same moment and stared at each other.

* * *

Later, Cat listened to the clocks of the town striking three. She had expected to fall asleep at once. But her mind would not release its hold on the waking world. There was no sound from the parlour, where Marwood was propped up in the big chair under a mound of blankets, his feet resting on the footstool. He was probably asleep. That irritated her. Why should he be asleep and not she?

She was cold. She had curled herself into a ball, but it did little good. The bed was damp. Her feet and hands were icy. Memories from the last few weeks paraded through her head. If only she could cut off the flow of her thoughts, as a tap stopped up the ale in a barrel. She had made a fool of herself over Meg Daunt. And how could she have been so foolish as to trust Van Riebeeck? She had allowed him into her life, and now he wouldn't leave. Even in death, he insinuated himself between her and oblivion.

Time passed. She became a little warmer. She drifted imperceptibly into the shallows of sleep.

Something wrenched me from sleep.

I opened my eyes. It was completely dark. I struggled to get my bearings. The only sound was my own breathing. I was cold and my muscles ached. I lifted my stockinged feet from the stool and placed them on the floor. I patted my chest. I had lost at least one of the blankets, as well as my cloak.

No sign of dawn. I stretched my right hand to the floor and swept the fingertips across the boards until I felt the outline of the sword. My back ached. I rose slowly and awkwardly to my feet and stretched. I stooped and gathered up the blankets and the cloak.

Something had wakened me. A noise from the street? I

435

wrapped myself in one blanket and sat down again. After a moment, I summoned enough strength to put my feet back on the stool. I draped the other blankets and the cloak over me as best I could. I was desperately tired. Tomorrow would be a busy day. I closed my eyes and commanded myself to sleep.

A scream cut through the silence.

I was on my feet again. I snatched the sword.

Then a cry: 'No . . .'

I blundered through the darkness towards the door of the bedchamber. I reached the wall instead. I fumbled my way along the panels until I reached the door jamb.

'No, no, pray don't . . .'

I found the latch at last and burst through the doorway. There were movements in the bed. Something scuttled over the boards near the fireplace.

'Cat? What is it?'

The sounds stopped. I felt my way towards the bed and tore apart the curtains. 'What ails you?'

'Oh . . . It's you.'

'Who else?' Relief poured over me, bringing a touch of irritation with it. 'You were screaming,' I said tartly. 'Fit to wake the dead.'

'Someone touched my face . . .'

'A rat perhaps. I heard something by the fireplace.'

'I – I was dreaming.'

'You sound terrified.'

'I . . . I couldn't escape . . .' Her voice was tremulous. 'I . . .'

From the darkness there came a sharp intake of breath, followed by a sniff.

'Dear God.' I sat down on the edge of the bed and patted what I thought might be her arm. 'A foolish dream, no more.

436

I'm here. It will soon be dawn, all will be well.' I was talking to Cat as if she were a child. 'In the morning you can send out for arsenic. That will deal with the rats.'

Her hand brushed my arm and then gripped my wrist. Her skin was cold, slightly clammy. She found my fingers and squeezed them as if to make sure they were real.

'I dreamed I was at Dover again. And the Dutchman, and my knife . . .'

'Hush,' I said, thinking of her words: *someone touched my face.* 'A dream. Nothing more. He's dead. He can't trouble you now.'

'I'm scared,' she said. 'Keep me company. Just for a while.'

When Cat swam like a fish from the depths of sleep, she was much warmer. It was absolutely dark, for the heavy bed curtains blocked all the light. She had been dreaming, she thought, not of Van Riebeeck, thank God, but of something he had made her feel.

She heard Marwood's breathing in her ear. In a rush, the memory of the last few hours returned to her. To her horror, she found that her hip was now resting against his. Worse still, his left hand lay on her right thigh. She gave an experimental wriggle. The hand didn't move.

Before settling, they had placed a pillow between them to form a barrier. It had slipped down the bed. She felt it resting against her knee.

Still half asleep, she lifted Marwood's hand between thumb and finger. She transferred it to his own thigh, only to find that his shirt had ridden up and she touched his bare flesh. The side of her hand brushed against something that wasn't his leg.

The rhythm of his breathing changed. He stirred and turned. His arm came over her. Automatically she moved, but that only made the arm tighten its grip. Suddenly they were facing each other. She felt his breath on her cheek.

Slowly, like a pair of sleepwalkers at a dance, they drew closer. The softness of Marwood's lips surprised her. He tasted salty. The dance accelerated. She clung to him. He pulled her toward him, twisting his body until he was lying underneath. The dance slowed again, and then speeded up once more.

In the morning, Cat was first to rise. She dressed quickly and summoned Josh, who lit the fire. Afterwards she went back into the bedchamber. Marwood was sitting up in bed. The curtains were tied back. His head was bare. Without the wig, she could see the full extent of his scarring, the blemishes left by fire. She had touched the scars last night, her fingers running over their complicated contours and pressing down on the skull beneath.

'Madam.' Marwood smiled at her. 'Good morning. You make me the happiest of men.'

She wished he had left the words unsaid. 'The boy's lit the fire.' She avoided his eyes. 'He's bringing hot water.'

He swung his legs off the bed and stood up. He was nothing but his shirt, which came down to his knees. He stepped swiftly towards her and took her hands.

'Will you marry me? And soon? There's no reason to wait.'

'Sir, you go too fast . . .'

'I can afford a wife,' he interrupted. 'You could leave Brennan here to manage the business. We'll find a better house, and—'

She pulled her hands away. 'I don't want to marry you.'

'But – last night – I thought . . .'

'That was then, this is now.'

'Forgive me.' He stepped back and smiled. She liked his smile, she always had. 'I blunder in like a fool,' he said. 'There's no hurry. You need time to think. Of course you do.'

'I don't need any time. I know my mind.'

Marwood's face changed. His expression made her waver in her resolve. After all, would marrying him be such a bad idea? She liked him a great deal, and she trusted him as much as she trusted anyone. He could give her security, insofar as any man could give a woman that. Moreover, after last night, she knew he would provide something else too, something she had never had before, certainly not with her husband, not like that; something she wanted.

'Is it me? Or is there someone else? Or that damned Dutch—'

'There's no one. But why should I marry again? What would I gain?'

'Cat, listen—'

'I've tried marriage, sir,' she said as coldly as she could manage, being cruel to be kind. 'It does not agree with me. And there's an end to it.'

CHAPTER FIFTY-SEVEN

ON SUNDAY MORNING, Mr Fanshawe was taking his ease among the cushions in the Fanshawe pew at St Bartholomew the Less, while the sermon floated gently down from the pulpit. The vicar's voice was soft and hesitant, as if anxious not to intrude upon the pious reveries of his congregation below.

The morning was fine, and shafts of sunlight cut across the church. Sitting in state by her grandfather, Maria watched motes of dust dancing torpidly in the air. After half an hour or so, the motes became indistinguishable from the preacher's words, and each were as meaningless as the other.

Maria fell into a doze. She realized this only when Mr Fanshawe snuffled and twitched in his sleep, with the result that his arm fell heavily on her shoulder. She woke with a start and edged away from him. His arm came to rest on a tasselled cushion instead, and he emitted a gentle snore.

The sermon was short as sermons went, and the service ended earlier than usual. By virtue of their position in the parish, the Fanshawes were among the first to leave the church.

The vicar was already waiting outside to welcome them back to Smithfield. He asked after Mistress Fanshawe.

'The journey from Kent fatigued her,' Fanshawe told him. 'No doubt you will see her here next Sunday.'

His thoughts were already running ahead to dinner, and he did not wish to linger any longer than necessary. As he and Maria were setting off home, however, Mr Thrumbull, his wife on his arm, made a beeline towards them. Or rather his wife did, for she towed her husband along as a tiny rowing boat tows an overladen lighter to shore.

'Mr Fanshawe, sir, good day,' the apothecary said, bowing low. 'And little Mistress Maria, eh? I hope we find you both in good health after your journey into Kent.'

'Perfectly, thank you,' Mr Fanshawe said, acknowledging Mistress Thrumbull's curtsy. 'But we're pressed for time, I fear, and—'

'Sir,' interrupted Mistress Thrumbull, 'a word in your private ear, if we may.'

'Of course, of course.' Mr Fanshawe's eyes strayed across Smithfield, towards his house.

'My husband thought you would want to know.'

'Know what?'

Confused, Fanshawe stared at her. Mistress Thrumbull was younger than her husband, an upright woman with a permanently pursed mouth and small, bright eyes. She kept her husband's accounts, placed the orders and dealt with both creditors and debtors. In all but name, the business was hers.

'A gentleman called at the house this morning,' she said. 'He was asking some very strange questions.'

'He came into the shop before,' Thrumbull put in. 'A month or two ago. I remember it distinctly because he wanted

441

unicorn horn, and I had to tell him that's not something you can pick up any day of—'

'His name's Marwood,' Mistress Thrumbull said firmly. 'He had a warrant. Signed by my Lord Arlington.'

'Marwood?' Fanshawe said uneasily. 'Yes, I know – one of my lord's clerks.'

'In fact, that first time, I don't think he wanted unicorn horn at all,' the apothecary said wonderingly.

Mistress Thrumbull raised her voice. 'He was asking whether anyone in your household had bought arsenic from us. In the last few months.'

'How should I know?' Fanshawe asked. 'And why the devil would this man Marwood want to find out something like that?'

'I couldn't remember,' Mr Thrumbull said, looking proudly at his wife. 'But Martha could. You've a wonderful memory, haven't you, my dear, quite remarkable.'

'Mistress Fanshawe's brother came in for arsenic,' she said. 'The Dutch gentleman. The twenty-first of February. I looked it up in the account book. We saw the gentleman here in church with you once. I never forget a face.'

'That's right,' her husband said. 'I remember now.'

'He gave it to a servant girl outside,' Mistress Thrumbull went on. 'That's what fixed it in my mind. I saw it quite clearly, because I was standing over the road outside the glover's. I wondered why the gentleman had bothered to come at all, if he could have sent the girl instead. And another thing – he paid for the arsenic when he bought it. He didn't want it put on your account.'

'What servant girl?' Fanshawe said.

'About as tall as that.' Mistress Thrumbull raised her hand

about five feet in the air. 'I've seen her about when your cook sends her out for something. Is she your kitchen maid, perhaps? An ill-favoured thing, poor soul.'

After I had left the apothecary's shop, I walked to the Slaughter Stone. Earlier this morning, when I was at Whitehall, I had arranged for a file of soldiers to meet me there.

The soldiers were under the command of Lieutenant Thurloe of the Foot Guards, a man I had worked with before; a former New Model Army officer, he was puritanical by nature, awkward in company and as honest a man as I ever knew.

I had not been able to talk to Thurloe beforehand, so I drew him aside for a brief conference. First I swore him to secrecy, which he would not agree to do until he had examined my warrant. That was typical of the man.

'Mr Fanshawe's a wealthy merchant,' I told him, 'a citizen of repute. That's his house up there. His widowed daughter-in-law is Dutch, and we recently apprehended her brother as a spy. That I tell you in confidence, sir, for your ears alone. He's dead now, but I must search the house. I'm looking for papers he may have left behind, or any other evidence.'

'And what do we do while you search? Stand about and watch?'

'More or less. I want the whole household under guard while I search. There's no other family apart from the grand-daughter. She's only a child. We'll put them all in the hall. I need a man or two to cover the garden and the old stables at the bottom. There's a side gate in the garden, by the way, and another through the stables.'

Thurloe nodded towards his men. There were six of them. 'That should be enough.'

'By the way, there's a lion in the stables.'

'A *what*?'

'Fanshawe has a taste for such things. It's held securely but it's a savage creature. You'd better warn your men to leave it alone.'

'They're not stupid.' Thurloe peered at me. 'What's amiss with you, sir?' he said suddenly. 'You look sour as a dog's vomit.'

I had been trying not to think about Cat all morning. I said, 'Believe me, I'll be happy as a king when this is over.'

CHAPTER FIFTY-EIGHT

FANSHAWE AND THE granddaughter returned from church to find us in possession of the house and the sound of screaming in the air. All but one of the servants had been herded into the hall. We had put Mistress Fanshawe in there with them. She had spat at me as we escorted her downstairs. The hall doors were now barred, and a soldier was keeping watch from the gallery.

I came downstairs and found Fanshawe in the parlour. He was trying to lay down the law to Thurloe, who looked grimly amused. The old man was with his granddaughter. I wished she were elsewhere. This was no place for children, any more than Swaring had been.

'Mr Marwood!' Fanshawe swung his attention towards me in the doorway. 'This is too much! First Swaring, and now here. It's persecution! My Lord Arlington shall hear of it. What the Lord Mayor will say, I cannot think.'

'I regret I must ask you to—'

'What is the meaning of those screams? Are you torturing some poor soul?'

'Your kitchen maid has a pain in her belly.'

The girl was in agony. I had sent for the apothecary.

'This is an insult.' Fanshawe hesitated, and his outraged dignity modulated into something more querulous. 'And dinner is spoiling in the oven. I can smell it burning from here.'

He was right about that. The savoury odours of roasting meat were acquiring an acrid tinge.

'My lord has commanded that this house be searched,' I said. 'As Swaring was. You know full well that this is a matter of state. Here's the warrant if you wish to inspect it. The less you obstruct us, the faster we'll be done.'

Fanshawe sank into a chair. 'You must do as you wish, I suppose.' He passed a hand over his brow. 'Would someone at least bring me a glass of wine and a biscuit? I feel faint.'

'I must ask you to join the rest of your household in the hall.'

'What? Why?'

'And I must have your keys, sir. All of them. Otherwise we'll use a crowbar.'

The fight had gone out of him, and he made only token resistance when Thurloe led him away. His granddaughter trailed after them.

'Pray order your men to exercise the greatest care over my collection,' Fanshawe said over his shoulder. 'It's beyond price, sir – indeed there is nothing like it in this country.'

When they were gone, I went to the back of the house and down the steps to the kitchen. The smell of burning grew stronger. The screams were louder as well. Thurloe had left a single soldier to watch the back door, which lay through the scullery beyond. The man had also been commanded to keep an eye on the ailing servant, who lay on a mattress in an alcove to one side of the scullery.

'How is she?' I asked him.

'Mortal bad, your honour. As you can hear. And smell.'

The scullery stank, the smells of vomit and excrement mingling uneasily with the smoke oozing from the oven. I stood at the foot of the alcove and looked down at the poor wretch writhing on the foul mattress. Something stirred in the depths of my memory.

'Be of good heart,' I said to her. 'The apothecary will be here soon.'

Vomiting, I thought, pains in the belly and violent flux: wasn't this how Abbott had died?

The girl retched violently but brought up nothing to speak of. There was a mug of water on the floor. I crouched down, picked it up and held it to her lips. Her mouth was chapped and flecked with foam.

'I'm dying,' she croaked.

She swallowed a little water, and more ran down her chin. She retched again immediately, and cried out, her features contorted with pain.

'You'll be well again soon enough, I've no doubt. Listen to me. Mr Van Riebeeck gave you some arsenic. Months ago. Do you remember? In Cock Lane. He bought the arsenic from the apothecary. He gave it to you outside the shop. What was it for? What did you do with it?'

'I'm a sinner, sir,' she wailed.

'We're all sinners. Take more water. What was the arsenic for?'

I moistened her lips but she could drink nothing. She tried to speak but I couldn't make out the words.

'What?' I prompted. 'The arsenic?'

'I smell the fires of hell.' Her voice was so faint I could hardly make out the words. 'The Devil's got me. I shouldn't have mixed it with the sugar, I shouldn't have done it, it wasn't her, sir, it was me, and now I burn . . .'

'It's not you that's burning,' I said. 'It's your master's dinner. What's this about sugar?'

But she had started screaming again. Her body was convulsed. Her eyes stared at the ceiling, as though they were straining to burst from their sockets. 'He's coming,' she gasped. 'Devil's coming . . .'

I felt a touch on my shoulder and looked up. It was the soldier, bringing the news that the apothecary was here at last. I turned back to reassure the girl, to make sure she understood that help was on its way at last. She had fallen silent. Her eyes were still open. She was still looking up at the ceiling.

'He's come too late,' the soldier said.

In the distance, the lion roared.

'Caliban's hungry,' Mr Fanshawe said. 'He usually has his dinner now.'

I ignored that. I had sent for him and his granddaughter. I had asked for Mistress Fanshawe as well, but she refused point-blank to see me. The three of us were in the garden, standing in a patch of sunshine beside a summerhouse. I wanted to get the smell of the deathbed out of my nostrils. I also wanted to avoid the risk of eavesdroppers.

'Your kitchen maid is dead, sir.'

'What of? Not plague, I hope?'

I shook my head. 'What was the girl called?'

'I don't know,' the old man said. 'I've forgotten. Or perhaps I never knew. She was only the kitchen maid. I never saw her, except at prayers.'

'Her name was Hannah, sir,' the granddaughter said.

'Maria knows about her,' Mr Fanshawe with obvious relief. 'Mistress Fanshawe brought the girl with her from Fleet Street after . . . after . . .'

'After the death of Abbott, her second husband,' I said brutally. 'And in a very similar manner to the way this girl died. Vomiting. Flux. Pains in the belly.' I looked at Maria Fanshawe, who stared back at me with solemn brown eyes. There was a frown between her dark eyebrows. 'Had Hannah been with you long? Where did she come from?'

'My mother took her in before Christmas, sir, when our old maid left. She used to hold the men's horses by Temple Bar. Or run errands for people.'

'Her parents?'

'I don't know,' Maria said. 'Dead, I think.'

'Was she a good worker?'

'She did what she was told, sir. If she had to.'

'Your mother must have thought so. Otherwise she wouldn't have brought her with you.'

'I suppose so.' The girl shuffled her feet. 'I – I didn't much care for her.'

'Come, child,' Mr Fanshawe chided. 'You should not speak ill of the dead.'

'She stole money from me,' Maria said in a voice barely louder than a whisper. 'She said she'd put a spell on me if I told anyone.'

'What nonsense is this. Maria, you must—'

449

'One moment, sir, if you please.' I looked into the girl's soft eyes. 'Did she often steal?'

Maria swallowed, still with her eyes on my face. 'I saw her yesterday, sir, in the yard with the privy. I think she was hiding something.'

I frowned. 'You *think*? Did you not look yourself? Or confront her?'

'You don't understand, sir. She . . . she scared me.'

'A kitchen maid?' Mr Fanshawe said wonderingly. 'What nonsense is this?'

I said, 'Why?'

'Because she would find a way to hurt me, sir. She always did. And she knew how to curse people.'

It was such a strange, superstitious story that I was inclined to believe it. Maria was no more than a child, and clearly gentle by nature. The maid had been older, and the two girls must have been thrown into each other's company when they were living at Abbott's lodging.

'Show me this hiding place, or whatever it was,' I said. 'We'll put the matter to the test.'

She led us through a gate and into the yard where the necessary house was. She stood in front of the wall at the side of the privy.

'About here, I think. See — there's mortar dust on the ground.' She patted the wall gently with the palms of her hands. 'Sir, this brick is loose.'

I told her to step aside. With Mr Fanshawe watching, I eased the brick from the wall and pushed my hand into the recess. But it was too narrow for me to manage more than three or four inches. I withdrew my hand.

'Will you try for me, little mistress?'

She nodded. Biting her lip with concentration she put her hand into the hole. It went in further than her wrist. She looked up at me.

'There's something here, sir.'

She pulled out a narrow bundle, wrapped in a filthy cloth secured with a knot. She gave it to me. She and her grandfather watched as I untied it. The first thing I saw was a lace trim.

'But that's your handkerchief,' her grandfather exclaimed. 'The purple one.'

'Mulberry, sir,' I said. 'The one that was in the lion's cage.'

'I gave it to you,' Fanshawe said, frowning.

'Yes, sir.' Maria stared at it, her eyes wide. 'I thought I'd lost it.'

'The maid stole it?'

She nodded.

I unfolded the handkerchief. Inside were three farthings, a shilling and a gold piece. And a packet of paper with something inside it.

'That's gold.' Fanshawe was not a man afraid to state the obvious. 'She can't have come by it honestly. If the girl wasn't dead, she'd hang for it.'

I examined the gold piece. On the obverse was the familiar figure in armour, with a sword in one hand and sheaf of arrows in the other. 'A Dutch ducat, sir,' I said in a toneless voice.

Fanshawe took the coin and turned it over. 'Aye. Utrecht mint.'

'Indeed. But the question is, how did she come by it?'

'No doubt she stole it.'

'Or was given it,' I said. 'If so, by whom? Van Riebeeck?'

'I saw them once,' Maria said. 'My uncle and Hannah. They were talking together on the path down to the stable. She was taking the bucket down to the pigs.'

'Why would he want to speak to a kitchen maid?' her grandfather said.

I glanced at the child, who looked back at me with dark, candid eyes. 'Why indeed?' I said.

That left the paper. I put the coins, the handkerchief and the rag in my pocket. I unfolded the paper. Inside was a heap of white powder, caked with moisture.

'More thievery,' Fanshawe said, blinking. 'What is it? Sugar? Flour?'

'Mr Thrumbull will tell us if he's still in the house,' I said, folding the paper into a small, neat packet. 'I think it's arsenic.'

CHAPTER FIFTY-NINE

I T WAS NEARLY five o'clock by the time Thurloe and I left Slaughter Street, with the Foot Guards behind us. Bystanders watched us surreptitiously, and I was aware of movement at the windows of the houses we passed. No one dared ask what we had been doing in Fanshawe's house.

Thurloe marched his men back to their barracks in Whitehall. There was no point in my going with him – Lord Arlington was still at Dover – so I walked slowly back to the Savoy, to Infirmary Close. Sam and Margaret were expecting me, for I had sent my baggage there on my way to Whitehall this morning. I wished to God I were on my way to Henrietta Street instead.

But it was a relief to be in my own house again, though the absence of Stephen struck me with renewed force.

'Is Mistress Hakesby in Henrietta Street, master?' Margaret asked.

'Yes. I escorted her back from Dover. We arrived so late that I was obliged to pass the night at the sign of the Rose.'

I would have preferred not to mention this fact, but I knew

that Margaret would soon learn of it from Pheebs or Josh. I sensed that the Witherdines pricked up their ears at the news.

'She's not best pleased with her maid,' I went on, trying to divert attention. 'Jane, is it? The apartments had not been aired. There was sewing strewn about everywhere. She'd left the closet window open and let the rain in. There was not even coal in the bucket or kindling on the hearth. Mistress Hakesby was most put out.' I looked sternly at Margaret. 'I thought you agreed to keep an eye on the place while she was away.'

The tactic worked, and Margaret launched into a tirade against the maid together with a spirited defence of her own conduct. Afterwards I sent her away to prepare me something to eat. Sam lingered.

'What is it?' I said.

He cleared his throat. 'Stephen, sir.'

For an instant, I felt as though he had jabbed me in the belly with his crutch. 'What about him?'

'Margaret and I – well, we don't know where he's buried.'

'No. Nor do I. The matter was taken out of my hands.' For all I knew, they had dumped Stephen's body in a pit for paupers and plague victims when the coroner was finished with him. 'What's done is done.' I looked up at him. 'I'm sorry.'

'Master, could we put a tablet up to him? In a church? Only a small one. We've a little money put by, me and Margaret, and we could pay for a mason to do the work if you'd arrange it.' He stopped and swallowed. 'It's not for me, master, it's Margaret.'

I sat back in my chair. I felt shame rise inside me in a hot, tingling tide. 'That's an admirable idea,' I said at last. 'We shall do it together. I'll look into it.'

Sam ducked his head in his approximation of a bow, and stumped out of the room without thanks and without waiting to be dismissed. He closed the door as gently as he could.

After supper, I sat in my parlour until nearly midnight, trying to get my thoughts in order before I wrote the report for my lord. The Cock Lane apothecary and his sharp-eyed wife had told me that Van Riebeeck had bought arsenic from their shop and that he had given it immediately to Hannah, who at the time had been the Abbotts' maid in Fleet Street. Mistress Thrumbull had recorded the transaction in her account book: Monday, 7 February. By 23 February, two days after I had found Abbott drunk as a fish in the Strand, he was dead.

Van Riebeeck was a fanatical patriot with a grudge against the English and a personal connection to the Grand Pensionary himself, a man whose dislike of the English was well known. When his sister had grown disillusioned with Abbott, partly because his mania for gambling had brought them to the brink of ruin, Van Riebeeck had seized the opportunity to exploit the situation. Abbott was Lord Arlington's confidential clerk, and his mounting debts made him vulnerable to blackmail. Thanks to Abbott, Van Riebeeck learned something of the French treaty, including the existence of the proposed secret clause. But its precise nature still eluded him.

Van Riebeeck's sister, Alink and even old Fanshawe had helped him, though for different reasons, but without knowing what he was about. Others, such as Connolly and Johnson at the Blue Bush, acted as his instruments in return for money. He escaped detection for so long because he operated quite

455

independently of the usual Dutch intelligence-gatherers in England.

At the end of his tether, Abbott had threatened to confess his misdeeds to Arlington. Van Riebeeck bribed Hannah, the kitchen maid, to poison him, and he provided her with ample means to stop Abbott's mouth for ever. When Johnson took fright and talked to me, Van Riebeeck and Connolly conveyed him to Slaughter Street and showed him the lion. Perhaps they even unlocked the gate and thrust him briefly into the enclosure; hence the mulberry handkerchief which Maria Fanshawe had found. It was possible that they had meant only to frighten him into silence. Instead they terrified him to death. That left them with a body to dispose of. Under cover of night, they must have left the corpse briefly unguarded on the Slaughter Stone. Then they had bundled it into a coach or cart, and taken it for burial to the abandoned garden in Austin Friars.

Austin Friars. Where in all probability Van Riebeeck had killed Stephen to shut his mouth and allow him to escape unnoticed.

But where did that leave Cat?

I still did not know what Van Riebeeck had wanted from Cat, or she from him. Perhaps it was better so. But he had either known or guessed that the King was using her as a courier between himself and Madame. Thanks to Jane Ash, he had been able to intercept her party at Dover and attempt to search her luggage. Cat had been unaware it was him.

Probably. Possibly.

Had she known or suspected?

I thought then of my own condescending words to Johnson, which now rebounded on my own head: *You must*

weigh a mere possibility against a probability — nay, let us call
it a certainty. Ask yourself, sir, presented with such a choice,
what would Monsieur de Fermat and Monsieur Pascal decide?

What about the kitchen maid, Hannah? Had she died of
cholera or the flux? By some devilish irony, could she have
taken arsenic by mistake, perhaps mixed with sugar? That
was surely possible, for the mixture might have been the
residue of whatever she had given Abbott.

Even if I had her body opened up, we would never know,
for arsenic left no trace. But it was probable that it had been
one or the other. They were the obvious answers to the question, and the obvious answers were usually the right ones.

The fire had died down and it was growing cold. I tried
not to think of the alternative: that someone still at large had
poisoned the kitchen maid with arsenic.

Someone? At Slaughter Street who had known where to
find arsenic? Who had a motive? Who had shown me where
to find Hannah's hiding place?

That sweet-faced child, with her widely spaced brown
eyes. Maria Fanshawe.

At midnight, Cat was still at work in her parlour at the sign
of the Rose. She had spent the last few hours running her
eye over worksheets, site reports and accounts until her eyes
were sore.

The fire was burning bright and the room had been set to
rights. Foolish, willing Jane Ash, who had worked desperately
hard all day in the hope of avoiding dismissal, was snoring
quietly in the closet, which had been dried out. Next door,
the bedchamber was aired, the curtains rehung, and the sheets
changed on the bed.

Upstairs, in the Drawing Office, everything was in order, ready for work on Monday morning. She had conferred at length with Brennan during the afternoon. She was pleased with what he had achieved in Fenchurch Street during her absence. She had told him about Madame's projected mansion at St Cloud, and he had been wise enough to make no objection.

All in all, Cat was glad to be back in Henrietta Street. Money was a problem, but then money always was. It might be months before she received the hundred pounds that Madame had promised, if it ever came at all. She refused to let the matter trouble her now. She had learned the wisdom of dividing her thoughts, for she knew that otherwise her fears would rule her. She tried not to think about Van Riebeeck either, what he had been to her, what he might have been, and how he had died. His death had filled her dreams last night. But the Dutchman lay in the past now, she prayed, with the other detritus heaped up there and waiting to be forgotten.

'Better not to think about it,' she said aloud to the fire. 'Let the past rot.'

But she did think of last night. She had been harsh to Marwood this morning, and now she regretted it – not what she had said, but the manner of it. She pushed aside the accounts, took a fresh sheet of paper and dipped her pen in the ink.

At the sign of the Rose, Sunday

Sir,
I write for two reasons. First, to thank you for your Company on the Journey to London. Second, the last time we went to

the playhouse, I fear I was less than complimentary about the Dramatic Art. My Head ached woefully that evening. I may have dismissed Mr Etherege's comedy too easily. Perhaps we should put the matter to the Test again and see another play. CH

Cat read it over. On second reading the letter seemed too apologetic, as if she were ashamed of something and wished to make amends. But she wanted to see Marwood. He belonged in the present. Things had not been easy between them for the last few months, and it would be foolish to let the coolness between them continue.

And then there was what had happened between them in the night. Never again, of course. She thought about it now, though, and a comfortable languor stole over her.

CHAPTER SIXTY

A Month Later

EXTRACTED FROM THE Calendar of State Papers Domestic:

Charles II, 1670 With Addenda 1660–70:

Whitehall, 27 June, 1670

On the 22nd, at 10 a.m., arrived an express from Paris, with tidings of the sudden death of Madame, his Majesty's sister, at St. Cloud, of the colic, after coming out of a bath; it had such an effect on his Majesty that he immediately took to his bed, and has not since appeared at Council. Madame had taken chicory water on leaving her bath, being in great pain, and was immediately taken with colic, and declared she was a lost woman. There being some suspicions, the French King caused her body to be opened, in the presence of the English Ambassador and some English doctors, who found her vitals so much wasted that they wondered she had lived so long; but her liver was sound, which would not have been had she been poisoned. The French King acquainted his Majesty and Lord Arlington of this through an express, and also that he was about sending over Marshal Bellefonds to condole and give a more particular account, under the oath and hands of those present.

Mistress Fanshawe held the sampler to the light of the parlour window. 'It grows worse, not better. It's meant to look like a lion, not a smudge. And is that blood on the corner?'

Maria lowered her head and looked at her lap. 'I pricked my finger, Madam.'

'Why were you not using a thimble? Why did you let the blood dry?'

'I didn't think . . . I beg your pardon.'

Her mother loomed over her, black as a shadow in full mourning. She slapped Maria's cheek. Maria cried out, from shock as well as pain.

'Spare the rod,' Mistress Fanshawe said grimly, 'spoil the child. You must unpick the lion and do it again. This should be a compliment to your grandfather, not an insult. You know how he dotes upon Caliban.' She gave a harsh laugh. 'You should, I suppose. He takes you to watch the beast often enough.'

She swept out of the parlour. It was nearly time for dinner, and it was her habit to visit the kitchen and terrorize the servants before the dishes were brought up to the dining room.

Maria folded the sampler. She disliked the lion. Her feelings towards her mother were more complicated, but they could not be said to include liking, let alone love.

She opened her workbasket. Sampler in hand, she hesitated. She put her other hand in the workbasket, burrowed down to the bottom, to the hole in the corner of the lining. She touched the familiar shape of the paper packet. She had dosed Hannah with half of the arsenic she had taken from the hiding place in the wall. Half was left.

Caliban or her mother? Her mother was larger than Hannah, and the lion was larger still. Perhaps there was not enough to kill either of them.

Something snapped inside her head. She dropped the sampler into the workbasket. She closed the workbasket as quickly as she could, as if shutting the Devil himself inside. She put the basket on its shelf in the press and closed the door with a bang.

Her mother came back into the room. 'Wash your hands, child, or you'll be late for dinner.'

'Yes, madam,' Maria said.

Until the interruption came, Cat had spent the last two hours absorbed in a private world of lines and proportions, curves and angles. It was a calm, austere place, purged of everything that made life tiresome.

Then came the hasty steps on the stairs and the knocking on the door.

Cat swore quietly and laid her pen on the ledge at the bottom of the drawing board. She was alone in the office – Brennan was at the Fenchurch site, sorting out a shortage of roof tiles. If she ignored the knocking, the caller would sooner or later go away.

Instead the door opened, and Marwood came in, smart as the Devil in a new suit, his wig freshly curled.

'What is it?' Cat said crossly. 'I'm working.'

He came and stood beside her. 'News arrived from France this morning. Madame is dead.'

She stared at him. 'Madame? No. No, she can't be.'

'She is. There was an express this morning. The King is mad with grief. He's shut himself up in his private apartments. He won't see anyone.'

Cat said, 'But . . . but this is for her.'

Her eyes returned to the plan on the board. Since returning to London, she had heard nothing from Madame about the proposed mansion or about a second visit to France. Nor had Madame's treasurer yet sent her the promised draft of a hundred pounds. In the interim, however, Cat's mind had run wild, and she had drafted half a dozen designs, each more elaborate than the last.

Marwood frowned. 'It looks like a palace.'

'It is a palace in all but name.' Tears pricked Cat's eyelids, and she blinked them away. 'Or it was going to be. Madame wanted it built on a hill near St Cloud. What happened?'

'A colic or something. They said her vitals were much wasted.'

'Monsieur her husband hated her. Are they sure it wasn't poison?'

'They say not. But people are talking.'

Cat stared down at the plan, but the lines were blurred. 'She was happy at Dover,' she said. 'Happy to be with her brother.' She turned to face Marwood. 'And I *liked* her. Everyone did. Everyone loved her. Except Monsieur.'

'And the Dutch.'

She began to cry in good earnest. He put his arms around her. She leant against him and rested her head on his chest. She shut her eyes. Marwood stroked her face as if he were soothing a child or a horse. She wasn't sure if she was crying because Madame was dead or because the French poultry house would never be built, or because this glorious palace could only exist on her drawing board.

After a few minutes, Cat pushed Marwood away. It was the first time he had embraced her since the night of their arrival in London a month ago.

'Thank you,' she said. 'Pray go now.'

He lingered at the door. 'It's almost midday. Will you dine with me?'

She looked up from the plan. 'I've work to do. Supper? At seven?'

Marwood smiled, which transformed his face. He bowed and was gone. When she was alone again, Cat took up her pen and returned to the drawing board. Madame's palace was not yet finished.

HISTORICAL NOTE

THE SECRET TREATY of Dover was signed on Sunday, 22 May 1670. The four signatories on behalf of Charles II were Lords Arlington and Arundell, Sir Thomas Clifford and Sir Richard Bellings. In strategic terms, the alliance made sense to both England and France. Under the Grand Pensionary, Johannes de Witt, the Dutch Republic stood between the French and their territorial ambitions in the Spanish Netherlands. The Dutch navy posed a formidable obstacle to England's control of the sea and its desire to dominate lucrative trade routes.

Later in the year, after an elaborate charade that greatly amused Charles II, England and France signed an official version of the treaty. It was identical to the first apart from the omission of the secret clauses: Charles's promise to announce his conversion to Catholicism when he judged the time to be right; and Louis XIV's promise to pay his cousin a pension.

The Secret Treaty was the culmination of negotiations conducted under conditions of great secrecy for the better part of two years. Both Charles and Louis loved and trusted Madame. (Her brother's pet name for her was Minette.) She acted as a conduit between the two kings, enabling them to bypass official diplomatic channels. A devoted Roman Catholic, she fervently believed that she was acting in the best interests of both men in the spiritual sphere, as well as the political.

She and her brother corresponded frequently; they used a simple number code for extra security. During the negotiations, it often amused Charles to find unusual messengers to carry his letters to her. No doubt it was also another security device. Their caution was so effective that the secret clauses of the treaty remained unknown for more than a century afterwards.

Madame's sudden death, only a few weeks after her return to France, risked undermining the treaty before its terms came into force. It was well known that her husband, Monsieur, and certain of his friends, had hated her and wished her dead; and this gave rise to rumours of poisoning. Louis was desperate to demonstrate to Charles that her death had been from natural causes.

The autopsy was conducted before both French and English representatives, to ensure that there was no attempt to cover up evidence of foul play. Though Madame's 'vitals' were wasted, her liver was healthy. Chronic exposure to arsenic damages the liver. This was taken as conclusive proof that she had not been poisoned. Since the twentieth century, scholars have generally believed that her death was due to acute peritonitis, following a perforated duodenal ulcer.

Arsenic was cheap, easily available and effective. In the

nineteenth century, it was sometimes referred to as 'inheritance powder', a nod to its reputation as a recourse for impatient heirs. Until the invention of Marsh's Test in 1836, there was no reliable way for a physician to differentiate between arsenic poisoning and cholera, food poisoning or dysentery, since the symptoms are so similar.

Madame des Bordes, Madame's *femme de chambre*, served her mistress for most of the princess's short life. Charles never forgot her devotion. After his sister's death, he sent for her and gave her the position of dresser to his own queen.

In the later seventeenth century, the expansion of foreign trade led to a taste for exotic pets from distant lands. Charles II led the way: by 1663, the population of St James's Park included an elk, an Indian antelope, spotted deer from Asia, Arabian sheep, a white raven and (among a range of imported birds) a cassowary. Later there were ostriches, while the Royal Menagerie in the Tower of London housed an array of more dangerous animals including lions.

Where the King led, his subjects followed. Over the years, Samuel Pepys, the diarist and naval administrator, acquired a range of unusual animals, few of which lasted long with him. They included a monkey (which he almost beat to death in a fit of temper), canaries, and an eagle (which he was glad to give away because it fouled the house).

Best of all, though, there was a lion cub. This was sent to him by a Mr Martin, the consul at Algiers, who described it as 'a gift he had taken the boldness to send as the only rarity that the place offered'. Pepys welcomed it into his house in Westminster. He wrote to thank Martin for the present, adding that the cub was 'as tame as you sent him and as good company'.

There is unfortunately no record of what happened to Samuel Pepys's lion.